*It's not always what you did that
gets you sent down. It's what I can
convince the jury that you did.
You think everyone I sent to prison
was guilty of what they were sent
to prison for? They were all guilty,
though. Of something. You're
guilty of something. I just haven't
figured out what yet.*

—Jim Grant

MONTECITO HEIGHTS

MONTECITO HEIGHTS

A RESURRECTION MAN NOVEL

COLIN CAMPBELL

MIDNIGHT INK
WOODBURY, MINNESOTA

First Edition
First Printing, 2014

Cover design: Kevin R. Brown
Cover illustration: Steven McAfee

Midnight Ink, an imprint of Llewellyn Worldwide Ltd.

Library of Congress Cataloging-in-Publication Data
Campbell, Colin, 1955–
  Montecito heights: a Resurrection Man novel / Colin Campbell.—First Edition.
      pages cm.—(A Resurrection Man novel; #2)
   ISBN 978-0-7387-3632-7
  1. Police—England—Yorkshire—Fiction. 2. British—California—Fiction. I. Title.
  PR6103.A48M66 2014
  823'.92—dc23

                                                    2013042073

Midnight Ink
Llewellyn Worldwide Ltd.
2143 Wooddale Drive
Woodbury, MN 55125-2989

www.midnightinkbooks.com

For Dad
... still in my heart

And for Mam
... still here

PART ONE

Lying by omission is still lying.
I prefer to be more open and up front.

—Jim Grant

ONE

THE GIRL WITH THE pierced nipples and the row of tattooed stars on either side of her crotch squatted beside the cream leather settee and began to kiss the man's hairy chest. The hairs were sparse and wiry and matched the ones covering his back and shoulders. This was not a young man. The girl was maybe eighteen or nineteen. He was toned and well preserved. She was slim and gorgeous. Her short black hair, gelled into a short, spiky cut, bobbed slightly with the movement of her head. Her small, firm breasts didn't move at all.

She slid one hand up the side of the guy's stomach and made small circling movements just out of reach of where he really wanted her to circle. The strain of crouching next to him brought cords of muscle to the surface of her soft, tanned skin. Her stomach looked flat and solid, a testament to hours in the gym or a very active outdoor lifestyle. Riding would be a good guess.

The thing she would soon be riding trembled to life. Slowly. This was not a young man.

He moaned as her hand accidentally brushed his manhood— one of those accidents that are destined to be. Destined because that's what having sex is all about. She let her hand curl up like a

3

crab until only her fingertips touched his skin. Long, sharp nails, painted black, scraped his stomach. Sparks of excitement twitched his manhood even more. The hand flattened, the palm feeling warm on his flesh as it slid down his stomach, bypassing the erection that was finally beginning to grow, caressing his inner thigh all the way down to the knee.

Her lips kissed and sucked his chest. Hairs tickled her nose but she didn't stop. A wet, pink tongue flicked out. She worked her way from his chest to his stomach, then paused. The girl was staring victory in the face. A bobbing head that would have smiled if it had a mouth. She had a mouth. She blew gently, the cold air making the glistening head twitch. Her face remained impassive. Following the example of her hand, she bypassed the erection and began kissing his thigh, licking it a couple of times for good measure.

Then the scenic window behind them opened smoothly on its runners, and another woman came in. She appeared shocked to see the couple performing on the couch. Behind her, sunshine bathed the garden in warm light. A decorative arch framed downtown Los Angeles in the background. She closed the door quietly and watched for a few seconds. The girl had worked her head between the man's thighs and was licking all the way up to his testicles. Whenever her tongue flicked the sagging pink balls, his member twitched into full erection.

The woman near the window couldn't wait anymore. She unzipped her dress and slipped it from her shoulders, revealing a skimpy bra and a sequined triangle that barely covered the triangle beneath it. Her breasts were much bigger than the girl's and strained at the fabric of the bra. She quickly released them with a flick of the catch. The weight pulled the strap apart, and the bra dropped to the carpet.

The man was oblivious to the intruder. He was focusing else-where—until the woman knelt beside him on the settee and dangled her breasts over his face. That got his attention. Her nipples were hard as bullets, the crinkly areola dark and inviting. He didn't need a second invitation. He craned his neck upwards and clamped his lips over the first nipple he could reach.

The girl finally crawled up the man's thigh and licked his shaft. For an older guy it was borderline impressive. She wet her hand with spit and encircled him. Her lips nibbled and teased all the way up to the head, then she opened her mouth and—

JIM GRANT PRESSED EJECT. The DVD stopped, and the disc tray eased out the front of the machine. He'd seen enough. He took the disc and clicked it into its display case. The cover was gaudy and colorful, with naked women and erect penises and big red lettering. *The Hunt for Pink October*. He dropped the box on the smoked-glass coffee table and sat back on the Chesterfield settee. Dark leather, not cream. Old school, not modern.

The study was large and airy. The windows looked out onto a garden that was well tended and bordered by pine trees and palms. Grant thought the contrast looked strange, but this was Los Angeles. Everything he'd seen since he got here looked strange. There was a full-height bookcase against the back wall and a grandfather clock beside the door. A solid wooden desk with green leather inlay stood in front of the bookcase. The furnishings screamed money. The room should have smelled of cracked leather and cigar smoke, but instead the air was filled with the scent of flowers from the garden. One window was open. Grant could hear a lawnmower droning in the background.

"No need to ask which one's your daughter."

"No."

Dick Richards wasn't sitting behind the desk. The fifty-nine-year-old senator sat in a matching Chesterfield chair, one leg draped lazily across his knee. He was dressed casual, in slacks and an open-necked shirt, but his body language was anything but casual, despite the draped leg. He turned the TV off using the remote but didn't bother getting up to close the cabinet built into the bookcase.

Grant didn't speculate on what having two Dicks in your name must have been like growing up. The senator had obviously done all right for himself. Having his daughter working in the porn industry was proving more difficult. That was why Grant was here. Saving US senators from their excesses was becoming a habit for him. At least this time he was being paid. Not exactly official, but still a cop. Sort of.

As always, he went for the direct approach. "Why don't you just ask her to stop?"

Richards dropped the remote on the coffee table. "Do you have children?"

"No."

"Well, if you did, you'd know that asking a teenager to do anything results in them doing exactly the opposite."

"So, ask her to *keep* making porn films."

"Movies."

"Yeah, I keep forgetting. When I was a kid, me and some mates used to go to the pictures—Saturday morning matinees. Old black-and-white serials, a bunch of cartoons, and a short feature. It was always a picture house, not a cinema."

"They are called motion pictures for a reason."

"They move. Yes, I get that. But in Yorkshire it was still 'the pictures.'"

"You come highly recommended. I hope you have assimilated by now."

"With the American culture? I get by. It's not what you know, it's knowing who to ask."

"Asking implies other people being involved. Nobody must know about this."

"Her picture's on the video sleeve."

"DVD. Not an angle you'd recognize her from."

"True. She's not using her given name?"

"A pseudonym."

"And the makers don't know who she is?"

"I believe that is the case. Yes."

"That's a start, then."

The lawnmower was growing louder. The expanse of grass outside was the size of a soccer pitch. The gardener must be getting toward the end nearest the house. The mansion, Grant corrected himself. A helicopter throbbed away in the distance. Since he'd arrived in LA he didn't think there'd been a single hour without an eye-in-the-sky chopper buzzing around, either police or news. Between that and the constant airline traffic from LAX, the sky was alive with the sound of engines. Add in the intermittent sirens and the ever-present freeway traffic and you had a recipe for mechanical exhaustion.

Senator Richards uncrossed his legs. "Discretion is paramount."

"Like the studio?"

"Essential."

Grant detected a hint of disdain. The wealthy man was talking down to his servant and not liking the servant's tone. Grant didn't like to be talked down to. He didn't like people who thought they were better than everyone else. But this was a job.

"Discretion is my middle name."

"You weren't very discreet in Boston."

"Twenty-four-hour news. They got that here?"

"They showed that everywhere."

Grant leaned forward and picked up the glass of Pepsi he'd been drinking. Ice and lemon. The ice had almost melted. The lemon was still fresh. Senator Richards' butler or manservant or whatever he was couldn't provide a pint of Tetley's. It was too early for beer anyway. He took a swig and felt the coolness soothe his throat. Dry heat always did that to him. He'd been in drier and hotter places, dusty and dangerous places. Putting the arm on a porn movie producer should be a piece of cake. He nodded as he spoke.

"Looks like if you can't get her to stop, we'll just have to persuade the film company it's in their best interests to find somebody else."

"Movie company."

"I think that's elevating the porn industry a bit, don't you?"

Grant put the glass down and picked up the DVD case. The sleeve was faded and badly printed. A pirate copy. He opened the box and checked the disc. Same thing: badly printed adhesive disc label. He turned the case over and read the back. Phony cast names and a ridiculous plot summary completed the low-rent nature of the business. He remembered a disc jockey in Yorkshire who called himself Big Dick Swelling. It got a laugh on a Saturday night. He doubted Big Dick Richards would see the funny side.

What Grant was looking for wasn't there—the address of the production company that made the film. It might have been there on the original sleeve, but this copy was so bad that any small lettering disappeared in a haze of smudged ink and penises. Or was that peni? He gave up trying to read it.

"Better give me her address."

"I'd rather you didn't speak to her about this."

"And I'd rather be six feet four and built like a brick shithouse."

"You are six feet four."

"True. We sometimes get what we wish for. I won't talk to her. Just a precaution. After I've talked to the producer, *he* might want to talk to her. Helpful if I can head him off at the pass."

Richards stood up and went to the desk. He scribbled an address on a notepad and tore the top page off. He was tall and slim and had obviously been into sports as a young man. Probably ex-military. Many politicians were. He handed the address to Grant, who folded it without looking. He'd need to refer to the map back in his hotel room anyway—the first thing he bought wherever he went. He got up from the hard leather.

"You don't know what a brick shithouse is, do you?"

"I think the name is descriptive enough."

"Terrace houses in Yorkshire, before inside toilets—they'd have a brick-built privy out back. Bottom of the garden or end of the yard. Big, solid, square things. Being built like one means you're big and solid."

"That's two parts of your wish come true, then, isn't it?"

Richards pressed a button on the desk, and a bell rang somewhere in the house. Grant picked up the Pepsi and finished it in one gulp. The ice rattled in the glass. The lemon stuck to the side.

"Bet there's no outside toilets here."

"I'm sure there are places in LA you might find some. Not up here, though. I doubt you'd find many in England either nowadays. It's called progress and the wonders of modern plumbing. It's only bears that shit in the woods."

"Touché."

Grant put the glass down. Richards didn't offer to shake his hand, but he did come round the desk and lead Grant toward the heavy wooden door.

"Please. I love my daughter. She needs protecting from this vile industry."

Grant was almost moved by the display of parental concern. It would have been more convincing if the daughter's indiscretion wasn't so harmful to Richards' career in politics. The door opened, and the guy who'd served Grant his Pepsi waited to take the guest out. Butler or manservant or whatever he was.

Richards ruined the illusion of being a loving father. "Be discreet. You come highly recommended."

Grant didn't answer. Sometimes discretion was the better part of anger. He followed the butler into the hallway and almost bumped into the most beautiful woman he'd ever seen.

IN KEEPING WITH THE pretension of greatness, the hallway was bigger than most people's houses. It wasn't exactly *Gone with the Wind* impressive, but the expanse of polished-wood flooring and the sweeping staircase came pretty close. The entrance hall was wide enough to park three cars with room to spare. Wood paneling and gilt-framed oil paintings completed the picture. This place reeked of money.

There was so much room that bumping into your host's wife was almost impossible. Grant wasn't surprised she'd been hanging around near the study door. His reading of wealthy families was that there were always secrets. He wondered if the mother knew that the daughter was making hardcore porn flicks.

He dodged sideways to avoid the collision. "Sorry."

The Englishman in him. Even though he considered himself a Yorkshireman. He always held the door open for ladies, gave up his seat for the elderly, and apologized even when it wasn't his fault.

She reciprocated. "No, no. My fault. Sorry."

Maura Richards' voice was as gorgeous as her face. It dripped sex appeal. The throaty cadence was deep and rich and nowhere near as affected as her husband's political delivery. She was tall and slim and elegant, but Grant suspected the elegance was something she had to work at. Money helped. Being drop-dead gorgeous helped even more.

Their eyes locked for three seconds, then the moment passed. The wealthy senator's wife and the man in faded jeans and an orange windcheater—a new one but nowhere near as pristine as the woman's summer dress. Mrs. Richards climbed the stairs as if on an escalator, gliding more than walking. Grant was escorted out the front door. It slammed shut behind him.

He stood on the front steps for a moment and took a deep breath to remove the oppressive atmosphere of the study. The smell was the same, flowers from the border on either side of the door, but fresh air and sunshine lifted the day. The lawnmower had stopped. He listened to the silence until it was broken by birdsong and the buzzing of insects. There was no traffic noise. It must have been the only place in Los Angeles where you couldn't hear the constant drone of the freeway.

Grant relaxed. This was the first commission in his new role, and if it wasn't what he would have chosen, at least being part of American law enforcement took the sting out of no longer being a West Yorkshire copper. He trotted down the wide stone steps and crossed the gravel turnaround in front of the house. The sun beat down. The sky was blue, not a hint of clouds on the horizon.

He should have known better.

He walked down the driveway between rolling lawns and well-groomed pine trees. Swaying palms reminded him this was Southern California. It was a long walk down the hill to the nearest bus route. He preferred public transport, especially in LA, where driving in a strange city was a nightmare times ten. The ornate gate slid open on silent runners as he approached. He waved to the cameras.

Ten minutes later, he was halfway there. He hadn't seen a single pedestrian. He wondered if wealthy people did any walking at all. He could imagine the twitching curtains and urgent phone calls to the police reporting the stranger in the orange jacket skulking around their neighborhood.

When the vehicle pulled up beside him, he wasn't surprised. He turned to explain to the cop what he was doing, then paused. It wasn't a cop car. The passenger door opened, and a big guy got out. He was smiling, but the smile wasn't friendly.

TWO

GRANT DIDN'T NEED TO do his breathing exercises to relax. The walk in the fresh air and sunshine had already done that. He kept his limbs loose and his mind sharp. The guy was about the same height as Grant but built like a brick shithouse. Broader than the brick shithouse that Grant resembled. He smiled at the analogy. Big Dick Swelling back at the mansion probably wouldn't have.

Grant slowed his pace but didn't stop. The vehicle was now just beyond him on his side of the road. The big guy was on the sidewalk. Grant would have to detour around him or go between him and the open door. He went for the gap. Relaxed. Ready to move fast as he drew closer to the threat.

Twelve feet.

Steady walking pace was maybe five miles an hour. Grant approached the rear of the car. It was a big shiny American thing with a sliding door along the side behind the front passenger door. A minivan kind of thing. The open passenger door obstructed half the sidewalk. The big guy stood three feet back and to one side, blocking the other half next to a tall conifer hedge. A narrow gap in between.

Eight feet.

Five miles an hour was pretty fast over a short distance. Grant glanced at the big guy, then squinted through the back window. Sun glared off the tinted glass. He couldn't see inside. Not good. He'd identified the threat outside the car but didn't know how many were hidden behind the reflective windows—a cop's worst nightmare. Caution dictated that Grant should keep his distance or go around the obstacle. Grant didn't hold with caution. He was more of a tackle trouble head-on kind of guy.

Five feet.

Since he couldn't see inside the car, he concentrated on what he could see. The big guy with the frosty smile. He was standing with his legs apart and arms folded across his chest. Bad positioning for close-quarter combat. Grant plotted the first moves in his head. Fast knee jerk between the legs, then a short-armed elbow strike up into the throat as the guy doubled over before he could unfold his arms.

Three feet.

Grant cleared his mind. His limbs were relaxed. Time to move.

Pffft hiss.

The sliding door pushed outwards a few inches, then slid open with a *pffft* of compressed air and the hum of an electric motor. A soft female voice came from the interior with a pleasant Midwestern accent. "Excuse me. Could you spare a minute?"

Grant stopped and looked into the roomy interior. John Travolta had been right in *Get Shorty*. This was indeed the Cadillac of minivans. He stared into the eyes of the second beautiful woman he'd met in less than an hour. This must be his lucky day. He bowed his head to see inside. "Not if you're trying to sell me something."

"Not sell—propose."

"You want to marry me?"

The woman laughed. It was infectious and completely uninhibited. The laugh lit up her eyes and exposed brilliant white teeth. A mop of unruly black hair framed her pleasant, rounded face. The dark complexion suggested South American or Italian descent. The accent discounted Mexican.

"Why don't you jump in? I'll talk while you ride."

"That's not an offer you get every day."

She laughed again. The big guy stepped away from the door, his smile less threatening now. Grant ducked into the back, and the door slid shut. The big guy got in the front. The driver pulled away from the curb. Grant settled into his seat.

"Home, James. And don't spare the horses."

Her laughter filled the interior as the minivan continued down the winding hillside road. Palm trees and Beverly Hills mansions showed through the windows. Somewhere overhead a helicopter throbbed in the pale blue morning sky.

"STEVEN SEAGAL?" Grant couldn't keep the surprise out of his voice.

"Yes. The show's called *Lawman*."

Robin Citrin's voice was almost as infectious as her laugh. The minivan was taking it easy, ignoring the nearest bus route and taking Grant all the way to his hotel. There were more palm trees outside now.

"That the one forced Elmore Leonard to rename his show *Justified*?"

"Right. That was originally called *Lawman*. I forgot about that."

"Saw it. First episode showed promise. Went downhill from there."

"*Justified* was fiction. *Lawman* is real. Cameras follow Seagal on patrol."

Grant snorted a laugh. It was nowhere near as infectious as Citrin's. "*Real?* You kiddin' me? A Hollywood actor playing at being a cop, and you think that shit isn't scripted? Fuck me. Pardon my French. But even if it wasn't, don't tell me that everyone he meets on camera doesn't act different than getting arrested by anyone else."

"It's advertised as real."

"Cher's advertised as real. She's more plastic than an Airfix model."

"Airfix?"

"Made plastic model kits when I was a kid. Spitfires. Tanks. Stuff like that."

"Steven Seagal's not an Airfix kit."

"He's not a cop either. Part-time special constable? Hobby bobby? Might as well stick Clint Eastwood on the street in a cowboy hat and a poncho and expect people to act like it's real."

"You're not Clint Eastwood or Steven Seagal."

Grant feigned hurt pride. "That's somewhere between an insult and a compliment."

"What I'm saying is, follow *you* around with a camera and we'll get more authentic responses."

"Reality TV?"

"Yes."

"Stick a camera in somebody's face, last thing you'll get is reality."

"The camera never lies."

"The camera always lies. Depends how you edit the footage."

Citrin backed off from trying to force Grant to accept. She tried flattery. "Bottom line is, we'd like to do a show using the Resurrection Man. The news got good coverage of you in Boston. Your name is known across America. And you look good on camera."

The snorted laugh this time was derisive. He diverted his embarrassment by looking out the window. They'd dropped down through Hollywood and were heading toward downtown along West Seventh. Not far from the hotel now.

Grant sighed and shook his head. "I'm a cop, not a movie star."

"Reality TV star."

"Not one of them either. I put bad guys in jail. Don't need cameras watching me do that."

"You could have the final cut."

"Final cut?"

"The final decision about what we show. Cut out what you don't want seen."

"Not very real, then, is it?"

"The camera never lies. Just don't show it all."

"Lying by omission."

"Technical point."

The driver called over his shoulder. "This it here?"

Grant leaned forward and looked through the windshield. The Mayfair Hotel was on the right up ahead. The lettering on the awning above the front doors read *The Historic Mayfair Hotel* but couldn't hide the fact that historic meant old and old meant faded. The Mayfair Hotel was old and faded.

"That's it. Thanks."

He sat back and looked at Robin Citrin. She was beautiful and intelligent. Grant could do a lot worse than spend time with her, but this wasn't for him. "Lying by omission is still lying. I prefer to be more open and up front."

"So leave everything in."

"Can't do that. Sometimes being open and up front isn't how the bosses want the job to work. I'm going to have to say no."

The minivan pulled up outside the hotel.

"Thanks for the lift though."

Pffft hiss. The side door slid open and, not for the first time, Grant thought he was getting out into traffic. Wrong side of the road. He swung one leg onto the sidewalk and turned to say good-bye. Citrin laid one hand on his forearm. The hand was warm even through the sleeve of his orange windcheater. It pained him to say no to her.

She held a business card in her other hand. "If you change your mind."

Grant took the card and read the name: L. Q. Patton. There was an address near Hollywood Boulevard and a telephone number. He flipped the card over and saw that she'd written her name and cell number on the back.

The warm hand was still on his arm. "You can call the office during the day"—she tapped the back of the card—"or if it's after hours."

He looked in her eyes to see if there was more to this than a business proposition but couldn't tell from her expression. This was Los Angeles. You had to take that into consideration. People acted different here.

He took the card though. "Thanks. But I doubt it."

He got out and stepped back from the open door. That's when he saw the black car parked across the street with two guys staring at him through the windshield.

GRANT FLICKED THE EDGE of the card with his fingers several times as the door hissed shut and the minivan pulled into traffic toward downtown. It crossed the freeway bridge and disappeared from view. The car opposite sat in the sunshine like a squat black toad. The two guys inside were pretty ugly too.

He stopped flicking the card and put it in his pocket. He walked from the edge of the sidewalk to the front door of the hotel. Under the awning. Two pairs of eyes followed him. Big square heads turned on thick necks. Broad shoulders. Grant stopped in the doorway and turned to stare them down. Thirty seconds. A minute. Two minutes.

The driver reached down and started the engine. The turn signal blinked before the car pulled into traffic, going out of town. The passenger kept his eyes on Grant as the car passed the hotel on the opposite side of the road. He smiled and nodded once. Grant watched them go, wondering what it was with everybody smiling at him today. Then he went inside.

LA was a strange place.

THREE

THE HISTORIC MAYFAIR HOTEL was a thirteen-story block of ugliness. Grant's room was on the twelfth floor, one room from the corner facing downtown. He fished the keycard out of his pocket as he entered the lobby, then paused in front of the twin elevators on the left. He threw a quick glance at the front door. The two guys in the black car had been waiting for him. That meant they knew where he was staying. He'd only arrived yesterday. His first visit with Senator Richards had been this morning. Whoever was interested in what he was doing worked fast. That kind of commitment seemed excessive for a small-time porn outfit.

Grant ignored the elevators and crossed the lobby to the reception desk. The high ceiling was carved and painted like a Michelangelo chapel. The expansive reception area took up two floors, with a balcony running around the first level, leading to a dining area and restaurant that advertised banquet facilities. Back in the good old days Grant could imagine the Mayfair hosting a banquet, but right now it could barely muster breakfast.

He stood at the reception desk until one of the staff noticed him and came over. The attractive Asian asked in broken English how she could help while another Asian took a booking over the phone. Grant asked if anything had arrived for him, and the girl said she would check. Checking entailed asking the guy on the phone, who shook his head. Grant thanked her before she could relay the message and turned toward the elevators. Passing the concierge desk, a third Asian asked if he could help. Grant reckoned there were more Japanese at the Mayfair than had attacked Pearl Harbor. Friendlier though. He thanked the valet and indicated the elevators. With no suitcases to carry and no likelihood of a tip, the valet let Grant go. Five minutes later he was checking the twelfth-floor corridor for strangers before slipping his keycard into the slot.

THE FIRST THING HE did was check the room for intruders. Having two heavies watching for him out front suggested there might be more inside. There weren't. Next thing he did was examine the room in case it had been searched. Not like in that James Bond movie where Sean Connery stuck a hair across the wardrobe doors and poured talcum powder over the briefcase catch—Grant just looked in the wardrobe and drawers for any sign of disturbance. Being ex-army meant his drawers were immaculate. In the military, tidiness was next to godliness. If you didn't keep your equipment and living space tidy, then your sergeant, who was God in the army, would make you pay. That made it easier to see if anyone had been rooting around in his drawers. Nobody had.

Out of habit he slid his hand beneath the neatly folded T-shirts. The velvet box was still there. He lifted it out and felt the comforting weight in his hands. He laid it on the dresser and opened the lid. The stethoscope lay curled like a sleeping snake. The battered blue velvet of the exterior gave way to the white silk lining of the inside. A faded American flag had been stitched into the inside of the lid. The stars and stripes added color to the plain white interior. The name scribbled beneath the flag had faded too but would never disappear—the female army medic who had served and loved with him. Killed in action. A stain on his heart. Grant touched it gently with one finger and smiled at a secret memory. Several memories. Then he snapped the case shut and put it back in the drawer.

Something caught his eye that he hadn't noticed when he came in. A red light was blinking on the phone beside the bed. He walked around the double bed and sat next to the cabinet facing the window. The curtains were open. Downtown Los Angeles stood out against the horizon, perhaps a mile away along West Seventh Street. Sunshine glinted off mirrored windows and polished chrome. A perfect blue sky powdered the background, the reason the movie industry had settled on Los Angeles to create the Hollywood legend. Good light and minimal bad weather.

A helicopter crawled across the sky. A second disappeared behind a skyscraper. Being a pilot in LA must be a nightmare, trying not to collide with all the other pilots hovering above the city. A siren started up on the freeway—the other thing that was a constant in the City of Angels. Grant turned from the window toward the red blinking light. A message on the phone. He picked up the handset, pressed the second button from the left, and listened to the voice he'd first heard in a hospital room at Massachusetts General.

The message was brief and to the point. Judging by the conversations Grant had had with him in Boston last year, that was the way he operated. Clear instructions and a confident manner were the signs of a strong leader, a man so powerful he didn't feel the need to belabor the point.

Grant listened to the message.

"Payment was delayed by internal considerations. It is now in your account. You can collect it from any bank or ATM. Any problems, you know how to contact me. Good luck."

Grant didn't need to listen to it again, so he hung up. Money was the first order of business. Figuring his next move was second. He decided to reverse the order and took the map he'd bought at LAX out of the bedside drawer. There was a narrow desk in one corner of the room, but he spread it open on the bed instead. It wasn't a close-detail street map, but it covered all of Los Angeles. Main roads and area names were clearly marked. Side roads and back streets were merely sketches of their true size.

He took out the torn page that Richards had written his daughter's address on. The street name was no use yet, but he found the area in the foothills west of Hollywood. A canyon road not too far from her parents' Beverly Hills mansion. He doubted it would be a log cabin rebellion against the wealth of her upbringing. Nothing on that side of town was exactly poverty row.

He slid his finger across the map toward town, past Beverly Hills and a little north: West Hollywood. Still an exclusive area. Then along the two best-known streets in LA: Sunset Boulevard and Hollywood Boulevard. He fingered the card Robin Citrin had given him. There wasn't enough detail on the map to locate the TV company's address. He didn't plan on visiting it anyway. Still, his finger lingered at the thought of seeing Citrin again.

The other address he needed wasn't available yet. Finding out which company made *The Hunt for Pink October* was his next move. The best place to find a video store was probably the heart of the place that made the most movies: Hollywood. His finger tapped the map. Maybe some things were meant to be.

ATM followed by a trip to Hollywood was the plan.

That's not how it worked out.

FOUR

THE SUN WAS HOT as Grant cut right off West Seventh up Alvarado. MacArthur Park was baked dry on his left, the grass practically scorched out of existence except for around the lake where residual moisture and spray from the fountains gave the grass at least a semblance of life. Most of the businesses he passed were Hispanic or Asian. The park was busy despite the time on a working day: half past eleven. Maybe the locals took lunch early. The smell of hotdogs and onions mingled with candyfloss and diesel fumes.

Grant crossed Wilshire and continued up the hill. The bank was at the intersection with Alvarado and West Sixth, the next junction up. Traffic was light on the roads. The sidewalks were busy. Grant reckoned the pedestrian population increased in direct proportion to the wealth of the area. He hadn't seen a single walker on his way down through Beverly Hills.

The bright red decal of the Bank of America stood out on the single-story building across the intersection. Grant waited for the walking man sign to show, then crossed the road. The cash machines were to the left of the main doors, covered with a clear plastic shelter for privacy. There wasn't a queue. If there had been, things might have turned out differently.

HE INSERTED HIS CARD and typed the password. It felt strange getting paid this way. When he'd been in the army, for the first couple of years anyway, soldiers had to attend pay parade once a week. The officer of the day sat at his desk at one end of the room while the squaddies stood in line at the other. Parade rest. At ease. A grizzled sergeant called the roll. Once your name was called, you had to stand to attention, shout "yes, sir," and march to the desk. Halt. Salute. Repeat your name and service number. The officer ticked you off the list and handed over your salary in a square brown envelope.

That soon changed when the Armed Forces moved to monthly payments, each soldier's wage being deposited in a bank account with Lloyds, the army's preferred bank. The West Yorkshire Police used the same system but with a bank of your own choice. You'd get a pay slip every month detailing the amount, your hourly rate, overtime worked, and total tax, national insurance, and pension deductions, etc.

This new position was better paid but a lot more slapdash. He'd had a brief discussion about the salary and career prospects with the man who'd recruited him when he'd been released from Massachusetts General. Bottom line was Grant was still in law enforcement. His deployment and the nature of that law enforcement was more flexible than in Bradford. Grant reckoned it was the fact that he was off the books that made employing him desirable. He could be attached to various departments or police forces or asked to work alone, but if the shit hit the fan, then Uncle Sam could deny he worked for him. That and the fact that Grant didn't always work strictly between the lines seemed to be the attraction for the man with the dark suit and quiet voice. Grant had no problems putting bad guys away with scant regard for the rules of evidence.

He waited for the machine to verify his account and glanced over his shoulder at the passing traffic. Not many cars. A single-decker bus like the one out of *Speed* but without the bomb and the fifty-miles-an-hour minimum speed. A blue and yellow taxi, the ugliest color scheme Grant had ever seen. There was no sign of the big black car or the two heavies who'd been watching him earlier. If they weren't following him, he wondered why he felt the itch up the back of his neck—Grant's early warning system for trouble.

He looked around again, scrutinizing passing pedestrians, any cars that appeared to be going too slow, and tourists sitting in the park opposite. Nothing seemed out of place. He looked to his left along West Sixth, checking out the front of the Moxa Medical Group building and the mini market next door. Then he looked to his right across the intersection toward downtown. Glass and chrome towers fringed the skyline. There was constant movement but nothing that appeared threatening.

He rubbed his neck, but the itch wouldn't go away. It was one of the instincts that had helped him survive desert skirmishes and criminal confrontations. Something was wrong, but he couldn't put his finger on what it was. The ATM beeped impatiently. He selected *cash with receipt* from the display menu, then typed in the amount he wanted. The machine whirred as it counted $500.

He looked around again. Still nothing.

The machine pushed his card out of the slot and beeped again. He took it. Crisp new fifty-dollar bills came out of a different slot, followed by a printed receipt. He took them all and put them in his wallet but didn't step out from the ATM shelter. When he got this feeling, it was best not to move until he'd identified the source.

Two and a half minutes later, he did.

The bank alarm went off.

"Aw, shit." He looked at the door and waited.

FIVE

THE ALARM WAS HARSH and annoying. That was the idea—make them hard to ignore. Grant didn't ignore it, but he didn't make any rash decisions either. He was unarmed and unprotected. No body armor. No gun. He hated guns but knew how to handle one. There were times when you had to embrace the thing you hated. Having a gun right now would have been helpful.

The ATM shelter was next to the front doors. Grant stayed inside it but shifted to the end nearest the door. Smoked glass made it difficult to see inside the bank, but he could just about make out violent movement. Two men. Fast and jerky. Not the smooth moves of veteran bank robbers. That was good and bad. Veterans were more ruthless. Amateurs were more difficult to predict. Grant didn't plan on giving them much choice.

The alarm was loud, but there had been no gunshots. Nothing bad about that. It suggested a modicum of self-control. Nobody wanted to go down for murder if they could help it. Armed robbery was practically an entry-level crime in LA nowadays. Killing people still took a lot of effort.

Grant judged speed and distance. The smoky figures through the glass door were coming this way but not fast. Not together either. They were separating. One holding back to cover the customers and staff, the other coming toward the door. Grant quickly scanned the curb. No getaway vehicle. Being right on the intersection, it would be hard to park for any length of time without drawing attention. A car would be coming, though. You could count on that. Even amateurs knew you needed a getaway car.

Traffic noises faded into the background.

Pedestrian chatter disappeared into silence.

The constant movement of the busy street slowed to a snail's pace.

Grant breathed easy, his heartbeat pulsing in his ears. Somewhere up above, the soft *thwup, thwup, thwup* of a distant helicopter droned across the sky. This was LA. He doubted if he'd seen the clear blue sky at any point without at least one chopper darting about like a dragonfly.

The smoked glass door began to open.

Six inches.

Grant stepped out from the shelter. Arms raised slightly but relaxed. Waist level. Hands open. Knees flexed, ready to move quickly.

The door opened outward. Good. It formed a barrier between Grant and the gunman.

Twelve inches and moving. Half open.

The sawn-off barrel of a pump-action shotgun poked through the gap as the smoky figure came forward. Grant kept his eyes on the dangerous end, the end that could kill you. As more of the barrel became visible, it seemed less rigid, not pointing at anything now but lowering as if the shooter felt safe now he was out of the bank.

Big mistake.

The door was wide open. A car skidded to a stop at the curb.

The first armed robber came out of the bank. Medium height. Scruffy clothing. Dirty blond hair and three days' growth of beard. His hands were grubby, fingernails caked in black, and his teeth needed brushing. This wasn't a top-of-the-range bank robber; this was a knobhead with a gun. Grant waited until he'd cleared the door. It began to close behind the gunman. Then Grant made his move.

He stepped forward and slapped the shotgun barrel down toward the ground with his right hand. His left came up swiftly under the trigger guard, grabbed the smooth black metal, and jerked it upward out of the guy's hands. He continued the sweeping movement until the shotgun did a complete circle, ending up the right way round in Grant's hands. His momentum carried him forward, and he jabbed his left knee into the guy's leading leg behind the joint. The leg collapsed, and the robber went down like a felled tree. Grant stamped on his balls.

One robber down. One to go.

The door opened again. All in one movement. The second gunman came out backwards. He held an ugly black handgun in one hand and a holdall leaking money in the other. He looked as dirty as the first robber, but at least he'd had a shave this morning. Grant heard a car door open behind him but couldn't worry about that now. First rule of engagement: face the most dangerous threat. The most dangerous threat here was the man with the semiautomatic.

The robber backed out of the door, and it began to close. His shoulders braced and he puffed his chest out. He gave a short little fist pump with his gun hand and blurted a victorious expletive: "Fuckin' *yes*."

The door closed. The guy stood facing the bank as the reflections in the smoked glass stopped moving. What he saw was a big guy in an orange windcheater pointing a shotgun at the back of his head. Grant kept his voice hard.

"Fuckin' *no*."

The guy's chest deflated like a pricked balloon. His shoulders sagged. The gun hand wavered, indecision stitched across his slack-jawed face. Grant jabbed the shotgun in his back, then stepped away out of reach.

"Ah, ah. I know what you're thinking. Did he fire six shots or only five?"

"What?"

"You don't need the rest of the *Dirty Harry* speech, do you? Drop the gun or your brains're gonna be spread all over the door. Probably break the window. Maybe injure somebody inside. And definitely leave you feeling light-headed."

The gun hand wavered, still undecided. Grant used the smoked glass to catch a glimpse of the car behind him. Nobody was getting out of the open door. He focused on the guy in front of him.

"Drop the gun. Bag too."

The guy's fingers tightened on the grip. His legs braced for one final roll of the dice. Grant recognized the danger. He pointed the shotgun skyward and fired one shot. He racked another round into the chamber and had the sawn-off barrel pointing at the guy's body mass before the expelled cartridge finished spinning to the ground. The next round wouldn't be a headshot. It would take out the guy's spine and vital organs.

"Now."

The fight went out of the robber all at once. He dropped the gun but lowered the bag gently to the ground as if it was carrying his baby. Banknotes leaked out of the half-open zipper and fluttered away. The man whimpered.

"On the ground. Face down."

He complied. Now Grant could focus on the getaway driver. The getaway driver was probably as uneducated as these two, but he wasn't stupid. He shoved the car into gear and sped off through the intersection, the momentum slamming the door shut. Grant didn't know the make but it was a big flat rust bucket with a Vote for Bush bumper sticker on the back. It was no doubt stolen and would end up dumped in a back street somewhere in the next half hour.

He dropped to one knee and picked up the handgun. Stood up again with the gun stuck in his belt and both hands back on the shotgun. The first guy was moaning in the fetal position, both hands cradling his swollen balls. The second simply lay still on his stomach, hands behind his head even though Grant hadn't asked him to. This was LA, the home of the movies. Everybody knew to put their hands behind their heads even though it was never what cops demanded. Hands in plain sight was what you wanted. Spread out, palms upward, away from any chance of reaching for a hidden weapon.

"I really think you should take up another line of work. You remember what film that was in?"

The first guy continued moaning. The second kept quiet.

"Charles Bronson in *Mr. Majestyk*. Another shotgun picture. I think Clint Eastwood got all the best quotes though. Maybe you should learn some of 'em. Or give up robbing banks."

With the danger over, Grant slipped into conversational mode. Remaining calm and relaxed meant he never got the shakes from the post-adrenaline dump that most experienced after combat.

"First crook I ever locked up back in Yorkshire—his name was Robin Banks." Grant smiled at the not strictly true memory. "Didn't have two brain cells to rub together. Stole a bag of sweets from the corner shop—Patel's on Ravenscliffe Avenue. Neither of you two are called Robin, are you?"

Neither of them spoke. One of them might have shook his head, but it was hard to tell with them both being on the ground like that. Grant saw movement through the smoked glass inside the bank. The customers and staff, who had been forced to lay on the floor, were getting up now that the threat had gone. There was movement behind him too. Cars pulling up at the curb and doors opening. Red and blue lights reflected off the front door but appeared darker in the smoked glass.

Gun slides were racked, pump actions pumped. A commanding voice shouted across the sidewalk without the aid of a loudhailer. "Put the guns down and keep your hands out where I can see them. Now."

Grant glanced at the two bank robbers on the ground and suddenly realized that he was the only guy armed and dangerous. A shotgun cradled in both hands and a handgun in his belt.

Traffic noises returned to full volume. A helicopter thumped away overhead. Pedestrians chattered. The voice became more insistent.

"*Now.*"

SIX

GRANT SET THE SHOTGUN on the ground and took the handgun out of his belt with just his fingertips. He laid it down beside the shotgun and stood up. He held both arms out straight, like Jesus on the cross. His reflection stared back at him in the smoked glass doors. The image was a familiar one. The orange windcheater was the icing on the cake.

"Aw, shit."

He didn't think that was overstating the point. He didn't have to look up to know it was a news helicopter hovering over MacArthur Park, zoom lens no doubt focused on the Resurrection Man making headlines once again.

Three LAPD cops came over to him, keeping a wide circle with one on either side of him and one down the middle. Shiny badges and heavy utility belts supplemented their smart black uniforms. All three kept their guns trained on the disarmed suspect.

Only one spoke. The one in the middle. "On the ground. Face down."

Grant complied.

"Hands out where I can see them. Palms open, facing up."

Grant complied.

Firm hands patted him down and came up empty for weapons. While he lay on the ground, backup units set up a perimeter around the bank. Just because there were three suspects in custody didn't mean there weren't more inside. Grant was impressed. He didn't try to explain. That would come later. Securing the scene came first. Protecting life and property was the priority.

Two officers, guns at the ready, deployed to the front doors. Both glanced through the smoked glass, one on either side, getting opposite views. One opened the door. The other darted inside. The first one followed, and the door closed. Grant could hear raised voices in the bank but couldn't see from his position on the floor. He didn't need to. The scenario was common sense. Get a quick first account from the witnesses. Confirm their stories with the bank staff. Ensure there were no further robbers hiding among the customers. View any CCTV footage.

There was some radio traffic from inside. Snippets of conversation. Then the officer standing over Grant spoke into his shoulder mike. "Two Adam Forty-Five. Scene secure. No casualties. Five-Six and Seven-Five on site. Request prisoner transport and crime scene."

The radio squawked. Apparently reception in LA was no better than parts of Ravenscliffe back home. Grant could imagine the consternation in the control room. If getting CSI was half as difficult as calling SOCO, then examining the crime scene would have to wait. In a city the size of Los Angeles, he reckoned the wait would be a long one.

The answer came amid a burst of static. "Negative on crime scene. Detectives en route."

As if on cue, an unmarked Crown Vic pulled up beyond the cordon of patrol cars and flashing lights. The front grill lights flashed twice, then stopped. Two detectives got out but didn't cross the line of armed officers. Preserving evidence meant not storming through the scene until you knew the common approach. Until the first responders told the detectives where they'd walked, the plainclothes officers would stay put. Once again Grant was impressed.

After a few minutes the two cops came out of the bank. "Clear."

They holstered their weapons and walked over to the detectives. There was a couple minutes of heads-together conferring, then the detectives approached the bank, keeping to the path the uniform cops had used coming out. The tall detective pointed at the two disarmed robbers.

"Have Five-Six and Seven-Five transport those two. Separate cars."

Two Adam Forty-Five waved officers from the other two cars over from the perimeter and repeated the instructions. They handcuffed the suspects and read them their rights. The first gunman was dragged to his feet, still moaning. He managed to find his voice.

"Officers. I was coming out the bank when this guy assaulted me. Unprovoked attack, man. Shotgun and everything. Fuck me. I was scared shitless."

The other robber followed his lead. "Yeah, man. We was, like, totally screwed."

Robber number one turned on his accomplice. "Shut the fuck up, man! We don't know each other. Remember?"

The tall detective jerked a thumb toward the patrol cars. "Take Shitless and Brainless back to Rampart. Separate rooms." Then, to the robbers, "And you two: put a sock in it."

They were dragged off muttering under their breaths. The detective indicated Grant on the floor as he walked past toward the smoked glass doors. "Sit this one up. Keep him here."

The detective glanced up into the clear blue sky above Mac-Arthur Park. The throbbing beat of the helicopter had become part of the local ambience and could almost be forgotten. "And don't forget the news is watching. This guy's a celebrity."

The detectives went into the bank. Grant shuffled against the wall and sat with his knees drawn up. He still didn't explain. He reckoned the uniforms had given a brief account of the CCTV footage, and the detectives would be checking it now. Grant craned his neck and smiled at the camera above the door covering the outside and the ATM shelter. The cameras inside would show the robbery in its entirety. No doubt the customers would confirm what happened. In a city as busy as LA, Grant reckoned they'd dispense with the crime scene technicians. Forensic evidence would only confirm what the cameras showed. CSI had more important crimes to solve.

Grant waited patiently. You can't rush a crime scene. Statements would be taken from the witnesses later. Thumbnail sketch accounts would be jotted in the detectives' notebooks for now. After a while the perimeter was withdrawn. By the time the detectives came back out, there was only 2A45 left guarding the last suspect, Jim Grant.

The tall detective lit a cigarette but didn't offer them around. He nodded to the uniform cop who'd been with Grant from the beginning. "Thanks, Tom."

He pointed at Grant. "We'll take this one."

"Okay. Those things'll kill you, y'know."

"They'll have to take a number. Street scum're always trying to kill me." He smiled at the uniform called Tom. "You pussies gave up too easy. Last smoker at Rampart. I'm proud to be an independent."

They got Grant to his feet and led him to the car. The helicopter pulled back, then banked left toward Hollywood. The action was over. The Crown Vic pulled away from the curb and did a U-turn back along West Sixth. Behind it the world returned to normal in the baking heat.

RAMPART POLICE STATION was just over a mile away along West Sixth toward the city. Everybody referred to it as New Rampart because it was brand new and clean as a whistle. The building was a long, low single-story cement structure with a half-dozen slitted blue windows on one side and a bank of mirrored glass at the other. It looked like Hitler's bunker apart from the terra-cotta vertical feature and the curved glass wall beside the front doors. Individual silver letters spelled out

LOS ANGELES POLICE DEPARTMENT RAMPART STATION

along the front wall. A tarmac visitors' parking lot nestled out front between an expanse of sprinklered lawns and flower borders. A well-established tree that must have been there long before the station provided shade to the entrance driveway.

The Crown Vic didn't use the entrance driveway, turning instead into the rear parking lot and prisoner reception area. The van bay doors stood open, having recently ingested the hayseed bank robbers. The Crown Vic parked in the far corner near the red and white communications tower. The taller detective let Grant out the back door and stretched his legs.

"Thanks."

"Welcome to Dodge."

"You want me to tell you what happened?"

"We know what happened. But, yeah, in your own words. Not out here though. In the office. I'm Bob Snow. My partner's Richard Wadd."

"You serious?"

Wadd shrugged his shoulders. "Go at it. I've heard all the Dick Wad jokes already."

"At least nobody'll forget you. I'm Jim Grant."

Snow nodded. "The Resurrection Man. Nobody'll forget you either, not even in that crazy disguise you're wearing. Orange jacket your favorite, is it?"

"Was. Last one got a bit torn up. This one's summer weight."

"Let's go in and get some coffee. Oh, hang on. You Brits drink tea, right?"

The trio crossed the parking lot into the van bay, leaving the sunshine behind. The heavy metal door in the side wall buzzed open. Five minutes later they were through the custody area and entering the detective bureau. Just like the CID office back home.

Grant smiled. It felt good to be in a police station again.

REMEMBERING THAT AMERICANS COULDN'T make a decent cup of tea, Grant settled for milky coffee with lots of sugar. He sat at one of the spare desks in front of the LAPD divisional map. Except they weren't called divisions; in LA, they were called bureaus.

The two bureaus across the middle of Los Angeles were the West Bureau, covering Wilshire and Hollywood, and the Central Bureau, which covered the east, including Rampart, even though it was just out of town to the west. Grant leaned back in his chair and took a sip of coffee. It was too hot, so he put it on the desk and surveyed the office. Rampart might be a new building, but the office furniture had obviously been carried over from the old place. The desks were dented and careworn. The filing cabinets looked a little newer. The swivel chair that Grant was sitting in creaked when he turned around. One of the wheels was bent and squeaked when it rolled.

"Nice place you've got here."

Snow looked up from copying notes out of his book. "I've heard about you English. Sarcasm drips from every word."

"I prefer 'dry sense of humor.'"

"Ironic, seeing as how we're in the dry season."

"I've heard Americans don't understand irony."

"I didn't say I understood it. Looked it up once though."

Grant tried his coffee again. It was still too hot. "What I'm getting at is, since they built a new station, you'd think they'd freshen up the desks for you."

Snow closed his notebook. "The new station isn't for us. It's for the populace. Looks good on the street. In here—where we live—they couldn't give a fuck."

"Modern policing. Same the world over."

"You're not going to give me that 'shit rolls downhill and cops live in the valley' thing, are you?"

"You heard about that?"

"I checked up on you."

"What did you find?"

"Something very strange."

"That's me, all right."

Snow picked his coffee up and came over to Grant's desk. He leaned against the wall map and looked down at the man in the orange windcheater. Steam drifted up from his mug. Snow didn't seem to mind. He took a deep swig of hot black liquid and didn't even wince. Maybe this was part of the pissing contest all new arrivals had to suffer.

Snow kept his tone friendly. "Officially you're not with the West Yorkshire Police anymore."

"Officially and factually. I was allowed to transfer."

"To the BPD."

Grant nodded. "Boston, Massachusetts, not Boston, Lincolnshire."

"So what are you doing out here?"

"At the bank? Getting cash out of the ATM."

"In LA."

"I love the movies. I'm on vacation."

Snow looked skeptical. He took another deep swig of coffee before speaking. "Because if you're here on official business, the courtesy is to let the local po-lice know what you're doing."

Grant smiled at Snow's impression of the Boston pronunciation of police. He reckoned it was intended as a put down of the northeastern force. He was sure the BPD had similar views of the LAPD.

"No official business. Just taking in the sights."

Snow nodded at the sheets of paper on Grant's desk. "You finished your statement?"

Grant swiveled in his chair and shuffled the five-page statement into a neat pile. "Signed and dated."

"Handwritten. I'd have thought you'd prefer to type it."

43

Grant threw Snow a sideways glance. It looked like the detective really had been checking up on him. His official army record showed him as being a typist.

"Back home—in Yorkshire—we prefer witness statements to be handwritten. Less chance of being accused of coaching. Just their own words." Grant smiled. "You've got typists, haven't you?"

Snow ignored the question and tapped the map behind him. "ATM at the bank—you want to keep your eyes open. LA's the bank robbery capital of the world. Over five thousand this year already."

"I hope they're not all as stupid as these two."

"Some are, some aren't, but they're all armed and dangerous."

"Yeah, I noticed."

"Those were impressive moves you put on them."

"Thanks. I got lucky."

Nobody in the room believed that. Snow reverted to his previous subject. "Not here on official business then?"

"That's right."

"'Cause I'm getting a vibe here suggesting something else."

"You're a gut instinct kind of cop, huh?"

"I am."

"Best kind, in my opinion."

"Thanks."

"But there's nothing for you to worry about. Just something I'm looking into for a friend."

"Anyone I'd know?"

"It's a small world. Never can tell." Grant stood up and handed the statement to Snow. "We finished here?"

Snow glanced at the first page. He didn't appear to be worried about the content. The CCTV and witnesses at the scene had cleared

Grant of any involvement other than being in the wrong place at the wrong time—the right time, as it turned out.

The detective waved toward his partner. "Need a ride? Dickwad'll drop you off if you like."

Grant smiled. Nicknames were incredibly personal among cops and only shared with trusted colleagues. Being included in that circle meant a lot to him. If Snow was a gut instinct kind of cop, then his instincts had given Grant the all clear.

Grant shook his head. "No, thanks, I prefer public transport. Get a better feeling of where I am."

"No direct route to your hotel from here."

"The Mayfair's walking distance. Bottom of Witmer, just over there." Grant indicated one block east and down the hill. "But I'm going up to Hollywood. Check out the Walk of Fame."

"Metro's back at MacArthur Park."

"I know. Walk'll do me good."

"This is Los Angeles. Walking's considered eccentric. You walk too much and you'll get a name for yourself."

"Already got one, it seems."

"Resurrection Man. Yeah, that's gonna stick."

Grant finished his coffee and set the empty mug on the desk. "Back in Bradford there's a guy who walks everywhere in a monk's robe and sandals. Weird fuck. I get like him, I'll start worrying. Thanks for the drink."

"You're welcome. I'll show you out."

Wadd looked up from his work and waved a hand in farewell. Grant waved back. Snow led Grant through a maze of corridors, bypassing the custody area, until they reached the reception counter. The curved glass wall let sunshine fill the room.

Grant paused at the front door. "One thing you could do for me."

Snow held the door open and waited. Most people would be suspicious of what favor they were about to be asked, but the detective appeared indifferent. "What's that?"

"Do you have any contacts in the movie industry? You know, who might have info about film companies and stuff?"

"You want an audition?"

"No. Just interested, is all."

"Not official business, though, right?"

"Right."

Snow took out his cell phone and began scrolling through the phonebook. When he found the one he wanted, he wrote it in his notebook and tore the page out. "Chuck Tanburro. Ex-LAPD. Works on *CSI: NY*."

"In New York?"

"In LA. Better weather. Tell him I sent you."

"Thanks."

They didn't shake hands, simply held one up in farewell. A familiar cop gesture. Grant stepped out into the sunshine and walked down the driveway. Once he was beyond the shady tree, he turned right, back along West Sixth.

SEVEN

THE NAKED WOMEN AND erect penises didn't stand out from all the other naked women and erect penises on display at Amoeba Music on Sunset Boulevard. The gaudy, colorful DVD sleeve didn't stand out either. Thankfully, Amoeba Music displayed its adult titles in alphabetical order. *The Hunt for Pink October* was filed under H, not T—standard practice for movie listings that treated *the* as a non-word when it came to titles.

Grant picked the empty case up and scanned the cover. Senator Richards had been right, you couldn't identify his daughter from the photo on the sleeve, but Grant recognized her from the clip he'd watched earlier. Pierced nipples. Small, firm breasts. A row of tattooed stars on either side of her crotch. Yes, that was definitely her. He turned the case over and read the back of the sleeve. The synopsis was the same. The cast names he couldn't remember. The lettering was so small he had to run his fingers across the production details until he found what he wanted. The film company was called Zed Productions, with an address in Long Beach. There was no telephone number. That didn't surprise him. He doubted there'd be one for Warner Bros. or Paramount on the back of their movies either.

He considered checking the Hollywood Street Guide he'd just bought from a guy who looked like Brad Pitt but knew the map was too local to cover Long Beach. Then a voice he recognized whispered in his ear.

"I didn't think that was your kind of movie."

Grant became aware of somebody standing beside him. Body heat transmitted like an oil-filled radiator. Understated perfume that smelled nice but not too strong. He half expected the infectious laugh to follow, but Robin Citrin kept a straight face. Grant held the case in one hand, refusing to hide what he'd been looking at. The smile he gave her was the only reason he couldn't keep a straight face too.

"I was looking for *Animal Farm,* but I think I'm in the wrong section. These are the only cocks I could find."

This time she did laugh, and it was not only infectious, it was downright dirty. "That joke doesn't work over here. Nobody knows what a cock is."

"*You* know what a cock is."

"I'm media savvy. Culturally cross-pollinated. The cock thing? Now that's a whole new reality show right there."

"You still chasing me for that?"

"Catching you, I think."

Grant put the case back and turned to look into Citrin's eyes. They were dark and sensuous. Sexier than anything on the gaudy video sleeves on display. She made the perfume smell sexy too. The mop of unruly black hair looked windswept and suggestive. The white blouse and black trousers looked even more so.

Grant held a hand up to his mouth and mimed a drinking motion. Citrin nodded and turned toward the stairs. He followed her down to the main shopping floor and out the front doors.

EIGHT

"How much?"

Grant was sitting at a table with his back to the wall, facing the plate-glass window. Outside, the street was busy. According to the street signs, Caffè Etc. was at the intersection of Selma and Cahuenga. According to the map, it was Selma Avenue and North Cahuenga Boulevard. If American sign makers abbreviated any more, you'd be guessing your location by initials.

Having coffee with Robin Citrin felt good. So good that Grant felt there were distinct possibilities. "You've got to be kidding me."

For now, he was more concerned with the money he'd just been offered to become the next Steven Seagal *Lawman* reality star. It was a sum that dwarfed his wages as a frontline cop and would probably rival the salary of the Chief of Police. He sat back in his chair and leaned against the wall.

Citrin leaned forward. "I'm not kidding."

Grant looked into her eyes. They were focused and serious. "I thought you said I wasn't Clint Eastwood."

"Eastwood's worth more. Seagal *gets* more."

"Jesus Christ."

"He'd get more than Elvis. Elvis would be top end."

Grant took a sip of his milky coffee. A latte. He was beginning to like it and would have to remember that's what to order. A latte. The cup was a large-scale version of a teacup in a saucer. It was bigger than a soup bowl back home. Any wider and he'd be able to swim in it. He put the cup down and stared out of the window to buy some time.

There was a street market along Selma Avenue, covered tables and temporary stalls running up either side of the street. Over the top of them he could just make out the red sign of Big Wang's. Considering what Wang was a euphemism for, he doubted there was a bigger prick in Hollywood apart from maybe Steven Seagal. Beyond the strip mall opposite, the skyline was dotted with enormous billboards advertising the latest movie or TV show. Practically every flat-roofed building had one built across the top. Even Caffè Etc. had a small billboard advertising Western Union and a stretch banner running the length of the building above the window with a giant bug-eyed frog and a wasp. Huge black letters read EYES? and BUZZ? Grant had no idea what it was promoting.

He couldn't think what to say so he simply repeated himself. "Jesus Christ."

"You become religious all of a sudden?"

"I believe that could be it. Yeah."

She leaned her elbows on the table. Her voice was low. "Your stock is rising."

He watched her eyes. "You noticed."

The dirty laugh came again, but she skirted the double-entendre. "Your other stock. Your value to any TV company willing to give you a show."

"Give *me* a show? I'm not Bob Hope."

"No. You're the guy who tackled a pair of armed bank robbers with his bare hands wearing an orange jacket and a smile."

"I didn't smile."

"Creative license."

"You see—it's that creative license that bothers me about reality TV."

"Getting shot doesn't bother you?"

"I didn't get shot."

"You could have."

"You could get killed by a falling block of ice from an incoming jet."

"But I wouldn't have provoked the incoming jet by confronting it with nothing but my dick in my hand."

Grant feigned concern, his face turning serious. "You've got a dick?"

"Figure of speech."

"Between creative license and figures of speech, what you're saying is you're full of shit."

"This is LA. We're all full of shit. The figure you should be concentrating on, though, is the one I just gave you."

Grant smiled. "And that's some figure."

Citrin grinned, exposing perfect white teeth and a brilliant California smile, then she turned serious. "The sight of you like Jesus on the cross outside the bank—guns on the floor, surrounded by armed police—that was priceless."

"It felt a lot worse at the time."

She shook her head. "I've watched the footage. Saw your face. Either you're the coolest guy under pressure I've ever met or you hide your fear very well."

"We all hide what we don't want people to see."

"Now you're beginning to sound like Steven Seagal."

"Steven Seagal, Lawman. I can't get over that."

"Jim Grant, the Resurrection Man. Get over that."

"With the orange jacket and my arms out wide?"

"It's your trademark."

"You reckon?"

"It's no coincidence. Boston, it happened twice. You've been here, what? Two days? And you're crucified again."

It was Grant's turn to shake his head. "My trademark is putting bad guys in jail. I told you: I'm a cop, not a TV star."

"You'd still be a cop."

"Have you ever seen anyone act normal when they know the cameras are on them? They either kick off or dry up. I can't do my job with half a TV studio behind me."

"We can be discreet."

"Not discreet enough."

She was losing him. The expression on her face changed from optimistic to hopeful to exasperated in a few short seconds. It was her turn to look out the window to buy time. Somebody had set up a wire cage directly outside Caffè Etc. Not the size of a zoo cage but big enough to house several dogs curled up on the sidewalk. A strange blue-haired girl with more piercings than Madonna sat on a foldout chair in front of a dog bowl full of money. Citrin appeared to take heart from the display. "You see that out there?"

Grant looked at the caged dogs and the woman guarding it.

"Yeah."

"What do you see?"

He sensed that was a trick question, so he examined the scene carefully. There were five dogs, one big cuddly thing, two medium-sized mongrels, and two midgets that hadn't walked anywhere in their lives. Glove puppet dogs, like the ones being carried around Hollywood by even stranger creatures with tattoos, spiky hair, and hoops through their noses. Like the blue-haired alien sitting on the foldout chair. Several people looked through the cage and made cooing noises before dropping cash in the dog bowl.

"I see a freak show. Somebody cashing in on a few stray dogs."

"You think they're stray dogs?"

He looked again. The dogs looked well groomed and cared for. The midgets looked expensive; the big dog, even more so. Now that he thought about it, the mongrels didn't look like mongrels at all, just breeds he didn't recognize. There was a lot of money in that cage. More than was in the dog bowl beside it. The blue-haired girl was still an alien species. Grant put a smile in his voice. "Expensive stray dogs?"

"Abandoned dogs. This is Hollywood. Most pampered dog owners in the world. They get bored; the dog goes out the door. That girl, she runs a free pet adoption service. Sets up on market day because there're more people who might take one home. Donations help feed the dogs until she finds them a new owner."

Grant looked at the girl with fresh eyes. "Real life hits La La Land."

"Reality. Not everything is what it seems."

He stifled a laugh. "Seagal playing at being a reality cop. You got that right."

Citrin leaned back in her seat, more relaxed. "You are a real cop. Reality will take care of itself."

"Discreetly?"

"Absolutely."

Something was running around in Grant's head. An unformed idea. Having a TV insider could prove useful. He took a deep swig of coffee and paused while he put his thoughts in order. He spoke slowly. "Hidden cameras. Long-distance zooms. Like that?"

"If that's how you want to play it."

"You know all about that covert stuff, then?"

Citrin looked him in the eye and lowered her voice. "I can do very undercover."

"You got a title?"

"Miss Whiplash."

Grant laughed. "For the show."

"It's got to be *The Resurrection Man.*"

Grant felt the mobile phone begin to vibrate in his pocket. He took it out and the vibration morphed into an increasing ring volume. He looked at the caller display but didn't recognize the number. He barely had any programmed in anyway. He was old school and preferred phones attached to the wall.

Citrin watched the pantomime and smiled. "I didn't see you as a cell kind of guy."

"A cell is where I put bad men."

"*Cellular phone* kind of guy."

"Used to keep it in my bag."

"That's okay—if I wanted to talk to your bag."

A moment of déjà vu washed over him, and he heard Terri Avellone saying the same thing back in Boston. His carnal thoughts about Robin Citrin made him feel guilty about the woman he'd left behind. Briefly. They weren't married. They were in different cities. Sex conquers all.

He flicked the Motorola open and answered. "Grant."

An educated voice spoke briefly. The butler or manservant or whatever he was. Senator Richards wanted to see him immediately. From the sound of it, the senator wasn't too happy about something. Grant closed the phone without saying goodbye and put sadness in his smile. "Got to go. Sorry. Let me think about the TV thing, okay?"

He left enough money for the coffees and went in search of a cab.

NINE

GRANT DIDN'T UNDERSTAND WHAT Richards was getting upset about, so he simply let the senator blow himself out without saying anything. The sun had moved round the garden since this morning but the view from the study window was just the same. The smell from the flowers had dulled. The lawnmower had stopped long ago. There was a fresh Pepsi on the coffee table, with ice and lemon.

Richards ran out of things to say, so he fell back on his main objection. "You were supposed to be discreet."

"I am being discreet."

"Discreet? You were plastered all over the news, getting arrested."

"I haven't seen that yet. They show the part where I disarmed two bank robbers first?"

"Yes, they showed that. Very publicly on national TV. Hardly discreet."

Grant took a drink of Pepsi and set the glass back on the table. He leaned back against the Chesterfield—the most uncomfortable settee in the world, in his opinion—and took a deep breath before he spoke. "Do you know the definition of discreet?"

"I know what it means. Yes."

Grant kept his voice monotone. Educational. "Careful and circumspect in one's speech or actions in order to avoid causing offense or revealing private information."

Richards glared across the coffee table from his position standing behind the desk. The grandfather clock ticked quietly. Birdsong drifted through the partly open window. Grant took his silence as permission to carry on.

"I was very circumspect in disabling two armed robbers and avoiding getting shot. That might have offended you, but, even with twenty-four-hour flying fucking news, it most certainly did not reveal any private information about your daughter or why I am in Los Angeles."

He took another swig of Pepsi. That was about as angry as he got without hitting somebody. Hitting the senator he'd been sent to protect wasn't a good career move on his first assignment stateside. Getting that off his chest calmed him down. "Pardon my French."

Richards chose discretion as the better part of valor, another variation of discreet that he didn't need a dictionary to understand. Instead he came round the front of the desk and leaned against the corner, one leg draped casually over the edge. Casual leg positioning seemed to be his specialty. His voice was calm and friendly, as if the previous conversation had never taken place.

"In regard to why you *are* in Los Angeles…have you made any progress?"

Grant crossed one leg over his knee. It didn't look anywhere near as casual as Senator Richards' pose, but it kept him from getting up and punching him on the nose. He was acutely aware that he needed to keep one eye on what the senator wanted and one on the real reason he'd been sent here.

"I've got a line on the production company. Somewhere down Long Beach."

The senator nodded as if that meant something when, in fact, he was just saving face and distancing himself from his explosive tantrum. The draped leg looked as if it was uncomfortable, but the pose had been struck for effect, not comfort. To divert Grant's attention from the feigned casualness, Richards got up and walked to the window. He took a deep breath because it seemed like the thing to do. Grant swiveled on the settee to follow the senator before speaking.

"In the interests of discretion, I assume you don't want me storming in there and ordering them to stop."

Richards looked mildly annoyed at the sarcasm in Grant's voice. "That's right. What do you propose?"

"I've got a couple of irons in the fire. First thing is to go see the producer. Get a reading on him. See what it'll take to divert his resources."

"You mean get him to use a different girl?"

Grant detected a note of disapproval in the senator's tone. "So long as they're consenting adults and he's not forcing anyone, yes."

Richards turned his back to the window. His shoulders didn't exactly sag, but they became less rigid. His eyes held a hint of sadness—and was that guilt? "My daughter is a consenting adult."

"They'll all be somebody's daughters. They just won't all have influential fathers with a reputation to protect."

"Point taken."

Richards went to the desk and pressed the call button. The bell sounded deep inside the house. The interview was over. It seemed that was how rich men and US senators dealt with things. Call someone else to do their dirty business. Grant got up but didn't finish his drink. He'd lost his appetite.

"You want my advice? Go public. Be open and up front. You're a concerned father. Use it to your advantage."

Grant said the words but knew they would fall on deaf ears. By protecting the senator, he was also protecting the man who had more to lose by association. If that wall came tumbling down, then more people would be hurt than a headstrong daughter and her family. He didn't wait for Jeeves to open the door. He went out by himself and slammed the door behind him. He was halfway across the hall when another door opened beyond the sweeping staircase. A husky voice called his name, and Maura Richards waved him over.

THE DAY ROOM WAS brighter than her husband's study. Grant reckoned that was partly by design but mostly because of the personality difference. Double Dick was stiff and unbending. Maura Richards was frothy and shapely. She wasn't so much bubbly as full of life. Not a dizzy blond, a sensuous woman with sandy-colored hair and the curves to match. She wore the same summer dress she'd been wearing that morning. It looked cool and airy and didn't hide her slim waist and curvaceous figure.

This wasn't Robin Citrin though, a flirtatious TV woman. This was a woman of substance.

He waited for her to indicate the comfortable patio furniture in the adjoining conservatory before taking a seat on a deep-cushioned wicker chair. Mrs. Richards sat opposite and crossed her legs. The elegant sweep of her calves was a million miles away from Double Dick's casual leg crossing. She wasn't striking a pose, she was simply relaxing. Her face didn't look relaxed though.

"Mr. Grant."

"Jim."

"Jim. I don't know where to begin."

Her voice was low and husky, as if she'd spent all her life smoking forty a day, but he doubted if she had ever smoked. She looked too healthy. Her skin was tanned and flawless. Her teeth were white, practically obligatory in California, and her eyes green and clear. This woman screamed healthy living and yet her eyes betrayed a darker side, a worry that was eating at her. So, Grant thought, she knows why I'm here.

He kept his voice nonjudgmental. "Mrs. Richards."

"Maura, please."

The perceived intimacy of being on first-name terms suddenly felt wrong.

"Mrs. Richards. I think you know exactly where to begin and just what you want to ask me. I'm fine with that. Ask away."

Her eyes flared briefly. Anger? Excitement? Grant assumed the latter. When you're a wealthy woman with a powerful husband, people don't disagree with you very often. This was something different than she'd been used to. Something different was generally more exciting than the norm. Jim Grant most definitely wasn't the norm. She leaned back in her chair and looked him in the eye. Direct. Unblinking. She appeared to make the decision to trust him.

"I want you to stop my daughter's self-destructive behavior."

"You mean stop her sleeping with men on film." It was a statement, not a question.

"You've seen the film. No sleeping takes place."

"Yeah. The nodding that goes on doesn't look like she's tired."

Her eyes flared again. Maybe he'd overstepped the mark. Maybe not.

"She does a lot more than head nodding. A lot of other things too. I am partly to blame for that. She is headstrong, free spirited—something she gets from me."

Grant gave her a quizzical look. "You're not a porn star, too, are you?"

The throaty laugh was pure Lauren Bacall. "Don't get free spirited mixed up with free bodied. Her career choices come from"—she paused in mid-sentence, taking a deep breath before continuing—"somewhere else."

If there was something to read into that, Grant missed it. Instead, he focused on the main reason children went off the rails. Age differences in second marriages.

"What happened to your husband's first wife?"

Mrs. Richards didn't appear surprised by the question. "She died before we met."

Grant didn't apologize for her loss. It was her husband's loss, not hers. As usual, though, one person's loss was another person's gain. "Either your husband's had a hard paper round or I'd say you're a lot younger than him."

"Is that a compliment?"

"Not for your husband."

"You don't like him."

"I don't need to like him."

"Do you like me?"

Grant smiled but wouldn't be drawn. "What are you, twenty years younger?"

She uncrossed her legs and stretched one arm across the back of her seat.

"You have a good eye. I am thirty-nine. My husband is fifty-nine. He made his fortune in oil. I married into that. Our daughter arrived around the same time. She is only nineteen, and I want her back."

Grant saw the concern in her eyes and softened his tone. He wasn't here to pass judgment on why people got married. It wasn't something he had any experience of. What he did have experience of was grieving parents. Angelina Richards wasn't dead, but she was lost to the family. It amounted to the same thing.

The sun was dipping toward the hills that gave Beverly Hills its name. Shafts of orange sunlight angled into the conservatory. For the first time, Grant noticed framed photographs dotted around the windowsills and wicker bookshelves. A smattering of family portraits. Several holiday pictures. A handful of official photos of the senator with various dignitaries. It was the man in the dress uniform and row of medals that caught his attention. The man who was inextricably linked to Senator Richards by virtue of each supporting the other's election campaigns: Richards to a position on the US Senate, the other to the highest role in modern policing.

The chief of police.

If Richards was torn down in a blaze of scandal, then the police chief would fall with him. The LAPD couldn't afford another scandal. Too much depended on the force regaining its good name and standing in the community. Too many people would be hurt if LA returned to the chaos that was the riots of '92. That's why Grant was sent to extricate the senator from the brown stuff. Get him out of the shit and the LAPD would be out of the shit.

Grant concentrated on the distressed mother. "She won't stop if your husband asks her?"

Mrs. Richards shook her head. "That would only drive her deeper into this…industry."

"Would she stop for you?"

She shook her head again, with more sadness this time. "She blames me…for many things."

Grant had never been married. The deep divisions between mothers and daughters were alien to him. That wasn't his area of expertise. Healing the rift wasn't why he was chosen. Closing the operation that was feeding off it was. "Well, let me see what I can do."

Mrs. Richards leaned forward and put a hand on his knee. The touch was warm; the emotion, cold. A practical manifestation of her plea for help. "Stop her. For me. Please."

He stood up, and her hand dropped away. She stood too. There was a moment's awkward silence, then she offered to have him driven to his hotel. Grant shook his head. "That's okay. It's a nice evening. I'll walk down to the Metro."

Mrs. Richards looked stunned that anyone would choose to travel on the Metro. She compromised with a counter offer. "I'll have Jeeves drop you at the station."

Grant stifled a laugh. "That's his name? Shit, I thought that was just in the books."

She smiled at him as she led the way through the day room to the hall. "Most things that find their way into books begin their life in reality."

"True fiction and reality. Story of my life at the moment."

The manservant or butler or whatever Jeeves was appeared from nowhere and took Grant out the front door. The sun was low in the evening sky. Insects buzzed around in the dying shafts of sunlight. A small car that looked foreign waited at the bottom of the steps. When Grant turned to say goodbye, Mrs. Richards had gone.

Twenty minutes later, he was dropped off on Hollywood Boulevard. Jeeves didn't offer his hand or say goodbye. Grant didn't speak either. He was too interested in the big black car that had been following them for the last two miles. The two big guys who'd smiled at him outside the Mayfair Hotel. Grant closed the door, and the little foreign car spun around and headed back toward the wealth and security of the hills.

The big car pulled up across the street. Grant stood on the sidewalk and waited. He'd had enough of this cat and mouse stuff. It was time to find out why Beavis and Butthead were shadowing him.

TEN

THERE ARE TWO GOLDEN rules to surviving a confrontation. Number one is avoid getting into a confrontation. Grant didn't intend to turn this thing into a showdown but was realistic enough to know that it could become one. That led to number two: choose your battleground and don't allow the enemy to dictate where you fight if possible. It was possible tonight. Crossing the street toward the big black car would give them home advantage.

There was a third rule that applied to all conflicts: divide and conquer. Grant needed to split the guys up and tackle them one at a time. He rephrased that in his head. *Question* them one at a time. To that end, he examined his surroundings while staying on the opposite side of the road, away from the two guys with square heads and no necks.

Hollywood Boulevard was still busy. Dusk was robbing the sky of the last vestiges of daylight, and the colored lights of night were already coming on. The street was crowded with shoppers and tourists, but a subtle change was taking place. Any semblance of conservatism was evaporating as the weird and wonderful took over. There was more colored hair on display than at a Star Trek convention.

Piercings and tattoos were the norm. Plastic breasts and miniskirts flooded the streets, and not all of them were female.

Grant scanned the intersection. The Metro station was on the opposite corner. Slow-moving traffic kept the crowds off the road. It would be a nightmare to drive around here; one of the reasons Grant liked using public transport. Navigating a strange city was one problem he could live without. The slow-moving traffic did something else. It blocked the big black car from coming across this side of the road. That dictated which direction Grant would take. If they wanted to follow him, they'd have to do it on foot.

There was a commotion in the crowd up ahead. A whole slew of heads turned in unison to the right along Highland. Grant noticed that the light coming from around the corner was brighter than the average street lamps. It was brilliant white light that could only mean one thing: somebody was filming on location. Whatever they were shooting, it had certainly got the crowd's attention.

Grant gauged angles and distances to the intersection, then glanced over his shoulder at the buildings along his side of the road. There was a narrow break in the building line leading to a parking lot round back of the El Capitan Theatre. The brilliant white light spilled around the back of the buildings from the parking lot. Whatever they were filming on Highland, this was a shortcut to get around behind it.

The crowd was growing at the intersection. There were people milling about the sidewalk all around him. Normally having so many people around would be a problem—witnesses to whatever he decided to do. Tonight he thought they might be a benefit. Witnesses worked both ways. Nobody was going to shoot him in the middle of this lot. It was time to make his move.

He locked eyes with the two guys in the black car and stared at them. Once he knew he'd got their attention, he turned sharply and darted down the alley, into the parking lot. He smiled as he heard the car doors slam behind him. Then he rounded the corner into the light.

GRANT'S FIRST THOUGHT WAS oh no, not again. At the far side of the parking lot, a pair of armed robbers were coming out of a single-story building mocked up to be a branch of the Bank of America. Cop cars screeched to a halt with their light bars splashing red and blue light across the scene. Uniforms dived out of the cars and leveled their guns at the robbers. Then somebody with a megaphone shouted above the car engines and the generator noise.

"Cut. Let's go again."

The parking lot was empty of parked cars, but one corner was crammed with Location Services trucks and mobile changing rooms. There was a catering truck with the serving hatch open along one side and a portable platform with steps for the diners. Nobody was eating at the moment. Everybody was busy capturing the fiction before them.

Grant was amazed at how much effort went into such a simple scene. It would be easier to commit a real bank robbery than make one up. There were several enormous lights with diffusers to take the sharpness off. Coils of electric cable snaked across the ground. On either side of the fake bank, two complicated structures fed water to a row of sprinklers across the top. It was raining in paradise. The tarmac was wet, reflecting the streetlights and flashing red and blue. The sky still had enough light in it to give a blue sheen to the action. The magic hour. Grant had heard of it. It was different to the magic hour at a crime scene, when evidence could be found or lost. In the movie industry it was that period when daylight became sunset and the wonderful images that could produce. He wondered what time of day it was supposed to be. The Bank of America didn't open at night.

A circle of technicians and actors surrounded the heart of the action. Some of the actors were dressed as LAPD cops but wore just the shirts and hats. Below the waist they wore faded jeans or track-suit bottoms. Grant thought they'd made a continuity error until they got in the cars for a second take. Stunt drivers. They wouldn't be seen in the shot except from the waist up. A miniature railroad track ran along the sidewalk with a complicated trolley-mounted camera rig. Grant noticed at least two other handheld cameras, no doubt for coverage from different angles. The guy with the mega-phone ordered everyone to their starting positions.

Grant turned left once he reached the parking lot and headed toward the nearest group of technicians. He heard pounding foot-steps behind him. Good.

The parking lot was clear of pedestrians. The only people here were cast and crew. Nearer the sidewalks of Highland it was a dif-ferent matter. The road had been blocked off, but beyond the barri-ers the rubberneck brigade was gathering in force. A thin blue line of uniformed cops kept them at bay. Off-duty cops getting a little overtime. Grant steered clear of them and headed toward the light-ing technicians and camera crew. The footsteps behind him slowed down. He threw a glance over his shoulder to confirm the big guys had followed him. They had.

Having the distraction of the location shoot was a bonus. Grant stood amid the outer circle of staff and hangers-on. There was still enough daylight for him not to be in the shadows, but so close to the brightly lit location he seemed to fade into the background. Except for his orange windcheater. Spillage from the arc lights picked it out like a red rag to a bull. Beavis and Butthead couldn't miss it. That was the idea. Grant wanted them to know where he was until it was time for them not to know.

Height and confidence got Grant past the outer cordon. He was now among the chosen few allowed close to the filming. Nobody asked who he was because he behaved like he belonged there. If Robin Citrin had her way, this would be his second home, only with fewer cameras. He watched the bank robbers come charging onto the street a second time. Patrol cars skidded to a halt. Armed police leveled their weapons. It all looked pretty realistic. No doubt one of the crew standing beside the camera was a police consultant, the guy who made sure the cops behaved like real cops and that operational procedures were followed. As long as it suited the story. Grant had seen enough movies where fiction was more important than reality.

He looked over his shoulder and saw the big guys standing on the fringes of the outer circle. They were tall and broad and built like tanks. It was the first time he'd got a good look at them outside of sitting in the car. He realized stereotyping them as wearing black suits had been wrong. The car was black. The shirts these two were wearing were not. Brightly colored Hawaiian monstrosities stood out even more than Grant's orange jacket. How could he have missed that? He thought back to this afternoon, when he'd had the itchy feeling up the back of his neck. He'd checked for a tail, but the tourists had all been wearing colorful shirts. Grant chided himself for not being more careful. The two Hawaiians exchanged a few words, heads together, then separated. One drifted toward Highland, the other around the outer ring toward the catering vehicles.

Divide and conquer. Good.

Grant moved deeper into the inner circle. Once he'd breached the outer ring, everybody assumed he had a right to be there even if nobody knew who he was. The only time they'd get worried would be if he took out a camera and started snapping away. He kept his hands loose at his sides and stepped into the spill from one of the lights. His jacket blazed, the orange almost too bright to look at. He waited a couple of seconds, then shifted sideways behind the aluminum reflector and quickly took his jacket off. He hung it over the corner of a light stand, then ducked into the crowd of watching crew.

The Hawaiian who had gone toward the catering truck breached the cordon first. He had collected a plate of pizza slices from the serving hatch and simply walked right through. Deep-set eyes scoped the shadowy figures standing behind the lights. They locked onto the orange jacket and moved to one side, keeping it in sight while pretending to eat.

Grant checked for the other guy. He was nowhere to be seen. Probably all the way over at the other side of the location making sure Grant didn't slip away. Grant had no intention of slipping away. With economical movements he stepped up behind the Hawaiian and stamped down on the back of his right leg with one foot. Just behind the knee. The Hawaiian's leg folded and he went down, hard. Grant took the plate before it dropped and knelt beside the big fella, who didn't look so big now. He set the plate on the ground, reached between the guy's legs, and grabbed his balls in a vicelike grip. Then he squeezed.

The big guy moaned.

Grant leaned close so he didn't have to shout above the generators. "Thought you'd go for ham and pineapple. That's a Hawaiian, isn't it?"

The moan formed into words. "I'm not Hawaiian, mother-fucker."

Grant tilted his head and scrutinized the flowery shirt. "The shirt is."

"You think Hawaii's the only place that has yellow shirts?"

Now that he thought about it, Grant reckoned the guy didn't have the Hawaiian look. Not Samoan either. He looked more Hispanic or South American. Enough of the small talk. He squeezed again, harder this time. "Short of you being gay and taking a fancy to me, why are you following me?"

The big guy smiled through the pain. "I'm gay. Have taken fancy to you."

Grant squeezed as hard as he could. "Why?"

The fallen heavy contained the scream of agony but couldn't control the whimper that escaped his lips. His eyes were watering. His face was red. But he was still smiling. He locked eyes with Grant but waited a moment to give weight to his words. "Keep a tag on you."

"Why?"

"So you don't leave, we don't know about it."

"Why?"

The big guy smiled and appeared to have conquered his pain. "You sound like my son, always asking why? Only not in English."

Grant released the squashed bollocks and wiped his hand on his jeans. It didn't look like this guy was going to answer his question. That was slightly worrying, but Grant was more concerned about how much the guy's boss knew about his business in LA. He picked up a slice of pizza and dropped it on the heavy's chest. "Don't eat it all at once."

Grant got halfway up, resting on one knee.

The big guy shuffled up into a sitting position. The pizza fell to the ground. He was smiling again. "He come for you himself. We make sure he no miss you."

"Who's he?"

The guy chuckled. "You think he forgot? He want talk to you. About Snake Pass."

"Dominguez?"

Grant was still swallowing that piece of information when he noticed the guy's eyes flick a glance up over Grant's shoulder. He spun round too late as the other guy came barging through the crowd.

Breathing exercises are one thing. Instant reactions are quite another. The fourth rule for surviving a confrontation is to act fast and don't think too much. Grant acted on instinct. It was why he'd survived so long. Everything happened in a few short seconds but felt like it lasted an age.

The other Hawaiian who wasn't Hawaiian was a charging bull. Seeing his friend on the ground enraged him. When anger takes over, clear thought goes out the window. The big guy's only thought was to get Grant. He lowered his head and beetled his brow and charged straight for him. He leaned all his weight into the charge. That was his first mistake.

Grant stayed down on one knee and picked up the plate. American football players have blockers and shoulder pads. With English rugby, it's all about positioning and timing. A good tackle takes away your opponent's legs. The opposition can't run without legs. Distraction is key. Grant flicked the plate upwards, sending pizza slices flying into the big guy's face. Not a dangerous prospect but enough to make him blink as he swiped a hand across his eyes.

A low tackle on an onrushing player the size of this guy can cause as much damage to you as the opposition. Grant needed to avoid taking damage. While the pizza distracted the charging bull, Grant got up and stepped over the first guy, who was still sitting up with his arms propping from behind. Grant kicked the arms away. He wasn't expecting that. The other guy wasn't either. His forward momentum ran him straight into the tangled body of his friend, and he suddenly found himself trying to change direction at full speed. That was his second mistake.

Grant darted to one side and snatched the orange jacket from the lighting frame. He flapped it like a bullfighter's cape and dumped it over the big guy's head. Blinded and disorientated, he lost his balance. As he went flying past, Grant grabbed his right wrist and yanked the arm outwards and down. The big guy had no choice. He either threw himself over into a forward roll or his arm would snap like a twig. He threw himself forward.

As he went sailing over his prone colleague, Grant stamped on the first guy's balls to disable him. The second guy landed on his back with a crash that shook the ground. Two of the pretending cops who weren't in the current scene looked on in shock. The guns in their holsters were replicas, but the equipment on their belts was real. Grant tugged a set of handcuffs from the nearest, and before the big guy had stopped rolling he had snapped one bracelet on his wrist and the other around the lighting stanchion. The second fake cop tried to step out of the way, but Grant took his cuffs too and shackled the first guy to the second.

Five seconds, tops. Two bad guys restrained and handcuffed.

Grant retrieved his jacket and slipped it on, aware for the first time that one of the filtered lights was now facing toward him. The orange windcheater stood out in the gloom. A lone Steadicam operator cut through the melee. The crowd of spectators applauded. They had just seen a stuntman perform a difficult combination in one take. Grant let them keep thinking that. He stepped aside with an embarrassed wave, then turned to one of the caterers who had come over to see what the commotion was all about.

"Sorry about the pizza. I'm sure it's very tasty."

He then spoke to the nearest play-cop. "I'd give it twenty minutes before letting them loose. They're not going to be happy with you."

The assistant director was shouting into his megaphone, but Grant didn't hang around to hear what he was saying. Cutting through the crowd, he was halfway to the Metro station before anyone realized he was gone.

ELEVEN

THE RED LIGHT ON the phone was blinking when Grant got back to his hotel room. It looked like an emergency warning light in the dark before he switched the lights on. If it had been a warning, then it had come too late. He'd already got the message. The Dominguez cartel weren't playing forgive and forget. They were coming for him. It would pay to be more careful for a while until he sorted them out.

He locked the door behind him and put the plastic bottle of water he'd bought on the bedside cabinet, then picked up the phone. He pressed the second button from the left and listened to the message. Hearing the voice made him smile.

It was Robin Citrin. "Hi. This is Robin Citrin for Jim Grant."

She paused, and Grant could hear traffic in the background. She must have been phoning from her cell. "Know how much you're worth now?"

Another pause.

"That's Clint Eastwood to Eli Wallach in *The Good, the Bad and the Ugly*. Poncho and everything. Actually, that scene was before he got the poncho."

Another pause.

"What I'm getting at is, your stock just rose again. I don't know what you were doing with those guys, but it's all over the news. You're giving better coverage than O. J. Simpson."

There was a throaty chuckle.

"Okay. Maybe not that good. Bottom line: the offer went up. Give me a call. We'll grab a coffee and talk about it. My treat this time. Just call, okay?"

She put on a phony newsreader's voice.

"This is Robin Citrin for LQ Productions, signing off."

The phone went dead for a second, then an electronic female voice said, "End of messages." Grant hung up and looked out the window. Downtown LA stood out against the night sky, all blinking lights and skyscrapers. A siren sounded somewhere in the distance, a regular night sound in any major city around the world but more prevalent in America. A police helicopter scooted across the sky, searchlight blazing. He glanced at his watch. It wasn't that late, but ringing from his hotel bed would be too provocative.

Instead, he opened the drawer and touched the velvet stethoscope box. That put everything in perspective. He closed the drawer, went into the bathroom, and turned the shower on. It had been a long, hard day. He got undressed and stepped under the hot spray. Tomorrow should be easier.

He was wrong.

TWELVE

ZED PRODUCTIONS LOOKED MORE like a 7-Eleven than a porn studio. That was because the plain concrete building at Alamo Court on North Long Beach Boulevard used to be a 7-Eleven. It stood in the corner of a parking lot that serviced Popeye's Chicken & Biscuits and the Road to Hana Hawaiian BBQ and Fish Grill. Alamo Court was a stubby dirt track that ran around the back of the food mall. Across East Tenth Street, a more upmarket concrete building housed Blockbuster Video, which stocked some of Zed Productions' softer adult movies.

Grant took the Metro Blue Line the following morning straight south out of downtown LA to Long Beach. The sun beat down out of a cloudless blue sky. High noon, the hottest part of the day, but he didn't see any point in visiting a porn studio too early in the morning. Sex stars weren't exactly early risers. Sex film producers were no doubt the same.

He slipped the orange windcheater off and slung it over his shoulder. The black T-shirt and faded blue jeans were still too warm, but even in LA you could only take so many clothes off before you got arrested. He cut across the parking lot, arriving outside the plain concrete building in the far corner at quarter past twelve.

ZED PRODUCTIONS

The discreet sign was underlined white letters on a black background. The only indication of what they produced was a silhouetted nude in white that reminded Grant of the Triple Zero matchbook condoms in Boston. Hardly surprising. The nude silhouette was a staple design in the sex industry. James Bond had even borrowed it for the teaser promotion of one of Pierce Brosnan's 007 movies.

The door was plain black-painted hardboard. There were no windows. What used to be the 7-Eleven shop windows had been bricked up and concreted over. They still showed through the yellow rendering that made the building stand out despite the covert nature of its business. A helicopter thudded across the sky over the yacht club marina farther south.

The door opened, and a midget came out. Grant stepped aside, trying to keep the surprise off his face.

The midget didn't look happy. He threw a disgusted look at the giant standing over him and stalked off through the parking lot. The door swung closed on its spring, and Grant caught the handle before it shut. He pushed it open and stepped out of the sunshine into darkness.

AN OLD GRAY-HAIRED GUY with a Van Dyke beard and an Elvis quiff sat behind a desk in the windowless office. The walls were painted dark red with black trim. Fairy lights blinked from the ceiling. Two wall-mounted spots illuminated the desk. The rest of the room was only lit by reflected light from the workstation. Half a dozen chairs lined one wall like in a doctors' waiting room. A filing cabinet, painted black to blend with the décor, stood in the corner behind the desk. The chairs were empty.

Van Dyke looked up from the papers on his desk. "At least you're the right size. Bilbo Baggins there must have got me mixed up with Vivid Inc. They do sex with primates movies."

Grant let the door close behind him and walked over to the desk. "Well, you know what they say about little fellas."

Van Dyke obviously didn't. He looked nonplussed, so Grant enlightened him. "Big guy, big cock. Little guy, all cock."

Van Dyke smiled but didn't laugh. "Muscles *and* a sense of humor."

Grant smiled back. "Of course it was probably a little guy said it."

The lighthearted banter did two things. It introduced Grant in a non-threatening manner, keeping the tone light and friendly, and it gave him time to check the room for threats and exits—the first thing he did whenever he entered a strange environment. The office was small and square. There were three black-and-white framed headshots of women on the wall above the chairs. There was a laptop computer open on the desk. Apart from the door Grant came in through there was only one other entrance, a door in the back wall beside the desk. There was a small surveillance camera high up in the corner above the filing cabinet. The wide-angle lens would cover most of the room from the desk outwards.

Any information Grant was looking for was likely in the desk drawers, the filing cabinet, or the laptop. He made a mental note of that for later. For now, he decided to keep things loose and see where they led him.

The rear door opened. The two guys who came in weren't midgets. They were as tall as Grant but built like Schwarzenegger. Skimpy cut-off vests exposed muscles that had taken years in the gym to produce. The bulging biceps were oiled and shiny. These guys had worked hard and liked to show the results. Judging by the way they glanced at each other, they were as bent as nine-bob notes. Grant wasn't sure how to translate that for the American market. He settled for gay. The look they threw at Grant told him they didn't like him.

Van Dyke jerked his head toward the first guy. "Mark Spitz."

Grant looked at Spitz. "Like the Olympic swimmer?"

Spitz smiled, but the smile didn't reach his eyes. "Only bigger."

Grant whistled. Van Dyke nodded toward the other guy. "Danny Swallows. They'll lead you through it."

Grant stifled a laugh. Barely. "Spitz or Swallows. Now there's a choice for the ladies."

Van Dyke nodded approvingly. "Humor. We could use that. The spits or swallows thing, though—we've heard it all before. You got your industry card?"

Industry card? Grant kept his face blank while he figured out what that was. If this had been the UK, he'd reckon Van Dyke meant the Equity Card that all actors needed to prove they were licensed to perform. There would no doubt be something similar in Hollywood, the Screen Actors Guild or the like. He was surprised they bothered with all that in the porn industry.

His best guess was that they didn't. "Not on me, no."

Van Dyke waved the minor irritation aside. "Doesn't matter. Nobody's working under their real name anyway."

"Not even Spitz and Swallows?"

"Them two. Yeah. Couldn't miss out on using that, could I?"

The two musclebound studs glared at Grant. They looked like they'd like to rip his head off and shit down his neck. They had the muscles to do it, too, just not the aptitude. Spitz and Swallows had pretty boy muscles, all bulk but no intensity. In a fight they'd be more worried about their hair and makeup than causing real damage. Grant slitted his eyes and glared back. He managed to hold back from growling.

Van Dyke noticed the atmosphere turning sour. "Okay, boys and girls. Let's not turn this into handbags at dawn."

Spitz and Swallows relaxed. Grant wasn't sure what they were going to lead him through but assumed Zed Productions was recruiting. A touch of luck. Maybe heavy laboring or security. Good. He could do either.

Van Dyke shut down the laptop and stood up. He glanced at the row of empty chairs and let out a sigh. Didn't look like there were many applicants for the job. That was good too. Standing up, the producer wasn't much taller than the midget who'd stormed off earlier. Short and round and as jolly as Danny DeVito. The Van Dyke beard and the quiff didn't suit him. They made him look like Pac-Man.

"Right, then. Let's show you around. I'm Stuart Ziff. That's the zee in Zed Productions, in case you wondered."

"I figured."

"Good. Muscles, brains, *and* humor." Ziff shrugged his shoulders and gave an apologetic wave. "We don't have any fluffers for the auditions. You'll have to work from cold. That a problem?"

Fluffers? Grant had heard of them. Non-performing females whose only job was to keep male porn stars erect between shots.

Hand jobs and fellatio were the tools of their trade. He suddenly realized Ziff wasn't looking for heavy lifting or security.

"No problem."

The back door opened again, and a woman stood in the entrance. Long dark hair and a figure-hugging dress. Tall and slim, with firm thighs and enormous breasts. He recognized her straight away. She was the woman with Senator Richards' daughter in *The Hunt for Pink October*.

THIRTEEN

THE STUDIO WAS BRIGHT and clean beneath the lights. Around the edges of the set, everything was shadows and darkness. The set was a replica living room with a beige carpet and a cream leather settee. It reminded Grant of the location in the movie Richards had shown him, only without the scenic background and the patio windows. Maybe they used this for pickup shots. More likely it was just for auditions or short films for the Internet.

Geneva Espinoza was absolutely stunning in a plastic and makeup sort of way. Her features were immaculate: dark eyes with long lashes; plucked and shaped eyebrows; small, straight nose; Angelina Jolie lips. If her skin and forehead didn't seem quite real, it could be the perfectly applied makeup or some other form of enhancement.

That took care of her face. The rest of her was equally impressive and almost certainly as false. The slim waist and strong thighs could be the result of rigorous exercise, as could the firm, round buttocks, but the breasts were twice the size of normal and as round as soccer balls. He'd have to reserve judgment on her nipples because she was still dressed, but the way her breasts didn't move as she walked onto the set, it would be a miracle if her nipples were in the same place they'd been naturally.

Ziff sauntered onto the set. "It gets hot under the lights, so we always keep plenty of bottled water handy. Sweat patches won't be a problem. Clothes are only for establishing shots. Danny here'll be running the camera."

Grant noticed the potbellied cameraman adjusting a large shoulder-mounted camcorder. There was no film cartridge. Everything was digital nowadays. Even so, the camera was bigger than anything Grant had seen on vacation. This wasn't for catching fun moments with the family.

Ziff waved Spitz forward. "Give him a rundown of the positions, then we'll get going."

Spitz came over to Espinoza, and they stood in the middle of the fake living room. They embraced without passion. She moved around him and slid her hands over his body, all the time aware of where the camera was and which angle gave the best view. Spitz followed suit. He feigned oral sex, masturbation, and doggy style before switching to several other positions, ending with Espinoza on top swinging her breasts over his face. They didn't swing much.

Grant recognized every position from porn films he'd watched over the years. He was no prude, and it all looked very interesting, but he never thought he'd be going through his paces on camera with a beautiful porn star. It was like every guy's dream come true. He wasn't sure how he was going to get information from her with everybody watching though. He might have to play this string out until he got her on her own.

How hard could that be?

To begin with, not very hard at all. He stepped under the lights and stood in front of the cream leather settee. Espinoza came into his arms like a long-lost lover. The figure-hugging dress contained her curves, but even in high heels she was much shorter than Grant. Her breasts crushed against his stomach but didn't flatten. Her hands snaked up his back and she tilted her face to be kissed. He obliged. It was the most pleasurable falsehood he'd ever committed.

Ziff nodded his approval, then went to the door. "I'll go watch on the link out front."

Ziff left, and Spitz went with him. That just left the cameraman and Espinoza. Still too many for a private talk. After a few minutes Espinoza stepped back and tugged the T-shirt out of Grant's jeans. Her fingers teased his stomach before yanking the black cotton up over his head in one expert movement. Playing his part, Grant reached behind her back and unzipped the dress. It peeled off like a second skin, revealing a skimpy bra and a thin cotton triangle that covered her sex.

Espinoza's stomach was flat and toned. She must work out almost as much as the Spitz and Swallows twins. Her fingers undid Grant's belt before slowly unzipping him. She slid one hand into the waistband and moved it around to his left hip, then slid her other hand around to the right. Delicate fingers began to ease the jeans off his hips.

The door burst open, and Ziff came charging onto the set. "Get that fucker out of here. What are you playing at? He's a cop."

Being caught with his pants down was bad enough. The atmosphere changed from lust to aggression in a split second. Grant swiveled sideways and moved Espinoza out of the way. He turned and was ready for action before the office door slammed shut.

Ziff stood between Spitz and Swallows, but Grant wasn't worried about them. It was the other three bruisers they'd brought with them. Five against one. All big guys. All fully dressed. That swung the odds in their favor.

FOURTEEN

GRANT TOOK HIS TIME getting dressed. The fact that he didn't seem intimidated gave the three heavies pause. They bunched together in the doorway as if they didn't want to be parted. Amateurs. If they'd been serious about getting Grant, they would have separated on entry and taken him from three sides at once before Grant could get his bearings. They hadn't. They simply stood like three bumps on a log and waited for Ziff to set the agenda.

Ziff stepped to the edge of the set. "You think anything you learn here isn't going to be tainted in court?"

It was a rhetorical question. Ziff was transmitting, not receiving. "Fruit of the poisoned tree's got nothing on what's poisoned here."

He barely paused for breath before continuing. The porn movie producer had kicked into defensive mode, and, like most small men, when he felt threatened, he talked. A lot.

"Here I am trying to run a legitimate business. Undercover vice come in trying to bust me up. Harassment, that's what it is. Picking on the little guy."

Grant was careful pulling the T-shirt over his head, but they didn't take advantage of his momentary blindness. The three heavies watched Grant with hooded eyes. Spitz and Swallows just watched, knowing smirks playing across their lips. Grant wondered if it was true what they said about bodybuilders, that their dicks shrank in direct proportion to their muscles expanding. If so, it was no wonder Ziff was recruiting fresh talent.

Ziff was still talking.

"Next time they want an undercover, tell 'em not to use somebody whose been plastered all over the fuckin' news. Didn't recognize you without the orange jacket."

Grant picked the windcheater up from the settee. "I've got the orange jacket."

"You weren't wearing it. That's what threw me. Sly fuck."

"Like you said. Clothes are just for establishing shots."

"Very fuckin' funny. If they hadn't just replayed the location shoot scuffle, I'd never have recognized you without the jacket."

Ziff mimicked Grant swishing his jacket while stepping aside. "What do you think you are? A bullfighter?"

"No. I'm a pit bull. Once I get my teeth into something, I never let go."

"What you want your teeth in me for?"

Grant considered telling him, but this wasn't the time. Even if five against one was only really three against one, they still weren't the best odds for intimidating Ziff out of using Angelina Richards. That needed to be one on one. Spitz and Swallows were out of the equation. The other three were getting restless. Grant reckoned Ziff was about to lose control of them. He put the jacket on to keep his hands free.

Ziff was still talking. "Resurrection Man." He snorted a laugh. "Erection Man is what they'll be calling you if this footage hits the streets."

Espinoza nodded a smile. "We could still use him. That could be his stage name."

Grant smiled back at her. "I wondered about that—what stage name to use. Thought I'd go with Big Dick Swelling."

Espinoza laughed. Ziff let out an exasperated sigh. "You're not taking this seriously. We got you on film."

"Thought you didn't use film anymore."

"We've caught you on camera. You didn't read any rights or nothing."

"I haven't arrested anybody either. The recording's yours. Go for it. I've got nothing to hide."

The three heavies were getting impatient. Grant saw them bunching their fists. The tallest took a step forward. "Come on, Zed. We kicking ass or what?"

Ziff looked worried, like maybe he'd unleashed a beast he couldn't control. "I just want him out of here."

That was all that the leader needed to hear. He took a step toward Grant, flexing his shoulders. Grant kept his voice friendly. "Zed? Last time I heard that was in *Pulp Fiction*."

The tall guy tilted his head, a quizzical look spreading across his face.

Grant smiled. "Bruce Willis and that squeaky-voiced girl. He's just come back for her on a great big Harley Davidson. She says, 'Whose motorcycle is this?' He says, 'It's a chopper, baby.' She says, 'Whose chopper is this?' And he says, 'It's Zed's.'"

Everyone was listening now. Grant relaxed his arms. Kept his knees loose.

"She says, 'Who's Zed?' And Willis says, 'Zed's dead, baby.'"

Grant looked the leader in the eye.

"'Zed's dead.'"

He took one pace forward and jerked his knee up fast, right between the big guy's legs. The single most painful assault a man can sustain. He doubled over, his face dropping straight onto Grant's elbow as it swung upwards. Bone crunched as the nose spread across his face. Grant kept moving, using the big guy's downward momentum to shove him into the next thug. He was too slow to move out of the way and got his legs all tangled up.

The third guy tried to step around his fallen colleague, but the sideways movement took his weight in the wrong direction. Grant went with him, forward momentum doubling his fighting weight. He clapped both hands together, one on either side of the guy's head, bursting his eardrums. As Grant leaned forward, he kicked backwards with one leg. His foot connected with the last heavy's right knee. Not hard enough to break it, but with enough weight for it to hyperextend. He went down on top of the first guy, clutching his knee. That only left one man standing, and he was bleeding from the ears and howling in pain.

Spitz and Swallows stood behind Ziff, who stared in disbelief at how fast things had changed. Espinoza stared, wide-eyed and panting. She looked ready to go at it on the settee again. Grant threw a glance at Danny the cameraman.

"You get all that? Be sure to leave that bit in about kicking my ass."

Danny lowered the camera. Grant turned to Ziff.

"There's a Medical Mall Pharmacy round the back on Elm if anybody needs aspirin. I'm sure you've got employee coverage."

Espinoza put an arm around Ziff's shoulders.

"Are you sure we can't use him? We're short of a man."

Ziff glared back at her. "Geneva. You for real? For crying out loud."

Grant walked around the heap of fallen humanity and opened the door to the office. Fairy lights still blinked on the ceiling. The laptop screen added a splash of color as the news feed replayed his exploits from last night.

He turned toward the porn producer and his star. "I can send the midget back in if you like."

Ziff looked like he could burst into tears of frustration at any second.

THE HEAT HIT GRANT the minute he stepped outside. He took the windcheater off and slung it over his shoulder. He wished he'd stayed long enough to get a shower but wasn't sure if Zed Productions provided shower facilities. Probably did, if only to wash off all that baby oil and love juice. At least he'd been spared the baby oil.

He considered what he'd learned. Not much. What he did know was that Stuart Ziff wouldn't take much persuading to stop using Senator Richards' daughter in his porn output. That conversation was for later. For now he wanted to get a professional perspective on the porn industry from the police side of things. But not with an official request. He had to be discreet.

There weren't too many numbers he could call, so he flicked his cell open and dialed the one most likely to help. He stood in the shade of Popeye's Chicken & Biscuits while he waited to be connected. The phone rang for several seconds. Just when he thought the call was going to switch to voicemail, a familiar voice answered.

"LQ Productions. Robin Citrin speaking."

"Howdy. How you doin'?"

"Jim Grant. As I live and breathe."

It was good to hear her voice.

"You mad at me?"

"No. I'm glad you called. You get my message?"

"I did. Thought about calling last night, but it was late."

"After your latest newsflash, I'm not surprised."

There was only a hint of admonishment in her tone. He imagined her smiling on the other end of the phone.

"I haven't seen that. How'd it play?"

"It played great. Don't know what the police made of it though."

"Those fellas pressing charges?"

"Said not on the news."

"Good, 'cause it was self-defense."

"Came over that way. The big guy charging at you like that."

"Pleased to hear it."

There was a pause on the other end of the line, and Grant could picture her building up to the big question again. She didn't wait long.

"So. Are you ready to talk business yet?"

"Won't be long. Just got a couple of things to sort out first. Hoped you could give me a hand?"

"Come arrest somebody with you?"

"Share your infinite knowledge of the movie industry with me."

This time the pause was longer. Citrin was no doubt weighing her options and wondering how much leverage helping Grant could provide. The ever-present helicopter hovered over downtown Long Beach. He couldn't tell if it was police or news.

Citrin kept any suspicion out of her voice. "What do you need?"

Grant nodded even though she couldn't see him. "Is there a listing of who's filming where around LA?"

"You want to know what they were filming last night?"

"I want to know what's filming today."

"You want to meet Clint Eastwood?"

"He around?"

"Doubt it."

"Shame. No. Can you find out where they're filming *CSI: New York*?"

FIFTEEN

GRANT STOOD ON THE fringe of the crew activity and tried to figure out which one was Chuck Tanburro. It didn't take long to identify the retired LAPD cop turned technical adviser. Tanburro was standing behind the camera position looking at twin monitors showing the previous shot. He was shorter than Grant but broader. His shoulders were solid and his neck strong. The way he held himself gave him away as an ex-cop. Grant wondered if he gave off the same air of authority and knew that he did.

The *CSI: NY* crew were filming on West Sixth near Pershing Square. There were cars with New York plates and buses displaying destinations two thousand miles away. A couple of NYPD patrol cars and an FDNY ambulance were parked along the curb, waiting to be deployed.

Grant waited until Tanburro appeared satisfied with the footage, then dodged between a yellow NYC taxi and a family sedan that had been given their final positions and walked up to the monitors. The temperature had dropped in the shade. Grant slipped his orange windcheater on so he didn't have to carry it. Tanburro sensed Grant coming and turned to face him—another instinct that marked him as a cop.

Grant nodded a greeting. "Chuck Tanburro?"

"Jim Grant? Bob Snow told me you might be dropping by."

They exchanged a warm handshake. Tanburro lowered his head as if looking over glasses on his nose. He wasn't wearing glasses.

"You're not gonna start assaulting the crew today, are you?"

"Self-defense isn't assault."

"Everything physical's assault. Self-defense is justified assault, is all."

"Spoken like a true police officer."

"You never lose it. I'll be a cop until I die."

Tanburro smiled as a woman pushed through the camera position, shouting above the noise. She pointed across the street, then held both hands up with her thumbs out to form a frame. The thin guy with the baseball cap she was talking to was obviously the director. Two Steadicam operators were standing beside the main camera. They looked at where the woman was pointing. A street sign high up on the opposite building line that was clearly Los Angeles.

Tanburro translated for Grant.

"Set dresser has most of the shop fronts with bits of New York stuff to set the background. Street signs we haven't bothered with. Just need to keep a tab on the camera angles, make sure they aren't in shot."

Grant looked across at the West Sixth Street sign on the wall. Unlike the modern blue signs up in Hollywood, they had an addendum across the bottom in small letters that identified the street as being in Los Angeles. He leaned one hand against the black director's chair with *CSI: NY* on the back.

"Wouldn't it just be easier to film it in New York?"

Tanburro took a drink out of a small bottle of water. "For street signs, yes. For weather, no. They can get three seasons in one day over there. There's a reason they chose California for the movie studios."

He turned his hands palms upwards and looked at the sky. "Back in the day when they first started making movies, they didn't have all these lights and reflectors and stuff. Indoor sets were built, three-wall. No front wall and no roof. They used natural light. Needed good weather."

"You know a lot about the movie industry?"

"I've picked a fair bit up."

"Then you're just the man I need to talk to."

There was a flurry of activity beyond the camera, and Tanburro held a hand up for Grant to wait. The next setup was ready. It was time for Gary Sinise to strut his stuff.

THEY FILMED A SCENE where Gary Sinise and his female partner dashed across the road to an injured boy on the sidewalk. Two NYPD squad cars skidded to a halt and the FDNY ambulance pulled up. The sirens were turned off. The lights kept flashing. A booming voice shouted above the chaos: "Cut."

Suddenly everybody was moving. The hurry-up-and-wait brigade went into action, redressing the set, repositioning the vehicles, and touching up Gary Sinise's makeup. Traffic cops in fluorescent waistcoats directed annoyed travelers past the location, the street only blocked off on the half they were filming, an LA ordinance that precluded the complete closure except for major action scenes.

The director gathered his camera operators to discuss the next setup. Tanburro came over to Grant, who had watched with interest from behind the monitors, where he could see each camera's view of the fast-moving scene.

Tanburro was smiling. "And that's what we do. A hundred times a day."

"Makes you miss dealing with proper crime scenes, doesn't it?"

"With real blood and dead people? Naw."

"You're right. Try gathering evidence after that lot have trampled over it."

Grant stood back with his arms folded and watched the carnage of a movie set being dressed for a different angle of the same scene. They were setting up for a shot from the ambulance doors that only involved the paramedics and the casualty.

A small group of people sauntered away from the set, one wearing a blue open-necked shirt and sunglasses. A wardrobe assistant slipped Gary Sinise's jacket off to protect it between takes. The attractive female partner had to take her own jacket off. Tanburro put an arm on Grant's shoulders.

"You want to meet Gary?"

GRANT HAD NEVER MET any movie stars before. They didn't move in the same circles, so he wasn't sure how he'd react being introduced on first-name terms with the star of *Apollo 13* and *Forrest Gump*. Like anyone growing up on a council estate in Yorkshire, he had viewed all things American through the eyes of Hollywood. He'd heard about all those temper tantrums by petulant stars and was prepared to be given the cold shoulder as soon as politeness allowed.

Gary Sinise wasn't petulant and appeared to be in no rush to escape the surprise visitor from across the pond. He smiled when the introduction was made and gave Grant a handshake almost as warm as Tanburro's. When Tanburro explained that Grant was a cop from the UK, he seemed genuinely interested.

"Oh yeah? You do any of this stuff?"

"Crime scenes? I've attended a few."

"You'll be able to tell us if we're getting it right, then."

Grant shrugged. "Procedures are different over here. Principle's the same though. Don't walk all over the evidence. Make sure they're dead before you start a murder investigation. You know. Basics."

"That ever happen?"

"What?"

"The dead thing."

"Almost. Once. I went to a suicide in a domestic garage where this fella'd hung himself from the roof beam. It was only a small garage, not very high. His feet were dragging on the floor when I arrived. Second officer along with SOCO."

"SOCO?"

"Scenes Of Crime Officer. CSI, they call them now. Would you believe? Anyway, first thing you should always do is make sure the deceased is deceased. If he's hanging there, cut him down and try and revive him."

Sinise shook his head, still smiling. "And they didn't do that?"

"No. They left him hanging for the photograph. His wife was in the kitchen, making tea for the police."

Sinise shivered. "Don't tell me he was still alive."

"No. First officer didn't follow procedure but he had a pretty good idea the guy was dead. His neck had stretched an extra six inches. That's why his feet were dragging on the floor."

Sinise sighed a half laugh. "We'll have to remember that if we ever do a hanging. You seen the show?"

"Bits here and there. Time's a factor when you work shifts."

Grant realized he might have just slighted the star of *CSI: NY*. "I've seen a lot of your movies though. Not many actors can pull off being a cop, but in that one with Mel Gibson"—he flicked his fingers, trying for the title; Sinise got it first.

"*Ransom*."

"Yeah, *Ransom*. I nearly said *Payback*. Well, in that you really nailed being a cop. Especially his dark side."

"Do all cops have a dark side?"

"Everybody's got a dark side. You just either control it or you don't. That's the difference between the good guys and the bad guys. Step to the wrong side, guys like me and Chuck put them away."

Tanburro spoke up. "Used to put them away."

Sinise patted him on the back. "Now he makes sure we look good while we put the bad guys away."

Grant waved toward the set. "Well, the way you jogged across the street, holding the traffic up. You got that right too."

Somebody called Sinise over for a consultation, and the star waved that he'd be right over. He smiled and shook Grant's hand again.

"Got to go. Nice to meet you. Stick around—I'll introduce you to the others."

"Thanks."

Sinise joined the director on the side of the street, and Grant turned to Tanburro, who was leaning on a pile of yellow equipment cases.

"Seemed a nice fella."

"One of the best. They're not all so obliging."

Grant looked across at the star, then back at Tanburro. "First time I saw him, in *Forrest Gump*, I thought they'd got an actor with no legs. For years. Then I saw him in that Stephen King thing, *The Stand*. With legs. Surprised the hell out of me."

Tanburro pushed off from the equipment cases. "Movie magic. Things aren't always what they seem."

"Sometimes feels that way, don't it?"

Tanburro took another swig of water. He glanced over his shoulder at the camera position. His demeanor changed. Duty called, and the self-confident posture returned. He turned back toward Grant.

"I'm on deck again in a minute. Now I've shown off with the stars, what is it I can help you with?"

Grant watched the traffic cops marshaling the commuters. The glass towers overlooking Pershing Square were still in the sun, but the shadows had crept across the park. He considered how to phrase this, then decided to just come right out with it.

"I want to pick your brains. What do you know about the porn industry?"

SIXTEEN

GRANT HAD TO WAIT until the shoot broke for an afternoon snack before talking to Tanburro again. They each grabbed a coffee in Styrofoam cups and sat in one of the NYPD squad cars for privacy. The interior was almost as authentic as the exterior but without the computer terminal and police radio. There was no shotgun clipped to the ceiling either. Grant reckoned if they were filming inside the car they'd have a special one with the props added.

Tanburro sat in the driver's seat, sipping coffee. "Porn movies? You're not branching out, are you?"

"No. It's just that thing I'm looking into."

"For the friend you're here to help out."

It wasn't a question. Grant threw him a look. Tanburro shrugged. "Bob mentioned it."

"You two are close, huh?"

"Partners for six years until I retired."

"How come he's still in, then?"

"I know it's hard to believe, but he's younger than me. Didn't join until later. His time's not up yet."

"And you'd swap with him in a flash."

That wasn't a question either. Tanburro shrugged again but added a shake of the head. "Naw. I've got a good job here."

Grant didn't believe him. Tanburro would be a cop until he died. He'd said so himself. You never stopped thinking like a cop. As if to prove the point, Tanburro put his coffee in the cup holder on the console and turned to Grant.

"So if the porn industry's something to do with what you're helping your friend out with, I'm guessing somebody's daughter got mixed up with the dirty Mac brigade."

Grant was impressed. "If you can teach Gary Sinise how to do that, they'll have a show that's halfway realistic."

"You don't think it's realistic?"

Grant sipped milky coffee that was nowhere near as good as Starbucks.

"I watched ten minutes of an episode once. All jumpy camera moves and flash cuts. Cops find a homeless guy torched in an alley. CSI turns up, Sinise and some other guys, and within seconds they've got this handheld machine sniffing all over the place. It proves not only that accelerants were used, which my nose would have told me anyway, but the exact chemical makeup of the petrol and a trail leading to the mouth of the alley."

He put the coffee down and tapped the dashboard for emphasis. "Sinise finds a cigarette butt on the ground and says it's probably what started the fire. Pardon me, but a cigarette butt in an alley? Last alley I went in was full of fuckin' cigarette butts. Anyway. They lift prints off the butt, run it through the computers back in this high-tech control room, and immediately come up with the guy's name, address, and driver's license photo. Next thing they've got him in custody, sweating him about smoking in the alley."

Grant snorted a disbelieving laugh. "This was within three minutes before the opening credits. I mean, fuck me. Forensic lab would be backed up three months before they even looked at the cig butt, and even then all it would prove was that the guy smoked in the alley. No way you could prove it was the butt that started the fire."

Tanburro picked his coffee up and took a drink. "How'd it work out in the end?"

"Never got past ten minutes. The alley looked real though."

"Glad you didn't tell Gary about that."

"It's not his fault. He's not the technical adviser."

Tanburro threw up his hands and almost spilled coffee all over the seat. "Hey, I just make sure the cops act real and don't shoot themselves in the foot. The rest of that stuff, it's movie magic."

"Things aren't always what they seem. Yeah, I remember."

Tanburro smiled. "So? This girl—she gone missing or something?"

"Not missing. Father wants her out of the business."

"Understandable."

"Does it work the same as prostitution? You know—are girls forced into this stuff? Intimidated into it? Drug habits? Pimps? Anything like that?"

"Some of the back-street outfits might work that way. This is Hollywood. Any studio making movies here is going to be legitimate. There's no shortage of girls that have come here looking for the dream of stardom, only to end up waiting tables or working the streets or making porn movies. Puts food on the table."

"I don't think this girl needs food on the table."

"Family got money?"

"Yeah."

"Film guys using her to get to them?"

"They don't know who her family is."

"Well, then. Like I said. They're probably legitimate. Budget for an average porn movie is maybe fifty grand, tops. Sell that around the world on DVD and then satellite, they'll make going on a million profit. Easy money."

Grant whistled. Tanburro continued.

"Safer bet than going mainstream. Small-scale movie would cost twenty to fifty million. Distribution and advertising, another twenty. To make a profit you've got to do double that in business on theatrical release and video sales, then pay the taxman. Anything big. Hundred million's entry level for a blockbuster these days. Do the math."

"Jesus Christ on the cross."

"Mind blowing, ain't it? Somebody once said that the most lucrative form of writing was ransom notes. Well, around here, the best way to make money is robbing banks. Less risk than making a movie."

"You don't get shot making a movie."

"Bank robbers don't get shot. There're five thousand bank robberies a year in LA. We've got more banks than security guards. More freeways than England. I bet one in a hundred gets shot. Even if they get caught, it's minimal jail time because the jails are full. Judges are falling over themselves trying to keep guys out of jail."

"Easy money."

"Bank robbery and porn movies. Like minting your own."

The crew began to filter back to the set. Hurry up and wait. The lighting crew adjusted the arc lamps, the camera operator adjusted the angle, the actors had their makeup touched up, and the director coordinated them all. A stunt driver tapped on the window, and Tanburro gave him a thumbs up. Grant got out the passenger side and joined Tanburro around the back. He finished his coffee as he watched the traffic cops directing the afternoon rush. Angry faces glared through their windshields at the disruption but didn't argue with the armed cops.

Grant shook his head. "They let those guys carry their weapons even though they're off duty?"

"They're not off duty. They're retired. Cheaper than using off-duty cops."

"Retired? They've still got their uniforms and everything."

"Guns and badges too."

"You can still carry your gun and badge after you've retired?"

"For certain jobs. Police union are up in arms about it, no pun intended. Movie companies always used to employ off-duty cops. Single guys could double their salary. Now it's mainly retirees."

"Christ. Back in Yorkshire, they don't even let you keep your socks."

"Welcome to Hollywood."

Grant dumped his empty cup in a bin beside the monitors. Tanburro did the same, then jerked a thumb toward the director. "Back in the saddle."

Grant indicated it was time for him to leave. "I'd better be getting off. Thanks for your time."

"You're welcome. If there's anything else I can help you with…"

Grant thought about that, then nodded. "You still got contacts in the department?"

"A few. Yes."

"Think you could run down the porn fella's record?"

"Shouldn't be a problem. What's his name?"

"Stuart Ziff of Zed Productions. Don't have a date of birth."

"Can't imagine there's going to be too many with that name. Give me your number. I'll get back to you."

Grant gave Tanburro his cell number, and Tanburro programmed it into a phone more complicated than most people's laptops. He dialed the number, then cut the call when Grant's cell began to ring.

"There. You've got mine too. I'll be in touch."

"Thanks."

HALF AN HOUR AND a brisk walk later, he was back at the Mayfair. The first thing he checked was if the black car was parked opposite. It wasn't. There was no sign of the two Hawaiians who weren't Hawaiians either. Grant walked through the front door but only made it halfway across the lobby before the concierge dashed over, flapping his hands. It wasn't until the hands stopped flapping and pointed toward the middle of the lobby that he understood.

Maura Richards was sitting in a threadbare chair with her legs crossed.

SEVENTEEN

"Mrs. Richards. How the devil are you?"

Mrs. Richards didn't stand up as Grant approached but simply indicated for him to sit down in the chair opposite. "Is that your approximation of an English accent?"

He pulled the chair closer to hers and sat down. "That is an English accent. I'm from England."

"You are from Yorkshire. That hardly qualifies."

"That's what I keep telling everyone. You've been doing your homework."

"This is my daughter we're talking about. Naturally I wanted to learn everything about the man my husband entrusted with protecting her."

"What else did you learn?"

Mrs. Richards shifted in her seat and laid both arms along the rests, palms down, fingers splayed. She looked Grant in the eyes as if trying to divine the truth from what she saw. She would have made an effective Gypsy Rose Lee, reading tarot cards and telling the future.

"You are an only child. Your mother died in childbirth, so your father, who was a naval commander, brought you up. You enlisted in the Army, probably to spite your father, and later joined the West Yorkshire Police, where you served for twelve years. While on assignment in Boston you prevented a suicide bomb attack on a US senator and the Crown Prince of Saudi Arabia. You are now employed by the Boston Police Department."

Grant was impressed. "They tell you my inside leg measurement and that I dress to the left?"

"I can see that you dress to the left."

Her eyes never left Grant's face. If she could see he was hung to the left, it was with peripheral vision. The husky voice made everything sound suggestive.

"You could have earned more money working for the Crown Prince."

"I've been there before. Didn't work out. I prefer America. I'm a cop, not a bodyguard."

"You're protecting a US senator."

"It's more of an investigative role. Detective work, not close order protection."

"But this is about my daughter."

"It is. So why not tell me why you're here?"

She shifted in her seat again. Uncrossed her legs and crossed them the other way. She laid her hands in her lap and closed her eyes. When she'd composed herself, she opened them again and let out a deep sigh. "I want her to stop all this nonsense and come home."

"So does your husband."

"My husband wants her to stop jeopardizing his career."

"Is she jeopardizing his career?"

"What do you think?"

"I told your husband what I think. This is only a political disaster if he hides the truth. As a concerned father trying to protect his daughter from the porn industry, he could end up looking better rather than worse."

"What if he were the reason she started in the porn industry?"

"Then he'd have a problem."

"A problem that would require your kind of help to keep things quiet."

Grant didn't answer straight away. He sat back in the chair and drummed his fingers on the armrests. He didn't like the sound of where this was going. Senator Richards was only a secondary consideration. The fallout of any scandal would more than likely destabilize the chief of police, and that would have a knock-on effect for the LAPD. That was who he was really here to protect. Protecting Dick Richards to achieve that was beginning to leave a bad taste in Grant's mouth.

"Did he start her in the porn industry?"

"I can only go on my female intuition. A mother's intuition."

"What does your mother's intuition tell you?"

She tilted her head back to stretch her neck. Bones cracked in the quiet of the hotel lobby. The tall square pillars surrounding them were clean and white. Ornate carvings around the top were touched up with gold paint. Maura Richards appeared to be examining the gold fretwork. When she looked back at Grant, her eyes held more than a hint of sadness.

"I think he may have driven her to it, yes."

Grant softened his tone. Put a touch of friendship and compassion in his voice. "What makes you think that?"

Mrs. Richards was having trouble remaining calm and clearheaded. Her voice was strong, but there was a quiver in the lip and hesitation in the words that betrayed her.

"In recent years—the last three or four, perhaps—there has been tension between them that was never there before."

Grant made rapid calculations. Angelina Richards was nineteen years old. That would make her fifteen or sixteen when the trouble started. A dangerous age for a young girl. Ripe and ready for the plucking, any predatory males might think. The age when your cute little girl becomes a voluptuous Lolita with all the accompanying complications that entailed.

He lowered his voice. This was a very delicate matter and not his field of expertise. He'd dealt with a couple of rape victims and a few child-abuse cases, but they were usually taken over by specialist interviewers. Since most abusers were men, it was better to have someone smaller and less intimidating than Jim Grant ask all the intimate questions.

"Did she ever tell you why?"

"No. But I could sense the division. The hostility."

There was no way around this next question, so he tackled it head-on. "Do you think he was abusing her?"

Mrs. Richards appeared shocked. Her eyes flew open and her nostrils flared. She shook her head but screwed her hands up into clenched fists.

"No. I saw nothing to suggest that. They displayed no…closeness. Intimacy. Anything like that. Quite the opposite, in fact. She began to draw away from him."

"That can sometimes be the first sign."

She shook her head more vigorously. "No. No. I do not accept that. I would have known. She would have told me."

Grant didn't belabor the point. The only saving grace was that while some abused children grew up to be abusers themselves, none ever started having sex with strange men. Avoiding sex was the norm.

"So you think she might have gone into this to spite him?"

"At the moment she would do anything to spite him. She has too much of me in her. Too free spirited."

She stopped shaking her head and lowered her eyes. This is where the sadness was coming from. Not because she hadn't noticed what her husband may or may not have been doing with their daughter but the fact that the daughter might have inherited the mother's sexual behavior.

Grant resisted the urge to pat Mrs. Richards on the knee. "Leave it with me. I'll pop in and talk to her tomorrow."

"You have her address?"

"Yes. Up the canyon, isn't it?"

"It is."

"Don't suppose there's a bus runs up there."

"No."

"Never mind. I'll take a cab."

"I could have Jeeves run you up there."

This time it was Grant's turn to shake his head. "Me and Jeeves don't see eye to eye. Besides, having a familiar car pull up might spook her. A cab'll be best."

They both stood up. For the first time, Mrs. Richards appeared less than strong. She wavered slightly, and Grant put a hand on her shoulder and one on her waist. She froze, and her eyes flashed something that wasn't anger. He'd last seen that look in Geneva Espinoza's eyes when Grant had disabled the three thugs at Zed's. Angelina could well have inherited the sexuality from her mother.

Once Mrs. Richards was stable, he let her go. "Can I call you a cab?"

"You can. But I won't answer to the name."

She had recovered her confidence as well as her balance. Grant was glad. He didn't like to see the mighty fallen. She said her driver was outside, and they walked to the front doors together.

She turned to face him. "Thank you. For understanding."

"Understanding is my middle name."

"I thought that was discretion?"

He smiled and waved her off. "You have a safe journey now."

The car took her away, and Grant was glad to be alone again. The beautiful woman with the damaged mind depressed him. It was sad to see. He went up to twelve in the elevator, his mind still pondering the conundrum that was the Richards family. He was about to slide the keycard through the lock when he noticed the light beneath the door and stepped back.

Voices sounded through the door. Some ambient noise and a little night music. Not very loud. Whoever was waiting for him in there wasn't hiding in the dark. If it was the two Hawaiians, they were even worse at surprising somebody than they were at tailing them.

Grant had to make a decision. Going through a door where you knew somebody was waiting was a dangerous proposition, especially now that the Dominguez cartel had come into play. A single

113

shotgun pointed at the door and Grant would be splattered all over the hallway. Two men waiting with handguns would have him pinned in a murderous crossfire.

He had two choices. Go in and face the music or find another way and surprise his attackers. He could drop down from the balcony of the room above, but climbing through the window would be the danger point. He would be vulnerable to attack and/or a long drop to his death. That didn't feel like a good idea.

The first option appealed to his sense of tackling things head-on. Simply open the door and walk right in. Feign surprise if he needed a delaying tactic or anger if he needed to counterattack. He wasn't getting that tingling up the back of his neck that signaled danger. This was something else. He weighed the odds and came down in favor of option one.

He slid the keycard through the reader and heard the electronic click of the lock. Then he opened the door and went in.

EIGHTEEN

Downtown Los Angeles stood out against the early evening sky through the windows. Blinking lights and mirrored glass painted a picture of tranquility in the background. The ambient noise and voices came from the TV on the corner of the dresser. The music had been the opening jingle to the evening news. It wasn't long before the outstretched arms and orange jacket signaled a rerun of the bank robbery folded into a follow-up on the location shoot fracas behind Hollywood Boulevard. It must have been a slow news day.

"They'll be checking you for stigmata next."

Robin Citrin was sitting in the chair next to the bedside cabinet. She smiled at Grant as he closed the door behind him, the brilliant white teeth complementing the twinkle in her eyes. The black hair looked even blacker and more unruly in the dull light from the wall lamps.

Grant dropped his keycard and wallet on the chest of drawers. "Well, Miss Citrin, you are a forward wench. Waiting in a gentleman's room."

"If I was a forward wench, I'd be sitting on the bed."

"Good point."

"And I am relying on you being a gentleman."

"Then your honor is safe with me."

He wasn't sure if he was disappointed or relieved. There had been too many women making eyes at him today. As irresistible as Geneva Espinoza had been and as beautiful as Maura Richards was, he found Robin Citrin more attractive than both of them put together. He felt a connection with her he didn't feel with the others. She flicked her head to get the hair out of her eyes.

"Did you find the *CSI* guys?"

"I did. Thank you."

"It helped you out, then, me giving you their location?"

"It did."

Grant could feel a proposition coming. He switched the TV off with the remote because he could never find the off button on American sets and went to the open window. He preferred fresh air to the recycled stuff they always pumped into hotel rooms. A siren sounded in the distance, forcing a smile. In every city he'd ever visited, sirens always started up after dark. LA added helicopters throbbing around the sky instead of distant railway noises, the other staple of city nightlife.

He looked down twelve floors to the street. He could see West Seventh all the way into town, but he concentrated on the chunk of sidewalk opposite the front of the hotel. The favored spot for the Dominguez cartel's spotters to park. There was still no black car parked across the street. He turned to face Citrin and leaned against the wall, legs crossed at the ankles and arms folded across his chest.

Casual. Relaxed.

His heart rate was slow and even, but he could feel the effect of having a beautiful woman sitting next to his bed. He hoped that dressing to the left wasn't as obvious to Robin Citrin as it had been to Mrs. Richards. If Citrin smiled at him much more, he feared it probably would be.

She spoke quietly. "So, if I helped you out, you should help me out, right? That's the way it works, isn't it?"

"Not exactly. You see, that implies an agreement made at the time to share information, like swapping. Not you doing me a favor, which is more of a helping-out-a-friend kind of deal."

"We're friends now?"

"I think we are, yes."

"But you don't owe me a favor."

"Favors are bestowed, not owed. It's like if I give you a present, then ask for something in return, I'd be an Indian giver. See what I mean?"

"An Indian giver's somebody who asks for the same gift back, not something in return. I'm not asking for the same favor."

"You want a favor? I'll give you a favor. Just not because *you* did *me* a favor."

"So you'll do me a favor?"

"Of course. Before we get to that, though, you want a bite to eat?"

"You got snacks tucked away in here?"

"Not in here. Go out for dinner. It's been a long day."

"Are you asking me on a date?"

"Does that count as another favor? 'Cause you don't get two in return."

"I thought favors didn't get paid back. They were bestowed."

"Glad we got that sorted. Dinner?"

"I'd love to."

Citrin stood up and walked to the window. Grant was blocking the way. He stepped back to let her pass but there still wasn't enough room between the foot of the bed and the dresser. They stood facing each other for a couple of seconds, their movement at an impasse. Her head was level with his chest, and she had to raise it to look into his eyes. He lowered his head to look into hers.

"Know what I like about you?"

"My sparkling personality?"

"Besides that."

"You like dusky South American types?"

"Like John Wayne did? No. I had you more for Italian."

"Very good. Italian, way back. I get mistaken for South American a lot."

"What I like about you is the way your nose crinkles up at the top when you smile. Like a mischievous pixy."

Citrin laughed to hide her embarrassment.

"When you laugh too. It's cute."

He raised a hand and stroked her chin. The contact froze her laughter and her smile vanished. Instead she just stared into his eyes without blinking. She didn't pull away. She didn't move at all. Encouraged, Grant reversed his hand and stroked the side of her face with the back of his fingers. She tilted her head up even farther and let out a deep breath but didn't close her eyes. He took hold of her chin gently and touched her lips with one finger.

Then he bent slowly and kissed her. A single kiss. Softly on the lips. Her lips puckered but didn't respond. He kissed her on the cheek. He kissed her forehead. He kissed her eyes, each one closing at the moment of contact. He kissed the other cheek, then her lips again. She still didn't respond.

He stopped and looked into her eyes.

She smelled real, not flowery. Her perfume wasn't as cloying as Geneva Espinoza's or as expensive as Mrs. Richards', it was just nice and clean and erotic. He reckoned that last part was more to do with the woman than the scent. Her eyes never left his. They were examining him as if looking for deeper meaning behind the kiss. For the first time in a long time he thought she could well be right. He nodded, then bent to kiss her again. Her reluctance was more exciting than being embraced by Espinoza. It added weight to what was about to happen.

When he kissed her this time, her lips responded. They nibbled and kissed and ate his mouth. She rested her hands on his waist but didn't pull him toward her. He did the same. Neither of them made the first move; it happened naturally as their bodies closed together. Her breasts pressed against his stomach. Her arms came up around his neck, and his arms tightened around her waist. Her kisses grew hungry, but then she stopped and looked into his eyes.

"Please. Turn the lights off."

He nodded and stepped over to the switch.

THEY DIDN'T SO MUCH undress as divest their clothes in a slow dance toward the bed. The lights were off but the room wasn't dark. It was just darker than outside. Streetlamps twelve floors down reflected off the ceiling. The evening sky had descended from dark blue to black, or as black as the downtown skyline ever got in LA. The soft light bouncing off the ceiling deepened the shadows but smoothed out the lines between light and dark.

Citrin's blouse was white.

Her skin was dark.

Grant saw everything as she unclipped her bra and fell backwards onto the bed. His T-shirt was already off. His jeans quickly followed. He didn't remember taking his shoes and socks off, but they had gone too. Citrin slipped out of the black trousers and what lay beneath and suddenly they were naked in each other's arms.

The feel of her skin against his was electric. Soft velvet warmth enveloped him as he took the weight on his arms and let his chest brush the hard tips of her breasts. The dark, crinkly areolas he had glimpsed through her blouse at Caffè Etc. crisped up as his body caressed hers. Goose pimples sprang up along the smooth lines of her stomach. The soft hairs of her bush invited exploration, but tonight was not the night for that. Instead of parting her legs and laying between them, he opened his own and sat astride her, still crouching forward to kiss her face and nose and lips.

Slowly he raised himself up from her until he was sitting up. Her eyes followed him all the way up. One hand, which had been draped around his neck, stroked his chest and stomach as he moved out of reach. His own hands began to play. Fingers toyed with Citrin's ears, then slid down the line of her jaw to caress her long, slender neck. She tilted her head back and closed her eyes. A small moan escaped her lips.

The strain of leaning forward from the waist tightened his stomach and the bands of muscle across his back. He left one hand stroking her neck and used the other to trace the angle of her shoulders. They caressed the hollow at the bottom of her throat, then the protrusions of her collarbones. Her skin was so smooth it was like touching silk. He flattened the palm and the full contact absorbed the warmth as it smoothed its way down to her breasts. When it passed over the first nipple Citrin let out a gasp. Her hand clamped over his, holding it against her. He squeezed gently. Once. Twice. The nipple became a bullet pressing into his palm. He moved the hand slightly and the friction sparked another gasp.

He cupped one breast and then the other, one at a time. With each new contact Citrin became more agitated beneath him. He let his other hand slide down her body while the first continued to tease her breasts. He cupped and squeezed and tweaked the nipples between finger and thumb. Her body shifted and pressed upwards against him. She twisted one way and then the other, a low-powered bucking bronco. His hand traversed her stomach, caressing and scratching all the way, until it stopped at the edge of her sex. The hairs were short and dark and neatly trimmed. He wanted to touch her there, to kiss her there, but it didn't feel right tonight. Tonight was for more traditional pleasures.

Citrin's hands rested on his thighs. They made no move to touch his shaft as it bobbed with excitement. He sensed that she too felt tonight was an introduction, not a full performance. Some forms of intimacy had to be worked up to. One form could not wait.

She doubled upwards from the waist and grabbed his head. He came down willingly and they kissed again, her hands holding his face to hers as she shifted one last time. Her legs began to open slowly and he took the hint. He shifted one leg and then the other into the gap she was creating and found himself lying between her legs with the warmth of her sex pressing against his stomach.

She lowered her hands to his waist and held him tight. Pulled him forward until the tip of his member touched soft, wet flesh. She gasped in his ear. He paused, not wanting to force himself on her. She had reached that point where pausing wasn't an option and scrunched her stomach muscles to push upwards. The tip went in, then out again. She bit his ear. Now that he had been given the okay, he slowly eased forward. All the way. Warm softness enveloped him. He stopped and felt the muscles between her legs tighten to squeeze him. Her hips began a gentle swaying motion. Her breath was coming in short bursts.

The rhythm became more pronounced. Her hips became more aggressive. Grant withdrew and thrust forward. Withdrew and thrust forward. She matched his movements in the opposite direction. They achieved perpetual motion. Short of a nuclear attack, nothing was going to stop them now.

She gasped louder but didn't speak. He remained mute.

Their bodies did all the talking, and the talking was loud. It was frenetic. It was hot, hard sex that had more meaning than a dozen sessions with a porn star with plastic breasts. This was real. The emotion made it more intense. When she began to explode, Grant finally let go. The noise they made was like animals howling. The release they felt was exhausting.

"So, what was the favor?"

"You're going to give me something else?"

"I haven't agreed to the favor yet."

They were sitting in the restaurant on the first floor of the historic Mayfair Hotel. Second floor, Grant corrected himself. Their table overlooked the lobby, with its tall white pillars and threadbare chairs. The place looked opulent but faded. It had definitely seen better days. Grant took a drink of water while he waited for their meal to arrive. He waved a hand and nodded toward the lobby.

"You know that Raymond Chandler stayed here in 1939? Wrote a short story set in the hotel."

"I didn't know that."

"Can't remember what it was called."

"You're full of interesting facts, aren't you?"

"Full of shit, some would say."

"Do you like Raymond Chandler?"

"Love the Marlowe books. Not read his short stories. Some of the films were pretty good."

"Movies."

"Yeah. I sometimes slip back into English."

"We speak English."

"A derivation thereof. What's that famous quote? 'Two countries divided by a common language'?"

"Are we divided?"

"Will be if you don't tell me what this favor is."

Citrin laughed, crinkling her nose the way he liked. When she stopped smiling, the twinkle of it was still in her eyes. She rested her elbows on the table. "I'd like you to come in and see L. Q. Patton. He's dying to meet you."

"Excited, is he? I haven't said I'll do the show yet."

"That would be a bigger favor. I don't feel I can ask."

Grant looked into her eyes and smiled. "The jury's still out on that one. I'm not against it as much as the first time you asked if that's any help."

She was about to say something when a Japanese waiter brought their food over. Something hot and steaming that was in keeping with the rest of the hotel, functional but not very appetizing. Breakfast was something they couldn't really fuck up. Fuel to start the day. Dinner was supposed to be something better, and he wasn't sure that this qualified. The steam said the meal was hot. He reckoned they should be thankful for small mercies.

He glanced over the balcony at the waiting area below. The mock carved pillars were impressive but the threadbare chairs were not. He wondered what Mrs. Richards had made of the place. Thinking of her reminded him he'd made a promise for tomorrow. Going to see L. Q. Patton might have to wait. Still, the favor didn't specify a timeframe, so he wouldn't feel bad about agreeing to it.

After they'd eaten.

NINETEEN

THE RIDE IN THE cab the following morning was long and informative. Grant sat in the back watching the miles tick away. Coldwater Canyon Drive was just past Beverly Hills and up the side of Franklin Canyon Park, but the length of the journey gave the driver plenty of time to talk.

"And ugly too. I tell you. America don't know how to make a decent car no more. And when they make one? Ugly as a squashed bug. Look at them Crown Victorias. Big, square, ugly sumbitches. Never sell any if the police didn't use 'em. Ain't surprised. Don't know why they don't copy them sleek, nice-lookin' cars, like what the Japanese do. All they cars are modeled on your Jaguars and BMWs. That Mercedes is a beautiful car. All them Jap cars, they copied the Germans. Americans, we copied some bug ugly tank or somethin'. Ain't a sleek line on any of 'em."

He was still talking as they followed the winding valley road that was Coldwater Canyon Drive. Grant looked for house numbers but couldn't see any. There were big houses and secluded houses. There were even houses on top of the ridge that jutted out into space, held up by angled stanchions that didn't look strong enough to support the square port-a-cabins.

They passed tennis courts and swimming pools and houses with electronic gates and security cameras. Grant was beginning to think he'd got the wrong address. For a runaway daughter, Angelina Richards had certainly landed on her feet. The road continued to climb and the houses became sparser, the barren hillsides more frequent. Eventually they came to a gentle right-hand curve in the road with houses on the left but open space on the right. An unmade driveway curled up the hillside with a mailbox on a stick beside the road.

2421A

The black letters stood out against the stylized white box. It was the only indication that anyone lived up the hill. The driveway ran a short distance, then swung left behind a large house with a swimming pool up beyond a stand of trees. The hillside was the familiar parched grass and scrubland.

Grant slapped the back of the passenger seat. "This'll do just fine."

The cab driver pulled into the drive and spun the car around, sending up clouds of dust and gravel. It was a wide entrance. The car managed to face front again in one go, despite it being a bug-ugly tank with the turning circle of a bus. One thing you could say about the cabby, he knew how to drive ugly.

Then he ruined the illusion by opening his mouth. "Can't wait for you, if'n that's what you want. Got other calls to make."

"Don't worry about it."

"Ain't worried. Just saying, is all."

Grant paid the fare and got out. The shade of the canyon tree line made the temperature passable. He was glad the orange windcheater was summer weight. It was thin and airy, with hidden vents to let it breathe. He unzipped it anyway and let it flap open. The cab pulled back onto the road and sped down the hill, leaving another cloud of dust swirling behind it. Grant coughed and wafted the dust away with one hand, then set off up the drive.

ANGELINA RICHARDS' ADDRESS WAS 2421A because it was built on land behind number 2421, the house with the stand of trees and the swimming pool. That house looked like it belonged on Coldwater Canyon Drive. The Richards residence looked like it belonged in a Western.

Grant followed the drive up the hill, coming out of the shade into sunshine as it curled behind the main house on the roadside. Puffs of dust exploded with each footstep, and he wondered when they'd last had any rain. The grass on the hillside was dry and brown. The only green came from the watered lawns of the big house and the trees along the canyon bottom. Up here, in the full glare of the sun, life had curled up and died.

The cabin was halfway up the hill.

Grant paused on the final bend and examined the approach. The cabin was a solidly built single-story building with a porch out front and wooden shed to one side. It nestled in a fold in the hillside that meant there was no access from the sides, where the slopes were too steep. He could just make out the winding road across the top of the escarpment that led to a hilltop mansion on Gloaming Way two bends farther on and hidden by a small forest of mature trees.

Angelina's place was much smaller, with a turnaround outside the front porch that could only fit one car at a time. The turnaround was empty. Grant wasn't sure if she had a car of her own, but she certainly didn't walk here so it was either a lift or a cab. Three windows looked out across the canyon from the porch, two on the left of the door and one on the right. The windows were closed. He couldn't tell if the curtains were drawn because of the sun glaring off the windows. He didn't have an angle on the side walls, which presumably held the bedroom windows.

There was no movement. No sign of anyone being home.

Satisfied, Grant walked the rest of the way to the front porch. He paused at the foot of the stairs, four heavy wooden risers that looked to be intricately carved and smoothed. This was good wood, not a cheap extension. A solid porch, not some teenage getaway. He wondered where she'd got the money to buy it. He surmised it was probably part of the Richards family properties.

He glanced across at the wooden shed. No movement there either. It wasn't big enough for a car. More than likely tool storage or chopped wood. He couldn't imagine a wealthy senator and oil tycoon having to chop wood. Or use tools either, for that matter. The shed had no windows and the door was padlocked from the outside, so there was no threat from that direction.

Time for the front door.

He climbed the steps and crossed the porch. His feet sounded loud on the hollow boardwalk. He glanced at the windows on either side of the door. No movement. He knocked on the door. No response. He knocked louder. Still nothing. Grant resigned himself to the fact this was going to be a wasted journey but knocked again just for completeness. He always knocked three times before kicking a door in.

The third knock was his Yorkshire copper knock. It was loud enough to wake the dead and denied any miscreants the opportunity to say they didn't hear him at the door. There was still no response. He went to the single window to the right of the door and squinted through the glass. The interior was in shadow, and all he could see was a reflection of the canyon behind him. He did the same with the other two windows. Same result, except one of the rooms had another window around the side that threw some light into the lounge.

Grant stepped back sharply. It was difficult to tell, but the living room looked like it had been tossed. There was a measure of disturbance near the TV cabinet, items strewn across the floor. Teenage girls weren't necessarily the tidiest of breeds, so that wasn't conclusive. What was more damning was the broken window around the side of the cabin.

He walked around the corner. The porch wrapped around the side of the house right to the back, where it butted against the hillside. One pane in the window was broken, a scattering of glass on the floor beneath it. He went to the front door and tried the handle.

It wasn't locked.

Warning bells began to sound in his head. In every movie he'd seen, nothing good ever came of somebody finding the door unlocked. It was almost as clichéd as the single woman walking up the stairs to the bedroom with the lights off. The reason things become a cliché is because they happen so often, they get typecast.

The unlocked door was typecast as bad news.

Grant opened the door and stepped aside. Nobody shouted at him to get out. No stray cat came screaming onto the porch. Nobody shot at him. That was good. He worked on the theory that people only shot at you if they felt threatened. Grant adopted a very nonthreatening stance and poked his head around the doorframe. There was nobody inside.

"Hello?"

The other cliché that was real: first thing you do if you enter a stranger's house and you're not burgling them is announce your presence. You don't want to be surprising somebody into taking a snap shot. You don't want to be embarrassing somebody on the toilet.

"It's the police."

Without a partner to cover the back, Grant wasn't going to catch a burglar in the act unless he was a stupid burglar. He'd met plenty of them in his time. This didn't feel like the window-breaker was still in the house. This didn't feel good at all. He scanned the living room with eyes that were rapidly adjusting to the gloom.

That was when he saw it.

He took two paces into the room. The floor was highly polished wood with a single beige throw rug in front of the settee. He shifted his angle so light from the window gave him a better view. There was an uneven stain at the edge of the rug. It had already turned a darker color. He didn't need to look closer. Grant knew what dried blood looked like.

PART TWO

Some of the things I've seen—they are exactly what they seem to be: real and hard and painful. Everything you film—it's just entertainment.

—Jim Grant

TWENTY

IF GRANT HAD BEEN the first officer responding to a concern-for-the-neighbor call, this is where he would be treating the lounge as a crime scene. Careful where you step and careful what you touch. Even then, first priority would be to make sure there was nobody injured on the premises and nobody dangerous at the scene. He wasn't the first officer; he was a visiting officer from a foreign force trying to keep a US senator and the chief of police out of trouble.

That burdened him with divided loyalties.

It didn't change his priorities.

He reckoned priority number two was already taken care of. There was no dangerous criminal lurking in the cabin. Whatever had taken place here happened some time ago. The blood had dried. There were no tire marks or footprints in the driveway. The turnaround was dusty and shifting. Only very recent activity would leave its mark. His own footprints coming up here were probably already disappearing. More importantly, Grant's spider senses—his innate ability to smell danger—hadn't been triggered.

That left checking for injured parties or deceased victims. Judging by the amount of blood, about six inches across and several spots leading across the floor, he didn't think he'd be looking for corpses. He glanced at the TV cabinet but ignored the scattered DVDs. That was for later. He turned his attention to the other rooms, starting with the adjoining kitchen. He wasn't worried about leaving prints but he was still careful how he opened the doors. Using the handles would overlay any prints left previously. He only touched the extremities. This could still turn into an official crime scene depending on what he found.

The cabin appeared small from the front but was bigger once you got inside. There were two large bedrooms and a medium-sized bathroom at the rear. There was a study to the right of the front door and a guest toilet beyond that. It didn't take long to check them all. They were empty. There were no dead bodies. There were no injured parties. There were also no signs of the house being ransacked, apart from the TV cabinet.

Angelina Richards wasn't home.

That led him back to the blood on the throw rug. He crouched beside it and rubbed two fingers over the edge of the stain. It was dry. He did the same in the middle of the stain, the last part of a pool of blood to congeal. That was dry too. Next, he went to the window and examined the broken pane. The window was a side-opening log cabin–type with six panes of glass and a single handle halfway up the frame. There was a scattering of glass on the sill, about the same amount as outside. If you watched all those cop shows like *Columbo* and *CSI*, you'd get the impression that broken glass only fell on the inside at a burglary. If the glass was on the outside, then it was a set-up job.

Wrong.

The glass in a window is flexible. If it is hit by a brick, it first flexes inwards until it reaches breaking point, then it shatters and the flex springs back into position, catapulting shards of glass outwards, hence the glass outside. The general rule of thumb is there'd be more on the inside than outside, but during a burglary the intruder would often pick out the pieces left in the frame to reach through. Those pieces ended up on the outside, sometimes neatly stacked, sometimes thrown across the garden. The glass on the outside here was inconclusive. What was conclusive was that the broken pane of glass was farthest from the handle. Either the intruder was an idiot or the window hadn't been the point of entry.

As strange as it might seem, the girl might always leave the front door unlocked. It was unlocked now. The other possibility was that whoever came in here was someone she knew. That left the question of where she was now. That was a more worrying development.

Grant stepped back from the window, his change of position giving him a fresh angle across the porch. He stopped. There was one other possibility. He glanced around the room. He found what he was looking for on a hook beside the door. The key for the padlock on the wooden shed outside.

HE'D BEEN RIGHT ABOUT his footprints. The dust and gravel turnaround was already pristine and virginal. There wasn't much of a breeze, but what little there was stirred the dust into swirling clouds scurrying across the drive. Grant stood on the porch and looked down the hill at the houses on the opposite side of Coldwater Canyon Drive. They were shielded by mature trees and high fences. Hastain Fire Road gave access to the hills via narrow trails and footpaths behind them.

Considering he couldn't see much of the houses opposite, it stood to reason the residents over there wouldn't be able to see much of what went on up here. No point doing house to house enquiries. Even the house with the swimming pool at the bottom of the drive was hidden behind a stand of trees, no doubt intentionally to preserve the owner's privacy. Something glinted behind the trees, then disappeared. He heard water splash in the pool. More light glinted off the ripples.

There were no side steps from the porch. Grant went down the front four and turned toward the shed, scrutinizing the ground all the way. There were no footprints and there was no trail of blood. He didn't expect any. This was simply covering all the bases. He stopped in front of the padlocked door and paused with the key in his hand. Scrutinized the lock and the doorframe with his eyes. Visual examination: the first step at any crime scene. See what you can see and photograph it before disturbing things that can't be undisturbed, contaminating evidence with outside interference.

There was no bloody handprint on the wall. There was no four-fingered scratch on the woodwork. The doorframe was smooth and undamaged. The padlock was shiny and clean. Grant stepped around the side of the shed. There was no window. He went around the other side. No window there either. He couldn't get around the back because the shed was cut into the hillside. Back to the front door. He slipped the key into the padlock and opened it. It dropped into his hand. It was a heavy lock. Closing his fist around the padlock, he pulled the door open. It creaked even though the hinges were as shiny as the lock. The wooden shed groaned under the weight of the door.

It was dark inside.

Grant waited for anything that might jump out at him to jump out. Nothing did. He stared into the gloom for a moment to allow his eyes to adjust, then stepped onto the wooden floorboards. They creaked and popped, not as solid as the porch steps. The shed was basic and matched the frontier spirit of the cabin it supported, but this was Beverly Hills, or near as damn it. If there was one thing he'd learned about the rich and shameless, it was that they liked their creature comforts. They wouldn't be coming out to the shed in the middle of the night with a kerosene lamp or a flashlight. He found the switch on the wall beside the door and turned the light on.

He let out a heavy sigh, then leaned against the doorframe.

BACK IN THE LIVING room, Grant flipped open his cell and prepared for an argument. He scanned the numbers programmed into the memory and hit the button for the Richards residence. The other Richards residence, not the one they no doubt owned but let their daughter live in as part of her teenage rebellion.

He hung the padlock key on the hook while he waited. The shed had been empty apart from a backup generator and some essential tools. It wasn't a workshop with tools hanging from the backboard inside tool-shaped outlines. It wasn't a storage shed full of supplies for the winter either. It was a rich man's plaything, simply there because if you've got a cabin, you've got to have a shed.

The phone at the other end of the line began to ring, not the distinctive *brrring-brrring, brrring-brrring* of an English telephone but the strange single, long tone that he thought he'd never get used to. He glanced at the scattered DVD cases while the tone played in his ear, dropping to one knee and carefully sifting through them.

They were standard Hollywood movies. The kind of thing any teenager might have in her collection. Nothing Grant had seen. Teenage girls didn't watch the classic cinema that he loved. There were no Bond movies, no spaghetti Westerns. The only one he'd heard about but not seen was *Mamma Mia*, a film he'd need tying down and drugging before he could be forced to watch it.

The butler answered the phone. Grant asked to speak to Richards.

There was a pause while Jeeves went to find him.

The shelf in the TV cabinet was deep. The DVDs scattered on the floor were from the front row of movies on the shelf. The second row was almost intact. Movies in the second row were more interesting. Even from the narrow artwork on the spines, Grant could see these were more adult in nature. Very adult. The thumbnail image at the top of each title was either naked women, naked women's breasts, or naked women sucking cock. The lettering of each title was as florid and colorful as the one Richards had shown him in his study.

"Yes? What do you want?"

There were no polite introductions. Senator Richards got straight to the point. Grant wondered if he'd interrupted his daily Scrabble game or something. He bit down on his anger and spoke calmly. "I'm at your daughter's. She isn't here."

"So? Call back when she's home."

"There's blood on the carpet and the window's broken."

That shut him up. There was a long silence before Richards spoke again. "Has she been taken?"

Grant considered that. Apart from the scattered DVDs, there was no sign of a disturbance. Discounting the broken window, if somebody had taken the daughter against her will, there would be signs of a struggle—furniture upended, the throw rug dragged to one side. Especially if the blood came from a struggle to control an unwilling victim. There was none of that.

"I'm not sure. Could be. Could be something else."

"That is rather vague."

"The evidence is rather vague. There's no obvious sign. No."

There was another pause. Grant leaned forward and pulled one of the porn films out of the stack. It was hardcore but nothing you couldn't buy at any adult video store. XXX just meant you had to be eighteen to buy them nowadays. Angelina Richards was nineteen. Grant opened the case. The disc was as gaudy as the cover. An original, not a copy. He shut the case and slipped it back into place.

"Has anything been taken?"

"Apart from your daughter, you mean?"

"You said she hadn't."

"I said I wasn't sure. Rule of thumb when it comes to kidnappings is treat them as worse-case scenario until you know different. You can always scale back if it's less serious."

"Is that your discreet side showing? Your middle name being discreet."

"It's my concern for a neighbor side. Until I know she's safe."

"My daughter has gone missing before. She used to run away to spite me before we let her use the cabin. She can be…dramatic."

"What you're saying is, don't involve the police?"

"For now. Your focus was supposed to be the producer."

"I'm working on that."

"Then work on it away from my daughter's house."

"Your house."

"My daughter's place of residence."

Richards sounded impatient. "Now. Has anything been taken?"

There was no reason not to mention the scattered DVDs, but Grant suddenly felt that tingling up the back of his neck. He looked at the back row of adult movies. They were neatly arranged like books on a bookshelf, from left to right. They almost reached the full width of the shelf, with the last few leaning into the rest to form a kind of bookend. There was no way to know if they were all there. Except there was a gap in the middle of the row. Space for a single DVD case. The movies on either side of the gap were pulled forward slightly as if the missing film had been tugged out in a hurry.

Grant focused on the gap as he spoke into the phone. "Doesn't look like it. House wasn't ransacked."

"Then get back to the job in hand. Zed Productions."

The gap wasn't completely empty.

"Okay."

He closed the cell without saying goodbye. Two things were going through his mind. The first thing was wondering what the single disc without a case was doing in the empty space. The second was he hadn't told Richards the movie company was Zed Productions.

Grant slid the disc out of the gap with one finger, then poked the fingertip into the hole in the middle. He held it up to read the title and wasn't surprised by what he found. The colorful lettering was the same as the pirate copy he'd seen two days ago, only this was an original. *The Hunt for Pink October*. The disc was adorned with naked breasts and erect penises, just in case you got it mixed up with the film about the submarine.

He doubted Sean Connery was in this one.

One last scan of the TV cabinet, then Grant stood up, the disc still balanced on his finger. His left knee popped loudly. The leg he'd broken in Boston. He reckoned that was something he was going to have to live with and knew that cold weather was going to be a problem for the rest of his life. He wasn't thinking about the rest of his life at the moment. He was thinking about what disc was in the missing DVD case if the original disc was still here.

Something glinted on the front window from outside. He popped the disc off his fingertip, put it on the shelf, then went to the door. The sun hit him with heat like an oven as he stepped onto the porch.

The glinting reflection flashed again. From the trees at the bottom of the hill, not from the swimming pool this time. Maybe it hadn't been the water before. Grant suddenly felt very exposed. He'd quartered the area coming up the hill for any threats but not considered the house at the bottom of the driveway. Anybody waiting for him would have been in the cabin, not one of the neighbors' houses.

He stood next to the railing, leaning on the porch roof support, and turned sideways to give a narrowed target. He breathed in through his nose and out through his mouth twice. Knees were flexed for quick movement if he needed to dive for cover. Just a precaution. Then he squinted into the sun and glared at the stand of trees and shrubbery.

The glare from overhead was beyond the trees. That threw the area he was searching into shadow. Good positioning, like fighter pilots watching for bandits coming out of the sun. Well, the bandits of Coldwater Canyon Drive were coming out of the sun. Grant couldn't see for shit while he was being highlighted like a movie star on the red carpet. He didn't want the red to be blood.

Something moved.

Grant's eyes swiveled like gun sights, even though he hated guns. There was another glint of light from the foliage, then a hand waved at him through the trees.

"Okay, you've got me."

Robin Citrin stepped into the open with her cameraman.

TWENTY-ONE

GRANT SAT ON THE porch steps and waited for her to come up the hill. The cameraman disappeared back through the trees, and Grant heard car doors open and shut. Robin Citrin walked up the drive, producing the same little puffs of dust with each footstep that Grant had an hour or so earlier. She reached the turnaround and stopped, head bowed and arms held out in apology.

"I enjoyed dinner last night."

An opening gambit that Grant reckoned was an olive branch even though it was clearly a lie. Dinner had been average, and that was being generous. What she was doing was reminding Grant of what else had happened last night. That had been far better than average, and they both knew it. Grant wiped sweat from his brow with the side of his finger and flicked it across the porch.

"If you'd stuck around for breakfast, I could have saved you a trip."

"It would have been the same trip. Different driver."

"Could have saved me the cab fare then. And the longest list of complaints since the Bradford riots."

Citrin lowered her arms and walked to the foot of the steps. "One step at a time. I didn't mean for that to happen."

"A happy side effect of sneaking into my room?"

"The sneaking was to persuade you about the job. The rest was happy, yes."

"But not enough to stay overnight."

"Like I said, one step at a time."

Grant patted the porch step, so she came and sat beside him. He glanced at her, then stared off into the distance with his best Clint Eastwood squint. No poncho or stubby cheroot but the same idea. He didn't have the ponytail to glare like Steven Seagal, although he didn't think Seagal had the ponytail anymore, just four stone of extra padding—about fifty-odd pounds, since Americans didn't work in stones.

Grant waved at the stand of trees down the hill. "What do you think you're doing?"

Not, "What the fuck do you think you're doing?" which he could certainly justify. Anybody else skulking around with a hidden camera and he'd be truly pissed off. It was hard to get angry with someone as beautiful as Robin Citrin. She was wearing tight gray trousers and a white blouse today. Sensible shoes, not high heels. Business clothes if sneaking around with a camera crew was your business. She wasn't a TV news reporter, the face of Fox News or CNN or any of those networks. Citrin was a working stiff. Another reason he wasn't annoyed at her.

She turned to him and smiled. "Proving a point. How discreet we can be."

"Sneaky, not discreet. Discreet means to be careful and circumspect in one's speech or actions in order to avoid causing offense or revealing private information."

"You read that lately?"

"Had to point it out to somebody else the other day."

"I was circumspect in my actions."

"There's no way you can argue it was discreet."

"Covert, then."

"Oh, you were covert, all right. Thought you were a tree for a minute there."

"What are you doing all the way out here?"

"Visiting a friend."

"What for?"

"For something private."

"Friend not home?"

"None of your business. Could be in there right now, making lemonade and ice cream."

"You don't make ice cream. You buy it."

"You scoop it, though. Into a bowl to go with the lemonade."

"That would be nice right now. Funny way you've got of visiting, though—that door thing you did."

He didn't reply.

Citrin glanced up at Grant, then joined him in staring off into the distance. Not far off, being a female Clint Eastwood but without the squint and the cheroot. Squinting encouraged wrinkles. Tobacco gave you bad breath. She spoke calmly, but not to him. As if she were talking to the wind.

"Should see the footage we got. The Resurrection Man in his orange jacket, unarmed, checking the windows. Cautious at the front door before ducking inside. Very dramatic. With a trailer-man voiceover, that would sell right there. The reality of life on the edge."

Grant spoke to the wind too. "You liked that, huh?"

He nodded at the dusty hills. "Reminds me of all those old black-and-white Westerns they used to churn out here. Saturday morning serials we watched at the local cinema club. Supposed to be in the big wild country, but you could see the same trails and hillsides. The film speeded up to make it look like the horses were galloping."

He turned to look at Citrin. "I saw a Batman serial one time, was filmed in exactly the same place. Car chase along the winding trail. Ruined the illusion for me. Couldn't watch another Western without thinking about Batman escaping from the car as it crashed over the cliff."

Citrin patted Grant's knee, the little boy who'd lost his faith in movies. "Nothing is what it seems."

Grant put his hand over hers. "Some things are."

He squeezed it as he stared into her eyes. "Some of the things I've seen—they are exactly what they seem to be: real and hard and painful. Everything you film—it's just entertainment."

He sensed the atmosphere taking a dip and quickly broke into a smile. "But we all need a good laugh now and again, don't we?"

Citrin joined in the charade.

"That's what Hollywood's all about. Let the good times roll."

"You're serious about this TV thing, aren't you?"

"Why d'you think I was hiding in the bushes?"

Grant stood up. His bad knee cracked again but didn't sound as loud outside the enclosed space of the living room with the blood on the carpet.

"Tell this L. Q. character I'll pop in to see him this afternoon sometime."

Citrin stood up too, one step down from Grant. It made the height difference even more pronounced. They were looking into each other's eyes when the tires squealed off the tarmac onto the dust and gravel driveway. A cloud of dust followed the patrol car up the hill. There were no red and blue lights flashing. There was no siren. They were only needed if you wanted to clear traffic out of the way or scare the crooks off before you arrived.

The car skidded to a halt in the turnaround. The cloud of dust swirled around the front porch. It wasn't until it settled that Grant realized it wasn't an LAPD black and white. It was plain white with blue detailing and a Police Department City of New York shield on the side.

TWENTY-TWO

Chuck Tanburro eased the patrol car along the winding canyon road toward Beverly Hills with Jim Grant sitting relaxed in the passenger seat. Twenty-five minutes after scaring Robin Citrin and surprising the Resurrection Man. Tanburro glanced across at his passenger.

"Sorry about that back there. Couldn't resist."

"Been that long, has it?"

"It's been a while. Yes. You were right. You kinda miss it."

"Doesn't teaching Gary Sinise to walk right fill the void?"

"It fills my bank account. And nobody shoots at me."

"Nobody shoots at me."

"They did outside the bank the other day."

"Never got to that stage. Police nearly shot me, though."

Tanburro jerked a thumb back toward the cabin they'd just left and Robin Citrin.

"You in bed with reality TV now?"

Grant wondered if last night showed but then realized it was just an expression.

"They're courting me. I'm keeping my options open. How'd you find me?"

"Called by the hotel but you'd already left. Concierge said you'd taken a cab."

"You understood him?"

"Japanese guy. Not very good English. But yeah, enough."

"I bet you enjoyed the detective part, didn't you?"

"Tracking down the driver? Yeah. Gave me a bit of a buzz. Guy could moan for the Olympics."

"Didn't need to come out here. You could have given me a ring."

"We getting engaged?"

Grant mimed holding a phone to his ear with the fingers and thumb of one hand.

Tanburro shook his head. "I didn't want to talk on the phone."

Grant was intrigued. "What you got?"

Tanburro smiled, driving with easy movements and casual observation. He looked completely at ease behind the wheel of a cop car. His eyes took in everything around him. His fingers caressed the steering wheel. Grant could imagine the sense of pride and belonging that the ex-cop was feeling. He'd felt it himself when he used to chase the radio on patrol in Yorkshire. The knowledge that you were making a difference in the world, protecting the innocent and locking the bad guys away.

Bad guys. A phrase that was developing shades of gray. Grant was beginning to wonder what kind of father could brush off even the possibility of his daughter being kidnapped. Not a good guy, that's for sure, in Grant's book. Then there was the porn movie producer.

Tanburro's voice became all business. All cop.

"Stuart Ziff. Zed Productions, Alamo Court, Long Beach."

Grant nodded. "I nipped down to see him yesterday. Low-rent porn outfit. Seems to be making a decent living out of it."

"He might well be. But making dirty movies isn't his only source of income."

Now Grant was really intrigued. He began to wonder about the heavies that the producer had hanging around the studio. Not Spitz and Swallows—they were porn stars, not muscle—but the other three. You didn't need hired muscle if all you were doing was making sex films.

"That a fact?"

Tanburro recited from memory. Like most cops, he didn't need the sheet in front of him; memorizing a suspect's history was part of the job. Fine details he could research later.

"Real name: Franco Zeffirelli."

"Like the Italian movie director?"

"The same, but younger. Got a sheet for theft, armed robbery, and extortion."

"Armed robbery? Guy doesn't look big enough to carry a gun."

"Could have been acting in consort. Gets you the same sentence if you go in with the gun, drive the car, or just act as lookout."

"I can see him being lookout. Maybe organizing a job."

"Organizing would be the same."

"I thought he seemed to have more attitude than just a movie producer."

"You haven't been around Hollywood much, have you? Producers are bigger sharks than any bank robber you've ever met."

"Judging by the two I met the other day, I can believe it."

"These top guys, they're real ball busters. Grind you up and spit you out."

"Spit instead of swallow?"

Tanburro smiled. "I like that. Very funny. This guy Ziff though. He ain't so funny. He's in bed with worse than reality TV."

Grant stared into the distance. He was thinking his own thoughts but having to translate them into American. "Extortion. That's like blackmail, right?"

"Right."

Grant thought: influential female, a broken window, and blood on the carpet. "His sheet say anything about kidnapping?"

Tanburro scrutinized Grant's face as if trying to get a read on his thoughts.

"No. That would send him to Federal. Nobody wants to go that deep. Some of these young girls they use in the porn industry, an element of coercion sometimes might skate close, but nothing that would stand up in court as kidnapping. You thinking about your friend's daughter?"

Grant was thinking that he needed to have another chat with Stuart Ziff. "Just a thought. Can you drop me at the Metro?"

Tanburro glanced over at his passenger.

"You don't need the Metro. I've got the car for a couple of hours before they need it back."

Grant nodded, then shook his head. "Thanks, but it's better I go alone."

He smiled across at Tanburro. "I don't want them ball busters getting on your case."

"Why? What you planning?"

Grant stared out of the window. "Something they don't teach in detective school."

Tanburro didn't ask for any more. He just kept his eyes on the road and eased the patrol car through the sprawl of West Hollywood, looking every inch the dedicated cop he used to be.

TWENTY-THREE

IN THE END, GRANT didn't use the Metro. Tanburro took him all the way down the boulevard and dropped him in the parking lot of Superior Super Warehouse opposite Popeye's Chicken & Biscuits, a bit farther up and out of sight of Zed Productions. The parking lot was huge. Grant reckoned Superior Super Warehouse must be the biggest grocery store in the world. A store so big it had super in the name twice.

Tanburro became serious when he pulled into a space and parked. "You sure you don't want company? The guys Ziff hangs with can be rough."

"I met a couple of them last visit. They aren't so bad."

Tanburro tilted his head and shrugged in a have-it-your-way kind of gesture. The sun was beating down, bleaching the sidewalk and turning the buildings into concrete blocks that were hard to see without squinting. Grant understood now why so many people wore sunglasses in LA, especially the cops. You don't want somebody bearing down on you while you're squinting to see what's going on. Grant didn't like wearing sunglasses. He preferred people to see his eyes. That's where the core of his expression came from. Happy eyes.

I'm-cool eyes. Angry, don't-mess-with-me eyes. He'd stopped more than his fare share of trouble just by staring down the troublemakers. He thought he'd have to do more than stare this time.

Grant opened the door and put one leg out before turning back to Tanburro. "You don't want Gary Sinise seeing one of his cars on the news."

"A marked patrol car can give you an edge."

"If it looked anywhere close to an LAPD car, you might be able to blind 'em with red and blue flashing lights and some attitude. This thing looks like a cab."

Tanburro patted the dashboard as if calming a horse. "You'll hurt its feelings."

"Not its feelings I'm worried about. You turn up with bullet holes and broken windows, you'll be in deep shit."

"Thought you said they weren't so bad?"

Grant got out and closed the door. He bent to look through the windshield and grinned. He gave an energetic thumbs up. Then he slapped the car roof twice and set off across the parking lot, squinting at the concrete building behind Popeye's.

HE CROSSED THE ROAD and walked around the back of the food mall via Alamo Court. The tall palms on East Tenth threw exotic shadows across the dusty back street. The back door of Zed Productions was anything but exotic.

Grant stood in the shade of a dumpster in the alley. The medical center parking lot behind Zed Productions was almost empty, just two small patient transports three bays up from a Cancer Care minibus. There were no pedestrians cutting through Alamo Court.

There weren't many walking past the end of the dusty back street along East Tenth either. A few cars drove past but didn't stop.

The front entrance of Stuart Ziff's empire had the silhouetted nude sign above the door. The back door simply had plain lettering that said STAFF ONLY. Grant ignored the front. This was going to be a back-door entry, something he was sure Ziff's wonder boys knew all about. A narrow wire enclosure ran along the length of the back wall with a small industrial dumpster and a pushbike. He couldn't imagine anyone he'd met inside riding a bicycle.

Grant stepped out of the shadows and crossed the dusty track. He glanced across East Tenth at the clapboard houses with their porches and American flags. There were no faces at the windows. No twitching curtains. Nobody was paying him any attention at all. There were a couple of cars in Blockbuster Video's parking lot next door to the houses.

He walked straight up to the fence. The gate wasn't locked. Once inside the enclosure, he smiled at the small camera above the door. If nobody was monitoring the CCTV, they would be in a minute. Grant knocked on the door. The rhythmic cop knock that was unmistakable. He paused to let the first broadside dissipate, then knocked again. Hard.

The door opened outwards. The staff entrance obviously doubled as a fire exit. Fire exits always opened outwards. Mark Spitz stood in the doorway. He looked nervous. Somebody shorter stood behind him in the shadows. No prizes for guessing who that was.

Ziff spoke from behind his protective muscle. "What the fuck d'you want?"

Grant kept his tone light, his eyes soft, giving Ziff the I'm-cool look. "Now, that's not very polite. And to someone who was nearly your latest sex stud."

"Granted, you could've got the job. Don't think the chief of police would have been happy about it though."

"I'm from out of town. The LA chief doesn't worry me."

"He worries me. Doesn't pay to shit on your own doorstep."

The fence rattled behind Grant as the gate opened. Danny Swallows closed the gate and stepped in close, a small silver gun in one hand. Spitz moved to the side of the doorway, smiling now.

Ziff came out of the shadows. "You, on the other hand, don't worry me at all."

GRANT KEPT THE I'M-COOL look in his eyes, but his mind was focusing on the man with the gun. He hated guns. They had brought nothing but pain into his life and today didn't look like being an exception. He calculated angles and distances, weighing up his options while keeping Ziff occupied.

"D'you remember that film with Sean Connery? Not the submarine one where he plays a Russian with a Scottish accent, the Al Capone one."

"*The Untouchables*. Yeah, I remember that."

Grant relaxed his body. Arms loose. Knees flexed. "He gives that speech about the Chicago way. You know, 'If he brings a knife, you bring a gun. He puts one of yours in the hospital, you put one of his in the morgue.' That speech."

Ziff could play this game. "The Irish cop with the Scottish accent."

"That's the one. Well, that's not the line I liked best."

"It's not?"

Grant kept his breathing smooth and even, his eyes soft, not betraying what was coming next. "No. I like the bit where the Italian climbs in the window with a knife, and Connery comes out with a sawn-off shotgun or something and says, 'Just like a wop to bring a knife to a gunfight.'"

Ziff leaned against the doorframe. "If that's supposed to be symbolic, you don't have a knife."

Angles and distances. Grant didn't need to look behind him to know Swallows was only a couple of feet from him. There was no room in the narrow enclosure for him to keep his distance. Being that close meant less reaction time. Grant spun round in a flash, his leading arm knocking the gun hand to one side and his second arm, all elbow, slamming into Swallows' throat. The big lug hadn't even cocked the gun. In less than three seconds, Grant had taken the chrome-finished Smith & Wesson and was back facing the door, two steps to one side to keep out of reach.

"And he doesn't have a gun."

Swallows was clutching his throat and gasping for air. Grant slipped the pistol in the back of his belt and nodded to Spitz. "Want to get him a glass of water?"

Spitz darted inside. Ziff looked smaller than before, and that wasn't easy for a short, fat midget. Grant switched from the I'm-cool eyes to the angry, don't-mess-with-me look.

"Now, let's go inside and talk about the submarine movie."

The Hunt for Pink October didn't have a submarine in it. Grant had been right about that. Ziff gave him a brief rundown of the plot, which included lots of sex with men in naval uniforms and women in nothing at all. There were plenty of up-periscope references and a few torpedo and depth-charge jokes. There was nobody with a Scottish accent and nobody who could act.

Grant asked about the cast.

Ziff snorted a laugh and shrugged his narrow shoulders. "What can I tell you? Oscar material, every one of 'em."

"I don't mean how good they are. Who are they?"

"Regulars. Spitz was in it. Swallows had a sore throat, had to stay in bed—missed that one. Geneva played the Secretary of Muff Diving Affairs. She was the nearest thing to a submarine in the movie. Always going down with sailors."

Spitz laughed at his boss's joke. Swallows was still drinking water to calm his latest sore throat. All three were sitting on the leather settee in the living room set. The studio lights weren't on, just the standard lighting. Grant stood in front of them, a leg length away in case one of them decided to launch a kick. Ziff made a gun shape out of two fingers and a thumb.

"Aren't you supposed to threaten us at gunpoint?"

"You want me to?"

"Not really. Just doesn't seem right giving you information without being threatened."

"You think I'm not threatening you?"

Ziff looked up at the big man from across the pond, then glanced at the muscle on either side of him, Swallows massaging his throat and Spitz giggling like a girl.

"Point taken."

"You know all the girls on that film?"

"Most of 'em, yeah. We always throw a couple of new faces in there if we have an orgy scene or something away from the main plot."

"What about the girl with the short, spiky hair? With the gray-haired fella on the cream settee?"

Ziff opened his eyes wide as if a light had just gone on inside. "This settee. I remember that scene. Geneva walks in on 'em and joins in."

"That was filmed here?"

"Most of it. Some establishing shots on location. Scene's supposed to look like it was captured on CCTV from a static camera." Ziff patted the settee. "Close-ups."

Grant twirled a finger, indicating the studio. "The girl was here?"

"Yeah."

"What's her name?"

"How the fuck should I know? They're not with the Screen Actors Guild."

"You asked for my card."

"Didn't get it, though, did I?"

Grant looked down at the unholy trio. Ziff's laptop played to itself in the front room. There was nobody else in the building—first thing Grant had checked when they came in the back door. The front door was locked so they wouldn't be interrupted. It was time to increase the pressure.

"I was at the girl's house this morning."

"Why are you asking me for her name, then?"

Grant took the gun out of his belt.

"She was gone. Broken window and blood on the carpet."

Ziff's eyes opened wider, and not because a light bulb had just gone on in his head. Panic flickered across his face. He held his hands up.

"Whoa. You can't lay that one on me. That's kidnapping. That's Federal. Me? I'm just a filmmaker."

Grant brought the gun round front. "And a bank robber, thief, and extortionist."

Ziff was staring at the gun and trying to push himself back into the settee. "History. We all make mistakes. I've got a good life now."

"A lowlife good life. Where's the girl?"

Grant spun the pistol's cylinder as if preparing for Russian roulette. Ziff threw his hands up like a cartoon bandit, straight up above his head. Spitz stopped giggling. Swallows gulped. Ziff was sweating even though the studio lights weren't on.

"I swear on my mother's grave. I don't know nothing about no kidnapping."

Grant cradled the gun across the front of him, one hand beneath the other for support. He stared into Ziff's eyes and reckoned he was telling the truth. He didn't know the girl's name and it wasn't him who had kidnapped her. Ziff was just a dirty moviemaker with a background in crime. Judging by the way he was cowering on the settee, Grant guessed it was not a very active background either. He couldn't imagine Ziff robbing a bank at gunpoint.

"You ever see the girl again—you even dream about her—she's off-limits. You understand?"

"I do. I do."

"She's not in anymore of your stroke flicks."

"Definitely not."

Grant raised the gun and popped the cylinder out of the side. He tipped the bullets out and quickly dismantled the mechanism. Bits of Smith & Wesson dropped to the studio floor. Ziff's eyes transmitted his relief. He let out a sigh that trembled close to tears.

"Thank you."

Grant nodded, then went to the back door. He couldn't think of a suitable witty response so he simply opened the door and stepped out into the sunshine. One thing was certain: Ziff might not have taken Senator Richards' daughter, but he was lying about something. Grant could see it in the way his eyes went blank in the middle of the interview, trying to hide what was going on in his head.

He pulled the dumpster across the door as a precaution but didn't think anybody would be coming after him. It wasn't until he was out of the wire enclosure that he saw the big black car parked across the end of Alamo Court.

THE TWO HAWAIIANS WHO weren't really Hawaiians didn't look any worse for wear after their tussle off Hollywood Boulevard the other night. Grant recognized them straightaway. They were hard to forget. They were both staring through the side window, the driver leaning forward to see past the passenger.

Grant smiled at them and began to walk toward the mouth of the alley. He'd stopped thinking of Alamo Court as a back street. The dusty shit tip didn't deserve that title. Coming out from Zed Productions probably had something to do with the change of mindset.

The driver gunned the engine. It let out a throaty roar.

Grant continued toward the car.

The nearest Hawaiian raised one hand and formed a gun shape like Ziff had done inside. He pointed it at Grant and grinned through the open window. Then the car sped off along East Tenth and disappeared beyond the building line. Grant reached the mouth of the alley just in time to see it turn right up North Long Beach toward the city.

He stood on the sidewalk and took a deep breath.

A car door slammed in the Blockbuster's parking lot opposite. Grant smiled and crossed the road toward Robin Citrin. He jerked a thumb over his shoulder.

"You get all that?"

"Close-up and in glorious Technicolor. The guy with the gun had me worried for a minute, though. Nifty moves."

"Most times, a fella with a gun doesn't really want to shoot you. I knew him from before. Left his lipstick at home."

Citrin formed a gun shape with her hand and pointed it at Grant. The third time in an hour. Grant put his hands up like a cartoon bandit, straight up above his head, and smiled.

"Take me to your leader."

It was time to go meet L. Q. Patton.

TWENTY-FOUR

FROM THE OUTSIDE, SUNSET Television & Film Inc. didn't look much different than Zed Productions. The square building was red brick up to eight feet off the ground, then rendered beige plaster from there to the flat roof, instead of Zed's plain bleached concrete. Other than that, the TV studio was just as ugly and functional, 1430 North Cahuenga Boulevard round the back of the Cinerama Dome and next door to Amoeba Music. No wonder Robin Citrin had been able to find Grant when he'd been checking the adult DVDs. At least it hadn't been a 7-Eleven in a past life.

They all got out of the car and stretched their legs. The driver, who doubled as the cameraman, reached in and dragged his equipment bag off the passenger seat.

Robin Citrin held out her arms, palms up. "Welcome to the dream factory."

"I thought we were talking about reality TV."

"Reality TV is a dream."

"I'm glad we've got that straightened out."

"You still complaining about truth versus fiction?"

"I'm coming round to it."

Grant followed Citrin through the double doors from the baking tarmac of the parking lot. If the outside of Sunset Television & Film Inc. looked as downbeat as the exterior of Zed Productions, once you stepped inside it was a very different story. The reception area was plush and expensive. Deep piled carpet, tan wood corner desk, and polished brass fittings. Even the blond receptionist looked like a million dollars. She was already alert to their arrival and smiled a welcome that could send strong men weak at the knees.

Citrin noticed Grant's eyes exploring the curves, and not the ones on the desk. She threw him a look that said "down, tiger" and guided him to a door in the back wall. Even the door was expensive. The receptionist nodded to Citrin that the man inside was expecting them. Grant wondered if she always communicated using telepathy.

Citrin pushed the door open and led the way. Grant liked following her in her tight gray trousers. It took his mind off the receptionist. There was a corridor with three doors down one side and two on the other. Grant glanced at the three on the left.

Citrin explained. "Editing suites. We don't have a studio here. All our work's on location."

Grant pointed at the other two doors. Citrin nodded at the far one first. "Sound mixing."

Then at the last door.

"And L. Q. Ready to meet the boss?"

She didn't wait for an answer. She didn't knock. She simply opened the door and walked straight in. Grant followed and walked into his first experience of TV money.

LAWRENCE Q. PATTON WAS nothing like Stuart Ziff. He was tall and slim and permanently tanned and possessed a smile that extended from ear to ear. He had more teeth than Burt Lancaster—gleaming white Hollywood teeth. His salt and pepper hair was swept back in a tasteful quiff. His clothes were casual but very expensive. Open-necked shirt with exotic patterns. Beige chinos. Pointy-toed cowboy boots. A suede jacket with Davy Crockett tassels hung over the back of his chair. The image screamed phony bonhomie and yet the man came around the desk as if greeting an old friend. The handshake was firm and the welcome genuine. Grant liked him at once.

"I thought it was James Coburn. Back twenty years."

Patton grinned. The comparison had obviously been made before. "Not as far back as that."

"I wasn't thinking of the cowboy with the knife in *The Magnificent Seven* as much as the boss in *True Lies.*"

"That was Charlton Heston."

"Shit, you're right. Maybe that other Western then—the Sam Peckinpah one with Kris Kristofferson."

"*Pat Garrett and Billy the Kid.*"

"That's it. James Coburn more distinguished but still with the smile."

"I'm honored, but really more like Stephen J. Cannell. Only taller."

"The TV producer? Never saw him. Just his name at the end of *The Rockford Files.* James Garner at his best."

Patton grinned even wider and finally let go of Grant's hand. "See how I got that around to TV producers?"

"You mean, letting me know you're a TV producer? I noticed that, yeah. Nice piece of misdirection. You should be in the room interviewing burglars and robbers."

Patton nodded at the open door, made a drinking gesture with one hand, then twirled his fingers to include everyone in the room. Grant saw the receptionist accept the instruction, obviously receiving by telepathy as much as transmitting.

She finally spoke. "Hot or cold?"

Patton raised an eyebrow at Grant.

"Cold, please. Orange juice?"

Citrin asked for the same. Patton made that three juices, then looked at Grant. "You think I'd be able to get them to do what I want?"

Grant raised his eyebrows. "Prisoners? Without 'em really knowing it. I'd say you could."

"And that would be, what? Interview technique?"

"No. More like people skills—get them wanting to please you."

Patton didn't look convinced. "Did prisoners usually want to please you?"

"They didn't want to displease me."

"I'm sure. So, using the same technique, have I got you wanting to please me yet?"

Grant smiled. "Not quite, but you're getting there."

"Good. Let's talk business."

Patton waved toward a group of comfy chairs in the corner of the office. There was a low-slung table and an expensive laptop linked into the local news broadcasts with the sound turned down. Three glasses of orange juice were already on the table. Grant took the far seat facing the door. Citrin sat opposite. Patton sat between them and indicated the laptop.

"I've been watching the footage Robin shot the other day up at the cabin, and catching up on the news archives all the way back to

Boston. You've got a screen presence that could work very well for us."

Grant didn't say anything. He always found compliments harder to take than criticism. Criticism he could argue about. Praise was harder to swallow. Instead, he glanced around the room. Framed posters of TV shows he'd never heard of adorned the walls. Judging by the artwork, they stretched from deep-sea fishing to teenage angst and celebrity cooking. The connecting thread seemed to be they were all reality based.

Patton waved a hand to include all the posters. "These are all ours—documentaries, behind-the-scenes, fly-on-the-wall."

"Celebrity chefs?"

"We've done celebrity chefs, yes."

"I'd like to do a few celebrity chefs myself. Lock 'em all up and throw away the key."

"Not your favorite TV?"

"I loved *The Rockford Files*."

"You could be our *Rockford Files*—reality TV version."

Grant leaned back in the chair and spread his arms across the back. "Mr. Patton."

"L. Q. Everybody calls me L. Q."

"L. Q. I've got to be honest with you. This whole having a camera follow me around thing doesn't sit well with me. I'm a cop. Reality is what I deal with. Cameras change all that."

"Because people don't act normal with a camera on them, right?"

"You've noticed."

"This is Hollywood. People don't act normal around here at the best of times. Everyone wants to be in show business."

"I don't."

"Almost everyone. The camera situation—I'm sure Robin explained we can be unobtrusive."

"She proved that, yeah. Acting like a tree."

"So part of your argument goes away right there."

Grant leaned forward and picked up his glass of juice. "You using that interview technique on me now?"

"I'm using my people skills."

Grant smiled and took a drink. Ice clinked in his glass. "Keep trying."

Patton took a deep swig of his juice and let out an appreciative sigh. He licked his lips, then grinned across the table. The TV producer looked more like James Coburn with every change of expression.

"Let's cut to the chase, shall we?"

Grant waited for the proposition. Citrin watched with anticipation. This wasn't her pitch. Patton put his glass on the table and crossed one leg lazily over the other, exposing a length of hand-tooled leather cowboy boot. All he was missing were the spurs and a battered Stetson.

"Robin mentioned the sum I offered?"

Grant nodded but kept quiet.

"Based on the footage I've seen, and having met you, I think this could blow that Steven Seagal shit right out the water—playing at being a cop. How's that going to rival the Resurrection Man?"

It was a rhetorical question. Patton was on a roll.

"The sum Robin mentioned—I'm prepared to double it."

That stopped Grant's objections dead. What she'd offered him before was more than he could earn in a year with the BPD, even allowing for special assignments and expenses. He took another drink as a delaying tactic. Glanced at the posters again. Avoided looking at Robin Citrin, who he could sense getting agitated in the corner. He took one last drink, then set the glass on the table.

"You deal with all the permits and stuff?"

"For filming? Yes."

"Everyone filming around Los Angeles—they need location permits?"

"They do. We do."

"Like *CSI* the other day? And porn movies?"

"Everybody needs a permit."

"Are they all registered? Permits and locations and stuff?"

Patton looked unsure where this was leading. He looked like a detective whose interview subject was getting away from the preferred path.

"From now until eternity."

"And retrospective?"

Patton uncrossed his legs but remained calm. On the outside. "The money not enough? What do you want?"

"I want information." Grant smiled at the TV producer. "Did you ever see *The Hunt for Pink October*?"

HALF AN HOUR LATER they'd reached an agreement, and the tension that had been building in the room evaporated. Grant would allow Sunset Television & Film Inc. to film a pilot episode of a show to be called *The Resurrection Man*. They would pay him an advance immediately, amounting to ten percent of the agreed salary. Nonrefundable. Everyone signed a confidentiality agreement that gave Grant control of what could be used in the final cut, just in case any sensitive issues were recorded.

That last bit was very important, considering his current investigation.

There were other benefits that weren't in the contract. Having everyone he encountered filmed could prove useful, especially if Grant managed to guide the circumstances of those encounters. There were strict regulations governing the use of covert surveillance by the police. Back in the West Yorkshire Police, he would have had to fill out numerous application forms detailing the exact reasons why it was necessary and any collateral intrusion into the subject's private life. Then he'd have to get them approved by a magistrate. TV just went ahead and filmed everything, then worried about it later.

There was another benefit of working with a Hollywood insider. You were suddenly on the inside.

Patton agreed to look into the locations that had been registered for *The Hunt for Pink October* and when it had been filmed. He would also check the financial records to see who paid for, and benefited from, the distribution of the movie.

The trio in L. Q. Patton's office was on their second round of orange juices by the time everything was concluded. The receptionist was as adept at gliding in with refreshments as she was at communicating telepathically. The laptop continued to play the news. There was a live news feed at a day shelter for the homeless. Grant's eyes caught it out of the corner of his eye, then quickly focused on the computer screen. Senator Richards was doing something official at the day shelter. Right now. That meant he wasn't at home.

Grant finished his juice and stood up. "There's somebody I've got to go see. Before you start filming."

Patton stood up too. "Don't worry. Now that it's a go project, we'll start tomorrow."

They shook hands again. The strong, dry handshake that James Bond used as a litmus test when meeting somebody new—in Ian Fleming's books, not the films. Villains always had a glint of red in their eyes. Friends always had a strong, dry handshake. L. Q. Patton had a strong, dry handshake, and he always grinned like James Coburn.

"Porn movies aren't the only ones with financial backers. I'd like you to meet our moneymen. Give them a chance to meet the star they're bankrolling."

"I'm not a star."

"You will be."

"Should I wear a poncho and chew a cigar?"

Patton looked nonplussed. Citrin stood and smiled at him. "An in-joke. Ponchos instead of ponytails."

Patton nodded as if he understood and waved the distraction aside.

"They're throwing a party tonight—up in the hills. Why don't I have Robin bring you along?"

"I don't have any party clothes."

"Informal party. Come as you are. Beautiful views of the city."

"I've been in the canyons today. Might as well do the Hollywood hills as well."

Patton shook his head.

"Same view, different angle. Across town at Montecito Heights."

TWENTY-FIVE

CITRIN DROPPED GRANT AT the gates of Senator Richards' house in Beverly Hills. Grant was getting used to being ferried around but still preferred public transport. The exception was being run around by Robin Citrin. He could definitely get used to that. She'd left the cameraman behind and did the driving herself. Grant sat in the front passenger seat. He was impressed. She drove like a cop. Even when she was talking, her eyes never stopped moving, covering the road, assessing obstructions, anticipating traffic movements. She was confident but careful, even when she was talking.

"This is where we picked you up the first day, isn't it?"

"You picked me up, did you? How shameless, Miss Scarlet."

"I do feel shame. Just not if the circumstances are right."

"Are the circumstances right?"

She slowed to allow time for congestion up ahead to clear instead of rushing up to it and breaking. A tangle of cars trying to turn left melted away, and Citrin picked up speed.

"Not this very minute. But, overall, I'd say yes."

"You did say yes."

"I didn't mean to."

"Me neither. Some things just happen when the time is right."

"Is the time right for you to tell me what you're doing at Senator Richards' house?"

"That would be something that doesn't make the final cut."

"Just asking."

"Thanks for the lift."

The car pulled up at the sidewalk, and Grant opened his door. He glanced across at Citrin and smiled but didn't get out. He looked into her eyes, and she nodded. This was one of those circumstances-are-right moments. He leaned across and kissed her on the cheek, then patted her knee. "See you tonight."

"I'll pick you up at Pearl Harbor."

"You noticed that, huh?"

"More Japanese than a sushi bar."

"Meet you in the lobby. Bye."

He got out and closed the door. She threw him a wave as she pulled away from the curb, then Citrin only had eyes for the road. Grant walked to the gate and pressed the buzzer.

Jeeves showed Grant into the study, then left. That surprised Grant. He'd expected to be taken to Mrs. Richards' day room and wondered if he'd got the timing wrong. Maybe Double Dick had got home already. That would be a pity. It wasn't the senator he'd come to see. Sunshine and birdsong came in through the open window. Scent from the flower border filled the room. The grandfather clock ticked in the corner.

Grant went to the window and looked at the lush foliage and carefully shaped trees surrounding the manicured lawn. Garden sprinklers stuttered an intermittent spray across the well-trimmed grass. The lawnmower was silent, but the alternating stripes of cut grass reminded Grant of Wimbledon's center court. Roger Federer would feel at home out here. Everything was green: the lawn, the bushes, the trees. It was a stark contrast to the parched hills above Coldwater Canyon Drive and the dried lawns of the rest of Los Angeles. If in the land of the blind the one-eyed man is king, then in the city of angels the rich get all the water—celebrity homes and golf courses. He thought about Jake Gittes and the water scandal in *Chinatown*. Sometimes fiction highlighted reality. Maybe that's where reality TV was going wrong, trying to do it the other way around.

"Make you feel at home, does it?"

Maura Richards closed the door behind her. She went to the other window and looked outside. A wave of the hand indicated the expanse of lawn.

"Green trees and verdant lawns. The striped grass of Wimbledon."

Grant turned to face her. "Wimbledon's two hundred miles south of home. I've never been."

"But you have grass and trees in Yorkshire?"

"And lots of rain to water them. Yes."

"It hasn't rained here for months. Summer gets like that."

"Doesn't look like water's a problem for you."

"No, it doesn't, does it?"

"We expecting Jeeves with the lemonade?"

"You remembered. Yes. We have routines at chateau Richards."

"Then we'd better wait until he's gone."

Mrs. Richards didn't ask why. She simply nodded and waved Grant toward the Chesterfield. He sat in the uncomfortable leather settee, and she took the chair opposite. There was a knock on the door, and Jeeves came in without waiting for a reply. He put a silver tray with a pitcher of lemonade and two glasses on the coffee table and left without speaking.

Grant watched the pantomime, then glanced at Mrs. Richards. He was getting the impression that she wasn't so much the lady of the manor as a bird in a gilded cage. He wondered how much it would take for her to fly away—how much she wanted to leave this life behind her. Judging by her demeanor, not enough. A gilded cage was still a pretty good place to live if you didn't mind the restrictions.

"Your husband kept you up to date about your daughter?"

"About her doing another vanishing act? Yes."

"I'm not sure it's that simple."

"What makes you think that?"

Grant leaned forward and poured two glasses of lemonade. He handed one to Mrs. Richards, then sat back with his own. He didn't drink it.

"The broken window. Blood on the carpet. Some stuff had been searched."

He didn't mention the DVD he thought might have been taken. When fishing for information it was always best to hold something back. He still wasn't convinced that Senator Richards was sharing everything with his wife.

"It doesn't add up to a burglary. Not quite right for that. But it's a bit elaborate for faking your own disappearance. When she's gone missing before, did she ever set things up like this?"

Mrs. Richards took a drink of lemonade. It gave her time before replying.

"No. She just vanished for a few days. Stayed with friends. Two weeks, once; that was the longest."

"Which friends?"

"She never said."

"She just came home, and you didn't ask where she'd been?"

"We asked. She never said."

"What friends do you know about?"

Mrs. Richards put the glass on the table and took a deep breath. She closed her eyes and appeared to be plucking up courage before answering.

"We don't know anything about our daughter. She had few friends as a child. Has even fewer as a teenager. She walks her own path. Like her mother."

"That's why you blame yourself."

It wasn't a question. He lowered his voice.

"Don't. We all inherit stuff from our parents—not all of it welcome. It's no more your fault than her sharing your blood type or hair color."

She smiled her thanks but didn't look like she believed him. Another drink of lemonade delayed her having to respond. Grant took a swig himself. It was cold and wet, blessed relief on a day like today. Ice clinked in his glass. He leaned back against the stiff leather. It was time to get down to basics.

"Have there been any ransom demands?"

Mrs. Richards appeared shocked at the reality of the possibility.

"No."

"Any threats?"

"No."

"Would you know? If they came to your husband?"

"I would know."

"Then it doesn't make sense, taking her. Kidnappings are for a reason. Either money or influence. Senator Richards carries plenty of influence. He knows a lot of powerful people."

He indicated the photos dotted around the study. Richards with sports stars. The senator with Arnold Schwarzenegger, the actor-turned-governor of California. A candid shot of Richards with the chief of police beneath a decorative arch that framed downtown Los Angeles. Lots of people Grant didn't recognize but who exuded power and influence. Any number of targets for coercion if the kidnapping aimed to use Richards in that regard.

"Have you tried calling her mobile?"

"Her cell is turned off."

"Give me the number, just in case."

He wrote the number beneath the Coldwater Canyon address in his notebook. It was something he should have asked for before, but this hadn't been a kidnapping back then. He wasn't convinced it was a kidnapping now. If he had been, no matter how much Double Dick protested, Grant would have brought in the police. This felt like something else, and he wasn't sure what it was yet.

He put the notebook away and took a final drink of lemonade. Mrs. Richards looked like a beaten woman. Her eyes were downcast and her shoulders stooped. He wanted to reassure her, but there was nothing he could say or do that would release the guilt she felt at having failed her daughter.

He stood up.

She stood up too. "Thank you for coming."

"It was on my way."

A little white lie. She shook her head.

"No. In the first place. Thank you for coming from Boston."

"You're welcome."

He said it and he meant it. Helping Senator Richards had been his remit. The real reason was to protect the chief of police from any fallout of the scandal. But this, right here, was the most important reason of all: helping a trapped woman recover her self-esteem and save her daughter from bad men. Bad men were his specialty.

"I'll get her back for you."

Another little white lie, but one he believed he could achieve. They didn't shake hands and there was none of that phony double-dip kiss on the cheeks. She didn't press the buzzer for Jeeves, showing him to the front door herself instead. Grant was halfway down the drive before the oppressive atmosphere of the study left him. He was glad to be back in the fresh air and sunshine.

TWENTY-SIX

Dusk had slid toward full dark by the time they arrived at the house in Montecito Heights. The view across Los Angeles was spectacular as they came around the bend where Montecito Drive doubled back on itself. Dodger Stadium was lit up like an alien invasion; the LA Dodgers were playing a home game against a team Grant had never heard of. Beyond that the downtown towers stood out against the skyline, red lights blinking on the rooftops to warn low-flying aircraft, which included the ever-present news helicopters. The lights of Willowbrook and West Athens sparkled in the distance, a vast plain of twinkling jewels.

The gate to 1042 Montecito Drive was plain and functional. It was set between white walls and a row of cypress trees on the right and some kind of flowering bush on the left. Bright pink flowers shone in the headlights as Citrin pulled up to the small black intercom in the wall. She identified herself. The gate slid open on rollers with an electronic hum.

The driveway wasn't a driveway. In keeping with everything Grant had learned about America, it was the mother of all driveways. Nothing succeeds like excess. The drive was actually a road that skirted the wooded hilltop and almost came around full circle before reaching a promontory jutting out from the hillside. The view was the same as from the bend in Montecito Drive but appeared even more spectacular with the canyon foreground below.

What was truly spectacular, though, was the house. If Dodger Stadium was lit up like an alien invasion, then the house at Montecito Heights had already been taken over. Grant braced himself for the onslaught of his first Hollywood party.

Robin Citrin locked the car in the turnaround that had become a temporary parking lot. This wasn't the dusty turning circle out front of Angelina Richards' frontier cabin; this was an expanse of tarmac that could have landed a private jet. Or at least a helicopter. The double beep of the power locks was almost lost amid the music coming from the house. Even from here, the sound of laughter and talk mingled with the cicadas from the canyon and music from the hidden speakers.

Citrin held her hands out to indicate the mass of people up the hill. "Welcome to party time."

Grant felt uncomfortable already. He wasn't a party animal. He preferred intimate gatherings with only two people. One female and one male. Tonight, that would have been him and Citrin.

"I'm gonna get eaten alive."

Citrin arched an eyebrow.

"Not while you're with me."

She led the way up the stairs to the house. People were milling about all over the place. Some on the stairs from the parking lot. Some around the outside of the house. Quite a lot in the hallways and living rooms of the split-level home. A couple came out of a bathroom holding hands and giggling. Further along there were couples chatting in the open-plan kitchen. Citrin looped her arm around his, and they drifted through the melee like ghosts. Nobody noticed them. Nobody spoke. By the time they'd wandered through two of the three levels, he'd had enough.

"Maybe this wasn't such a good idea."

Citrin patted his arm. "It's not my scene either. Haven't spotted L. Q. yet."

"You sure he's coming?"

"He'll be around somewhere. He wants to show you off to the money."

"I'm not spiking my hair and dying it blue."

"That was the disc jockey."

"Can't we get out of the crowd?"

Citrin looked around and noticed a row of doors farther along the corridor.

"Let's try up there."

She led him by the arm, and he went willingly. She knocked on the first door and pushed it open. It was a large room with a king-size bed and a smattering of furniture—a chaise longue, a single chair, and a coffee table. The built-in wardrobes were tan wood and mirrors. The bedclothes were smooth and tidy. There were no personal items on display. A guest room, Grant reckoned. He closed the door behind him, and the noise level dropped to a murmur. He let out a sigh of relief.

"That's better. Now what shall we do?"

Citrin sat in the chair and slipped her shoes off.

"We relax until you've built up your immunity."

"To that lot out there? I think I need vaccinating."

He turned the lock on the handle and walked to the middle of the room. Subdued lighting painted the beige carpet and cream furniture with soft tones. Smoked-glass mirrors and a built-in dressing table complemented the tan wood of the wardrobe doors. Grant's reflection was darker than he actually was. His orange windcheater shaded down toward ochre. He draped himself across the chaise longue—a settee with one end missing, as far as he was concerned. He glanced at the bed but didn't want to appear pushy. This was Citrin's party. Sort of.

Grant held a hand up to his face, the forefinger and thumb forming a circle. He looked at her through the circle like a spyglass.

"Want to play I-Spy?"

"The sixties TV show?"

"The party game. I spy with my little eye something beginning with…"

"Oh, that game?"

"Or we could just get out of here and see L. Q. another time."

Citrin got up from her chair.

"Or. We could not."

She sat next to Grant on the chaise longue. He had to shuffle over to make room and nearly fell off the end. The missing end, if it had been a settee. She leaned into him, put one arm around his waist, and rested her head against his chest. If she were a cat she'd be purring.

Grant rested one arm across her shoulders and gave them a gentle squeeze. "I thought you said you were a shy girl."

"I said I'm an old-fashioned girl."

"Is this old-fashioned? Like dating your high-school sweetheart?"

She spoke into his chest.

"You think I'm not a sweetheart?"

He squeezed her shoulder harder.

"I think you're beautiful."

She raised her head and smiled up at him. Grant lowered his to meet halfway. They looked into each other's eyes and neither spoke. Citrin snuggled her body into his, getting comfortable. Grant used his free hand to stroke her cheek. He touched her lips with one finger, then took hold of her chin and tilted her mouth so he could kiss it. She responded straightaway this time with soft, gentle nibbles of his lips in return. It felt good, this intimacy that wasn't going to lead to sex. Not here. Not now. This was simply getting-to-know-you time. Like a first date with your childhood sweetheart. Except it was their second.

She closed her eyes as he kissed her.

Grant kept his open and watched her face become calm and happy.

He saw something else as well.

He kissed her on the forehead, then sat up. He could see their reflection in the mirrored doors on the middle wardrobes. They both looked tanned and healthy. She looked darker than him. The Italian heritage. He moved his head slightly to one side and then the other. At a midway point their reflections dulled slightly and there was a glint from behind the glass. Citrin raised her head.

"Was it something I said?"

He quickly kissed her on the nose, then slid out from beside her.

"You ever see *From Russia with Love*?"

She sat up.

"The one with Sean Connery? A British secret agent with a Scottish accent?"

"As opposed to the Spanish immortal or the Russian submarine commander with a Scottish accent?"

"Point taken. The one where he sticks a hair across the wardrobe doors and pours talc on the briefcase catch?"

He stood up and walked over to the wardrobes.

"That's the one."

"You spotted a hair across the wardrobe?"

Grant stood in front of the mirrored doors. He stepped to one side so the light could reflect off the smoked glass. He held a hand up in front of the center door and moved it up and down. The reflection changed when the light was blocked out.

"It's also the one where he makes love to Tatiana Romanova in the bridal suite. She fingers his scar and he turns her over in front of the mirror. The shot pans up and you can hear an old cine-camera behind the glass."

He yanked the door open. There were no clothes rails inside. The middle shelf had been removed and a small CCTV camera fastened in its place, angled down toward the bed. Any romantic thoughts he'd been having on the chaise longue vanished. He hadn't even begun life as the latest reality TV star yet and he was already fed up with being caught on camera. The intrusive photographer had already cramped his style with Geneva Espinoza. Being filmed with Robin Citrin was a step too far. He moved aside so she could see the miniature camera.

"Smile. You're on *Candid Camera*."

Citrin didn't smile. She looked mildly embarrassed. Not like she'd been caught in a compromising position but like she'd rather keep her private life private. Grant nodded at the impartial observer.

"Boot's on the other foot now, huh?"

She stood up, annoyance creasing her brow, and slipped into her shoes. Grant realized it had been the wrong thing to say and tried to dig himself out of the hole.

"That wasn't a swipe at you, by the way."

"What was it a swipe at, then?"

She still sounded angry. He closed the wardrobe and walked over to her. Took her face in both hands and bent to kiss her forehead and nose and lips. By the time he reached her lips she'd calmed down. He stepped back and looked into her eyes.

"A swipe at the inequities of life."

It was a good line. It seemed to appease her. Grant wasn't worried about the hidden camera in the wardrobe, though. He was thinking about a static camera view of a gray-haired man on a cream settee and the pert-breasted teenager keeping him company. Smoke and mirrors. Not so much a porn shoot as a hidden camera.

FIFTEEN MINUTES LATER. MUSIC thumped into the night, a mixture of modern classics and tuneless rubbish. Grant yearned for the soundtracks of Lalo Schifrin and Ennio Morricone. If he ever got introduced to the host, he might suggest that for the next party. After their brief spell inside, they'd come out of the side door.

The house was a long, low structure with peaked roofs and dormer windows. It was built on three levels climbing up the hillside into the woods. There was a traditional Hollywood swimming pool and acres of sculptured gardens with patio lights scattered along the winding paths. The pool had underwater lighting and naked female swimmers.

Grant followed Citrin around the pool and along the garden path toward the extensive patio. People were mingling and laughing and exchanging stories while drinking fancy cocktails that looked more alien than some of the people drinking them. The colors were ghastly. They reminded Grant of those scenes in the *Star Trek* movies that were supposed to be the Star Fleet bar. The only things missing were a handful of Tribbles and Captain Kirk. The rest of the alien quotient was provided by some of the females wandering the decking. Grant leaned close to Citrin so she could hear him over the music.

"Maybe we should just leave and find somewhere a bit more peaceful."

She looked as if she was about to say yes when her eyes suddenly darted across Grant's shoulder. He turned to follow her gaze and saw the tall man with a Davy Crockett jacket and cowboy boots coming toward them through the decorative arch. The grin was unmistakable. James Coburn in his heyday.

It was too late to escape.

"It's life, Jim, but not as we know it."

L. Q. Patton was standing on the patio with a cold beer and a grin. One hand was indicating the wildlife around them. Citrin was standing to one side. Grant was in the middle.

"Is that from the song or from *Star Trek* proper?"

"What song?"

"*Star Trekkin'*. A spoof."

"Never heard the song. The quote was from the TV show. Doc McCoy to Captain Kirk."

"*T. J. Hooker.*"

"That wasn't one of mine."

"One of yours if you were Stephen J. Cannell?"

"Which I'm not. I'd have loved to have done *The A-Team* though."

"I preferred *The Rockford Files.*"

"Yeah, you said."

Grant glanced around the patio. The decking was crowded but not as full as the house. Picture windows ran all along the south-facing walls, giving Grant a reverse view to what they could see from inside the house. People standing and talking, some kissing and cuddling. At least two snorting coke on a glass-topped coffee table. The scene it reminded Grant of was that one in *Kiss Kiss Bang Bang* where Robert Downey Jr. was at a Hollywood party full of weird and wonderful people. Whenever Downey was asked what he did, he made up a different story. Nobody listened. Nobody cared. They just said yes, then drifted off. Grant felt like he'd been kidnapped by aliens and dropped right into the middle of that scene.

Aliens were a recurring theme tonight. A woman who was practically naked had been painted completely blue. She was wearing a skimpy bikini that no doubt hid patches of bare flesh to allow her skin to breath. The blue woman was only one of many strange sights wandering around the split-level house and grounds. Grant shook his head.

"So, is this how the rich and shameless spend their Saturday nights?"

Patton surveyed the crowd.

"It isn't Saturday night."

"Figure of speech."

"You see? You're getting the hang of this. Reality TV is just a figure of speech for the visually impaired."

"TV for the blind, you mean?"

"TV for the less intellectually inclined."

Grant smiled. "TV for thick fucks."

"On the scale of human achievement among the great American viewing public, there are more thick fucks than rocket scientists. And they all pay to watch TV. This is show business. We go where the money is."

Citrin tugged at Patton's sleeve and jerked a thumb toward the barbecue deck. Three chefs were busy grilling steaks and burgers and sausages. The smell of cooked meat and sizzling onions drifted across the patio. Smoke swirled around the cooking area. A man walked out through the smoke like a wraith from the mist.

"Talking of money. Here he comes."

Patton turned to look at the figure swathed in smoke who was talking to everyone he met as he crossed the barbecue deck. He was patting people on the shoulder. He was grinning almost as much as L. Q. Patton. Grant followed their gaze and watched a solid, athletic guy who was on the wrong side of fifty but the right side of healthy. If Patton was James Coburn, then the newcomer was Burt Lancaster. Patton's grin broadened.

"Perfect timing, Jim. Here comes the man I want you to meet."

The man cleared the smoke and spotted Patton's upraised hand. He came across the patio with measured strides. Unlike Patton, he was wearing tan loafers, blue jeans, and an open-necked shirt revealing a triangle of hairy chest. The hairs were tinged with gray like the short-cropped haircut but were sparse and wiry. Grant thought there was something familiar about him. Something other than a passing resemblance to Burt Lancaster.

Then it came to him, and a shiver ran down his spine. It was hard to tell because he'd only seen the guy from behind with a fixed camera angle. The general shape was the same—the well-groomed hair sliding toward gray. The hairy chest. Grant wondered if they matched the hairs on his shoulders.

TWENTY-SEVEN

SMOKE AND MIRRORS. THAT'S what Grant was thinking as Nathan Burdett came through the smoke to greet L. Q. Patton. The smoke part was obvious. The mirrors went back to what he'd discovered in the guest room. Smoke and mirrors. A technique used by illusionists to make a trick look like one thing when it was really something else. Everything was different depending on how you looked at it.

Grant managed to contain the surprise at where he thought he recognized the guy from. Not from *The Scalphunters* or *Birdman of Alcatraz* but from the static camera pointed at the back of his head while a naked Angelina Richards sucked his cock. Patton introduced them, and Burdett held out a hand. Grant shook it. James Bond's friend-or-foe detector worked a treat. The handshake wasn't firm and dry. Burdett's hand felt as clammy as a just-shit turd, not easy in the dry heat of Southern California. There wasn't a hint of red in his eyes, that was something, but Grant distrusted him straightaway.

None of that showed in Grant's face as he smiled at his host. "You sure know how to throw a party."

Burdett grinned his appreciation of the compliment. "This is LA. It's a party town."

He let go of Grant's hand. The guy had the limp grip and sweaty palm of a banker that was at odds with the tan and movie-star grin. Burt Lancaster would be spinning in his grave if he knew this guy modeled himself on the Hollywood legend. Grant kept the smile relaxed and friendly.

"I particularly like the synchronized swimming team."

Citrin narrowly avoided digging him in the ribs again. Burdett glanced across at the swimming pool.

"Not exactly Busby Berkeley, but they get by."

"Did you know that silicon implants are heavier than natural breasts?"

Citrin looked away. Patton grinned. Burdett laughed and shook his head.

"I didn't know that. I guess we'd better employ more lifeguards. We don't want anyone drowning. This is LA—there's more plastic here than in Silicon Valley."

Grant waved at the view of downtown Los Angeles through the decorative arch. There were at least two helicopters buzzing across the night sky, searchlights lancing into the dark.

"LA seems to have more of everything. Actors. Film crews. TV shows. It's the bank robbery capital of the world, I've been told."

"If robbers wanted to make real money, they should steal the budget of any Hollywood movie. Hundred million average these days."

"Not rob the budget of a reality TV show?"

"That would still net them a decent profit. Not the big league, though. The money I've put up for some projects would make your eyes water."

"You don't just do TV, then?"

Burdett held one hand up, fingers spread.

"See those fingers? Covered in pastry, the number of pies I've got them stuck in. Keep hoping that one of them will come out with a plum. Like in the nursery rhyme."

"My dad never read me nursery rhymes."

"You get the picture, though? My projects are diverse and wide ranging."

Grant didn't mention that diverse was the same as wide ranging. He realized that in Hollywood it was all about how it sounded or how it looked, not the reality of the words. He wondered if Burdett had a finger in the porn industry.

"Well, the party-throwing pie looks pretty healthy."

"Thanks. Glad you could come."

"Just a thought, though"—Burdett's grin faded to a half smile that looked strained. He didn't like having his judgment questioned. Grant kept his tone light.

"This being Hollywood"—he indicated the horizon to the west—"over there, anyway. But this being the movie capital of the world, you throw a party like this, how about using film soundtracks instead of dance music? A bit of Morricone or Schifrin. Elmer Bernstein. Jerry Goldsmith. The theme for *Lonely Are the Brave* would fit perfect in the background. Then you could hear yourself think."

Burdett appeared to consider that for a second, then his grin returned.

"The plaintive horn solo with guitar. Like he used in *First Blood*. The first Rambo movie? Yes, I see your point. Maybe *Bullitt* or *Dirty Harry*."

"If you wanted to throw in some Brit influence, there's always *Get Carter* and *The Long Good Friday*. Gangster stuff with a difference."

Burdett was back to his old self. Grinning like a fool.

"I'll look into that for next time. See if there're any soundtracks in the house."

Grant glanced at the split-level home. "Nice house, though. Can't argue with that."

Burdett followed Grant's eyes. "Not bad, is it? I've used it before."

Grant was surprised. He was thinking about the camera behind the mirror. "It's not yours?"

"Hell no. Don't want all these airheads fucking up my carpets."

"That's a point."

"Or drowning in my pool." Burdett waved an arm to include everything around him. "In this business, you can always find someone who'll lend you their house."

"So it seems."

Burdett offered his hand again, and Grant shook it.

"Mr. Grant. Nice to meet you. Everything L. Q. has told me about you is true. I think you're going to make me a lot of money."

"More than robbing banks?"

"Enough to keep the wolves from the door."

Burdett let go of Grant's hand and slapped Patton on the back. He spun on his heels and marched back across the patio, greeting and backslapping all the way. Grant wiped his hand on his jeans. Citrin noticed and smiled. Patton said farewell too, and pretty soon Grant was alone with Robin Citrin. Alone in a houseful of heavy drinkers.

"Can we go now?"

She nodded and began to walk toward the parking lot. Grant fell in step with her. Citrin took his hand.

"Want to come back to my place for a nightcap?"

"I don't wear a nightcap."

She laughed. The laugh was dirty and full of promise.

TWENTY-EIGHT

ROBIN CITRIN LIVED IN a bungalow on Los Grandes Way at the foot of the Griffith Park hills. She had the corner plot just off Winona Boulevard. At the top of the hill behind the housing development the Griffith Park Observatory searched the night sky for stars, while below and slightly west of the bungalow Hollywood catered to stars of a more earthly nature. If Nathan Burdett and L. Q. Patton had their way, Jim Grant would soon become one of those stars.

Grant still wasn't a hundred percent sold on the idea.

It was late but nowhere near midnight when Citrin pulled the car into the carport at the side of the house. They'd been chatting all the way across town but now they fell silent. This felt like a more important moment than being picked up from the hotel or making love in his room. Grant got out and walked to the corner of the house. The slope of Winona meant the houses lower down the hill didn't obstruct another perfect view of downtown Los Angeles in the distance. He wondered if there was anywhere in LA that didn't have that view.

The car door slammed behind him.

"You're a bit of a night gazer, aren't you?"

She was standing beside the car, twisting the keys nervously around her fingers. It was the only sign that she felt the tension building. Other than that, she looked calm and collected and drop-dead gorgeous. Her smile looked genuine enough. Her body language exuded self-confidence. Apart from the keys. He turned and walked back toward the car, never taking his eyes off her.

"I'm just a gazer."

He stepped in close, put one hand behind her head, and kissed her nose.

"No pressure. I'm just here for coffee."

She smiled up at him. "Thought you preferred tea."

"I don't want to offend you, but Americans can't make tea for shit."

"Is that like those camel-dung cigarettes?"

"Could be. Anyway, I'm getting used to this latte culture. Plenty of sugar."

Citrin broke off from him and went to the front door. She unlocked it and quickly disabled the alarm at the keypad. She flicked the lights on and beckoned him inside.

"One latte coming up."

THEY DRANK IN SILENCE, sitting in poolside furniture on the concrete patio round back. The pool didn't qualify as a swimming pool, but it was big enough to get wet if you fell in. The patio was small and intimate, with a shield of bushes between them and the next house along Los Grandes. The bushes were necessary because each house along the street was only three feet from the next one in line. Grant had looked over the hedge before sitting down. He'd struggle to walk down the gap between the houses without having to turn sideways. Three quarters of the houses had pools out back. Every single one of them had a spectacular view across the city. Not as high up as from Montecito Heights but clear and unobstructed. It must have been getting late because Grant only saw one helicopter now. There were no jetliners coming in to land at LAX. The night was at peace, apart from the occasional siren over in West Hollywood.

This was a hundred times better than the noise and bustle of Nathan Burdett's party. This was what he'd wanted all night. To spend some quality time alone with the woman he was growing close to. Unattached sex was fine. He could live with that. Sex and a laugh was better, giving Terri Avellone the edge over many of the ships-that-pass-in-the-night one-timers. This thing here with Robin Citrin was shaping up to be something different. Something he hadn't experienced since…

Grant finished his coffee and put the empty mug on the concrete, pushing any thoughts about army medics and stethoscopes out of his mind. The past was history; that's why they called it the past. Live for now and die later. That was Grant's motto. He didn't look ahead and rarely looked back. Enjoy the moment.

He heard Citrin's cup clink on the concrete and glanced over at her. She was draped across a sun lounger with the back raised. The night air was cool after the heat of the day. He could see goose bumps along her forearms and hard evidence of the chill through the cotton of her blouse. She swung her legs off the lounger and sat up. She held out a hand for him to help her up. Grant stood without using his hands, the muscles of his thighs screaming with the effort from the low seat, and pulled Citrin to her feet. She glanced up at the starry sky.

"Maybe I should have ordered a violinist."

"Or a full moon."

She shook her head.

"I don't think I could manage you on a full moon."

"The beast inside me, you mean?"

She put her arms around his waist and snuggled up to him.

"Yes."

His arms folded around her like a protective wall. He got the feeling she needed protection more than she showed. There was hurt behind the façade. From a previous lover perhaps.

"Not tonight. Tonight I'm a teddy bear."

She squeezed him, then stepped back, taking his hand.

"Let's go inside and find out."

Without looking back, she led him through the patio doors.

THE MASTER BEDROOM WAS to the left, off the living room. It also faced the patio and had its own picture window with full-length curtains. They didn't turn the lights on but left the curtains open. Grant ignored the room and focused on the woman standing in his arms.

Citrin's face looked up at him with bright eyes and a beautiful white smile from the slightly parted lips. The unruly mop of black hair looked even darker in the shadows. The white of her blouse became luminescent in the starlight and the reflected glow of the patio lamps. He let her make the first move.

Gentle fingers tugged the T-shirt out of his jeans, and her hands slipped inside the cotton to caress his back. They ran up his spine and sideways around his waist. The touch of her palms was hot. The goose pimples on her arms were no longer because of the cold but something else. She snaked both arms around his back and pulled him toward her, flattening her breasts against his stomach. The cotton blouse was soft but intrusive. She stepped back and looked into his eyes, then down at the little pearl buttons. He got the message.

He unfastened the buttons one at a time. Unhurried. From top to bottom. With each released button, another two inches of tanned flesh became visible. Cleavage first, then a snatch of skimpy bra followed by the soft, flat plain of her stomach with the exquisite indentation of her belly button. Below that the rest of her was hidden by the waistline of her trousers. Grant stopped at the trousers. Citrin slipped the blouse off her shoulders and reached behind to unclip her bra. It fell to the ground and firm, dark swellings jiggled slightly.

They both stood still for a moment, eyes locked together. Peripheral vision showed her long, slender neck and bare shoulders. Her breasts and stomach were not the focus of his attention. Citrin broke the spell. She looked down as her hands unfastened his belt and jeans. Once again her fingers slid inside the material and slid round behind him. Her hands took one buttock each and squeezed. The forward movement drew her closer to him, and this time when her breasts touched his stomach electricity sparked a joint reaction.

She gasped under her breath. Her nipples became bullets pressing into him. His own reaction became firmer. She pushed his jeans down to release it but didn't look. Her eyes were back on his face, watching the look in his eyes. Grant kicked off his shoes, then quickly bent to remove the jeans, underwear, and socks. When he stood upright again, Citrin had taken the rest of her clothes off.

They stood naked in the subdued light from the street. Grant explored her body with his eyes. She did the same with his. Her initial shyness was evaporating fast. The self-confidence was returning. Grant put his hands on her waist.

"You are beautiful."

"Thank you."

When they came into each other's arms this time, the full-body contact provoked a chemical reaction that saw erections firm up on both of them. Her nipples became even harder. His erection stabbed at her stomach halfway to her breasts. That secret place between her legs grew hard. Their hands slid across naked flesh and felt the sleek firmness of muscle and bone. Before, in his hotel room, Grant had proceeded carefully, not wanting to rush her. Tonight it was Citrin who was pushing matters forward.

With a gentle shove, she guided him backwards onto the bed. She fell forward over the top of him but held herself up on stiff arms. She straddled his middle. His middle was waiting to be straddled. She leaned forward and kissed his chest, the unruly mop of hair adding friction to his skin. She kissed and teased and flicked her tongue across him but didn't move down his stomach. Instead she moved upwards, kissing his neck and collarbone. Her breasts swayed gently over him, nipples brushing flesh and forcing little moans from her lips.

Grant reached up and took the breasts in his hands. He squeezed gently. Then harder. She gasped. She rubbed her sex across his stomach and pressed her thighs tight around him. Behind her, farther down his body, his manhood waited. Slowly, she backed up. Her thighs moved down his sides. Her buttocks pinched together over his stomach. The soft, wet lips of her sex moved toward him. She reached behind herself with one hand, the other straining to keep her upright, and took hold of his shaft. It felt hot to the touch.

Then she guided it into her and sat down slowly.

All the way.

"Oh my God."

Her voice was a whisper. It was the only thing she said. Everything else was movement and muscle control. Pretty soon all control was lost, and they fucked each other hard and fast and very, very long. She gasped and screamed and tore at his hair as she came. He gritted his teeth and breathed out through clenched lips. Then she collapsed into his arms.

It took half an hour before they did it again. Another hour after that for the third time. After that, they were spent. Citrin's hair was plastered to her head. Grant's muscles quivered as if he'd run a marathon. They lay in each other's arms, and she fell asleep on top of him.

THE HELICOPTER WAS BUZZING over Hollywood Boulevard as Grant took a drink of bottled water from Citrin's refrigerator. He was leaning on the patio rail wrapped in a bath towel. The faintest hint of blue was feathering the eastern horizon. A siren sounded in the distance, coming closer. He reckoned the chopper was for police support. Even twenty-four-hour news would find little to cover at this time of night. The searchlight scoured the ground, looking for something the police wanted to find. A burglar disturbed in the act? A car thief running from an abandoned vehicle? It could be any number of incidents the night watch had to deal with.

His eyes ran across the twinkling lights of Hollywood, then strayed farther south toward Long Beach. Somewhere in between, the glass and concrete towers of downtown jutted skywards. Somewhere near them was the Historic Mayfair Hotel. Somewhere in the vastness of sparkling jewels and darkness a teenage girl was either hiding or being held captive.

Grant took another drink of water.

The helicopter searchlight switched off abruptly. The sirens stopped. They'd either found whatever they were looking for or given up. Grant hadn't found what he was looking for, neither the answers nor the girl, but he hadn't given up. He knew it was only a matter of time before he solved the puzzle. A puzzle that was shifting with each move he made, because the only thing he was certain of was that everyone was lying.

Almost everyone. The patio door to the bedroom slid open. A tired voice that was still sexy despite the fatigue called out quietly, "Come back to bed."

He turned round and saw the ghostly face in the opening. Beside that, reflected in the window, the entire cityscape glinted across the plain. He ignored the twinkling lights and concentrated on Robin Citrin. He smiled even though she couldn't see his face and went back to bed.

TWENTY-NINE

CITRIN DROPPED GRANT OFF the following morning after breakfast. Not at the hotel but in a dusty vacant lot two blocks from the Mayfair. West Seventh was busy with commuter traffic avoiding the freeway. Broken clouds provided sunshine and shade in equal measures. Grant wasn't sure why he'd suggested being dropped off at the vacant lot, but the itch at the back of his neck told him it was time to be careful. He always paid attention to the itch.

She swung the car through a gap in the chainlink fence and stopped amid a cloud of dust. An overgrown palm cast a shadow across the windshield. The urgency in his voice when he'd told her to pull over precluded her asking why. She looked the question at him instead.

Grant shrugged. "Probably nothing. But best be on the safe side."

The dust settled. The sun went behind a cloud that threw the vacant lot into shade. They looked at each other for a moment, unsure how to say goodbye, then Grant leaned over and kissed her on the lips. She kissed him back. When he opened the door, he preempted her protest.

"In private. That feels right. When it's work, I'll be more..."

He didn't finish. She nodded and looked a little sheepish. The professional woman caught with her guard down. Then she leaned over and kissed him again one last time before waving for him to get out.

"I knew there was a reason you wanted to park behind a tree."

"The privacy couldn't hurt. See you later."

"Bye."

He shut the door. Citrin spun the car around and pulled back onto West Seventh out of town. Grant watched her go, then walked in the opposite direction, still wondering about the itch and the growing sense of foreboding. A helicopter thudded across the sky above the Staples Center farther south. The sun came out, turning up the heat. Freeway traffic, noisy and constant, sounded in the distance. He was halfway to the hotel when he spotted the big black car parked opposite.

GRANT CROSSED THE ROAD toward the Mayfair but walked straight past the front entrance. He went into the Seventh Street Dollar Store next door instead to buy a bottle of chilled water. There was a display of fruit near the door consisting of bruised apples, discolored oranges, and several bunches of bananas going brown in the heat. The car was chugging exhaust fumes across the road. Grant smiled as he looked at the ripe bananas, then at the car again. He remembered Eddie Murphy disabling a car in *Beverly Hills Cop* by stuffing a banana in the tailpipe and briefly considered doing the same. He dismissed the thought as unworkable because they'd already seen him, and paid for the water.

Then he changed his mind. He bought a selection of rotting fruit and asked for it bagged, then stepped back out into the sun. Traffic had eased. A smile broke out on his face as he trotted across the road humming Harold Faltermeyer's "Axel F" theme. The jaunty tune lifted his mood. He eyed the tailpipe as he approached but knew stuffing a banana in there wasn't really an option, so he walked past it and slapped the passenger door.

Hawaiian number one didn't flinch in the driver's seat. He'd been watching Grant in the rearview mirror and leaned over to wind the window down. Grant was still humming. The Hawaiian smiled through the open window.

"You think you pretty funny, don't you?"

Grant stopped humming and shrugged. The Hawaiian nodded as he spoke.

"I like that movie. You too big and white to be Axel Foley, though."

"It was originally going to be Sylvester Stallone."

"You too big for him also. Guy's a fuckin' midget."

"No. The guy played R2D2 was a midget."

This time the Hawaiian shrugged.

"You are no midget."

Grant held up a hand in appreciation.

"I'll take that as a compliment. Where's your friend?"

There was nobody else in the car.

"Gone walkabout. Like Crocodile Dundee."

"I like the theme for that too, but I can't whistle it."

Grant held up the bag of fruit. "There'll be too much just for you. Some fruit since you're always out here watching on stakeout. Couldn't afford the sandwiches and stuff like in the film."

"*Crocodile Dundee*?"

"*Beverly Hills Cop.*"

He handed the fruit through the window and immediately realized his mistake. Cold, hard metal pressed into his back, and the second Hawaiian spoke quietly.

"Not walkabout. I'm more like that boomerang in *Crocodile Dundee*. When it goes away, it always comes back."

Grant dropped the bag on the passenger seat. The gun felt big. It was pushed firmly against his spine. Rule of thumb about holding somebody at gunpoint is to keep out of that somebody's fighting arc. The closer you are, the more chance of being disarmed with a rapid spin and defensive arm strike. Rule of thumb doesn't apply when the gun is shoved right in your back. No matter how fast you are, you're never going to be quick enough to prevent the gun being fired at point blank range.

Grant let out a sigh. Rule of thumb about a situation like this is not to worry about what you can't control. If they'd wanted to shoot him, they would have done it already. If they didn't want to shoot him, then a proposition was coming. He waited with his knees flexed and arms relaxed. Just in case.

The proposition was more of a demand.

"Get in. Somebody wants to talk to you."

Hawaiian number two opened the back door, and Grant got in.

The gunman got in with him and the driver nodded. He threw the bag of fruit out the window, then set off down the road, humming the "Axel F" theme. Badly.

THIRTY

THE DRIVER FLICKED THE turn signal on Santa Monica Boulevard and waited for traffic to clear so he could turn left. There was an ornate chapel at the entrance. It had a red-tiled roof and a stained-glass oriel window on the gable end. At first glance it reminded Grant of the Alamo except without the battle scars. He read the sign on a patch of neatly trimmed lawn next to the chapel.

HOLLYWOOD FOREVER

Cemetery

Funeral Home

Flowers & Gifts

6000

To Grant it felt like turning into the drive of an exclusive golf club, and he supposed Hollywood Forever was as exclusive as it got. You had to be dead to get in there, but more importantly it helped to be famous.

The black car drove slowly and respectfully as if leading a funeral procession and turned left at the chapel through the gates. A wide tarmac road network encircled the cemetery with two extra driveways, one running up the spine and the other going across the middle, forming a crossroads near the crematorium. The car followed the left-hand driveway along the northern edge behind the strip mall. The tall, thin palms formed an honor guard on either side of the road.

Grant scanned the horizon for possible threats. There were no drug cartel gunmen waiting to greet him. There were no long black limousines with tinted windows. Even the Hawaiian sitting next to him had put his gun away. The car crawled past marble tombstones and ornate crypts. A scattering of tourists and well-wishers sauntered around the graves, taking pictures. Spectacular flower arrangements turned the open spaces into a riot of color and relaxation in the sunshine. Scent from the blooms was only spoiled by the fried onion and candyfloss smell from a concession stand near the gift shop. Having a gift shop and burger joint seemed incongruous in a place of worship, but that didn't appear to discourage Americans. As if to emphasize the point, Grant could see the Hollywood sign on the hills in the background and several rooftop billboards advertising the latest movie blockbusters.

The car stopped at the junction with the drive that cut across the middle of the cemetery. A twin marble tomb marked the grave of Cecil B. DeMille, king of the religious epic. The driver ignored it and turned right toward a manmade lake. A crypt the size of a small house stood on an island in the middle of the lake with swans and lily pads. A man whom Grant had never seen before stood on the bridge to the island. He turned at the sound of the car but didn't wave. Inside the car, the atmosphere turned frosty. Both Hawaiians tensed in the presence of their boss.

The driver pulled over, and the gunless gunman indicated for Grant to get out. He did. The door was yanked shut behind him, but the car didn't drive away. The engine purred, adding exhaust fumes to the smell of burgers and candyfloss. Fresh air and the scent of flowers fought a losing battle. Nobody moved. The man on the bridge stood still. The Hawaiians sat frozen in the car. Grant grew bored waiting for instructions, so he walked toward the bridge.

He was halfway there before the man nodded at the visiting Yorkshireman. Grant nodded back and stepped onto the bridge to meet the head of the Dominguez drug cartel.

"YOU HAVE COST ME a lot of money."

Rodrigo Dominguez spoke in measured tones with only a hint of an accent, but there was weight in his delivery that went way beyond the words. Dominguez was maybe sixty years old but carried himself with the easy grace of a much younger man. He was medium height and medium build and possibly the most dangerous man Grant had ever met. He could feel the power emanating from him like a force field. There was no outward display of anger or violence, but it was there in the steely glare and deeply etched lines across his face. This man wouldn't think twice about ordering Grant's death if business required it.

Grant didn't speak. He decided to tread carefully.

Dominguez's expression didn't change. His chiseled features were as craggy and tanned as dried parchment. His eyes were hard and gray. There was no emotion in them, just fierce concentration.

"I do not like losing money."

Grant didn't speak.

Dominguez cast his eyes around the cemetery, nodding at certain grave sights to punctuate his words. The first was on the eastern shore of the lake, beneath a neatly trimmed conifer and a tall, slim palm tree.

"That is the tomb of Tyrone Power. Hollywood star that played Zorro."

He indicated a much simpler marble grave shaped like a park bench on the opposite shore behind them.

"Fay Wray. A personal friend of King Kong."

He nodded across the right-hand driveway toward the crematorium, where a more impressive memorial overlooked a long, narrow water feature and fountain.

"Douglas Fairbanks, Junior and Senior. Zorro multiplied by two."

Grant didn't speak.

Dominguez raised an arm toward the house-size crypt on the island across the bridge. It had the Doric marble pillars and angled roof of a Greek temple and stood perhaps twenty-five feet tall. The walls were hand carved white stone with two slitted windows in the side elevation and a door from the patio at the end of the bridge.

"William A. Clark, Junior. Founder of the Los Angeles Philharmonic." Dominguez lowered his arm and turned his stare on Grant. "Do you know what they all have in common?"

Grant couldn't resist. "They're all dead?"

Dominguez wasn't swayed. "They all generate money even though they are dead." The stare intensified. "You, on the other hand, would just be dead. Worth nothing but a handful of dust and a prayer."

The eyes hardened.

"That is the only reason you are still alive."

Grant wasn't easily spooked, but he felt the short hairs bristle up the back of his neck. Goose pimples broke out on his forearms despite the heat. This was like staring death in the face and knowing there was nothing you could do about it. A swan drifted past on the lake and made a squawking call to its mate amid the lily pads. A helicopter thudded across the sky somewhere over the Hollywood Freeway. A tourist took a photograph of Tyrone Powers' memorial.

Grant didn't speak.

Dominguez's tone didn't change. He could have been discussing the weather.

"You are worth nothing to me dead."

Grant decided to test the water. "You haven't just threatened an officer of the law, have you?"

"I don't make threats. I make promises."

"To cops?"

"Cops. Priests. Mothers and their babies. The world is a dangerous place."

"But you didn't just threaten me?"

"Would you like a confession? Want me to speak into the microphone like in all those TV cop shows? It wouldn't do you any good. The wire would be buried with your ashes, and the only benefit would be the worms and the flowers that you would fertilize."

"I don't wear a wire to the banana shop."

"Yes. The fruit. I heard about that. Very considerate of you. I also don't think you wear a wire to your lover's bed. The beautiful Robin Citrin."

This time the bristling hairs sparked all over Grant's body. He managed to keep the shock out of his voice but wasn't sure his eyes hadn't flared.

"Too dangerous. The battery can give you a shock."

"I agree. I do not believe you are recording this conversation. So let me get to the point. Walk with me."

Dominguez walked across the bridge to the island and stood in the shadow of the mausoleum. Grant followed, keeping pace with the man from south of the border. He waited for the proposition because he was certain one was coming. The car doors opened, and the Hawaiians got out. A second car pulled up behind them. Same type, same color, tinted windows; nobody got out of that one. Grant stepped into the shade. The amorous swan squawked loudly, and its mate squawked back. There was a commotion in the water. Dominguez ignored the disturbance.

"You are moving in opulent circles."

Grant looked into Dominguez's eyes, trying to gauge how much he knew and how much was speculation. The slate-gray eyes gave nothing away. He would make an excellent poker player. The craggy features remained impassive as he spoke.

"Senator Richards is a wealthy and influential man."

"He is. I'm not."

"Don't do yourself down. By association you have acquired a modicum of that wealth. You are being paid, are you not? And by helping him, you are also exerting an element of influence over his future."

"Not as much as you'd think."

"It doesn't matter what I think. What matters is how much that knowledge is worth to me. You have a debt to pay."

"Snake Pass? Papers valued the shipment at something like fifteen million."

"An exaggeration. The press cannot be relied upon, as I'm sure you know."

"Still, more than pocket change, that much powder."

"An inconvenience. Cost price to me was nowhere near fifteen million."

"Money like that—not even a low-budget Hollywood movie. You'd be better off robbing banks. LA's the capital of both."

"I don't watch movies. And I own a bank. What this is, is a debt. And you are the one who owes it."

Grant shrugged. "I'm just on a street cop's salary."

"You are doing yourself down again. You are currently employed by one of the wealthiest men in Southern California. A man who wants to keep certain things quiet to protect his political career."

"You thinking of blackmailing him?"

"No. I am blackmailing you. Richards is the leverage and the money man."

Grant thought about something else. "You into kidnapping as well as drugs?"

"In my time as the executive officer of our business, it cannot be ruled out."

"So is this a ransom demand?"

If Dominguez was surprised, he didn't show it. His face remained placid and his voice calm.

"The Richards girl? I have no interest in her foolishness. She is wherever she is and has nothing to do with me."

Grant believed him. "Why d'you think I'm bothered about Senator Richards' reputation, then?"

"If the senator's problems become public, he is not the only one who will fall."

The goose pimples returned. Grant wondered just how much Dominguez knew about why he was in Los Angeles.

"Whoever falls, it won't be me. I'm just an honest cop."

"Honest but not exclusive. You now have a very lucrative TV contract."

Again Grant was forced to wonder how much the drug lord knew. "Not yet, I don't."

"The contract yes. The money no. But to keep you happy, they will pay you in advance because they know you give good copy."

"You sound like a newspaper man."

"I am a practical man. You should try it sometime."

Dominguez nodded toward the second car. The door locks popped, and a big guy in a dark suit got out. He wasn't wearing a chauffeur's cap, but he was the driver. Two more guys got out of the back, dressed in dark clothes and carrying machine guns held loosely across their stomachs.

"You will pay me one hundred thousand dollars."

One of the gunmen came across the bridge. Dominguez began to walk toward him and waved a hand at Grant.

"You have three days."

The two men crossed paths on the bridge, and the guy with the machine gun walked up to Grant. Grant was in the open. No cover. Even with his relaxed stance and flexed knees, the nearest place he could reach was the corner of the mausoleum ten feet away. A guy with a pistol might miss with a snap shot. A machine gun would cut Grant down before he got three feet away.

Dominguez stopped on the bridge and turned back toward Grant.

"And just in case you really aren't worried about Senator Richards, remember there are other people who could get hurt because of this. One of them I am sure you do care about. She would find it difficult to work a camera without hands."

The normal reaction would be to lunge at Dominguez. Grant wasn't normal. In a situation like this you had to focus on what you could control and not worry about extraneous matters. There was a man with a machine gun between Grant and the drug lord. The man with the machine gun raised his hand.

Dominguez walked to the open car door and got in. The raised hand held a blank business card with a cell number written in ink. Grant took it, and the guy turned and walked away. He crossed the grass and got into the second car, and all the doors closed at once. The Hawaiians smiled across the lawn, and the passenger winked. He pointed a finger at Grant like a makeshift gun and dropped the thumb like a hammer. Bang.

The cars pulled away slowly. They didn't spit gravel as they sped off. That only happened in the movies. They crawled, slowly and respectfully, like a funeral procession taking grieving relatives away from the graveside.

Grant watched them go back down to the bottom of the cemetery and out the main gates. The sun had moved across the sky without losing any of its ability to bake. The two swans kissed and made up. The tourist photographing Tyrone Powers had disappeared. The helicopter had drifted across the Hollywood Freeway.

Grant looked at his watch. Almost twelve. He walked back to the driveway and headed for the concession stand. Confrontations always made him feel hungry. He bought a burger and a Pepsi. Ten minutes later, he dropped the empties in the trashcan and opened his cell. Robin Citrin answered on the first ring.

"You get all that?"

That was becoming his catchphrase. The helicopter returned and hovered over Santa Monica Boulevard. Citrin gave the thumbs up through the window.

THIRTY-ONE

GRANT WAS SITTING ON an ornamental stone beside the Hollywood Forever sign when Citrin pulled up at the curb in the minivan. The side door slid open with the usual *pffft hiss*, and she waved him in. When Grant was sitting on the back seat, the driver closed the door and set off toward downtown.

Citrin was busy working the controls of a portable video monitor. Grant saw a long shot of the Hawaiians letting him out of the black car in the cemetery. The angle was shifting slowly as the helicopter kept its distance. The orange jacket stood out in the sunshine against the bright green lawns. The zoom lens followed Grant to the bridge. Crackly audio came out of the twin speakers. There were snatches of dialogue, but the predominant sound was the loud, thumping beat of the helicopter blades.

Citrin turned the volume down.

"The directional mike works better on the ground or in a static vehicle. In a chopper—too much noise. That didn't look friendly, though."

Grant considered how much to say without panicking her. There had been an implied threat against the woman in his life, but he had three days before that would become a problem. Seventy-two hours was a long time. He reckoned he'd have this thing sorted before then. He had to tell Citrin something, though.

"It goes back to an old case. I don't think he likes me very much."

"I'd say that's an understatement."

Grant smiled. "Understatement is my middle name."

"Bull's-eye should be your first. Lot of guys with guns down there."

"You worried about me?"

Citrin wasn't smiling. "I am, yes. This is reality TV. Don't want you really getting shot."

"That's reality for you. People carry guns, somebody's gonna get shot."

"Doesn't seem to bother you."

"Funny thing about guns. In the movies, everybody's a crack shot unless it's one of those *Die Hard* films, spraying machine gun fire everywhere and only thing they do is shatter the windows. But mainly, in the movies, a quick-draw gunslinger can hit a running man or shoot a gun out of his hand and never miss. In reality, if you're more than six feet away, it's a lottery."

"Some people win the lottery."

"Most people lose."

"With handguns?"

"Yes."

Citrin pointed at the video monitor. "Those guys from the second car. They're not carrying handguns."

The screen showed the two men in black cradling machine guns across their stomachs. One of them walked toward Grant while Dominguez crossed the bridge.

"Strictly speaking, they are. Handheld weapons that can be fired single-handed. But I get your point. Machine pistols. I'd have trouble dodging the shit storm they'd be able to unleash."

"Exactly. Maybe we should run this past L. Q. This is getting deeper than just following your daily routine."

"Hang fire for a bit. They were for show—to put the willies up me."

"Put the what?"

"Scare me. They weren't going to shoot. The head guy wants my help."

"Didn't look like he was asking for help."

"More like demanding it. Anyway, the next three days should be fairly quiet."

"And after that?"

"After that, you'll have a great show."

"Jim. Don't go doing anything stupid."

Grant waved the objection aside and took the notebook out of his pocket. "Did you see where they went?"

Citrin seemed happy to change the subject.

"Hollywood Freeway, heading south. We lost them in traffic after they split up near Echo Park."

"Lost them? You were in a chopper, for Chrissakes."

"D'you know how many black cars there are on the freeway? Most popular color in America. Big ugly square things."

Grant shrugged and smiled. "Turning circle of a bus. I know. You sound like my cab driver."

"I'm turning into your cab driver. Where d'you want to go?"

Grant was busy leafing through the notebook until he came to the numbers he'd jotted down in the cemetery as soon as the cars had driven off. The plates of both cars recorded before he forgot them. Good police practice. It was only in TV shows and movies that cops could remember car numbers off the top of their heads. He flicked open his cell phone.

"Hotel will do fine, thanks. Just want to get someone to run the plates."

He scrolled the settings until he found the phonebook, then selected Chuck Tanburro's number. He was about to hit the call button when the phone began to ring. The caller ID showed it was Tanburro. Grant answered the call.

"What's up? I was just going to call you. Can you run a plate for me?"

"I'm not a cop anymore. Remember?"

The minivan was dropping down through Wilshire Center toward West Seventh. There wasn't much traffic on the surface streets, most of the through travelers preferring the freeway system. The driver was taking it nice and easy. Grant smiled into the phone even though Tanburro couldn't see him. He knew the ex-cop would help.

"You've still got contacts on the job, though."

"I do. And that's why I'm calling."

Grant felt a tingle of gooseflesh up the back of his neck. Tanburro obviously had some information, and that could only be good. Citrin sensed the change in mood. Grant listened.

"The girl's bank card just got used in East LA. She's at the ATM now."

THIRTY-TWO

Citrin's driver got the minivan to the bank on East Cesar E. Chavez Avenue in record time. The bank was part of an L-shaped strip mall at the junction with East Cesar and Gage. The L wrapped around two sides of the parking lot at the intersection. The smallest branch of the Bank of America was in the angle of the L. It used to be PLS Check Cashers, and the building retained the low-rent nature of that business while adding the familiar red signage and a single cash machine beside the door. The ATM had the same transparent shelter for its customers as the MacArthur Park branch.

There was nobody at the cash machine.

The minivan cut across traffic and swung straight into the parking lot. The side door did its *pffft hiss* thing, and Grant was scouring the pedestrians before his feet hit the ground. Most appeared to be Mexican or Spanish American. There were no blacks and only two white Anglos. One of them was male. The female didn't have short spiky black hair. Angelina Richards was nowhere in sight.

Grant crossed the parking lot to the ATM and stepped under the shelter. The screen had settled back into advertising mode after the last transaction, but a paper receipt stuck out of the slot like a tongue poking fun at him. He took the receipt and read it. Some-body had withdrawn two hundred dollars just eight minutes ago. The card details were blanked out except for the last four numbers. There was no customer name. He screwed the paper up and balled his fist.

Above him, a CCTV camera looked down into the shelter. Grant glanced at the bank door. There was another camera in the angle of the wall. A customer walked into the bank, the door swinging both ways as it shut. Grant turned to Citrin, who was standing beside the minivan.

"Keep an eye out for her. I'll check the cameras."

He turned toward the door, fishing out his badge wallet. It wasn't an LAPD badge but it still made him official. Kind of. The door was working down to the last flip flaps and he was about to push the handle when it opened outwards. A dark-skinned woman and a white guy wearing a Dodgers baseball cap came out side by side. Grant stepped between them but was shoulder charged by both. The woman waved an apology. The white guy did not. One of the few things that angered Grant. He felt like snapping a retort but focused on the job in hand.

He pushed the door and entered the bank.

THE INTERIOR WAS AS low rent as the outside. PLS Check Cash-ers clearly had been a poor man's financial institution before the Bank of America realized the potential of having a bank in even the roughest parts of town. No wonder there were so many armed rob-beries. A sign inside the door advertised money transfers around the world, and it reminded Grant of the corner shops and travel agents in Bradford. Immigrant families from India and Pakistan could save money through the welfare system and send it to the next member waiting to move to England. It was a growing industry, right up there with furniture manufacturers who supplied at least four settees per household for all the extended family living in a two-room semi.

CCTV cameras covered the main room, but it was outside that interested Grant. There were only a handful of customers at the dark wood counter with anti-climb windows. Grant held up his badge and shouted over the glass.

"Police officer. I need to speak to the manager."

There was a muttering of excitement from the customers and bank tellers. A short man in a dark suit stood up and pointed to the side of the counter. He looked nervous. Grant moved toward the end of the counter, and a door opened in the wood-paneled wall. The short guy stood in the opening.

"Please. Not another robbery."

Grant put his badge away and made a placating gesture with the hand not holding the receipt. He kept his tone calm but insistent. "I'm a cop, not a robber."

"But please. You not here because of another robbery?"

"Have you had another robbery?"

"No."

"Then I'm not here about the robbery you haven't had." He glanced around the room. "Don't you have armed security guards anymore?"

He remembered seeing movies where even the smallest branch had a geriatric ex-cop standing guard in the corner.

"Sadly not. Cutbacks, you know."

Grant shrugged and held the receipt up.

"Can your system pull up the details of the last half-dozen ATM transactions?"

"Only the same as on the receipts."

"Not who the customers were?"

"No, that is private information. I cannot reveal that to you."

"But head office could do it? Else how d'you know whose accounts to debit?"

"Yes. But without—"

Grant interrupted him. "I've got a missing girl. Could be in deadly peril. I need to know if she just used the machine outside."

He was overstating the case, but it was worth a try. The short, nervous bank manager shook his head, wringing both hands as if pleading forgiveness.

"I am sorry, officer. Without a court order I cannot release that information."

It was what Grant expected. Time was of the essence. Unless he could persuade the manager to circumvent procedures, the girl would be long gone before he found anything out. That just left the one thing he could check. He waved at the cameras dotted around the room.

"Your CCTV cameras. They on time lapse or full record?"

The manager looked confused. He stopped wringing his hands and began to rub his head with one hand while stroking his chin with the other.

"I cannot show—"

Grant's tone ratcheted up a notch.

"Deadly peril. If this girl dies, d'you want it on your conscience that you could have helped save her and didn't?"

"But procedures are—"

"I don't want to seize the tapes. Just have a quick look."

"But—"

Grant lowered his voice and feathered a knowing smile across his lips. "If there's anything on the tape, we'll get a court order straightaway. These are exigent circumstances. I'm sure you've got them in your manual. Life or death. Choose life."

The manager was weakening. He stopped rubbing his head and stroking his chin. He began to nod, slowly. The sad look in his eyes remained, but he forced a weak smile. He was about to step back and let Grant through the office door when his expression changed. His eyes flared panic as he looked toward the front door.

"I thought you said this wasn't a robbery."

Grant turned to follow the manager's stare. Red and blue flashing lights showed through the glass. Several police cars were pulled across the parking lot. Armed cops racked shotgun actions and handgun slides. They formed up across the hoods of their cars. The only thing they didn't do was shout, "You're surrounded. Throw down your weapons and come out with your hands up."

He glanced around the room. Of the handful of customers, three were short dumpy women, one was an elderly Mexican who looked too thin to hold himself upright, and one was a housewife with her baby son. No prizes for guessing who the police were here for. Grant let out a deep sigh and walked toward the front door.

THE PARKING LOT HAD become a war zone. Three marked units blockaded the entrance, red and blue lights flashing, and a plain Crown Vic was parked behind them on East Cesar. A square black SWAT van pulled up outside the Spanish church across the intersection. The only thing missing was a police helicopter. It was the first time Grant had seen the sky empty.

Grant opened the door slowly and stepped outside. He held his arms out straight at shoulder height, hands open and palms forward. Half a dozen gun barrels swung in his direction. The lead officer shouted over the hood of his car.

"Sir. Get on the ground. Facedown. Now."

Grant lowered himself to the floor, facing the threat, and lay flat on the ground.

The lead officer walked around the front of his car. "Hands out where I can see them. Palms up."

Grant already had his arms outstretched, palms up. He watched the lead officer nod to his colleagues from Hollenbeck Division, and two of them approached the bank. The same procedure as before. A quick recce inside, then they came back out, holstering their weapons.

"Clear."

The lead officer kept his gun pointed at Grant and spoke into his shoulder mike. "Four Adam Fifty-Three. Scene secured. Suspect detained. Call off SWAT."

The other cops lowered their weapons behind their cars. A black-clad SWAT commander visibly sagged. Another siege he hadn't been able to send his team into action for. The heavy mob were the same the world over. Couldn't wait to get into combat. Grant didn't mention that the suspect wasn't detained until he'd been searched and handcuffed. This wasn't the time for flippancy.

Two Hollenbeck detectives came through the cordon. Grant half expected to see Bob Snow and Dick Wadd, but he didn't recognize these two. The lead uniform dropped to one knee and began a weapon search. He read Grant his rights as he checked each pocket. The American version he'd heard a thousand times on TV and in the movies. He doubted if anyone in the States didn't know their rights, but it wasn't the knowing so much as the having them read to you. Procedures. Fall down on the little things, and an entire case could crumble to dust.

"Sit up."

Grant rolled over and sat on the edge of the curb.

"Cross your legs at the ankle and put your hands behind your head."

Grant crossed his ankles.

"Interlock your fingers."

Grant linked the fingers of both hands behind his head. He was now sitting in an unstable position. It would be hard for him to cause trouble, and he could be easily pushed over if he tried. A solid base would be to have your legs apart, but with them crossed he was top-heavy and vulnerable. He didn't like feeling vulnerable. Four Adam Fifty-Three began a more detailed search of Grant's pockets while asking if Grant understood his rights. Grant nodded. The officer holstered his gun.

"You are under arrest for the abduction of Angelina Richards."

"What?"

Grant had assumed this was another robbery call. He turned toward the detectives crossing the parking lot. They weren't smiling. Grant knew better than to start arguing his innocence. This would get sorted out at the station. Until then, it would be wiser to keep quiet. He kept quiet. Beyond the police cars he saw Robin Citrin next to the sliding door of the minivan. The door was open.

He couldn't tell if she looked worried or excited. The cameraman wasn't in the driver's seat.

A short, fat detective with a moustache stepped around the lead uniform and reached for Grant's interlaced fingers. He pulled the ATM receipt out of his hand. The second detective was concentrating on the pocket search. He looked at each item as it was laid on the concrete. The usual stuff—wallet, coins, handkerchief. Grant's notebook and pen. Grant felt the lead officer's hands go into the side pocket of his windcheater and saw him put a small plastic card on the curb. The second detective picked it up by the edges.

A bankcard.

He held it up to the light to read the name.

"Angelina Richards."

He looked over at his partner, who was still holding the ATM receipt. They nodded at each other, then the short, fat one spoke to the lead uniform.

"Cuff him."

Grant was helped to his feet and handcuffed behind his back. The suspect had now been detained; there was no arguing that. Grant wasn't thinking about being arrested though. He was thinking about the person who'd sent him here in the first place. A man he'd trusted. Chuck Tanburro.

PART THREE

*I've got a tattoo just above my butt-
hole says No Entry. Rubber or not,
nobody fucks me in the ass.*

—Jim Grant

THIRTY-THREE

It was hard to know who to trust in a foreign land. That was something Grant had learned through bitter experience in desert climes. There was nowhere more foreign than Los Angeles and nothing that looked more alien than Hollenbeck Station at 2111 East First Street. If Rampart Station was a new building, then Hollenbeck was modernity gone mad. It looked more like a gallery of modern art than a police station. The pink and orange squares arranged along its sides obscured the fact that none of the windows seemed to correspond with a regular floor plan, and the hideous brushed-steel panels of the frontage looked like a kid's Lego construction gone wrong.

Four Adam Fifty-Three swung into the back yard beside the red and white communications tower, the only thing that identified the building as a police station apart from the strange sign on the brushed-steel panels, and pulled up at the van dock to the cells. Grant was handcuffed in the back seat. Nobody spoke. The unmarked Crown Vic parked in a vacant space marked Detectives.

The arresting officer, the uniformed cop guarding his arrest figures by insisting the collar was his, led Grant through the metal door with the peephole window, his partner bringing up the rear. There was no queue at this time of day. The custody sergeant inspected the handcuffs as a matter of routine before ordering them to be removed. If anybody complained about them being on too tight, the custody sergeant could refute the claim, having checked them himself. In the litigious society that was America, deflecting a lawsuit was as important as presenting the evidence. Grant reckoned it was the evidence that would clear this matter up. It would just take a little time.

Grant was booked in at the counter and his property bagged and listed. His badge wallet drew close inspection, but nobody discussed it. Bad cops were nothing new, and since the charge desk was being recorded, nobody wanted to speculate on the matter until they knew which side of the coin Grant was on. He wasn't fingerprinted—that was the only discretion the custody sergeant had exercised—but he was placed in a cell without his belt or shoelaces.

He sat on the hard wooden bench and waited. He wasn't worried. As soon as the detectives checked the CCTV, they would see it wasn't Grant who had used the card. The problem was that if somebody had enough clout to send Grant to the bank, then what else had they managed to arrange? There was nothing to do but wait.

He didn't have to wait long. Half an hour later, an overweight jailer opened the door with a rattle of keys and told Grant to get up.

"I'VE SEEN THIS BIT on TV. Good cop, bad cop. That'd make you Sipowicz"—nodding at the short, fat detective with the moustache—"and you Jimmy Smits"—nodding at the taller, more smartly dressed cop. "I can never remember his character."

The tall one spoke first. "Bobby Simone. But I'm not Hispanic."

The short one joined in. "And neither of us are with the NYPD."

Grant was sitting at a metal table bolted to the floor in an interview room that looked more expensive than his hotel room. The chairs were bolted to the floor too. Grant wasn't handcuffed to the table, so that was a good sign. He kept his tone conversational.

"Don't tell me they filmed that in LA as well? I bumped into them making *CSI: New York* downtown, and it ruined the illusion."

The short one shook his head. "No more of an illusion than a Boston cop working in LA."

Grant corrected Sipowicz. "Not working. On vacation."

"But keeping busy."

Grant shrugged. Until the detectives got down to business, he was going to play his cards close to his chest. Sipowicz sat in the chair opposite. The tall one stood beside the closed door and made the introductions.

"I'm Detective Laudati, and this is Detective Costillo."

Costillo rested his elbows on the table. "We're investigating a reported abduction. The daughter of a very fuckin' prominent figure in the community."

Grant folded his arms across his chest and said nothing. Laudati came and sat in the chair next to his partner. He wasn't smiling, but his expression wasn't as serious as Costillo's. That marked him as the good cop—the one who would claim to be Grant's friend. Laudati relaxed in his seat, leaning backwards, not forwards. Giving Grant some space.

"We're three cops here, so we all know how this works. Your record is pretty impressive. No criminal history. So this is no doubt some prime-time fuck-up. Help us clear you out and look for the real bad guys."

Costillo offered the stick instead of the carrot. "Otherwise you're fucked up the ass without a rubber."

Grant unfolded his arms and rested them in his lap. He looked at Costillo, then Laudati, before settling on Costillo again. When Grant had enlisted in the army, the training had been brutal. The drill sergeants could put the fear of God into a young soldier. Later, after mustering out and joining the police, the West Yorkshire version of a drill sergeant tried to do the same. After the army, it was laughable. The two detectives trying to put the arm on him now were the same. After some of the desert interrogations he'd endured, this was chicken feed.

"I've got a tattoo just above my butt-hole says No Entry. Rubber or not, nobody fucks me in the ass."

Laudati took the friendly approach. "Jim. We're not the enemy here. Somebody else has put you in the frame. Not us. We just need to understand how come. You tell us what happened, then we can start working it out."

The pattern had been set. Soft soap and hard rock. Grant lowered his eyes and took a deep breath, as if considering his options. The detectives waited patiently for the enormity of Grant's situation to sink in; patiently in Laudati's case, Costillo less. Grant leaned on the table.

"Isn't this where I ask to see my lawyer?"

Laudati took the lead.

"You can go that route if you want. You're a cop. You know how that goes. If you lawyer up, then we can't ask you anything. Also means we can't help you. Right now, we want to help."

Grant nodded.

"You got one of those yellow pads for me to write everything down?"

Laudati slapped a yellow legal pad and a pencil on the table. He must have had it ready beside his chair. Grant pushed the pad aside with a smile, shaking his head.

"Just checking. They always did that in *NYPD Blue*. I didn't think anybody was dumb enough to confess on the strength of a promise and a Diet Pepsi."

Costillo smacked the table with one hand.

"Okay, you want to be a smart-ass, go ahead. Right now we've got you at the ATM using the missing girl's bankcard and with no good fuckin' reason why."

Grant leaned back in his seat.

"You've got me at the ATM with a receipt. The bankcard was in my pocket."

"Same thing."

"You were careful handling it. Got it printed yet?"

"In the pipeline."

"Well, when you do, it won't have my prints on it."

"Doesn't matter. Cops know to wipe them off. Possession. It was in your fuckin' pocket. Fly that one."

Laudati tried to rein the situation in. Grant was impressed with how calm he could appear when inside he must have been as frustrated as his partner.

"What were you doing at the bank?"

An open question. Good. Nothing Grant could say yes or no to. It was a question that required an answer or a refusal to comment. Grant decided to loosen his grip on the interview.

"Looking for a friend."

"What friend?"

Another open question. Good. Part of the four Ws: when, where, why, how. That last one only counted in the abstract, like the three Rs of reading, writing and arithmetic. Grant was impressed.

"Can't say."

Costillo put a spoke in the wheel of Laudati's progress.

"This ain't no PI gig, Fuckface. You can't claim detective-client privilege."

"I won't say then."

"Same thing applies."

"Does it? I thought one of my rights was to remain silent."

Laudati put on a strained smile. The smile was wearing thin. His voice remained affable, but there was steel in the words.

"Okay, Jim. I can understand you not wanting to say too much until you know what's going on. Let me lay it out for you. After one more question."

Costillo huffed in the corner. Grant folded his arms across his chest. Laudati leaned forward on the table. He spoke slowly so that each word could carry its full weight.

"What were you doing at the girl's cabin yesterday?"

The room fell silent.

You could have heard a pin drop, even on the very expensive carpet. If there had been a clock on the wall, it would have been ticking quietly in the background. If the two detectives had attempted to bribe Grant with a Diet Pepsi, he would be taking a drink of it right now. He felt thirsty.

"Looking for a friend."

"Same friend you were looking for at the bank?"

"Could be."

"Same friend who has gone missing and whose cabin has been ransacked?"

Ransacked was putting it a bit strong, but Grant didn't fall into the trap of disagreeing. Any admission of seeing the inside of the cabin would put him at the scene of the crime.

"Could be. Doesn't mean she's missing."

"There's blood on the carpet. When we get it analyzed and it comes back as Angelina Richards' blood, you're in deep shit."

Grant couldn't argue with that, so he fudged around it instead.

"Hope they're as fast as *CSI: New York* then. 'Cause back in Yorkshire it used to take weeks."

Laudati finally put a hard edge into his voice.

"You're not in Yorkshire. You are in the U S of fucking A. And I'm trying to find a teenage girl who looks to be missing with extreme prejudice."

Grant didn't correct the mixed metaphor. He was beginning to get worried about Angelina Richards himself. His primary motive for not reporting the disappearance before was because he didn't truly believe she'd been abducted from the cabin. He still wasn't convinced. But the situation had developed beyond having to protect the reputation of a US senator and the chief of police. Maybe it was time to come clean.

There was a loud knock on the interview room door. Laudati got up and opened it a crack, then stood back, shocked. He waved Costillo to step out of the room with him and closed the door. Grant waited, concern furrowing his brow. This didn't look good.

When the door opened again, it wasn't Laudati and Costillo who came back in. A lone man in dress uniform entered and closed the door behind him. A powerful man in the Los Angeles Police Department. Grant leaned back in his chair and waited to hear what the police chief had to say.

THIRTY-FOUR

Sherman Gillespie was fifty-five years old and had been the LAPD chief of police for the last three of those years. Grant recognized him from the photos in Senator Richards' home and from snippets he'd seen on the news. Grant's research before coming down from Boston suggested the chief was neither the best nor the worst that the LAPD had endured. Endured was a term he always applied to bosses who had climbed so far up the ladder that they'd forgotten what police work was all about.

The best chiefs allowed street cops to get on with their jobs with minimal interference while deflecting the shit heaped on them from the politicians. Target figures. Changes in the law that benefited criminals over victims. Budget cuts and tighter reins. The worst chiefs were simply rubber stamps for whatever the politicians wanted to do while feathering their own nests and fermenting political ambitions. Chief Gillespie fit somewhere in between.

Until now.

"Senator Richards is a good friend of mine."

Grant watched Gillespie cross the room and stand in front of the table.

"And I will not tolerate or condone any action that puts either him or his family in jeopardy."

Grant watched Gillespie's face for any hint of the chief's true meaning. Men with political leanings always had two agendas: the one they declared and the one behind the scenes. Declaring an interest in protecting Angelina Richards was simply covering the fact that if Richards fell, so did the chief; therefore, his hidden agenda was self-preservation. That didn't show on his face. He seemed genuinely concerned.

"My first priority is finding his daughter before harm befalls her."

Gillespie sat in the chair opposite and tugged the razor-sharp creases of his uniform trousers so they hung neat and straight. He shot the cuffs of his tunic for the same reason. It was an affectation almost as blatant as Senator Richards' casually draped leg and open-necked shirt.

"I need you to tell me what you know."

Grant leaned back in his seat and rested one arm across the back of the chair next to him. He rested his other hand on the table.

"I know that if you're such a good friend, then you know he hasn't reported his daughter missing."

Gillespie's tone hardened. "But missing, she is. Isn't she?"

"Could be. Richards seems to think she might be staying away to annoy him."

"A broken window and blood on the carpet suggest otherwise."

"Evidence of a disturbance only shows there's been a disturbance. We need more than that to indicate a kidnapping."

The chief played along.

"More than that, how?"

"Ransom demand. Threats for him to do something or not do something. Any kind of reason why she might have been abducted. There hasn't been anything like that."

Gillespie's eyes never left Grant's. They were searching and inquisitive. Good interview technique. Always watching for the smallest tick that would give away the lie. Grant was reminded again of how some people found it disconcerting having a conversation with a cop because the eye contact was so intense. The chief watched Grant's eyes as he spoke.

"She is the daughter of a wealthy man; therefore, she is wealthy herself. You were caught using her bankcard. That could be reason enough."

The room was getting warm. If it was air-conditioned, then the air-conditioning was turned off. Grant knew they sometimes did that to get suspects sweating. Make them feel uncomfortable and more likely to slip up.

"Aren't you supposed to offer me a drink or something? Build up rapport?"

"I'm not interested in building rapport. You are a police officer."

"Be a nice touch, though."

Gillespie went to the door and asked for a cold drink, then sat back down. He went through the clothing pantomime again. Thirty seconds later, Laudati came in with a bottle of chilled mineral water. Still, not sparkling. There must have been a vending machine outside the interview rooms, probably for just such an occasion. Laudati's eyes betrayed their curiosity, but he couldn't exactly ask how it was going. Since he wasn't instructed to stay, he left and shut the door.

Grant unscrewed the lid and took a drink of cool, refreshing water, then put the bottle on the table. He toyed with the pale blue lid in the fingers of one hand.

"I remember a job once. Back in Bradford. Woman at a cash machine with her boyfriend. Outside Tesco on Canal Road. They were bundled into a car and driven down a back alley. Bad guys threatened to kill the boyfriend if she didn't go and withdraw the maximum amount. Made her do it three times before the transactions flagged her account and the police were called."

Grant took another drink.

"She got away from the guy shadowing her at the ATMs and stopped a patrol car. Full-scale kidnapping alert went out. The car circulated, helicopter deployed, everything. When I took her statement, it didn't ring true. Checked the boyfriend's record, and he came up a wrong 'un."

Gillespie shifted in his seat. Grant continued.

"Long story short: she hadn't been kidnapped at all. She was scamming the machines and going to claim coercion so the bank wouldn't debit her account. Boyfriend was found in the boot of a stolen car for effect, but he didn't have a mark on him. Both got locked up."

The chief grew impatient. "Your point being?"

"My point is, they managed to get six hundred quid. Found it later hidden in her clothes. And they sparked a force-wide manhunt. It was the most ridiculous plan ever. Nobody gets kidnapped for a few hundred quid."

"Senator Richards is worth more than a few hundred."

"But you can only draw so much out of the machine at a time. Maximum daily limit. Only an idiot would risk doing Federal time for that amount."

"They did it in Bradford."

"That's Bradford. Place is full of idiots."

"Los Angeles has its fair share of idiots too."

"Not idiots capable of taking a senator's daughter."

"Are you saying Angelina Richards is trying to scam the machines?"

"I'm saying the card has nothing to do with her being missing."

"You would say that since you're the one with the card."

Grant screwed the lid on the bottle. "I've thought about that. Whoever wanted me out of the picture made sure I had the card."

"And how did they do that?"

"When I went in the door, a guy bumped into me. Nudged me into a woman he followed out so I'd be concentrating on her. Must have slipped it in my pocket."

"A bit far-fetched, don't you think?"

"Check the CCTV. It'll show the contact."

"We've checked the CCTV."

Grant felt a cold shiver run up his spine. Neither Gillespie nor the detectives had mentioned the bank recording. They might have been holding it back until they got a confession from Grant or it could mean something else. Gillespie watched Grant's face.

"The manager hadn't set it right. There is no recording."

GRANT LET OUT A sigh. The room closed in around him. To cover the awkward silence, he unscrewed the lid and took another drink. Gillespie never took his eyes off Grant's face. Grant could keep a poker face with the best of them, but he was sure his concern was showing.

"Nothing from the cash machine?"

"Convenient, wouldn't you say?"

Grant lowered his voice. "Under the circumstances, I'd say it's extremely inconvenient since the recording is what would prove I'm telling the truth."

Gillespie leaned on the table, creasing his tunic. "Your mystery man is invisible now, isn't he?"

Grant considered the alternatives. Other shops on the strip mall might have cameras. Lee's China Express on the corner or the Spanish church across the road. Then he remembered the rundown neighborhood. Sneakers dangling from telephone wires. The low-rent shopping mall. No, the bank was the only building that could afford recording facilities.

In a situation like this, confronted by evidence of possession and interviewed by the chief of police, a lesser man might crumble. A member of the public facing such insurmountable odds might feel the walls closing in on him. Caught at the cash point with an ATM receipt and the missing girl's bankcard, the evidence was stacking up. A civilian could buckle and either admit a lesser charge to get a better deal or demand to see a lawyer.

Grant wasn't a member of the public. He wasn't a civilian either. Hadn't been a civilian for the last twenty years if you added military service to his police career. That was half of his life. Being in the services, the first thing they taught you was how to think on your feet. How to assess a situation and act accordingly. He weighed all the evidence. He contemplated the possibilities. Then he decided what line to take and took it.

"I think you should let me go now."

Gillespie smirked back a laugh. "Why would I do that?"

"Because you've got no evidence."

"No evidence? What do you call the bankcard and receipt?"

"Proves I was there, that's all. The cops who arrested me can confirm I was there. A good lawyer will be able to discount the receipt. The next in line is always screwing up the previous customer's receipt. With no prints on the card and a TV crew watching from the parking lot, that'll get tossed as well."

Grant considered something else.

"Everybody keeps telling me that LA is the bank robbery capital of the world. That Hollywood is the movie capital of the world. Well, don't forget this: America is the lawsuit capital of the world. And I'll sue your ass off."

Gillespie didn't back down, and he didn't bluster. He simply stated the facts as he saw them.

"You are in possession of property belonging to a missing girl."

Grant shook his head. "Doesn't matter."

He took a drink of water, then screwed the lid back on. When he spoke again, he ticked each point off on his fingers.

"You have nobody reported missing."

One finger.

"You have no report of a burglary."

Two fingers.

"You have no money reported stolen from the ATM."

Three fingers.

"And no report of the bankcard being stolen."

Four fingers. He didn't bother ticking anymore off on his hand.

"With no CCTV, you can't put withdrawing the two hundred on me."

He jerked a thumb at the door.

"And when they searched me, they didn't find two hundred dollars."

Grant leaned forward, moved the bottle of water to one side and rested both elbows on the table.

"You have got nothing except a steaming bag of shit. And if you don't let me go, the smell is going to waft all over city hall."

The threat didn't fit with the remit he'd been given when taking this job. It was an empty threat anyway, but Gillespie didn't know that. Protecting the chief of police from any fallout from the scandal with Senator Richards required Grant to be on the streets and free to act. Threatening the object of that protection was a small price to pay. Somebody out there knew more than they were saying. The worry was if that somebody was Rodrigo Dominguez. The drug cartel had its fingers in many pies. If Grant was wrong and it had a hand in this, then Angelina Richards could be in more danger than Grant had originally thought. At the moment there were more questions than answers. In order to find the answers, Grant needed to be released.

Gillespie still didn't back down, and he still didn't resort to bluster. Grant was impressed. Maybe Gillespie was a better chief of police than he'd given him credit for. The chief leaned farther forward, ignoring the creases in his tunic and lowering his voice to an urgent whisper.

"I will have you locked up and throw away the key."

"In the good old days, maybe. Before the riots. Not anymore."

Gillespie didn't waver but simply changed tack.

"You are an Englishman abroad. I can have you deported as an undesirable."

"I work for the Boston Police Department."

"Doesn't matter."

"And you've got no crime to hang me with."

"That doesn't matter either. I'm the police chief. I can do anything."

Grant looked the chief in the eye. Anger flared a hint of red in the depths of Gillespie's corneas. Reflections from the interview room lights. The calm façade was beginning to crumble. Grant was sorry to see that. He had hoped that this chief of police was worth the effort of trying to save. Now he wasn't so sure. But it was still his job.

"Chief. Before you do anything foolish, you need to know I've got friends in high places too. And they don't want me deported."

A flicker of concern crossed Gillespie's eyes. The chief leaned back in his chair and straightened his tunic cuffs. The creases wouldn't drop out. His face settled into a mask of calm with a mischievous twist to the mouth.

"You could be right. Deportation might be more than I can arrange."

The smile vanished and the face became hard as stone.

"But I can still arrange a lot. Justice moves slowly. Especially when organizing your release. You're going to spend time in my jail before that happens."

Gillespie stood up and walked to the door. Grant waited for the parting shot, but there wasn't one. The chief of police left the room and slammed the door behind him. Grant took another drink of water. He resigned himself to spending time in a holding cell while Gillespie slow-balled his release. He could manage that, no problem. What he didn't expect was who he'd be sharing that cell with.

THIRTY-FIVE

THE HOLDING TANK WAS huge and well appointed, befitting Hollenbeck's status as the newest refurb in the LAPD. Rampart was an upgrade of an existing station, but Hollenbeck was a completely new build. As such, the architects had considered issues that refurbishing an old station couldn't address, the main issue being the size of the custody suite. Rampart's was just big enough to accommodate the local miscreants. Central Station on East Sixth had barely enough room for overnight detainees. But when they redesigned Hollenbeck, they included a custody area the size of a small prison. It was therefore the holding tank for anyone waiting for court or being held for enquiries from neighboring divisions.

The holding cell was the jewel in Hollenbeck's crown.

Grant was led past the charge desk in handcuffs. If Gillespie had had his way, he'd be wearing chains and leg irons. The custody sergeant looked up from amending Grant's custody record with the change of location and nodded for the jailer to continue. They came out of the corridor from the interview rooms and past the cell where Grant had waited the first time. Individual cells were important prior to the interview. You needed somewhere you could keep prisoners apart so they couldn't cook up a story. Post interview or after being charged prisoners could be put in general population. That meant the holding tank.

The central area of the tank was a larger version of the traditional jailhouse cell. Bars surrounded the cage on three sides, with benches and tables for the inmates to sit and eat. The back wall had two doorless openings. One led to the concealed entrance to the tank. The other led to the communal washroom and toilets. The entrance was separate from the main cell so that new admissions could have a moment of dignity and privacy before being gawped at by a cell full of morons.

Grant's handcuffs were removed in the antechamber. He rubbed his wrists even though the cuffs hadn't been on tight, a reflex action he hadn't understood before. The gate was locked behind him, and he walked round the corner into the cage. The room was filled with cursing and wild conversation. There were raised voices and urgent whispers and they all blended into one unruly symphony of noise. Metal cups rattled on the tables, the preferred jailhouse container so they didn't have to throw out a mountain of used paper cups. A water fountain hissed against the back wall.

The room smelled of sweat and tobacco even though nobody was smoking. The average criminal smoked forty cigarettes a day. The smell of it was ingrained deeper than the tattoos that most of them wore. Some smelled of used marijuana. A couple smelled of vomit. Nobody smelled of soap and aftershave.

Grant felt unclean already.

The noise didn't abate when he entered. There wasn't a pause in conversation while everyone eyeballed the new arrival. That only happened in the movies and even then only for effect. The rest of the inmates couldn't give a shit who was dumped in the holding tank unless it was somebody they'd done a job with.

Somebody Grant had done a job with was sitting with his back to the door when Grant came in. Two somebodies facing each other across a table in the far corner. That meant that the second guy was looking directly at Grant as he walked through the doorless opening. The two hapless robbers Grant had disarmed outside the Bank of America on West Sixth and Alvarado. The second guy nudged his partner, and Grant knew he was in trouble.

THERE WAS NO CHANGE in the rhythm of conversation, but the atmosphere turned frosty in an instant. Grant weighed up his options. Call for the jailer and ask to be removed. Go straight up to the robbers and flatten them in a preemptive strike. Or find a more defensible location to fight. That last one was number two in Grant's golden rules for surviving a confrontation. Number one, avoid getting into a confrontation, wasn't an option today. Number three, divide and conquer, would be difficult too. But at least he could choose where to fight, and being in the middle of general population wasn't the place. Prison fights might only start with two or three combatants, but they invariably spread like a virus as everyone else joined in. Especially when the rest of them realized it was open season on an incarcerated cop.

Grant checked through the bars for the jailer, but he was nowhere in sight. That made Grant's decision for him. He turned right and walked through the second doorless opening into the communal washroom. Somebody was taking a leak in the first cubicle. The other toilets were empty. There were no doors. Half a dozen clean white washbasins stood empty along the tiled wall, each with a barely used bar of soap. The mirrors were metal, not glass. Two electric hand dryers were fastened to the wall.

There were no roller towels.

There were no toilet seats.

There was nothing he could rip off and use.

Hollenbeck's designers had thought of everything. Even the floor was smooth and free of sharp edges. All the washbasins were rounded and lightweight. The doorless doorframes were preformed metal without a single sharp angle or protrusion. The best Grant could do was stick his finger across the cold faucet and direct the jet like a water cannon.

Grant looked at the faucet. That wasn't such a bad idea. He quickly turned the first two faucets on and used his thumbs to direct the spray across the smooth tiled floor. It didn't take much water to turn the tiles into an ice rink. The faucets shut off automatically when he removed his hands. This was high-tech for a prison facility. He remembered going into a museum restroom in Denver one time and the faucets not only came on when you put a hand under the spout but it played music while you washed. Only in LA could they have automatic faucets in the jailhouse.

Grant stepped away from the door. There was nobody behind him. There was no room either side of him. It was the best he could do under the circumstances. When the two guys plucked up courage to come for him, they only had one way to go. The narrow entrance also meant they couldn't come more than two abreast, so if they brought their friends with them, it was still only two against one at any given time.

Grant stood and waited.

He didn't have to wait long.

The two hayseed robbers didn't come alone. Whatever they'd said to the rest of the inmates, it was obvious they all knew that Grant was a cop. Eyes gleamed with malice as the general population crowded the entrance. Tweedledee and Tweedledum led the way, two abreast. One had a metal cup in his hand, flattened to form an improvised knuckleduster. The other just had his fists. Both had ample backup just itching to get in on the action. The doorway filtered them down to two at a time.

The first two were Tweedledee and Tweedledum.

Grant kept his feet planted shoulder-width apart for balance. Knees flexed. Arms loose and ready. He focused on the robbers' eyes, the first indicator in any conflict. The man hadn't been born yet who didn't show at least a flicker of intent before charging. Gunslingers always blinked as they drew. Boxers always creased their brows before throwing the first punch. Clint Eastwood might have been able to fake it in his poncho, but Steven Seagal almost certainly could not. Both men acted in a fictional world, though. Even in Seagal's so-called reality show. This was real life. Tweedledum blinked first.

Grant stepped forward to close the fighting arc and threw a sweeping leg strike low across Dum's front leg. The strike took his leg sideways, away from his partner, and his second leg followed on the slippery floor. Both legs went from under him. He flung his arms out for balance, but all that did was swing his body in the opposite direction to his legs. His body slapped wet tiles and tangled with the legs of Tweedledee. Dee tried to step over his partner, but the floor was so wet his front foot went left and his back foot slid right. He did the splits and grabbed his groin as he hit the floor with a splash.

Grant took one pace back to maintain his distance. The preferred wisdom would have been to step forward and stamp on both attackers' balls, but the floor was too wet. Stamping would risk Grant slipping over too. He stayed on the dry floor at the end of the cul-de-sac. The dead end. He was acutely aware that there was nowhere for him to go and the natives were restless.

Dum thrashed his legs as he tried to get up. Dee groaned and cupped his strained groin. A big guy with a beard and Nazi tattoos kicked Dum in the back to keep his legs still and stepped over the barrier. Three more followed, one on his own and the other two side by side. Two big guys and one little fella with a mean face. The little fella looked the most dangerous. He also looked like he was in charge.

Grant backed away, but he was up against the wall.

The little fella clicked his fingers and pointed to one side. The guy with the Nazi tattoos moved to that side. The little guy directed the other two to separate, and all three formed an arc that gave Grant too many angles to cover. Now they were through the narrow doorway the space inside the washroom opened out. It was no longer restricted to being two abreast. The three big guys were evenly spread, just out of Grant's fighting arc. They knew what they were doing. The little fella stepped between them and held one hand out behind him like a relay runner waiting for the baton.

Somebody handed him a knife.

Now Grant knew he was in real trouble. It never ceased to amaze him how easily prisoners managed to fashion weapons out of everyday items. The knife wasn't a knife. It was a sharpened blade made from a hard plastic comb with the teeth removed and a torn handkerchief tied around to form a handle. Grant took his orange windcheater off and wrapped it around his right arm for protection while leaving his dominant left for attack.

The blade glinted in the light.

The rest of the inmates crowded the doorway.

There was no escape. Grant's only hope was that the jailers would recognize that something was wrong and come in to investigate. The last time Grant had seen the jailer, he'd been going in the opposite direction. Grant wasn't confident he'd be coming back anytime soon. The only other thing in his favor was that the floor was dry beneath his feet, while the others had tracked water across the tiles. They outnumbered him, but their base was less stable. It was small comfort.

The knifeman moved forward.

The big guy on Grant's right feigned an attack, then stepped back. The one on his left did the same. Grant had to defend against three positions at the same time. It was only a matter of time before two attacked together, and then his goose would be cooked. Once they got him facing one direction, the little fella could move in with the blade and—

"Hold on there, Shorty."

A black guy with a shaved head and a deep voice that Grant hadn't noticed before stepped in behind the little fella and grabbed the knife hand. He yanked it backwards, twisting the arm up the midget's back and taking the blade. He passed it behind him, and the knife disappeared into the crowd.

"That's no way to treat a celebrity."

THE BLACK GUY WASN'T as big as the other three, but he was more powerful, both in build and personality. The three stepped aside.

The black guy kept ahold of the little fella and shook his head. Grant had just met the alpha male of the holding tank, but he still wasn't sure of his intentions. Grant stayed in the ready position, protective arm forward, attacking hand loose. The black guy introduced himself without holding a hand out to shake.

"I'm Julius Posey."

Grant nodded.

"But everybody calls me Jewel."

"Everybody calls me Officer Grant."

"In here, man, that ain't no good idea. Resurrection Man—now that has a ring to it. I'd stick with that one."

The crowd filtered out of the washroom. Tension leaked out of the air. Posey let go of the midget and there was a moment when Grant thought there was going to be a confrontation, but the little fella backed off without a word. His three cronies followed him through the door into the holding cell. Two slim and relatively well-dressed black guys flanked Posey, half a step behind him and to either side. Posey waved them away, and they left.

Grant unraveled the coat off his arm and shook the creases out.

"Posey? Like Clint Walker in *The Dirty Dozen*?"

"That guy shoulda been a bigger star."

"He was pretty big."

"Yeah, but he had the looks and the voice. You know, kinda low and rumbling."

"Like yours, you mean?"

"Naw. Mine's more Ving Rhames deep."

"Or Samuel L. Jackson. That's a black thing, though, isn't it?"

"It's no Clint Walker thing, that's for sure."

"Don't do yourself down. You're cool enough to be Clint Walker."

"Against dwarfs and prison riffraff I can be. But you, man—walking into the jaws of death with your arms out—that shit in Boston? That was real cool."

Grant held out a hand. "Thanks for the help."

Posey shook the outstretched hand. A warm, dry handshake that belied the fact that he was obviously a crook or he wouldn't be in here. Grant considered that. He was a cop, not a crook, but he was still in here. Maybe he needed to reassess some of the judgments he made on a daily basis. Grant nodded toward the doorway.

"Buddying up to a cop. Isn't going to give you trouble, is it?"

"Day I worry what these mopes think, *that's* when I'm in trouble."

They walked through the door, back into the general population. The tables were occupied again, and conversation had settled back to its unruly norm. One or two inmates gave Grant the evil eye, but most ignored the black guy and the cop. Grant knew he shouldn't ask but couldn't help himself.

"What you in for?"

Posey smiled. "I got caught."

Grant laughed. "Let me guess. You're innocent, right?"

"Hell, no. I'm a dyed-in-the-wool bank robber. Everybody around here knows that. They ain't gonna be able to prove this last one, though, so I'll be moving on out presently."

"The hayseed boys who had it in for me—they were bank robbers. Thought you guys stuck together."

"Them boys is foolish dunderheads. Piggybank robbers. Deserve whatever the state of California throws at them. Me? I only do real banks. They're insured against it anyway. Insurance companies and injury lawyers, they're the real crooks. Fuckin' the country over with their blame-and-claim culture. Them and drug dealers. I hate drug dealers."

"You gonna tell me you've never shot nobody?"

"I ain't no angel. But I ain't never laid my gun on no civilian."

"You sound like Omar."

"Bin Laden?"

"Not Osama. Omar. From *The Wire.*"

"Oh, yeah. Guy with the shotgun who robs drug dealers. Has that little whistle when he's coming."

"You got a whistle?"

"Can't hold a tune."

"I thought all you black guys could hold a tune."

"Now there goes that racial stereotyping. Like saying white men can't jump."

"Shove a cattle prod up their ass. Anybody will jump."

Keys rattled in the lock, and the gate swung open. One jailer waited outside with a clipboard while a second came through the antechamber. He glanced around the cell before settling on Grant.

"Grant. Follow me. You're out of here."

Grant smiled at Posey. "Looks like I'm more innocent than you are."

"Didn't say I was innocent. Said they couldn't prove I was guilty."

They shook hands again.

"Well, thanks anyway."

"Off you go, man. Resurrected again."

The jailer grew impatient. "Come on. I'm gonna cry. There's someone here to pick you up."

With that, Grant was led out of the holding tank. The gate slammed shut behind him, and the keys rattled in the lock. The symphony of angry conversation continued unabated as Posey rejoined his crew. The smell of sweat and tobacco clung to the folds of Grant's orange windcheater. He wafted the coat to dislodge the smell, then slipped it on, thinking about the bank robber with a conscience. Then he concentrated on who could be waiting outside to pick him up.

It took almost as long to process him out as it had taken to book him in. Grant knew better than to just sign anything they put in front of him, so he read each piece of paper before scribbling his signature. The Property page listed everything in the bag. He signed it. The Condition of Prisoner page declared that he had no scars or injuries he didn't already have when he was arrested. At that time, his body had been mapped against any claims of police brutality. He signed that page too.

The Prisoner Release page stated there was insufficient evidence to support a charge but that he was subject to re-arrest if further evidence came to light. Grant paused over that one. He knew it was standard procedure, giving the police a second bite of the cherry if they could dig up any more evidence. He wasn't worried about that. There was no more evidence to find. He signed the page and put the property in his pockets. He flicked open his badge wallet and let the shield catch the light before closing it. The custody sergeant didn't react. The apology was in the look on his face but not outwardly expressed. All cops stuck together. Covering each other's backs was part of the job. But surveillance culture meant you had to be careful what you said and where you said it. Custody suites were recorded to prevent abuse of power. It meant the sergeant couldn't speak his mind. He pointed to an elderly jailer instead.

"Frank'll show you out. Watch your back."

"Thanks."

Frank led Grant out of the metal door, not into the back yard but through the station to the public reception area. Sunlight blazing in through the front windows was only partly shielded by the brushed-steel panels of the art installation across the front of the station. The vestibule looked even more like an art gallery than the exterior. The curved reception desk was pale wood with a lime green work surface. A metal staircase swept up to a balcony that overlooked the lobby. The room smelled of polish and air freshener. The officer performing desk duty glanced up from his work but didn't speak. Grant crossed the floor and went out the front door.

Blue sky and sunshine greeted him. The afternoon was hot and bright. The heat reflected off the glaring pink tiles of the front steps and open area that was broken up by low pink walls and tall, thin palm trees. A sign on the wall nearest the road said

2111
LOS ANGELES POLICE DEPARTMENT
HOLLENBECK STATION

just in case he didn't know where he'd spent the last few hours. Considering how long the roads were in America, the police station was one of the few buildings with a number on East First. As far as Grant could tell, neither Los Antojitos Café nor Zeeno's Nutrition opposite had street numbers. The only thing that made them stand out was the big black car parked outside with two big Hawaiians who weren't Hawaiians smiling at him through the windshield.

Grant held up a hand in greeting. He looked for the second car, but Rodrigo Dominguez wasn't there. Good. The drug baron had given Grant three days, and this was still only the first. His goons were obviously keeping tabs on him but surely they weren't the ones waiting to pick him up.

Grant looked each way up the street. There were no other cars parked out front of Hollenbeck Station. He was looking for the minivan, but there was no sign of Robin Citrin and her film crew. Then a car pulled around the corner from North Chicago where it had been waiting and stopped in front of him. Not the NYPD patrol car Grant had last seen him driving but a battered pickup with Special Effects Unlimited Inc. on the door panel.

It was hard to know who to trust in a foreign land, and there was nowhere more foreign than Los Angeles. Grant considered that as the passenger door opened and Chuck Tanburro beckoned for him to get in.

THIRTY-SIX

"I came as soon as I heard. Front desk said you hadn't been released yet."

Tanburro let the engine idle as Grant got in the pickup and closed the door. He didn't appear to notice the black car parked over the road, concentrating instead on his passenger and the police station beyond. Grant was focusing on the bridge two blocks ahead where East First passed under the Golden State Freeway. It gave him something to look at instead of the man who'd sent him to the bank in East Los Angeles. Grant didn't speak. Tanburro interpreted the silence correctly.

"It wasn't my fault. I don't know how it got fucked around."

A constant stream of traffic flowed along the freeway. The noise was a distant hum, but it seemed to Grant like it was in the background wherever you went in LA. A helicopter hovered over the Los Angeles River Basin in the distance. The river was another inaccurate description since it was really just an extra-wide concrete storm drain with a trickle down the middle that was the river. It was true what they said: nothing in LA was what it seemed.

Including the people you counted as your friends.

The black car pulled away from the opposite curb and drove slowly past the pickup. Two pairs of eyes watched Tanburro and Grant until the car turned left and disappeared up North Chicago. Grant watched the Hawaiians go, then turned to look at Tanburro.

"How come you told me to go to the bank?"

Tanburro looked like he'd been asked a question that had an obvious answer.

"Because you were looking for the girl."

"But why did you tell me to go to *that* bank?"

"Because the girl's card was used at the ATM."

"And who told you that?"

Tanburro squinted his displeasure at the way this was going.

"Hey. You asked me if I had friends on the force. Well, I reached out to them. And that's who gave me the heads-up when her card was flagged."

"And you trust him?"

"He had my back for six years. Yes, I trust him."

"Bob Snow?"

"Yes."

Grant stroked his chin as various scenarios played in his mind. None of them explained why a trusted detective would give false information to his former partner in order to get Grant arrested. None of them gave credence to the *CSI: NY* technical advisor fronting the bad guys or being involved in kidnapping and extortion. That simply didn't add up.

"Who told him?"

Tanburro shrugged. "I didn't ask. Assumed he'd been monitoring her details for me."

"So he'd been asking around?"

"I guess so."

"Well, guess this: who d'you think warned me to back off in there?"

Tanburro shrugged again. "Surprise me."

"Chief of Police Sherman Gillespie."

Tanburro let out a low whistle. Grant watched his eyes and was pleased to see that they registered genuine surprise. Whoever was pulling the strings, he didn't think it was Tanburro.

"Somebody told him about my visit to the girl's cabin. The broken window and the blood on the carpet."

"What blood on the carpet?"

Again, genuine surprise. Grant pressed the point.

"Not many people knew I'd been to the house."

"Don't look at me. I didn't tell him."

"Somebody did. And somebody made it official."

Tanburro narrowed his eyes.

"Somebody with friends in high places?"

Grant was thinking along the same lines but couldn't understand why Senator Richards would do such a thing if he wanted Grant to be discreet. In any case, the chief had suggested he knew Richards hadn't reported his daughter missing. None of this made any sense. Grant shook his head.

"I don't know. Something's rotten in Denmark."

Tanburro's brow furrowed as a fresh thought struck him.

"Why did they arrest you? Being at the bank isn't against the law."

Another gap in Tanburro's knowledge that indicated he wasn't involved. Grant felt a sense of relief that at least there was one person he could trust.

"They found the girl's bankcard in my pocket."

"How'd that get…"

Then Tanburro nodded his understanding. "Palmed it. Sleight of hand."

Grant nodded. "By somebody who knew I was going to be there."

He turned to look out of his window at the pink and orange obscenity that was Hollenbeck Station. Beyond that and two blocks north was East Cesar E. Chavez Avenue and the former PLS Check Cashers turned Bank of America. Farther north, across the San Bernardino Freeway and into the foothills, was Montecito Heights. The geometry felt too convenient to be simple coincidence.

"D'you think you can get Bob Snow to check an address without half the LAPD turning up on my doorstep?"

"Check where it is?"

"Check who owns it."

"Sure I can. Bob's not the leak. I guarantee it."

"Good."

Grant gave Tanburro the address of the party the other night. 1042 Montecito Drive. Tanburro didn't write it down. Addresses were easier to remember than car numbers.

"I'll have to call him later. He doesn't go on shift for a couple of hours."

"Thanks."

Grant faced front. The helicopter had lost interest in whatever was happening in the dry riverbed and had drifted off toward the west. No doubt another helicopter would replace it soon, maintaining the record of there never being a clear blue sky above LA without at least one chopper causing a blemish on it.

Tanburro pulled away from the curb toward the freeway underpass.

"Hotel?"

Grant thought about that for a moment, then shook his head. "I need to go somewhere else. Could you run me to Hollywood?"

"No problem."

The battered pickup with Special Effects Unlimited Inc. on the door panel went through the darkness of the underpass and came out into bright sunshine on the other side. It felt like a symbolic return to the light. Grant was glad he and Tanburro were friends again. In the police service, like the armed forces, your colleagues were your friends and your friends were your brothers. When shit hits the fan, they're all you've got.

THIRTY-SEVEN

Tanburro dropped Grant at Sunset Television & Film Inc. on North Cahuenga. Tanburro didn't pull into the parking lot, preferring to park on the street opposite the custard yellow brickwork of Stepan's Automotive.

Late afternoon sun blazed through the windshield, so they both had their side windows open. Hollywood traffic droned in the background. The lot between Sunset Television and Amoeba Music resembled the hanging gardens of Babylon with its row of cypress trees and pink flowers, no doubt intended to provoke memories of Kenneth Anger's book *Hollywood Babylon*, the underground classic about Hollywood's darkest secrets. Grant wondered what secrets he was going to uncover today.

Tanburro didn't turn the engine off. "You got your cell?"

"I just got out of my cell. I think I'll revert to calling it a mobile phone."

"Nobody'll understand you."

"I've got it with me anyway."

"I'll give you a call about the Montecito Heights address."

"Thanks."

Grant opened the door and got out, then leaned in through the opening.

"Be careful who you trust. Tell Snow to watch out too."

Tanburro nodded. Grant closed the door, and the pickup pulled away from the curb with a gentle roar from the twin exhaust. It turned right on Sunset and headed back toward town. Grant took a deep breath, inhaling the flowery scent that reminded him of Senator Richards' study, then walked through the gates into the TV studio parking lot. Robin Citrin's minivan was parked in the bay farthest from the door. Grant was glad. This discussion should involve all of them. With a brief nod toward the cameraman, who was leaning against the minivan, Grant crossed the lot and went through the studio door.

"You getting good coverage?"

They were sitting around the table in L. Q. Patton's office. Robin Citrin, Patton, and Grant. The blond receptionist had just brought a round of cold drinks and left. Ice clinked the glass as Grant took a drink of orange juice. Patton looked as cool and casual as ever, but it was Citrin who answered.

"Would have liked to see what happened inside."

"The bank or the police station?"

"We can hack the CCTV from the bank. The station is the mystery footage."

"The bank's a mystery too. Manager didn't set it right."

"No recording?"

"No."

"Well. I guess most of it happened outside. We got most of that. And yes, we're getting pretty good footage. You should get arrested more often."

"It's better than getting shot or blown up, I suppose."

"Like in Boston? Yeah. I should be careful what I wish for. Don't want you getting shot again."

There was a hint of compassion in her voice. Patton noticed but didn't mention it. He clinked the ice in his glass to bring the meeting to order, then put the drink down on the table.

"We can cut the footage together anyway we like. Add a voiceover and some back-story, make it tell whatever story we choose. But like Robin said, I'd like to know what happened in Hollenbeck Station."

Grant took a cool drink while he considered just how much to tell them. By the time he put the glass on the table, he'd made up his mind. He told them everything about Senator Richards' daughter and her porn career, including Grant's visit to the house in Coldwater Canyon Drive and the girl's bankcard being in his pocket at the ATM. He ended with his visit by the chief of police and the threat to have Grant deported. He briefly mentioned the knife attack in the washroom and the cemetery meeting with Rodrigo Dominguez but kept quiet about the veiled threat toward Citrin. He didn't see the point in worrying her just yet. He still had two days to sort that problem out.

When he'd finished talking, the room fell silent.

There was a collective clinking of ice as all three took a drink.

Robin spoke first. "Jeepers creepers."

Patton kept his voice low and even.

"Times ten. When you want to piss somebody off, you don't aim low."

Grant didn't mention that the guy he'd apparently pissed off was the same guy he'd been sent here to protect. In a roundabout sort of way, it didn't matter because L. Q. Patton had his finger on the pulse anyway.

"Richards campaigned hard to get Chief Gillespie elected. And Gillespie has been very vocal in his support of Senator Richards. The mutual backslapping means they are inextricably linked in the public's eye. If scandal befalls one, then it sinks them both."

Grant nodded.

"That's why I told Richards his best option was to come clean. Being a protective father would show him in a better light than trying to cover it up if he got found out."

Patton smiled. "You don't know much about American politics, do you?"

"I don't know much about any politics."

"Well, in America, we have a puritan streak. Doesn't matter to the voters how many countries we invade as long as we keep one foot on the floor and the price of gas down."

Grant rattled his glass and raised an eyebrow. "The Hays Code."

"The Hays Code of 1930: 'No picture shall be produced that will lower the moral standards of those who see it, therefore sympathy of the audience should never be thrown to the side of crime, wrongdoing, evil, or sin.' Before the MPAA rating system came in. Back in the dark old days, you couldn't have a man and a woman kissing on a bed unless they both had at least one foot on the ground."

"Origami sex."

"Kama Sutra could probably work something out. But in American politics, we pretty much stick to the Hays Code. We like our politicians squeaky clean. That means not having your daughter sucking cock all over Hollywood."

"Didn't seem to bother Clinton."

"Getting your cock sucked is different. Lying about it's what sunk Clinton."

Citrin kept out of the conversation, preferring to drink her juice and listen.

Grant played devil's advocate but already knew the answer. "And that's bad for Gillespie how?"

"Because cocksuckers will bring you down if you're in public office. The chief of police is a public office."

Grant shook his head.

"Getting the same way back in England. Chief constables used to rule their forces with a rod of iron. What they said, went. Politicians couldn't interfere because it would show the police service as being a tool of government and not the impartial guardians of peace that we should be."

He put his glass on the table.

"Nowadays, any copper gets above inspector and he's more interested in climbing the political ladder than policing the streets. If chief constables don't agree with government policy or meet targets, they get replaced. Job's fucked."

Citrin felt it was time to show she understood what the men were talking about.

"Having a chief that's above reproach is even more important now after the riots of '92. The public image of the LAPD is paramount."

"And their public image is what a Senator Richards scandal could tarnish."

Nobody answered because it wasn't a question. Everyone nodded and they all took another drink of juice. The statement put an end to that line of conversation. Patton changed the subject.

"I've been keeping a tag on Zed Productions since you asked about locations for that movie of theirs."

"*The Hunt for Pink October.*"

Patton grinned his best James Coburn grin. All teeth and crinkly eyes. "That's the one. They registered several locations for external shots. Somewhere up in the Hollywood Hills, a few in East LA, a couple of days at the marina at Long Beach."

Grant leaned forward, resting his elbows on his knees. "Tell me they didn't shoot sex scenes out in the open."

"I don't know what they shot out in the open. They only have to register locations, not what scenes they filmed."

"So, assuming that lot was for establishing shots, where did they film the sex scenes?"

Patton flicked through a sheaf of papers he'd picked up from the table.

"There are three houses they rented for a couple of days each. A boat at the marina they hired for a week. And two private homes donated by their owners."

Grant's ears pricked up. "Whereabouts are those?"

"Premises not hired or registered for movie shoots don't have to be disclosed. All they've got to give is the general area for budgeting records in case the IRS comes looking for tax."

"And?"

The sheets of paper were stapled in one corner. Patton folded the pages back one at a time until he found the relevant entry. "One in East Los Angeles. The other in Montecito Heights."

Grant took a final swig of his juice, then leaned back in his chair. East Los Angeles, where he'd been arrested at the Bank of America. And Montecito Heights. He thought about the house in the foothills overlooking downtown LA and remembered the decorative arch in the garden that he'd stood beneath with Robin Citrin. The same arch that had been in the background while a gray-haired man had his cock sucked by a teenage girl with stars tattooed on either side of her crotch.

Patton hadn't finished. "Zed Productions must be moving upmarket, though."

Grant brushed the previous revelations aside. "How's that?"

"He's upped his location budget by some mark for his latest extravaganza."

Patton ran his finger down the list and let out a low whistle. "They've got a permit to close two square blocks downtown tomorrow for a shootout, car chase, and bank robbery."

"Like the one I saw being filmed the other night?"

"Same but bigger. Stunt crews and vehicles, traffic control, the whole nine yards. More blockbuster than cocksucker."

"Where?"

Patton read out the location. Grant ran it through the map in his head. It sounded familiar. Then he remembered walking past it on his way to the *CSI: NY* shoot the other day. Tall buildings and mirrored windows. One building stood out in his mind, and he had to fight back a smile from breaking out on his lips.

The germ of a plan began to form.

Before Grant could give it too much thought, his cell started to vibrate in his pocket. He took it out, and the vibration gave way to the climbing ringtone. Grant checked the caller ID flashing on the display, then flicked the phone open and spoke into the mouthpiece.

"That was quick."

Chuck Tanburro sounded excited. "You know what they say. Once a cop, always a cop."

"What have you got?"

"That house you wanted checking. Up on Montecito Heights."

Grant felt a shiver that was nothing to do with drinking cold orange juice.

"Yes?"

"It's owned by Stuart Ziff."

The shiver turned into goose pimples. He didn't let his pulse race. He didn't show his excitement because he didn't get excited. He stayed calm and focused and nodded into the phone, even though Tanburro couldn't see him.

"Good work. Thanks. I'll call you later."

He closed the phone but kept it in his hand. Citrin recognized the look on Grant's face even though his expression had barely changed. He saw it in her eyes. She was more in tune with him than anyone else since…

He pushed that thought aside. Citrin waited for Grant to explain the call. L. Q. Patton wasn't that patient.

"Well?"

Grant put the phone back in his pocket.

"I know where they filmed in Montecito Heights."

Citrin nodded. She knew too.

"Let me guess."

"That's right."

He picked up his glass but it was empty. He held it up to his eye and looked through the bottom like he was using a telescope.

"And I think I know where the girl is."

THIRTY-EIGHT

IF GRANT HAD LET Citrin bring the cameraman along, then things might have turned out different, but he hadn't. There was no point crying over spilt milk. Grant rarely looked back with regret even though there were many things he'd like to have changed about the past. Occasionally he looked forward. Mostly he lived in the here and now. It was one of the reasons he was so effective in combat. No aspirations. No regrets. Only action or inaction. But there would be a moment later when he wished he'd let her bring the cameraman.

CITRIN SWUNG THE MINIVAN around on the scenic overlook so it was facing the gate of 1042 Montecito Drive. Dust swirled around them in the dying rays of sunlight. The sun was dipping below the horizon so fast you could almost see it moving. Soon it would be gone, and dusk would suck the light out of the day. In half an hour it would be dark. Grant looked through the windshield.

"I'm gonna do a recce first. Then call for backup once I've checked the lie of the land. Standard procedure—note defenses and enemy strength."

"You sound like you've done this before."

"I have done this before."

"Doesn't sound like police-type maneuvers."

"They're not."

"Where'd you learn this, then?"

"Somewhere else."

He focused on the twin gates of the houses on the ridge. The driveway for 1040 circled the wooded hill and headed along the ridgeline to the farthest house overlooking the valley. The drive of 1042 formed a tighter circle around the woods and led to the house where Nathan Burdett had hosted the Hollywood party yesterday. There was a narrow pedestrian gate and a dirt track that skirted the left of the hill for cyclists and joggers. Grant wasn't considering skirting the hill. He was going to take the direct route, straight ahead and through the trees. Frontal attack. Always his preferred option. He turned to Citrin.

"You wait here."

She was about to speak, but he held a finger up for her to stop.

"Do not follow me. I need you ready to drive as soon as I get back."

"Am I your getaway driver?"

"You got your phone?"

"Always."

"When I call for backup, I'll ring you too. Guide them in."

Citrin looked worried.

"Have you got a gun?"

"I hate guns. People tend to shoot at you if they know you're armed."

"Unarmed people get shot too."

"Not as often."

"Don't know if I'd be playing the percentages over something like that."

"That's why you film reality, and I live it."

Citrin's eyes stared into Grant's. Grant stared back. It wasn't one of those see-who-blinks-first contests. It was just saying goodbye. Grant leaned over and kissed her on the lips. Her arms came around and held him tight. She kissed him back with hunger and passion. They both stopped at the same time, and Grant got out. Citrin called through the open door.

"Be careful."

Grant shook his head with a smile.

"You really think I'm going to be careless? Anyway. I thought you were in the entertainment industry. Shouldn't that be 'break a leg'?"

"That's superstitious nonsense. Don't break a leg. Be careful."

He didn't answer. He simply closed the door, jogged across the road to the pedestrian gate, then disappeared into the woods.

THE TREES WERE THICK and heavy on the northern slope and provided perfect cover as Grant slid to his right from the dirt track toward the wooded hill. He didn't crouch or sneak or creep through the woods. They only did that in the movies. He would be more careful once he approached the brow of the hill overlooking the house, but for now the only prerogative was to be quiet.

Grant moved like a cat. Soft footsteps and perfectly quiet.

Ten paces in, and the woods engulfed him. The outside world became an alien planet, and Grant's focus was on the here and now. The absolute present and the single piece of land he was standing on. He loved night maneuvers. During military training his squad had been dropped in the middle of Salisbury Plain with a compass and a map and ordered to find their way from point A to point B without being spotted by enemy patrols. The silence and focus of being in the dark without a light had been exhilarating. He felt that same exhilaration now.

He stopped next to a sturdy tree and listened.

At first there was nothing. After a few short seconds he could hear the trees breathing around him, not the intake and exhalation of human breath but the tiny noises of living things moving in the dark. Leaves rustled in a nonexistent breeze. Branches groaned under the weight of their own burden. The smell of grass and bark and pine needles mingled with the scent of flowers in the distance. The pink blooms surrounding the gate to 1042 behind him.

He waited for his eyes to adjust to the gloom inside the woods. The sun had set, and the sky was dialing down the blue from its daytime brilliance to the darker blue of evening. Dark blue was the color for cops, even in police forces where the blue was nearer to black like the LAPD. Even in West Yorkshire, Grant's uniform hadn't been blue serge for many years. If dark blue was the shade for cops, then darker blue was more befitting Jim Grant, a man who erred on the side of getting the job done instead of observing the rules. He was straying well off reservation tonight, but his instincts told him it was the right thing to do. Results were the final test of any policing strategy. A result tonight would be finding Angelina Richards.

Night sounds began to include more than the life of trees. Birdsong filtered into the woods, something that had been there all the time but overshadowed by traffic noises and the world of people. Grant could see darting movement among the branches overhead. Small black shapes dashed from tree to tree. The faint *burrrring* hum of wings. A squirrel came down the side of a pine, stopped to sniff the air, then continued down to the ground, where it bounded across the bed of pine needles and grass to a neighboring tree. Nature was all around. The secret life of Los Angeles.

Satisfied that he was the only biped in the woods, Grant walked slowly up the hill. He watched his feet as much as the horizon, his eyes performing a cycle as they traced his progress while checking for obstructions. He avoided every fallen branch. He dodged every low-hanging bough and leaf. He maintained his course toward the house on the other side of the hill. Through a gap in the canopy he saw a red light blinking atop a triangular radio mast. It was painted red and white and reminded Grant of the radio towers at Rampart and Hollenbeck stations, only not as sturdy. Cell phone masts were everywhere, even in people's back gardens.

Grant flicked open his phone. Yes. Five bars. A strong signal. He set the volume to silent, closed the cell again, then let his eyes re-adjust. First things first. No point calling the cavalry until you had some Indians to fight. He continued up the hill. The trees began to thin out as he approached the flattened summit, so he slowed down, taking more care about what lay ahead. He dropped into a crouch, keeping low to the landscape and foliage. The cell phone mast stood in a clearing overlooking the house. That was his preferred observa-tion point. When he reached the tree line he knelt for a moment, checking for movement. The mast pointed its twisted finger into the sky. He could just make out the peaked roof and chimney of Ziff's house. The top section of the split-level structure farthest up the hill from the parking turnaround.

Beyond that, the view was breathtaking.

Dusk had brought out every streetlight in Los Angeles. They sparkled like jewels across the flatlands below. Down in the folds of Montecito Heights, the street lamps of East Avenue and Johnston Street shone the brightest. The glass towers of downtown stood out, each with its own red blinking light to protect it from low-flying aircraft and helicopters. As if on cue, the distant throb of chopper blades cut across Dodger Stadium. A police helicopter, judging by the searchlight beam lancing toward the ground. A siren confirmed a foot pursuit somewhere near Elysian Park.

Grant turned his attention to the cell phone mast. It was narrow and made of thin gauge metal struts with some kind of transformer box at its base. The box was painted green to blend with the surroundings, a pointless exercise since the mast itself was red and white. There were no lights on the top of the hill. Daylight was long gone, and the summit was dark and empty. There was nobody walking his dog. There was nobody having a late-evening cigarette, admiring the view.

There was nobody standing guard.

That was good.

Grant walked low and fast to the transformer box, then knelt behind it. The rest of the house came into view. Three levels stepped into the hillside. The party level from the other night was at the bottom, next to the patio and barbeque area and garden. The guest bedroom where he'd spent some time with Citrin before discovering the hidden camera was part of the second level, together with toilets and the dining room. The top level was no doubt private quarters for the owner and his family. Ziff had no family, so the question was, if the porn moviemaker had the girl, where would he keep her?

And how much muscle would be on hand to keep her under control?

Grant had already met some of Ziff's muscle. It would be easy to dismiss them as incompetent buffoons, but Grant never underestimated the opposition. He had encountered them at Zed Productions and caught them by surprise. His experience of conflicts around the world was that when you fought enemy troops on their home ground, the battle was harder and bloodier. Ziff was on home ground tonight. His boys would fight harder. This would be no pushover.

Note defenses and enemy strength.

That was the first order of business. Grant checked for movement down below. There was none. The hillside behind the house was sculptured garden and flowering shrubs. It was too steep for anything else. The true garden was around the front, where crazy paving and neatly trimmed lawns were complemented by flower borders and a decorative arch. Grant remembered standing beneath the arch in the dark with Citrin. He also remembered it being in the background of the sex scene with the gray-haired guy and the missing girl. Filmed on the cream settee in the living room facing the picture windows. The lower level of 1042 Montecito Drive.

There was no movement. Lights were on in a couple of the rooms, but most of the house was in darkness. Patio lights illuminated the front garden. The swimming pool had underwater lighting. The sky was dark blue and clear. The first stars were beginning to twinkle overhead. The helicopter had gone. A different siren sounded somewhere across the flatlands. The peace and tranquility of the woods was a thing of the past.

The turnaround in front of the house held two cars. Lights from the garden reflected off gleaming paintwork and polished chrome. Twilight robbed the cars of color, but they weren't black. One was a light-colored sports car and the other was a big silver 4x4. Grant didn't know what they called them in America. He was surprised it wasn't a Humvee. Since Schwarzenegger had started the trend, half of LA seemed to like driving around in tanks. Zed obviously hadn't got the memo.

Preliminary recce completed, it was time to put some flesh on the bones. Put personnel numbers to the vehicles. Grant moved slowly across the flat crown of the hill, keeping low so his silhouette didn't stand out on the horizon. He started with the top section. One bedroom light was on, but the curtains were closed. From his position up the hill he couldn't detect movement behind the curtains.

He moved down the rear garden to the second level. More lights were on here but still with the curtains closed. Grant wondered what possessed them to close the curtains on a secluded hillside in private grounds with a security gate. Maybe they didn't want someone seeing out. He marked the mid level as a potential holding cell, then moved down to the lower level.

The front of the house might have been wall-to-wall patio windows, but the rear only had small windows and a door to the terraced garden. Grant could see the swimming pool to the left—no naked swimmers this time—and the turnaround below. The curtains round back were open. He found a comfortable observation point and settled into a crouch for a few minutes, staring through the windows. The kitchen was bright and well appointed, as befitted a house of this caliber. It stretched along most of the back elevation. Steam rose from a kettle beside the twin washbasins.

A short, round figure moved through the steam like a ghost.

Ziff.

The movie producer pottered around the kitchen until the steam drifted away. Grant was surprised he didn't have some toady making coffee for him. Maybe he didn't want domestic staff knowing who he was keeping at the house. Grant looked beyond the kitchen into the open-plan living room. He could only see part of it, the cream settee and the patio doors beyond. There was nobody else in view. Time to check round the front.

Grant moved smoothly and silently down the back garden and bypassed the swimming pool. He kept his back against the house wall as he came around the side to the barbeque pit. The patio doors were slightly open, and soft music drifted into the evening air. Grant crossed the patio at the far end and stood beneath the decorative arch. The view out of the windows from the cream settee had framed downtown LA through the arch. The reverse view was just as enlightening. Grant could see the entire living room and the kitchen. The lights were bright and the furniture neutral colored. The scene blazed like the first night on Broadway. Or a brightly lit film set, which the living room had most certainly been, because there was no doubt that *The Hunt for Pink October* had been filmed there.

Ziff came out of the kitchen carrying a silver tray. A mug steamed beside a sugar bowl and a plate of biscuits. No wonder he was so fat. Grant scanned the room. There was nobody else. There was only one mug of coffee. That put a shadow of doubt over

Grant's calculations. He didn't let it settle. The best way to find anything out was to ask.

It was time to ask Stuart Ziff what he'd done with the missing girl.

Grant threw a glance to either side of the living room. The lights were off in the room to the right but on in the room to the left. The curtains were open. There was no movement. The sirens across the city stopped. Cicadas chirruped down in the valley. The gentle music from inside sounded familiar, but he didn't wait to figure out what it was. Satisfied there was nobody waiting to jump him, Grant walked swiftly across the patio and through the open doors.

THIRTY-NINE

"You sure you've got enough biscuits there?"

Ziff almost spilled his coffee when he saw Grant standing among the folds of the open curtains. Grant could tell it was coffee now that he was inside the living room. The smell was unmistakable. It was shock that almost upended Ziff's coffee, but other than that he didn't seem surprised to see the man in the orange windcheater.

"Walker's butter shortbread. Get it imported from the Lake District back where you come from."

"I'm from Yorkshire, not Cumbria."

"Near enough."

Grant took a step into the room and closed the sliding doors behind him. He didn't want any surprises coming up on his flanks. The background music sounded familiar. Ennio Morricone, but one of his obscure pieces. Nathan Burdett hadn't been kidding when he'd said there might be some film music in the collection. Grant looked at the tray on the coffee table.

"At least they're chunky shortbread fingers and not them puffy petticoat tails."

"I make porn movies. Puffy doesn't enter into it."

Grant threw Ziff a knowing look.

"Two of your helpers are. Spitz and Swallows are as big a pair of puffs as I've ever seen. Might as well rename 'em Patrick Fitzgerald and Gerald Fitzpatrick."

"You hold something against homosexuals?"

Grant shook his head.

"Not as long as they hold nothing against me. I've told you about my tattoo, right?"

"No."

"Of course. That was Dick Wadd. Anyway. Got a No Entry sign tattooed just above my backside. So there's no mistaking my sexual leanings."

"I saw you with Geneva. I don't think anyone's gonna make that mistake."

Ziff's show of bravado evaporated, and his shoulders sagged. He leaned back on the cream settee and let out a quivering sigh.

"I wondered how long it'd be before you came knocking on my door again."

"I didn't knock."

"Knew you wouldn't leave me be."

Grant stepped farther into the room, glancing at the corridor leading to the guest bedrooms on the second level. The lights were off and the shadows grew deeper along the hallway. Ziff pushed himself up off the settee.

"You want a coffee and a biscuit?"

"Can you make a latte?"

"Milky and tasteless. I can manage that."

"Then I accept. Thanks."

Ziff walked through the wide doorless opening into the kitchen and started boiling some milk. Grant kept station in the middle of the living room, protecting his flanks while keeping a safe distance from any approach on all sides. He glanced at Ziff to make sure he wasn't trying any funny business, then focused on the smoked-glass bookcase at the back of the room. The pale wood blended with the décor of the bright and airy room. The smoked glass reminded Grant of the room he'd been in on his last visit. The angle of this hidden camera was just right, the positioning ideal, for looking down on the cream leather settee.

Grant caught movement out of the corner of his eye. Ziff sidling to one side, stiff and awkward. A row of gleaming sharp kitchen knives hung from a magnetic strip on the wall. The coffee was nearly ready. There was no need for Ziff to be moving away. Grant stepped into the kitchen.

"You're not thinking of using one of those, are you?"

"Don't need a knife for coffee."

"Depends how thick you make it."

Grant noticed a drawer partly open next to Ziff's right hip. He reached past the producer and opened it wider. The chrome finish .38 snub gleamed brighter than the knives. Grant took it, checked the load, and slipped it in his jacket pocket.

"I thought you'd learned your lesson with guns."

Ziff stirred the coffee with a noisy spoon.

"I suppose you'll be wanting to ask me some more questions."

Grant followed the producer as he brought the second mug of coffee into the lounge.

"You suppose right."

Ziff handed Grant the coffee, then indicated a chair that matched the settee.

"Might as well make yourself comfortable then."

The music changed. Still Morricone but this piece Grant did recognize. Soft tinkling chimes played a simple intro from a scene in *For a Few Dollars More*. The pocket watch scene where El Indio challenges Colonel Mortimer to a showdown. Go for the gun when the music stops.

The chimes grew louder.

Ziff sat on the settee.

Violins bled in and augmented the chimes.

Grant sat on the chair.

They sat opposite each other and prepared to face off. Two pairs of eyes stared across the coffee table. Two sets of lungs took deep breaths. The showdown music grew into a sweeping crescendo, then it was simply the chimes again. Growing slower as the watch wound down.

GRANT STARTED WITH A direct question.

"Where's the girl?"

Ziff was taking a drink of his coffee. He stopped drinking and held the mug in both hands as if trying to warm them on a cold day. It wasn't cold in the living room, but the distraction allowed him time to think.

"I told you before. I don't even know the girl."

"What you told me before, when I asked the girl's name, was, 'How the fuck should I know? She's not with the Screen Actors Guild.' Something along those lines."

"Yeah, well, nothing's changed. She still ain't with SAG."

Grant lowered his voice but injected added menace.

"She might not be with SAG, but you're wrong. Plenty has changed."

Ziff selected a finger of shortbread and dunked it in his coffee. Another delaying tactic. He held the biscuit under while his mind scrambled for a suitable response. He waited too long. The biscuit broke off and bobbed about in his coffee.

"Shit."

Coffee splashed the settee. Ziff fished the floater out with three fingers and popped it in his mouth. The biscuit was too hot, and it burned his tongue.

"Shit."

This time the expletive spluttered wet crumbs across the cream leather. He put his coffee down on the table and took out a handkerchief to dab up the spillage.

Grant kept his tone light. "Considering the stains that settee's had to suffer"—but the menace was still there—"it's a good job you chose leather over fabric."

"Coffee stains leather as well."

"Semen stains it even worse."

Ziff stopped dabbing.

"What?"

"Don't know if you ever got it over here, but back in England we had a kid's TV show called *Captain Pugwash*. Cartoon about pirates and stuff. Kids didn't understand that half the crew of the Black Pig had suggestive names. Master Bates. Roger the Cabin Boy. And Seaman Stains. Became one of the great controversies of our time. Except it wasn't true. Just a rumor that spread like wildfire. The only truth is that semen does stain."

Grant leaned forward, careful not to spill his own coffee.

"And this settee has had plenty of semen."

With his short, round face, Ziff could have made a passable Captain Pugwash. All he needed was a skull-and-crossbones hat and the blustering red cheeks. The red cheeks he already had, and his protestations were bordering on bluster.

"I don't know what you mean."

Grant put his coffee on the table and stood up.

"Oh yes you do."

He walked around the back of the settee, forcing Ziff to crane his neck to keep him in sight. Grant continued.

"Reason that scene in *The Hunt for Pink October* was made to look like it was CCTV footage is because it was CCTV footage."

"What the fuck you talkin' about?"

The bluster had no conviction. Ziff knew the game was up. Grant crossed to the bookcase and opened the smoked-glass door. The hidden camera was small but perfectly formed. It was held in place by an adjustable bracket. Wires from the back of the camera housing disappeared through a hole in the bookcase.

"Smile. You're on *Candid Camera*. Did you get that show over here?"

Ziff ignored the question, trying one final distraction.

"I don't understand Roger the Cabin Boy."

Grant mimed holding onto somebody bent over at the hips and thrust his groin in and out, twice, doggy fashion.

"Rogering is slang for fucking. And you're fucked."

Ziff deflated like a slow-pricked balloon. He spread his arms across the back of the settee in an affectation of nonchalance, but it was really just to stop him falling sideways. The music changed.

Still Morricone but the piece used at the wedding chapel for *Kill Bill 2*. Slow and threatening while David Carradine sat on the porch. Grant couldn't remember what movie Tarantino had stolen it from. He preferred the beginning of *Kill Bill* part one, the instrumental prelude to "Bang Bang (My Baby Shot Me Down)." The cowboy boots in close-up, crunching along the bare wooden floorboards amid a litter of spent bullet casings.

Grant's black K-Swiss tennis shoes didn't crunch as he walked around to the front of the settee. His footsteps made no sound at all on the deep pile carpet but they kept pace with the music. Slow and threatening. The smell of coffee was as strong as the scorched blood and cordite of the wedding chapel massacre. He stood over Ziff and didn't need to threaten the smaller man. Ziff had seen Grant in action. Yet he still insisted on trying to play it cool.

"Is that why pirates always fly the Jolly Roger?"

Grant didn't respond. He simply stood with his legs shoulder-width apart, shoulders braced. Ziff knew what that stance meant. All the blood drained from his face. Grant tilted his head as if studying a strange creature.

"Zed Productions is about to go into liquidation."

He took half a pace forward.

"You remember what I said to your hired muscle? That bit from *Pulp Fiction*? The girl with the squeaky voice saying to Bruce Willis, 'Who's Zed?' And Willis saying, 'Zed's dead, baby. Zed's dead.'"

Grant looked Ziff in the eye, feeling a bit like a schoolyard bully but ready to take it to the next level if required. He didn't think it would be.

"Well. If you don't tell me where Angelina Richards is, Zed's going to be worse than dead."

Ziff gulped, his eyes wide open. Grant waited for him to spill the beans and was so intent on watching the diminutive producer that he didn't notice the movement along the hallway until the door clicked shut. He spun around toward the sound, arms relaxed and prepared to repel boarders.

The figure that came out of the shadows wasn't Mark Spitz or Danny Swallow. It wasn't one of Ziff's hired muscle either. Angelina Richards walked into the living room and stood beside the bookcase. She looked calm and relaxed.

"It's okay. You can tell him."

FORTY

ALL THREE SAT AROUND the coffee table, fresh drinks steaming in the overhead spotlights. Jim Grant, Stuart Ziff, and Angelina Richards. The tension had leaked out of the atmosphere, and they sat like a group of old friends chewing the fat or passing the time chatting about what they'd done this week. What Angelina Richards had been doing wasn't what Grant had envisaged.

Angelina sighed as if the pressure had been lifted.

"So I grabbed the master copy and came here."

Grant took a sip of milky coffee.

"Just that scene. Not the complete film."

"The uncut footage of that scene. Yes."

Grant pieced it together.

"In a hurry. Explaining the video cabinet being messed up."

"Yes."

"What about the window?"

"I broke it for effect. You know—in case anyone came looking."

"I did come looking. You should have broken it from the outside."

"I shouldn't have cut myself either. What can I say? I'm no burglar."

"I've met some burglars were dumber than you. One kid dropped his bus pass in the house he'd screwed. Name and address and a photo on it."

"That's dumb."

"Isn't it just? Told him he should try another line of work."

"Did he?"

"He didn't get caught again. So either he did or he got better at it. Prison does that to you. One way or another you change."

Grant looked across at Ziff.

"You could end up making decent movies."

Ziff jerked back like a startled rabbit.

"I'm not going to prison."

"You think?"

"You heard what she said. She came here of her own free will."

"And you filmed her having sex with a gray-haired guy. Now you've got the uncut recording. Extortion you got done for wasn't it? Before."

"I'm not blackmailing nobody."

Ziff didn't sound convincing. Grant ignored the double negative.

"It's not always what you did that gets you sent down. It's what I can convince the jury that you did. You think everyone I sent to prison was guilty of what they were sent to prison for? They were all guilty, though. Of something. You're guilty of something. I just haven't figured out what yet."

Angelina held her mug in both hands, fingers interlaced, as she spoke.

"What about pandering? That's a crime, isn't it?"

Grant turned his attention back to Angelina.

"Like grooming? Pimping? That kind of pandering?"

"That's right."

He nodded at Ziff.

"You saying that's what he did?"

"Not him."

"Who, then?"

Angelina stared into her coffee and shivered. It wasn't cold in the lounge. Her eyes lost focus and she looked as if her mind was somewhere else. Somewhere not very pleasant. This was a delicate subject. Grant wasn't a delicate cop. That's why he never specialized in sexual abuse cases. It took patience and sympathy to interview damaged girls. Sympathy he could muster, but patience wasn't one of his virtues. One thing he was certain of: Angelina Richards was a damaged girl. Grant decided to slide past the subject until later.

"What about your bankcard?"

The girl came back to life, her eyes back on Grant.

"At the ATM? That was my idea. To try and get you off my trail."

"You use it yourself?"

"No. That could have backfired. We got someone else to use it."

"But it was the police got the message to me."

"Yes. Stuart's got a police contact. To make sure the message got through."

Her eyes dropped to her coffee for a moment. Something about what she'd just said wasn't entirely true. Grant filed that away for later too.

"You might not know how to fake a burglary, but you've got a devious mind. I think you're learning all the time."

"Sometimes you've got to think on your feet."

"Daughter of a rich and powerful man—I wouldn't think you'd need to do much thinking on your feet."

"Then you'd think wrong."

A hint of anger entered her voice. The father-daughter schism exposed. Grant remembered her mother mentioning the gulf that was growing between the doting father and the headstrong daughter. It was time to approach the subject head-on.

"When your dad showed me the film…the reason he engaged me was because he wanted me to stop you making them. To warn the producer off."

Ziff stiffened. The girl's eyes sharpened. Grant continued.

"I told him he should ask you to stop himself."

Angelina stared at Grant but kept quiet. Grant continued.

"He said it didn't work that way. Your mother too."

"She would say that."

"You blaming your mother for this?"

"She knew what was going on."

Grant felt he was getting close.

"But didn't stop it?"

Angelina shook her head but didn't speak.

"What didn't she stop?"

She still didn't speak.

"What did she know?"

Three mugs of coffee steamed in the silence. Creaking noises echoed through the cavernous room. The house settling around them. A gentle breeze had sprung up outside, rustling the leaves in the garden, but the double-glazing dulled the sound down to nothing. Ziff sat completely still, holding his breath. Angelina stared at Grant, her eyes unblinking. Grant lowered his voice to a whisper.

"Why didn't he ask you?"

Angelina blinked. Tears formed in the corners of her eyes.

"Because there was no point."

One leaked out and ran down the side of her nose.

"Since he was the one who got me to shoot the video in the first place."

THE REVELATION SHOULD HAVE been a shock, but somewhere in the back of Grant's mind the answer had always been there. No wonder Maura Richards had been so upset. Guilt was a powerful motivator, but it could also cause complete paralysis: the inability to move or act or do anything to rectify the situation. It sucked you in and bogged you down. Angelina's mother had been bogged down and could no more act to save her daughter than she could admit to herself that she'd failed her.

Senator Richards was a different animal.

Grant hadn't liked him from the start.

"This was your first movie, wasn't it? *The Hunt for Pink October.*"

"Yes."

"Your only one?"

"Yes."

"Why?"

Angelina took a sip of coffee, the preferred delaying tactic of both Ziff and the girl. She warmed her hands around the steaming mug and lowered her eyes to stare into the swirling cloud. She looked like a woman lost in a cloud, unable to see a way out of the trouble she was in or the life that had been forced on her by an overbearing father. Grant disliked Richards even more.

She kept her eyes down and spoke into the mug.

"Why was it the first one? Or why was it the only one?"

"Take your pick."

Another sip of coffee while she gathered her thoughts. She raised her head and let out a long, deep sigh. Her eyes roamed across the ceiling, then the bookcase, and finally settled on the fireplace. Anything to avoid looking at the man who had come to save her. She was beyond saving.

"It was the first one because it became necessary."

Ziff placed a paternal arm across her shoulders, a gesture that seemed completely out of character for the small-time crook and pornographer. More fatherly than the father she had left behind. She appeared to take comfort from the contact.

"It was the last because it was no longer necessary."

Grant shifted in his seat and rested the mug of coffee on one knee. The heat warmed through the denim of his jeans. It counteracted the cold that was creeping over him.

"You get any more cryptic and you'll be compiling crosswords."

Her eyes fixed on his again.

"My life is cryptic."

She didn't blink.

"Has been since I was ten."

The cold feeling began to spread and sent a shiver running down Grant's spine. Angelina caught the look in his eyes.

"Not the way you're thinking. Just…complicated."

Grant wanted to get back to the point.

"Why was only one film needed?"

Ziff removed his arm. He appeared to shrink in on himself as if waiting for bad news. The paternal instinct morphed into self-preservation. Grant put his coffee on the table in case the little man made a break for it. He threw a quick glance toward the corridor. There was still nobody there. There was still no hired muscle hiding in the shadows.

Angelina changed tack.

"You mentioned extortion earlier."

Ziff stiffened. Grant split his attention between the pair of them. He nodded.

Angelina continued.

"You were on the right track. Only it was my father doing the extorting."

"He's one of the wealthiest men in the country. Must have been for a lot of money."

"Not money."

Grant's mind raced through the possibilities. Blackmail could be used for many things. To get more money. To get someone to do something for you. Or to get someone to stop doing something against you.

"He was blackmailing the gray-haired guy in the film."

It wasn't a question, but it raised a question.

"So, why did you take the master copy?"

"You saw the movie."

"*The Hunt for Pink October*. Yes."

"What did you see?"

Grant tried to be polite.

"A lot."

She didn't blush. Grant reckoned Angelina Richards' lifestyle had banished blushing from her repertoire. She continued probing.

"What didn't you see?"

Grant replayed the scene in his head, paying particular attention to the camera angle. He glanced over his shoulder at the bookcase with its hidden camera pointing down at the back of Ziff's head.

"The guy's face."

The girl saw understanding dawn on Grant's face but continued to make her point.

"You know that when they make a movie, they shoot a lot more footage than ends up in the final cut, right?"

Grant nodded.

"Well, the master copy has all that footage. Establishing shots of the set-up. The guy coming into the room. And his face."

"That still doesn't explain why you took it. Surely your dad has a copy."

Angelina shook her head.

"I switched them."

"The pirate copy he showed me?"

"That's right."

"He didn't make a duplicate?"

"Apparently not. That's the thing about powerful people. They start to believe their own publicity. Think nobody will dare challenge them."

"So you're protecting the gray-haired guy."

She shook her head again. Ziff looked like he wanted to squirm away from the settee. Grant waited for her to explain.

"We were going to use it to get him to shut my father out."

Ziff held his hands up in surrender.

"Wasn't my idea."

Grant focused on the girl.

"Out of what?"

"Out of office."

"He could do that? This guy?"

"Men in office need men in office."

"What office?"

"You didn't recognize him? He came to see you yesterday."

The cold feeling became a worm of doubt snaking up his spine. Angelina didn't wait for the penny to drop, or the American equivalent. She spoke the name with a bemused expression, as if it was so obvious it didn't need speaking.

"The chief of police."

Grant resisted the urge to jerk forward, partly to avoid spilling his coffee but mainly because he wasn't surprised at all. He'd sensed something a bit off about his visitor in the interview room at Hollenbeck, and he'd never liked the bosses in the police force. They were always too far removed from proper police work and too interested in playing the political game. This was a step too far, though, even for them.

He put his mug on the table with a clatter that jarred the silence.

FORTY-ONE

THE ROOM SHIMMERED WITH tension. Grant's mind raced. He wondered if the guy who recruited him back in Boston knew about the police chief's indiscretion and quickly concluded that he probably did. That's why it was important to have someone like Grant come down and sort it out. Somebody with a proven loyalty to the force. Not just the LAPD but any of the police departments or emergency services or armed forces. Anywhere that men and women put their lives on the line for others, mainly their fellow troops. In the trenches. On the frontlines. At the sharp end.

It would have been easier if Grant had been told in advance, but finding out for himself gave the information more weight. It also bolstered his determination to protect the service. His boss knew that. Grant had done the same in the army. In the dusty streets of the killing ground where he had saved the day but not his colleagues. He thought briefly of the stethoscope and all that it represented but brushed the memory aside.

The Chief of Police was dirty. His position was compromised.

That meant pressure could be applied and the most powerful man in the LAPD would be forced to comply. Not good for the cops on the ground. Not good for the citizens of Los Angeles. Not when the criminals could run the police. Shit rolls downhill, and cops live in the valley; a fact of life. Grant had been employed to deflect that shit.

Two things were immediately apparent. If this got out, the scandal would set the LAPD back twenty years. And if it didn't, then the LAPD would become toothless tigers with their leader compromised and the fight against high-end crime blunted. The department would be an open book to the crooks, with more leaks than the British Government.

The answer to both was on a silver disc the size of a beer mat.

The solution was obvious.

"Where's the disc?"

Angelina began to get up, but Ziff held an arm out for her to stop.

"Hold on. You're not thinking of giving him the disc, are you?"

Grant didn't need to brace his shoulders. He just glared at Ziff.

"You're not thinking of stopping her, are you?"

Ziff went pale and lowered his arm. Angelina glanced at the producer, then back at the cop in the orange windcheater.

"It's in my room."

"We'll get it in a minute. First, let me get this straight."

Grant paused to gather his thoughts. Ziff sat back against the settee, resigned. Angelina sat patiently, apparently content to let the big cop from England run the show. Grant interlaced the fingers of both hands and flexed them in reverse. The bones cracked, sounding like gunshots in the suffocating quiet. He separated his hands and formed them into fists. The knuckles cracked again.

"Richards set the filming up so he could get one over on the police chief."

He pointed at Ziff.

"He got you to arrange the set-up and used his daughter as bait. But you couldn't resist putting the scene in the movie. What the fuck were you thinking?"

Ziff blushed and shrugged his shoulders.

"It was good footage. A different angle on the sex scene. Edited down, nobody would know who the guy was. In my movies nobody's interested in the guy anyway. Just who he's…"

He didn't finish in consideration for the girl.

Grant continued. "So Richards has the master copy, but you"—Grant nodded toward Angelina—"switch the discs. Now the senator needs damage control, but you've got his leverage over the chief. You find out that I'm looking for you and decide to bring the disc here. I've got to ask again. What the fuck were you thinking?"

Angelina didn't blush or shrug.

"I had nowhere else to go. I thought it was the safest place."

"That's like a drowning man hiding underwater."

This time she did shrug.

"I haven't drowned yet."

"And what was he thinking? Hiring me to warn the guy off that he'd hired in the first place?"

"Like I said. Believed his own publicity."

"Or thought Ziff would keep his mouth shut to protect himself."

"That too."

Ziff, emboldened by the fact that Grant didn't look like he was going to punch him, put on a brave front.

"What is this? That Poirot scene where he gets all the suspects together in the drawing room and lays the plot out for anybody dumb enough not to have figured it out yet?"

Grant turned his eyes on the short, round producer. Ziff's false bravado vanished in an instant. Grant let the stare sink in before continuing.

"Mate of mine told me a story once. It goes like this."

He rested one arm across the back of the settee and crossed his legs at the ankles.

"Guy goes bear hunting in the woods. Hires a rifle and off he goes. Spots a grizzly among the trees and starts shooting. Leaves and branches everywhere. Dust settles and he goes to inspect his prize. Nothing there. Then he's grabbed from behind and the bear says, 'You've got two choices. You either take it up the ass or I'll eat you.' The hunter chooses number one, gets fucked up the ass, then limps back to camp."

Ziff looked bemused. Angelina smirked. Grant continued.

"Following day, the guy gets a bigger gun and goes into the woods again. Sees the same bear. Shoots like crazy. Leaves and branches everywhere. Goes to look. Nothing there. Bear hug. Same choices. Takes it up the ass again, then limps back to camp."

Grant's voice became conspiratorial and he leaned forward.

"Third day, guy's got a machine gun. Same trees. Same bear. Guy empties the magazine into the trees. Leaves and branches everywhere. Goes to look. Nothing. The bear grabs him from behind and whispers in the guy's ear, 'You're not here for the hunting, are you?'"

The girl laughed. Ziff was still bemused. Grant spoke firmly.

"You're not here for the girl, are you?"

ZIFF TRIED IN VAIN to appear calm. He gulped back his discomfort and spoke in a clear voice, but he couldn't prevent a tremble from quivering his words.

"You're gonna have to translate that. Or get an American interpreter."

"No, I don't."

"Seriously. I don't know what fuckin' accent that is, but it isn't English."

"It's Yorkshire and it's not that broad and you know exactly what I'm talking about."

"I have no fuckin' clue."

Grant raised one foot and slammed it against the coffee table. The table shot across the floor, leaving the three mugs hanging in midair for a brief moment before they tumbled to the carpet. The coffee wasn't steaming anymore but it stained pretty good all the same. Ziff jerked backwards. The girl was the calmest person in the room. She watched Ziff with the dawning realization that she had been played.

"You bastard. I thought you were helping me."

Ziff blurted a response.

"Don't listen to his bullshit. When d'you ever hear a cop tell the truth?"

Grant slid to the front of his chair and prepared to stand up. Ziff countered Grant's movement by sliding back as far as he could go. He couldn't go very far. The back of the seat stopped him dead, and the cream settee was too heavy to push backwards. Grant's face was only feet away from the moviemaker.

"You might have started out working for Richards—maybe even considered helping Angelina—but you've got your own agenda now."

Ziff threw up his hands and shook his head. He ignored the spreading stain on the carpet. He was trying to avoid staining his pants.

"Hey. No. You got it wrong."

Grant braced his legs. The muscles stood out across the top of his thighs, stretching the denim of his faded blue jeans. His back tightened in readiness for the push upwards. The trees outside threw dancing shadows across the picture windows as the wind grew stronger.

"Tell me about the location shoot tomorrow."

This time Ziff's face turned white, and Grant knew he'd hit the nail on the head.

"How come you're staging an armed robbery outside a bank downtown?"

"It's in the script."

"I've seen your movies. Anything that doesn't involve tits and pussy doesn't make the final cut."

Ziff kept quiet. The girl fumed in silence. Grant stood up.

"How many bank robbers you still in touch with?"

Ziff tried to melt into the cushions. The trees continued to thrash outside. The constant movement almost camouflaged the three men standing in the garden, but a glimmer of light reflected off cold black metal. Grant saw the first muzzle flash a split second before the window cracked, then all three guns opened fire.

FORTY-TWO

GRANT DIVED FOR THE settee, forcing Ziff and the girl backwards. Their combined weight tipped the couch over. Soft furnishings do not make an effective shield. If a police car isn't sufficient protection unless you kneel behind the engine block, then six feet of foam and leather isn't going to stop a bullet either.

The volley of gunfire was almost one continuous noise. Three men spraying bullets into the living room. The floor-to-ceiling windows didn't shatter like they do in the movies. This wasn't John McClane dashing across the office in Nakatomi Towers; this was an expensive house in northeast Los Angeles. Double-glazed patio windows. Laminated glass. Shatterproof. What the bullets did was punch holes through the glass in a ragged line across the top. Grant took one look and knew they were aiming high.

This wasn't a kill mission.

That didn't matter. Grant was going to make them pay. He nudged Ziff toward the bedroom corridor and jerked the girl in the same direction.

"The hallway. Stay low."

The warning sounded ridiculous, but you'd be surprised how many people stood up in their panic to get out of the line of fire. Even professional soldiers occasionally succumbed to moments of foolishness. Grant kept his voice calm and unhurried. Whoever these guys were, they weren't trying for headshots and they weren't aiming for the center mass. That didn't mean they wouldn't change their minds once they'd spooked the residents.

"Stay on the floor. As far along as you can get."

The living room was brightly lit. The garden was dark apart from a handful of low-level patio lamps. That made everyone in the house easy targets. Grant scanned the walls and spotted the light switches next to the corridor. While Ziff and the girl crawled into the comparative safety of the hallway, Grant sprang up from behind the settee. In one movement he flicked the lights off, then sprinted through the first bedroom door. Rear guest room. The one he'd visited with Robin Citrin.

That thought provoked another but he didn't have time to worry about her now. The gunshots became intermittent but didn't stop. The gunmen were moving along the building, shooting every window as they went, moving up the incline toward the wooded slope. Good. Grant yanked the bedroom window open and climbed out. He didn't dive or smash the glass or do anything to draw attention to himself. He simply slipped into the shadows and moved silently toward the sounds of gunfire. The last thing they'd expect.

THE COOL NIGHT AIR hit him like a slap in the face. It refreshed him and sharpened his senses. The wind was stronger than when he'd arrived, and the trees atop the hill swayed, the rustling of leaves sounding almost as loud as the gunshots around the front of the house. Almost but not quite. The good thing about continuous gunfire was that it deafened the shooters. The bad thing was you could get shot. They might have been aiming high in the lounge, but stray bullets and ricochets went wherever they pleased.

Grant climbed the tiered garden toward the transformer box at the base of the cell phone mast. He kept to the bushes and flowering shrubs as he traversed each tier one level at a time until he was at the top of the hill. He now held the high ground. The gunmen were in the valley, and Grant was about to roll shit downhill.

The three men were edging toward the corner of the house, keeping a safe distance apart to avoid getting into each other's line of fire. Beyond them, in the turnaround, a square black car spewed exhaust fumes into the night with its lights turned off. The engine noise was lost amid the barrage of gunshots.

Ziff's .38 snub was a close-quarter firearm. Not a target pistol and not a cannon. It held five rounds. Not ideal. From this distance, to hit three guys out of five shots would be miraculous. Grant didn't like guns, but he was a good shot. He'd have to be the second coming of Christ to take these guys out and survive unscathed. He might be known as the Resurrection Man, but he was no Jesus Christ. He'd have to lower his expectations. Send them packing instead of killing them.

The first guy came around the corner, still firing, using either a semi or full automatic. It was hard to tell from Grant's position. He hadn't noticed any pauses during the shooting, so they must be due to reload soon. The first guy began to work his way round toward the back of the house, bringing him up the hill to keep the safe distance from his partners. Twelve feet away from Grant. The second guy came round the side of the house.

Soon.

They'd have to reload soon.

Six feet away from Grant.

The slide of the first guy's gun jammed open in the empty position. He released the magazine and it dropped out of the butt. He caught it in his free hand and put it in his pocket. It was only in the movies that gunmen discarded their magazines. What were they going to reload with next time? He quickly took a fully loaded magazine from his other pocket and was halfway to slamming it home when Grant laid his gun arm across the top of the transformer box and fired.

One shot. Square in the back. The guy dropped like a puppet with its strings cut. Grant fired twice toward the second guy but missed, coughing up dirt and grass at his feet. Three shots. Two left. Grant was moving before the third shot slammed into the night and snatched up the first guy's gun. It was empty. He hadn't managed to insert the magazine. Grant fired a fourth shot to give him time as he scrabbled among the dried grass for the magazine.

Headlights came on full beam in the turnaround and the engine roared. Grant realized the other two gunmen had stopped targeting the house. He braced himself for a final assault on his position. One bullet left. Free hand searching in vain for the dead guy's magazine.

Two shots came from downhill.

Grant didn't dive for cover. From their position they'd have to be marksmen to hit him. Diving to one side could just as easily throw him into a bullet's path as out of it. Both shots went wide. The gunmen were covering their retreat. Grant had been right. This wasn't a kill mission. It was a warning. They hadn't reckoned on losing one of their own in the process, though.

Grant found the magazine and slammed it home.

Car doors slammed, and the headlights swept along the drive. They disappeared beyond the sharp bend as the driveway curved around the wooded hilltop. Grant was up and running with a gun in each hand. The trees slowed his progress. Even though he was cutting the corner by going over the top, he was no match for the speeding car. He had no shot. They were gone.

Grant stuffed a gun in each pocket of his windcheater and took out his phone, still moving through the woods. He flipped it open and selected Citrin's number. He felt slow and awkward. Grant wasn't a mobile phone kind of guy. He pressed call and held his breath. There was only one way into the drive of 1042 Montecito Drive. Right past the minivan parked at the overlook. If Grant had let Citrin bring the cameraman along, then things might have turned out different, but he hadn't. There was no point crying over spilt milk.

The phone kept ringing.

Nobody answered.

He was down the hill now, approaching the footpath where he'd first entered the grounds. He cut across the narrow strip of land and came out on the driveway near the front gate. The electronic gate had been smashed off its runners and lay in a twisted heap beside the road.

The phone kept ringing.

Nobody answered.

Grant wasn't out of breath when he jogged through the gateway. He wasn't winded and he wasn't tired. What he was, was anxious. He couldn't help it. He'd been in this position before. Twice. Supposedly protecting a woman in his care but failing miserably. Both times had turned out bad. The woman in Boston he'd shot in the head. The woman with the stethoscope he'd…

The phone stopped ringing.

Nobody answered but Grant could hear breathing in his ear. Another sound, the gentle purr of a powerful engine. The big American car. He turned left out of the gate toward the overlook. The minivan was still there, facing away from him as if staring at the view. The city of angels. It didn't feel like there were any angels around tonight.

Grant kept the phone to his ear but didn't speak.

He listened, knowing the cell wasn't in the parked minivan.

He circled Robin Citrin's car, expecting the worst, telling himself all the time this wasn't a kill mission, it was a warning. The driver's door was open. This would make one helluva warning. Grant kept his distance in case it was a trap and took the stolen gun out of his pocket. With the phone held to his ear and gun arm outstretched, he angled toward the opening.

The front seat was empty.

His eyes cycled through all the visible openings. The passenger footwell. The gap between the seats. The space behind them. He reached for the sliding door and yanked it open. Using manual instead of electric there was no familiar *pffft hiss*. The rear passenger compartment was empty.

He moved toward the front of the car.

A voice he recognized sounded in his ear.

"Now I have something you want more than to protect the senator. Yes?"

Rodrigo Dominguez sounded like he was ordering pizza. Grant stepped in front of the minivan and saw the bullet holes stitched across the top of the windshield. Aimed high. Not kill shots. Grant breathed a sigh of relief, but not a big one.

"You gave me three days."

"I did. But I thought you needed added incentive."

"Well, you didn't. So you can drop her at the bus stop."

"This fine lady does not look like she belongs on a bus."

"I agree. So get her a cab."

Grant put the gun back in his jacket pocket and stared at his reflection in the windshield. A tall dark silhouette against the starfield of twinkling downtown lights. He looked like a man adrift. A man who had lost everything. Dominguez spoke in a calm voice.

"Do you remember what I said about her working without hands?"

Grant felt a cold shiver run up his neck.

"Don't worry. That is a last resort. We won't start with her hands. Fingers. One at a time. Here is one on account."

The scream coming through the phone was agonizing. Grant almost crushed the cell in his hand. His silhouette against the twinkling lights expanded. Dominguez had just made the biggest mistake of his life.

FORTY-THREE

Dawn was already breaking by the time Grant parked Citrin's minivan down the side of the Mayfair Hotel. The Seventh Street Dollar Store wasn't open. He wasn't thinking of buying any fruit today anyway. Twelve stories up, on the east face of the Historic Mayfair, Grant's hotel room stood with its window open. Same as always. Only today it felt different. Life felt different.

One of Grant's strengths was his ability to deal with life's adversities. His ability to remain calm under pressure. To think clearly and act decisively. Since the scream over the phone, he had been busy making a few calls of his own. As was often the case with him, all the pieces came together in a blinding flash of inspiration. One of his army training officers had said it was sometimes better to be lucky than good. Grant was both. Regularly. But the secret is recognizing your good fortune and shaping it into a plan of action. Grant had already selected his plan of action.

Two of the calls he'd made were obvious. The call he didn't make was no surprise either. But it was the final call that would prove to be the most important one of all.

The black car was parked in its usual spot opposite the front of the hotel. Grant crossed the road in plain sight, hands in the open. He didn't want these guys getting nervous so close to the prize. He doubted they were among the shooters at Montecito Heights, but they would certainly have heard about the shooting. Might have even been friends with the guy that got shot. Grant didn't want this thing going off half-cocked.

He walked around the front of the car with his arms held out, palms upwards. Not full Resurrection Man pose, more like flags at half-mast. If the Hawaiians knew about the shooting, then they knew that Grant now had two guns. He wanted them to see he wasn't holding either of them.

The passenger window slid down as Grant climbed the curb onto the sidewalk. Not for the first time he wondered why Americans felt the need to make the curbs so high. There were black scrape marks all along it where cars had parked too close and scarred their tires. The depth of the curb gave Grant extra height. Even though the big American car was tall, he was looking down into the square blank face from a position of advantage.

The gun pointing at his chest negated that advantage.

These guys were taking no chances.

Grant lowered his arms and bent at the waist so his face was level with the gunman's. He rested one hand on the roof of the car. The driver glanced up at the sound of it. The passenger twitched his gun hand. They were nervous. After the scream over the phone, they had reason to be. They might not have been at the house, but these two were part of the team. That made them legitimate targets.

The streetlamps blinked off.

Daylight of the final day had arrived.

Grant leaned his head forward and spoke in low, measured tones. There was no small talk. No witty asides. He didn't offer the gift of fruit and they didn't talk back. They just listened to what he had to say.

"Tell him I'll get his money out of the bank today. He can meet me there. In a public place. Bring the woman. Eleven o'clock."

He gave the address. The Hawaiians didn't react. The passenger just nodded. The driver started the engine. The window slid shut. Message delivered in person, not over the phone. Grant stepped back from the car as it set off along West Seventh, then crossed the road to the hotel. He needed a shower.

GRANT FINISHED DRYING HIMSELF and wrapped the towel around his waist. He examined the two guns that were laid on the bed. The chrome finish snub nose .38 and the ugly black .45 automatic. One bullet left in the first and a full magazine in the other. Neither would be any use today. Go wandering into a bank carrying firearms and you were in deep shit.

Grant was already in deep shit.

He sat on the edge of the bed and quickly stripped both guns down to their component parts. Using a fresh handkerchief, he cleaned each component as best he could. He unloaded the magazine and cleaned each bullet, then reloaded the clip. Expert fingers rebuilt the .38, spinning the cylinder one notch at a time until the live round was one chamber away from the hammer. Cocking action would bring it into line should he need it. One bullet wasn't much use in a gunfight, but if it came down to him and Dominguez, one shot was all he'd need. The .45 fit back together easily. He didn't rack the slide, leaving the chamber empty.

Grant left the ugly black gun on the bed and tucked the .38 into the rolled-up hood that formed the collar of his orange windcheater. The pistol was small but still bulged inside the cloth. He took a pair of clean socks out of the drawer and padded the rest of the collar until it matched the bulge. The Velcro fastening held the entire thing together. He slipped the automatic in the pocket and zipped it shut.

The scent of shower gel overpowered the smell of gun oil, but he washed his hands again anyway. Body spray and aftershave completed the job. He felt fresh and clean and ready for anything. Still wearing the bath towel, he laid a clean pair of jeans and a black T-shirt on the bed, then looked out of the window. The view of downtown hadn't changed. He could still see the glass and concrete towers of the business district, but now those businesses carried more weight. Somewhere among the skyscrapers was a bank waiting for him to make a withdrawal.

Grant replayed the phone calls in his head.

The first one had been to Chuck Tanburro and the second to L. Q. Patton. Then he considered the call he hadn't made. Considering what was about to go down, calling the police was the sensible option. The only trouble was the police were compromised, and although Grant would trust his life with any cop on the beat, he had never trusted the bosses. It had been a running joke back in Yorkshire that you were more likely to get stabbed in the back from the senior management team than in the front by a street crook. And that was without the chief of police being caught on camera getting his cock sucked. Look what happened to Bill Clinton.

Grant didn't dwell on the past, and he rarely looked to the future. The exception to that rule was when he was planning ahead. He had been planning ahead when he made the third call. He smiled at the irony of it all and wondered if Dominguez would see the funny side. If Grant had his way, Dominguez wouldn't see anything ever again. With a little nod of satisfaction, Grant whipped off the towel and began to get dressed.

FORTY-FOUR

THERE ARE 794 BANKS in central Los Angeles; 115 of those are in downtown LA. At first, Stuart Ziff's choice of film location had seemed like a happy accident to Grant, but when he thought about it, Los Pueblo Trust and Banking was a perfect target. It was widely known that only the most powerful banks had any kind of decent security, and Grant had already witnessed how easy it was to rob one of them. The Bank of America must rank as one of the largest in the country, and yet two hayseed crooks had walked out with a bagful of money using a shotgun and a few harsh words. What possible threat could a small Mexican bank pose?

The sun was already high in a clear blue sky by the time Grant crossed the Harbor Freeway on foot. Constant traffic sped both ways on ten lanes of cracked gray tarmac beneath the bridge. A helicopter hovered over the Staples Center. A low-flying airliner circled low on its approach to LAX. The daily grind of California's biggest city continued as if nothing was wrong. In the flatlands of South Los Angeles, petty crimes continued to be committed. In West Hollywood, movies and TV shows continued to be made. And at West Sixth and South Olive, opposite Pershing Square, a film crew from

Zed Productions prepared to execute the most expensive shoot in porn movie history.

Los Pueblo Trust and Banking was a gray three-story building between the Millennium Biltmore Hotel and Domino's Pizza on South Olive. There was an underground parking garage next to the bank.

Grant came around the corner and half expected to be transported back to New York again, but there was no sign of Gary Sinise today. There were no NYPD patrol cars or FDNY ambulances. Today was pure LA. Hot and sunny and busy as hell. Grant found a bench in a shaded area of Pershing Square Park and settled down to watch the show. It wasn't time for him to make his entrance yet.

NOTHING MUCH WAS HAPPENING at the moment. There was a lot of milling around and not very much getting done. This wasn't the professional location shoot of *CSI: NY* or the movie bank robbery round the back of Hollywood Boulevard. This was a wolf in sheep's clothing. It was only supposed to look like they were making a movie.

There were two handheld cameras carried loosely over the operators' shoulders. Not quality Steadicam equipment but the sort of cameras that were more at home getting close-up sex shots while not disturbing the performers. From Grant's experience with Geneva Espinoza, he doubted if porn stars were ever disturbed by intrusive camera angles. Big Dick Swelling would still be swelling if they dropped a nuclear bomb on his dick. Arc lights and reflectors completed the picture, giving the scene being shot an authentic feel. South Olive was blocked to traffic at the intersection with West Sixth and halfway along the Millennium Biltmore. The hotel doors were still accessible. Closing a downtown thoroughfare was one thing; closing a major hotel, something else entirely. This was a recession. Business was tight.

Retired traffic cops manned yellow trestles at either end of the cordon. Two at each barrier. Chuck Tanburro stood chatting to one of them outside the hotel. Grant didn't know how the ex-cop had managed to get his own guys attached to the shoot, but Tanburro's stock just rose a few points. On the frontline you had to trust your partner. Grant trusted Tanburro. It was a good feeling. He hoped L. Q. Patton had been equally successful. The helicopter drifted over from the Staples Center. It was difficult to read the markings in the glare but its position suggested Patton had at least done part of his job.

The camera operators were talking to a man with a goatee beard and a flowered shirt. Stuart Ziff was nowhere in sight. The producer had learned from his previous robbery outings to be nowhere near the scene of the crime. After the shooting at Montecito Heights last night he was understandably nervous, but at least he only thought Grant was after the incriminating DVD. Grant had taken it. Nothing more had been said about the location shoot. Events had overtaken them, and that suited Grant just fine. He wished he hadn't mentioned it at all, but it appeared that the job was still on for this morning.

A group of fake cops dressed in LAPD uniforms crossed the street, checking their sidearms. Four heavyset guys wearing long coats slipped past the Millennium Biltmore and disappeared into the underground garage. Grant felt the short hairs bristle on the back of his neck. The four guys weren't part of the movie shoot. He glanced along South Olive in both directions. There was no sign of Dominguez yet. He checked his watch.

Quarter to eleven.

The helicopter hovered above the jewelry district east of Pershing Square. The traffic cops diverted traffic around either ends of the cordon. Tanburro kept to one side, just past Domino's Pizza. The arc lights were turned up and the reflectors deployed. The guy with the goatee beard and the flowered shirt shouted into a megaphone for everyone to take their positions.

Grant stood up and walked down the steps from the park.

Ten to eleven.

He crossed South Olive opposite the Millennium Biltmore. Height and confidence got him past the film crew. This wasn't an official SAG shoot. The crew didn't know who the hell anybody was. Grant stopped for a moment in Los Pueblo Trust and Banking's front door.

Five to eleven.

A big American car pulled up outside the hotel, and the traffic cops removed the trestle to let it through. The car went down the ramp, into the parking garage. Grant watched it disappear without a nod or a smile. He showed no emotion at all. It was showtime.

The guy with the megaphone shouted, "Action."

The fake cops played out the scene on the street.

Grant walked into the bank.

THERE WERE NO SECURITY guards inside. Grant would have been surprised if there had been. He stood just inside the doorway and scanned the room. Los Pueblo Trust and Banking had more in common with the Bank of America's East Cesar branch than the one at MacArthur Park. He doubted it had ever been a PLS Check Cashers, but it shared the same dark and dingy interior, with wood-paneled walls and a full-length bank tellers' counter. The counter had wired glass barriers to prevent robbers climbing over, but they were only three feet high. Two large ceiling fans twirled slowly, shifting warm air around the waiting area.

First order of business: familiarize yourself with the battleground. Grant ran his eyes over the high-ceiling room with practiced ease. Within sixty seconds he knew where all the exits were, how many staff manned the bank tellers' positions, and which customers were possible threats. The customers he discounted immediately. None looked out of place, and all were either female or too old to cause problems. The bank staff were all Latinos. They were slightly built and nervy types. Typical bank tellers. Money mathematicians, not protective services. The exits were obvious and clearly marked. The one behind him led into the street. One on the far side had an arrow pointing down to the parking garage. There was a wood-paneled door next to the counter for staff and two more doors beyond the counter, one into the manager's office and one into the side alley.

There were three CCTV cameras, one on either side of the public area covering the counter and the front door, and one in the main office looking out at the public area. Grant hoped Citrin had been right about being able to hack internal systems and that Patton was watching right now. That was more important for Sunset TV and Film Inc.'s finished product than Grant's tactical deployment.

Grant's tactical deployment was himself and nobody else.

For now.

Rodrigo Dominguez's tactical deployment appeared to be somewhat more. The head of the Dominguez drug cartel came through the door from the parking garage with three men and Robin Citrin.

In tactical terms, Citrin was a human shield. Grant kept any emotion off his face. He was almost as successful at keeping the anger from boiling inside him. Anger led to mistakes. Grant's strength was built on remaining calm under all circumstances. Calm and relaxed and ready to act in an instant. He checked his watch.

Eleven o'clock.

"Right on time. Maybe you should be running the railway."

Dominguez stayed with his entourage near the garage exit, his eyes doing exactly the same as Grant's had a few minutes ago. Scan complete, and keeping the exit close behind him, he beckoned Grant over.

"It's railroad in America. But nobody travels by train anymore."

"You know, history shows that whatever they say about Mussolini—mass murder, genocide, Hitler's bag boy—at least he got the trains running on time. I guess that's something we'll have to hold off on when they write about you."

"History is written by the victors. I intend to write my own history."

Grant kept his eyes on Dominguez, but his peripheral vision focused on Citrin. She looked bedraggled and pale. Her hair was a tangled mess, and dark rings showed beneath her eyes. One hand was wrapped in a bloodstained white handkerchief. The shape of the fist made Grant's blood run cold. It narrowed considerably where the little finger should have been.

"Written in blood, no doubt."

"All history is written in blood."

"Be careful it isn't written in yours."

Car tires squealed outside, and there was a flurry of gunfire. The customers threw worried glances toward the front door. A megaphoned voice shouted, "Cut. First positions again." Dominguez didn't flinch. His bodyguards kept position behind him, near the parking garage door. Grant smiled.

"Movie capital of the world, Los Angeles."

"So they say. But we have our own business to conduct here."

He waved toward the nearest bank teller station. Grant nodded his agreement and began to move over to the counter. Dominguez followed. Two bodyguards moved with them, one holding onto Citrin's arm. The other guy patted Grant down. He ran his hands over the main areas, body, arms, legs and ankles. He took the .45 out of Grant's pocket and showed it to Dominguez. The third guy stayed by the door. Dominguez glanced at the gun and tut-tutted.

"I believe it is a federal offence to bring a gun into a bank."

"Federal, is it?"

"Certainly illegal. The other gun?"

"Emptied it at Montecito Heights."

Dominguez indicated for the bodyguard to search Grant's crotch.

"Don't be shy."

The guy felt Grant's balls but came up empty and stepped back.

Grant glanced at the wall clock.

Ten past eleven.

He wondered what was holding them up. The irony of his phrasing wasn't lost on him. Whoever Ziff had employed wasn't as punctual as Dominguez. Grant knew there was no set timetable for Ziff's plan, but it must be close now. All Grant had to do was keep the ball in play until the action kicked off.

"I don't suppose a check will do?"

"No."

"A hundred thousand is a big bag of cash."

"You can transfer it to my bank."

They were in front of a teller now. A more confident-looking guy than the others. Bigger too. Grant selected a withdrawal slip from the counter.

"What bank?"

The teller waited for instructions.

Dominguez smiled.

"You're standing in it."

Grant kept the surprise off his face because it wasn't a surprise. The fact that Dominguez owned Los Pueblo Trust and Banking was the reason he'd chosen this bank for the meeting. It was also the reason Dominguez felt secure enough to do the deal in a public place. Because this wasn't a public place. It was a private place with a few members of the public sprinkled in.

"You really are branching out, aren't you?"

The front doors slammed open, and two LAPD cops marched across the floor, guns drawn. The older one beckoned for the teller nearest the wood-paneled door to let him in. The other raised his voice for the customers.

"Nobody move. We've had a report of a robbery in progress. Remain calm and keep your hands where I can see them."

A third cop stood just inside the door and closed it with his back. A short female teller let the first cop into the office, and he went immediately to the side door. When he opened it, another two cops came in from the alley and shut the door behind them. All five cops had their sidearms drawn. Two fired shots into the air, and the first shouted over the noise.

"This is a robbery. Everybody on the floor. Now."

The tellers dropped to the ground. A customer shrieked and was hit in the face by the second cop. Dominguez glared across the counter but didn't move. Grant kept his tone conversational.

"Robbery capital of the world too."

FORTY-FIVE

DOMINGUEZ STOOD RIGID WITH anger. The muttering of voices died to nothing as the customers got down on the floor. The teller at Grant's service window threw a frightened look at his boss, then slowly dropped to his knees behind the counter. Grant's attention was on the bodyguard holding Robin Citrin.

In a combat situation, timing was everything. Step the wrong way at the wrong time and you could walk right into a bullet that would have passed you by. Stay in the same position for too long and you were a stationary target just waiting to be shot. A bank robbery was just a combat situation from a different angle. Timing was still the key.

Timing and distraction.

The bank robbers were the distraction.

Grant quickly reassessed the battleground. The exits hadn't changed, but two of them were no longer available. A fake cop from the movie shoot covered the front door. An armed man also blocked the side door into the alley. That only left the parking garage. A cartel guy with a broken nose stood in front of that. Best choice. With the exits whittled down to one, Grant turned his attention to the enemy. The enemy was pretty much everyone in the bank apart from the innocent bystanders. The bank staff worked for Dominguez. The bodyguards worked for Dominguez. The armed cops had come to rob Dominguez. The upside of that was that the armed cops neutralized the bodyguards, making the robbers Grant's primary threat.

The bodyguards threw glances at their boss but didn't move.

Dominguez stood firm, glaring at the cop in the middle of the public area.

The cop glared back and came over to the only group left standing.

"You fuckin' deaf? On the ground."

Dominguez didn't move. Considering the situation, he kept his voice calm but threatening. Grant was impressed.

"Do you have any idea who you are robbing here?"

The cop raised his gun at Dominguez's face.

"A bank."

Dominguez ignored the gun, staring the cop in the eyes.

"A bank is a place. The owner is the most powerful drug cartel south of the border. And I am the owner of that cartel."

The cop blinked but didn't lower the gun. Grant divided his attention between the confrontation in front of him, the guy holding Robin Citrin, and the other cops distributed throughout the bank. They were evenly spread. He met Citrin's eyes briefly and winked. She didn't appear to notice. She was in shock. Overhead, the fans spun lazily, like slow-motion helicopters in some Vietnam War movie. The wall clock ticked away the minutes. Fear filled the room like bad sweat: the customers' fear on the polished wood floor, the bank tellers' fear sprawled across the office carpet behind the counter, the bank robbers' fear of having to open fire if this thing went bad. It was going bad right now.

The cop put a brave face on it.

"Then you should have opened a bank south of the border."

Timing. Grant used the standoff distraction to move half a pace to one side. Half a pace away from Dominguez and half a pace toward the guy holding Citrin. The move went unnoticed. It opened a gap and put Grant in the open. Dominguez continued to play his part, voice low and hard and nasty.

"Los Angeles is south of the border. There are more Hispanics here than any other part of the United States. And they will find you. And your family. And I will personally ensure every living seed of your tree is exterminated. I will have your sisters and daughters and granddaughters raped and killed in front of your mother's eyes before tearing out your living guts and staking them for the dogs."

The cop's eyes were wide open. They didn't blink. Water formed in the corner of each eye with the strain of not blinking. The gun hand trembled. The CCTV camera on the wall looked down on them. Grant slid another half pace to one side. The first cop came back through the wood-paneled door and joined his colleague.

"What's the holdup?"

Dominguez turned eyes as hard as flint on the newcomer.

"You are. Holding up a bank that you should have avoided like the plague."

The cop was dumbfounded. Nobody spoke to armed robbers like that.

"What?"

"You are all dead men in fake uniforms. If you leave now, I will spare the lives of your families."

The tension smelled almost as bad as the fear. Sour sweat and bad breath. The polish and air freshener smell of the bank couldn't compete. Somebody needed to light a cigar or open the windows, but what was going to happen was everybody was going to get shot. Grant sensed it. He glanced at the wall clock: 11:25.

Any second now. He checked the enemy positions again. One cop at the front door. One cop at the side door. Another one behind the counter. And two standing in front of Rodrigo Dominguez. That was the cops. The bodyguards were less spread out. One guy beside the parking garage door. One guy holding Citrin. And the third guy standing next to Dominguez. When the shit hit the fan, which Grant knew was about to happen, luck could take out Dominguez and one of the bodyguards straight away. It was better to be lucky than good.

Grant wasn't that lucky today.

The first cop raised his gun too.

"Are you fuckin' insane?"

The stare that Dominguez fixed on the cops proved what Grant had known all along. Rodrigo Dominguez wasn't insane, he was evil. The man had no redeeming qualities whatsoever. He was a cold-blooded killer of women and children and just about anything else that lived and breathed. He would shoot your dog. He would skin your penis. He was a very bad man. And very bad men were always incredibly lucky.

Grant prepared to make his move. He couldn't wait for the cavalry any longer. He glanced at Citrin and forced a smile, hoping that she would be all right but not believing it. His track record for rescuing endangered women wasn't good. When he saw the parking garage door open he breathed a sigh of relief. Then the breath went out of him as a big black guy with a pump-action shotgun walked through the opening.

Julius Posey worked the action to get the first bodyguard's attention. Then he shot him in the chest when he turned to face him.

THE SITUATION GOT FLUID real fast. Fluid situations were the most dangerous. The odds had shifted from the four-to-one that was Dominguez against Grant to five-to-four that was the robbers against Dominguez. Now they shifted to four-to-nine, which was the four shotgun-wielding black guys against everybody else. Four, because that's how many materialized in a split second after the first shotgun blast.

The side door was kicked in, and a second shotgun took out the cop standing guard. Another black guy in a long overcoat came in from the alley. The fourth stepped around Posey toward the front door.

Then everything happened at once.

The bodyguard holding Citrin drew his weapon and shot the first cop in the throat above his Kevlar vest. Grant swept a strong leg across the back of Citrin's ankles and dropped her to the ground. The second cop swung his gun away from Dominguez and shot the bodyguard in the chest. The black guy who came in from the alley let off two shots at the cop in the middle of the office, knocking him backwards and forcing the cop's reflex shots up into the ceiling. The cop at the front door raised his gun double-handed, but the fourth black guy got him in the chest with a single shotgun blast. He dropped to his knees with a comical expression on his face.

Then the odds shifted again. Fluid situation. Chuck Tanburro burst through the front door with four retired traffic cops. The traffic cops spread across the room, guns raised in the traditional short-armed two-handed stance. Tanburro was carrying a shotgun identical to the ones the black guys had. A police-issue Remington loaded with beanbag rounds. He noticed the spent beanbags on the floor, sturdy bags of shotgun pellets with rubber tentacles like a squid to slow them down in the air.

The only people dead were the ones shot by the robber and the bodyguard.

The body count was two.

But it wasn't over yet.

The second fake cop saw Grant come up from his sweeping leg strike on Citrin and identified him as another threat. Posey tugged a second shotgun out of the folds of his coat and tossed it through the air. Dominguez darted sideways and down, away from the fake cop. He brought something shiny out of his jacket pocket. The fake cop was momentarily confused as to which was the greater danger. The delay gave Grant just enough time to catch the shotgun and use its momentum to spin full circle. He fired from the hip at close range, lifting the cop off his feet and sending him backwards across the floor. The saggy little squid flattened against his Kevlar vest and dropped, still smoking, like a dead fish.

Dominguez dragged Citrin to her feet and clamped one arm around her waist. He held her tight and forced the fingers of her good hand out. Light glinted off the blades of the secateurs as they tightened around her forefinger. He backed away into open space.

Sirens began to sound across the city.

Silence reigned inside the bank.

The stunned robbers were disarmed quickly. The four traffic cops handcuffed the four survivors. The two wounded bodyguards moaned on the floor as they nursed bruised ribs. Body count was still just one robber and one bodyguard. So far. The three other black guys gathered in front of the counter. Posey kept station beside the parking garage door, shotgun leveled at Dominguez's back. Grant had the cartel boss covered from the front. The situation was tense. Tense situations provoked humor as a defense mechanism. Posey took two paces toward Grant.

"Thanks for the call. But next time you want my boys to step into a roomful of hot lead, we's gonna want more than shotgun condoms."

Grant kept his eyes on Dominguez but spoke to Posey.

"I'll be able to argue deputizing you. Giving four armed robbers live shotguns in a bank would be hard to justify."

He stared into the drug lord's eyes but still spoke to Posey.

"Back in England we used rubber bullets. Lots of controversy over that. These beanbag rounds are non-lethal but effective. Optimum range is thirty feet. They'll deliver a strike like being hit across the ribs with a baseball bat. Farther than that and they're not very accurate. Up close, like six feet"—Grant was six feet from Dominguez—"and they'll rip your balls off. Go for the central body mass, and they'll break your ribs. Raise it above that, and it's a kill shot."

The sirens were getting nearer and there were more of them.

Grant didn't smile. Humor was over. He spoke directly to Dominguez.

"You've got nowhere to go but hell."

Dominguez squeezed the secateurs, and Citrin whimpered.

"I have no illusions about going to hell."

He took two shuffling steps backwards, toward the parking garage, keeping Citrin between him and Grant like a full-length body vest. Grant had no shot at his body mass or his balls. Dominguez saw the indecision on Grant's face.

"But not today."

Grant took two steps, keeping pace with the drug lord. Posey had to step aside. Distraction. It was Grant's only chance. Keep Dominguez talking and hope he let his guard down.

"You just confessed to being the owner of the biggest drug cartel south of the border on national television."

Dominguez stopped in front of the door.

Grant nodded backwards to the CCTV camera on the far wall.

"Smile. You're on *Candid Camera.*"

He brought the shotgun up to his shoulder. This needed to be a more accurate shot than firing from the hip. Citrin's eyes flared in panic. Dominguez kept moving backwards. He was almost at the door. Posey had sidestepped to keep out of his way. Both shotguns were round the front of the human shield now. A tactical error that was too late to change. Posey glanced at Grant.

"Your call, man."

Grant knew the decision was his. The shotgun pointed straight at Citrin's face. Citrin was shorter than Dominguez, but he was crouching behind her. That put her face right in front of his throat. The kill shot. Trouble was, it would be a double kill shot. One to take out the hostage and the other to kill Dominguez. Grant had been here before. He had stared into a desperate woman's eyes and made the only choice available. Twice. It didn't look as if it was going to be third time lucky.

Dominguez butted up against the door.

He tightened his grip on the secateurs.

"Unless you want another finger on your conscience"—Citrin whimpered but didn't scream as the blades drew blood—"you had better lower the shotgun and back off."

The door wouldn't open. It wasn't a swing-both-ways door. It only opened inwards. And Dominguez didn't have a free hand to open it. Impasse. The drug baron couldn't go backwards and he couldn't come forwards. Grant weighed up the loss of another Citrin finger against letting a killer go free. He balanced the death of a single hostage against how many more people would die if Dominguez got away.

Citrin saw the calculations on his face.

Grant stared into her eyes. He blinked. Once. Slowly.

Citrin nodded. A half smile that was almost a grimace on her face.

Grant's finger tightened on the trigger.

Dominguez was a cold-blooded killer of women and children and just about anything else that lived and breathed. He would shoot your dog. He would skin your penis. He was a very bad man. And very bad men were always incredibly lucky.

The bad man's luck kicked in now.

The garage door opened, and a short man with wire-framed spectacles came in. A customer. He took one look at the armed men before him and threw up his hands in surrender. Dominguez slipped through the opening with Citrin before the door closed and disappeared.

FORTY-SIX

THE BESPECTACLED CUSTOMER SQUEALED and backed away as Grant lunged forward. Fearing imminent death, the customer bumped into the door, collapsed on the floor, then curled up in a ball with both hands wrapped around his head. Grant pulled the handle, but the door was blocked.

"Shit."

In one swift movement he dropped to a crouch, grabbed the little fella's collar, and dragged him aside. He yanked the door open and braced it against one leg as he bobbed his head through the opening. One quick glance, then back out again.

"Shit."

The stairwell was empty. Footsteps echoed in the distance, down in the bowels of the parking garage. The landing was brightly lit and freshly painted, but the corridor at the bottom of the stairs looked dingy and careworn. It reminded Grant of a mid-level restaurant where the front of house was beautifully decorated but behind the scenes was utilitarian and plain. The stairs were utilitarian and plain. The lack of good lighting made them dangerous as well.

Posey came up beside Grant.

Grant shook his head and pointed toward the front of the building.

"Make sure they cover the exit ramp. Nothing gets out."

Posey nodded, then turned to find Tanburro. Grant went through the door and took the stairs two at a time, shotgun leveled, ready for any more surprises. A short corridor at the bottom led to a pair of swing doors. Not as fancy as the ones into the bank. They were still swinging to and fro. Grant kicked the right-hand door open and stepped back. While it was still flip-flapping, he bent at the waist and darted through the left-hand door.

PARKING GARAGES ARE THE same the world over. Concrete pillars and dark ceilings. The ribbed floor was painted oxide red with direction arrows and instructions marked out in white. There was nothing nice about them. There was nothing safe. And there were lots of places to hide.

Rodrigo Dominguez wasn't hiding. He was standing next to a big American car with the turning circle of a bus. He still had Robin Citrin clamped in one arm, and he still held one finger in the jaws of the secateurs. Her head was slumped and she was breathing heavy. Dominguez had to hold her up to keep her from collapsing. What kind of human shield would that be?

Grant's footsteps echoed through the subterranean lair.

Citrin coughed. That echoed too.

Dominguez didn't have to raise his voice.

"Stop right there."

Grant stopped.

The fluid situation had solidified. The odds were down to evens. One on one, with a single piece of collateral damage. Grant had made these decisions before and always chose the greater good. Living with those decisions was just something you had to do if you were in the firing line. Whether it was a bleached-out desert street or a conference room in Boston, the decision was still the same. Take the shot. It was the only decision.

"Mushrooms."

Grant's voice echoed off the concrete pillars.

Dominguez couldn't help but respond.

"What?"

"Cops are like mushrooms. Keep them in the dark and feed them shit."

Grant used the conversation to cover him moving forward two more steps. Twenty feet became fifteen. Closer than the Remington's optimal range but not quite close enough for the kill shot. Not to be certain. Dominguez was intrigued.

"Shit for brains, it seems like."

Grant held the shotgun loosely across his body at waist level. Two more paces would be enough. He kept talking as he cleared the pillars on either side of him.

"Thing about mushrooms is this. You cut them down in the morning."

Twelve feet.

"But they keep coming back at night."

Ten.

"And the darker it is, the stronger they get."

Citrin's head came up. The time had come. Her face was dulled by acceptance but her eyes flared with panic. It was the human condition. No matter how hopeless the situation became, there was always a spark inside that forced you to survive. Grant tried to ignore the spark in Citrin's eyes. He raised the shotgun. Her eyes flashed a warning, but he had to be strong. It was the only way.

Dominguez spoke quietly.

"The only thing I know about the dark."

There was a smile in his voice.

"Is that you can't see in it."

Two hulking figures stepped out of the shadows on either side of the concrete pillars. Both held guns pointed at Grant's head. The two Hawaiians who weren't really Hawaiian. Citrin's eyes dulled over. Grant recognized the warning too late. He lowered the shotgun barrel and let out a sigh.

THE CONCRETE SUCKED ALL the light out of the parking garage. Even the red oxide paint couldn't lift the atmosphere. The room smelled of defeat. In the distance, toward the South Olive exit ramp, sirens echoed down the tunnel and tires squealed to a halt. The sirens were switched off. None of that was worth a damn to the hostage and her rescuer twenty feet beneath Los Pueblo Trust and Banking.

The two Hawaiians kept their distance.

Dominguez lowered the secateurs.

"Now, slowly—using the barrel—lay the shotgun across your foot and kick it over here."

Grant took his finger out of the trigger guard. He glanced to his right. The colorful Hawaiian shirt was the only brightness in the gray concrete tomb apart from the other colorful Hawaiian shirt. Grant glanced to his left. Both guns were aimed high. Head shot.

Bad move.

Grant nodded toward the exit ramp.

"Those are real cops out there, not retirees or movie cops. They aren't going to let you out of here."

Dominguez smiled.

"For a cop, you're not very observant. This is a one-way parking garage. South Olive is the entrance. Exit's on South Grand."

Grant could have kicked himself for being so blind. The entrance ramp had been in plain sight when he'd crossed from Pershing Square. It was a single-lane ribbed-concrete driveway. The parking structure ran beneath the entire block, coming out on the next street. In all the excitement of setting the trap, he'd overlooked the basic rule of engagement. Always reconnoiter the battleground.

Dominguez remained focused.

"The shotgun. Slowly."

There was no distracting the drug lord. Grant took hold of the shotgun barrel near the front sight and let the butt sink to the ground. Bending at the knees, he slowly lowered the barrel across his toes and let go. It balanced evenly on his left foot. The Hawaiian on Grant's right appeared to relax. His gun was still aimed at Grant's head but with less purpose. He took over prisoner control. Another bad move.

"Hands behind your head."

Grant was still flexed in a half crouch. He moved his hands out wide until they formed the Resurrection Man cross but kept them moving, slowly bending at the elbows until his hands came behind his neck. The muscles in his thighs tightened as he began to rise.

"They don't teach that at cop school. We prefer you to keep the hands out in the open until after the body search."

The second Hawaiian put his gun away and took the car keys out.

The first stepped forward, his gun arm lowered halfway to the ground.

Dominguez snipped the air with the secateurs.

"I think you've earned a few more fingers. You could keep them as souvenirs. Except you will be dead before she stops screaming."

The secateurs began to come up slowly. Citrin tensed but was held firm by Dominguez's clamped arm. Grant tugged at the Velcro collar that held the folded hood as he pushed upwards with his legs. The snub-nosed .38 came out easily. His fingers found the trigger as he snapped the gun forward and shot the gunman in the chest.

The gunshot echoed off the concrete walls. Blood and bone exploded out of the guy's back. Grant was already dropping the .38 as the other Hawaiian tried to get his gun out again. A coordinated jerk of Grant's foot and the shotgun sprang into the air. He caught and fired it in one movement, dropping the driver with a gut punch that took all the wind out of him. His gun skittered across the floor toward the car.

Dominguez brought the secateurs up too slow. Grant racked another round into the chamber and took aim at the center mass. The body. Dominguez smiled. The body belonged to Robin Citrin. He dropped the secateurs and reached for the gun beside his feet. Grant looked Citrin in the eyes. And pulled the trigger.

The shotgun spat flame, and the beanbag squid hit her full in the chest. It broke two ribs and doubled her forward. Her legs gave way. She went down like a dead weight. Grant worked the pump action, and the spent cartridge ejected through the smoke. It was still spinning when the next round was slammed into the breach, and Grant drew a bead on Dominguez.

Dominguez froze halfway up from the ground. The secateurs clattered at his feet. The gun looked alien in his hand. He held it out to his side to show it was no threat and slowly straightened his back until he was fully upright. Smoke hung in the air like mist. The smell was harsh and acrid.

Grant laid the front sight on the center mass. The body. From this range it would be like being hit by a double-weight baseball bat but would still be a non-lethal strike. Dominguez stared into Grant's eyes. Grant stared back. There was no anger. There was no compassion. Grant didn't have to think twice.

He raised the aim six inches and fired. Kill shot. The beanbag hit Dominguez in the jaw from five feet and split, sending shotgun pellets up into his brain like a splinter round. He wasn't dead when he hit the side of the car, but he was by the time he slid to the ground. The echo lasted longer than the dying drug baron. Then Grant was on his knees beside Citrin, holding her in his arms until help arrived. The echoes faded. The smoke cleared. Help felt like a long time coming.

FORTY-SEVEN

THE AFTERMATH OF THE Los Pueblo Trust and Banking robbery at Pershing Square played on every news channel across America. Grant doubted if it was covered on the BBC back in England. Los Angeles was the bank robbery capital of the world, and this was just another robbery. It wasn't even a successful robbery. When the Great Train Robbery made the news back in 1963, it was a rarity. Banks were two a penny in LA. Grant wasn't sure how that translated into American money.

The medal ceremony, three days later, was about to be given as much prominence as the robbery in California. All the local news stations prepared to televise it live from Parker Center, the LAPD administrative building. Grant felt a little embarrassed about that. L. Q. Patton was ecstatic, convinced it would enhance the ratings for his new show, *The Resurrection Man*.

Grant felt a little guilty about that.

He hadn't told Patton about his decision yet.

"You can't do that."

Not L. Q. Patton. Chuck Tanburro. He was standing open-mouthed in a private anteroom at Parker Center half an hour before the medal ceremony. Grant slapped him on the back, admiring the dress uniform Tanburro had been provided with to attend the ceremony. Grant was as smartly dressed as he ever got, clean blue jeans and an open-necked black shirt. No tie. No orange windcheater. He did wear a pair of highly polished black shoes he'd borrowed off Tanburro.

"I already have. PR guy threw a dickey fit."

"A what?"

"He wasn't happy. But it's done."

Tanburro let out a sigh and shook his head.

"You earned it. Ain't right just me and the guys getting ours."

"They're retired LAPD. So are you. It's appropriate."

"You couldn't talk 'em around about Posey and his crew?"

"Giving medals stuck in the LAPD's throat. Cleaning the slate made Posey's day. He's thinking of going into movies."

"What about you?"

"The movies aren't my thing. I'm a cop."

"I mean the medal."

"I've been given medals. Lost every one of them. I'll be proud to cheer you on, though. From the crowd."

They could hear the hubbub outside the door. Visitors and press gathering to salute the heroes of the Los Pueblo Trust and Banking robbery. The men who had foiled an armed robbery and brought down the biggest drug cartel south of the border. Dominguez's confession on CCTV had been silent, but a court-appointed lip reader confirmed what had been said. The drug lord's unfortunate demise meant he couldn't defend himself. The bank's assets had been frozen and would later be seized by the Federal Government. It was a big win for all concerned. Grant was pleased to be a part of it, but that wasn't why he'd been sent here.

"I've got a private audience coming up."

"With the pope?"

"The chief. In the police, that's the same thing."

A side door from the anteroom opened, and a smartly dressed aide beckoned Grant to follow him. Grant turned to shake Tanburro's hand.

"Great job. I'll see you out there."

"Thanks."

Grant followed the aide through the door and took a deep breath. It was time to have a private word with Sherman Gillespie.

THE OFFICE WAS SILENT. Tension bristled like static. Chief Gillespie stood with his back to the window and ignored the sunshine outside. The front lawn stood out in brilliant green five floors below. The squat black memorial to fallen officers was hidden behind Gillespie's back. It was just as well. Grant might have been provoked to violence. Those fallen officers deserved better than to have a disgraced chief of police running the LAPD.

Gillespie's shoulders sagged.

"You would do that to the LAPD?"

"I would do that to protect the LAPD."

Grant watched the most powerful police officer in California crumble. It wasn't a pretty sight. In Grant's view, the law of diminishing returns applied to cops when they climbed the ladder of rank. The further away from the streets they got, the more ineffective they became. God complex set in, and they invariably began to believe their own publicity. Gillespie wasn't the worst case of an authority figure being corrupted by power that Grant had come across. It wasn't as if the chief had been turned to the other side for money or power. He'd simply slept into the wrong crowd and been caught in their trap.

"I never wanted this to happen."

"Nobody ever does."

"I am not a bad man."

"Neither was Bill Clinton, but loose lips sink ships."

"Pardon me?"

Grant formed an O with his mouth and pouted his lips. He held one fist in front of his mouth as if holding a penis and with each thrust forward stuck his tongue into his cheek. Gillespie blushed.

"Once they had the recording…"

He didn't finish. The details weren't important. The only consolation was that it hadn't gone on for too long, and Gillespie's involvement had been minimal. Deep water had been beckoning, but he was only in the shallows. The corruption had only resulted in a bit of misinformation and Gillespie's threat to have Grant deported. It had been an idle threat. Grant leaned against the desk.

"There's nothing wrong with sex, just who you have it with."

"I know."

Grant almost felt sorry for the man who'd run the LAPD for three years. For two and a half of those years, he'd done a pretty good job.

"It's not always about being a bad person, just bad choices."

Gillespie accepted the olive branch with a nod of the head.

Grant didn't nod back. He didn't feel that sorry for him.

"And now you're going to take early retirement for health reasons."

"To spare the force. I know."

Grant moved to the window and looked down at the memorial to fallen officers. There were things he didn't like about the way this had shaken out. There were people who deserved to be punished but would get off scot-free. Zed Productions would continue making porn movies, but Stuart Ziff was out of the armed robbery and extortion business. Keeping his name out of the Los Pueblo Trust and Banking debacle would depend on his accomplices taking their punishment like men. That wasn't always the way it worked. Pressure had to be exerted and promises of leniency made, something else that stuck in Grant's throat. All for the greater good. The reputation of the Los Angeles Police Department. Because if that collapsed, then the streets would run with blood again. Appeasing a few bank robbers was a small price to pay. The judges were trying to reduce the prison population anyway.

The official line was that the armed robbers who had infiltrated the location shoot had used it as a perfect cover for the robbery. The producer had been cleared of any involvement. No mention was made of the suspected abduction of Senator Richards' daughter or the blackmail-by-sex-tape of the chief of police. The choice of bank tied in with Los Pueblo's involvement with the Dominguez Cartel, a happy coincidence that resulted in a major victory in the war against drugs.

There was a knock on the door, and the aide poked his head in the room.

"Five minutes, sir."

"Okay."

The aide closed the door.

Gillespie squared his shoulders.

Grant pushed off from the window.

"Time to honor your men. Retired cops who never forgot the job."

Gillespie winced and clenched his teeth.

"Nobody ever forgets being a cop."

"You did."

"No. I forgot to keep my dick in my pants."

"There but for the grace of God go many of us."

Gillespie picked his dress cap off the desk.

"One thing, though. If I hadn't fallen from grace, you wouldn't have come to Los Angeles. If you hadn't come to LA, then you wouldn't have foiled the bank robbery, and the Dominguez cartel wouldn't have fronted you there. So, really, destroying the biggest drug cartel south of the border was down to me."

Grant crossed to the main door.

"There goes the politician in you."

Gillespie put his hat on and pulled the gold-braided peak down over his eyes.

"No, there goes the cop in me."

"Once a cop, always a cop."

"I hope so."

Grant opened the door for Gillespie. The chief of police walked through. The hubbub of voices quieted, and dozens of flash cameras went off. TV news reporters read the lead-ins to their stories, and five retired cops stepped up to the podium. Grant closed the door behind the chief, then quietly blended with the crowd. Robin Citrin stood at the back of the room and waited. Grant kissed her on the cheek, careful to avoid the bruises, then joined in with the applause.

FORTY-EIGHT

THE SUN WAS HIGH in a cloudless blue sky when Grant came out of the wooden cabin on Coldwater Canyon Drive. He stood on the porch and soaked up the fresh air, his orange windcheater unzipped and flapping in a gentle breeze that dulled the afternoon heat. He took a deep breath, then turned back toward the open door.

"Bet this is a bit of a comedown after your other place."

Maura Richards stood next to her daughter and shrugged.

"It's only temporary while we sort out the divorce settlement."

She moved to put an arm across Angelina's shoulders, but the girl pulled away. This wasn't the Lassie moment at the end of the movie where everything worked out fine and they all smiled at the dog that had saved the day. It would be a long time before Angelina Richards let her mother put an arm around her again. There was a lot of hurt that needed healing first. Moving in together was a start, though.

Mrs. Richards covered her embarrassment by joining Grant on the porch.

"The announcement comes out tomorrow. The press release will say he's stepping down to concentrate on running the business."

"He'll need to work extra hard to cover paying you, I guess."

"We'll both need to work hard to pay back what we owe."

She spoke to Grant but the words were meant for her daughter. Angelina shifted uncomfortably in the shadows. Grant took all the judgment out of his voice.

"Don't beat yourself up about it. Doesn't make you a bad person. You just made bad choices, that's all."

There was an awkward moment when they didn't know whether to shake hands, hug farewell, or simply say goodbye. In the end it came down to a shared look and a half blink of the eyes. Mrs. Richards glanced past him down the porch steps.

"She has been very patient."

Grant followed her gaze to where Robin Citrin stood leaning against the minivan in the dusty turnaround. Without another word, he walked down the sturdy wooden steps and joined her.

THEY DIDN'T KISS UNTIL Grant heard the cabin door close behind him. Citrin pushed off from the side of the car, her hand freshly bandaged in that curious shape that all amputees had. He took her gently in his arms and kissed her upturned lips. She kissed him back, the defining moment of forgiveness for being shot in the chest with a shotgun condom.

Grant drew back and looked into her eyes.

"You get all that?"

"I got it. You're off the books now, though."

Grant nodded toward the bushes that surrounded the house with the swimming pool at the bottom of the hill.

"You sure he's not pretending to be a tree down there?"

Citrin opened the passenger door and handed Grant the keys.

"L. Q. wouldn't mind treating you like a tree. Thinking of doing a lumberjack show—you'll be the first thing he cuts down."

Grant helped her onto the passenger seat and closed the door. He climbed in the driver's side. The lack of working hands meant he was driving.

"He still mad at me?"

"It's business. You always said you were a cop, not a TV star."

"Didn't believe me, though, did he?"

"He does now. Footage will cut together for a great one-off show."

Grant closed the door and started the engine. The windshield had been replaced, and there was no evidence left of the violence that had taken place. Not on the minivan anyway. Citrin would carry the scars forever. He didn't allow himself to feel guilty about that. The things he had done in his life, the people he had hurt, were history. He would probably do the same again if necessary.

"Yeah, well. Seagal can have the limelight. I've had enough."

He set off down the slope, leaving a cloud of dust swirling behind him. The hills rose up beyond Coldwater Canyon Drive, dried grass and stumpy trees covering the place where Batman had once escaped from a crashing car and Saturday Western posses had chased bank robbers on horseback. It seemed that Los Angeles had always been the bank robbery capital of the world.

Citrin put her good hand on Grant's thigh.

"Forget Seagal. L. Q. is looking at Julius Posey as the next reality TV star."

"Posey? What you gonna do, follow him around while he robs banks?"

"Didn't you hear? Posey's going straight."

"Yeah. Straight back to jail."

"No, seriously. We're going to do a bounty hunter show."

"Thought they already had one. That biker guy with the long hair."

"Dog, yes. But Posey gives better footage."

Grant snorted a laugh.

"Now where have I heard that before?"

Grant stopped at the bottom of the drive, then turned left toward Hollywood and beyond. He never dwelled on the past and rarely looked to the future. He lived for today. Today he had a beautiful woman on his arm and money in the bank. What more could a man ask for?

ACKNOWLEDGMENTS

As I've mentioned before, writers write, but it takes a lot more people to bring that writing to the reading public. I won't go into Oscar-speech meltdown, but I can't go without thanking at least a couple of them: Terri Bischoff for believing in Jim Grant and the Resurrection Man novels, Rebecca Zins for once again doing a bang-up job of polishing the Englishman's prose, and Donna Bagdasarian for not only being an excellent agent but also for being my friend.

The following excerpt is from

ADOBE FLATS

The forthcoming book from Colin Campbell.
Available September 2014 from Midnight Ink.

Steam hissed up from Jim Grant's lap as scalding hot coffee shriveled his nuts and turned the front of his jeans into molten lava. At least that's what it felt like when his efforts to peel back the lid of his latte tipped the king-size paper cup over his nether regions and threatened to melt his gonads. Hot coffee in his lap and a swirl of white foam down the front of his T-shirt like a question mark. Not the best start but par for the course considering his reception since arriving in Absolution, Texas. About as friendly as the one those Mexicans got who visited the Alamo.

Grant's frosty reception began even before he arrived. On the train from Los Angeles. Not the main line express but the third change after leaving the city of angels. The parched scrubland passing outside the window reminded Grant of that other place—the one where devils ruled and angels feared to tread. When he asked the conductor how long before they stopped at Absolution, the conductor's reaction set the tone for all that was to follow.

"This train don't stop at Absolution."

"That's not what my ticket says."

The conductor examined Grant's ticket. The printout gave his journey as Los Angeles, California, to Absolution, Texas. The railroad official frowned and scratched his head.

"We ain't never stopped at Absolution. That's a request-only stop."

"Well, I'm requesting it. How long?"

The conductor handed the ticket back.

"Next stop after Alpine."

He pulled a pocket watch out of his waistcoat pocket. More for effect than necessity. Grant reckoned this fella knew exactly how long before the place the train never stopped at.

"Half an hour. Bit more, maybes."

"Thanks."

Grant settled back in his seat and watched Texas drift by through the window. Dry and brown and dusty. He couldn't remember the last patch of greenery he'd seen since changing trains. He didn't expect to see any more up ahead. Considering why he was here, that seemed appropriate. He glanced at the leather holdall in the overhead rack and thought about what was inside. Then he turned his attention to the scenery again.

Absolution wasn't anything he was expecting either.

STEAM DIDN'T RISE UP from the engine as the train pulled in at the one-stop bug hutch of a town. It wasn't that kind of train. This wasn't the iconic steam engine of the Old West with its cowcatcher grill and enormous chimney. It was the squat, bulky diesel of the Southern Pacific that hadn't changed shape since the '50s. Grant felt like Spencer Tracy stepping down from the streamliner at Black Rock. That was another place trains never stopped at.

Heat came at him like he'd stepped through an oven door. Dust kicked up from the boards of the platform. Calling it a platform was an exaggeration. A raised section of wood and nails with three steps at one end that led into the parking lot. Parking lot was an exaggeration too. The hard-packed sand and gravel might have been a parking lot once upon a time but nobody parked there nowadays. The ticket office was boarded up and closed. No wonder the conductor had looked nonplussed as he pulled the portable stairs back into the carriage. The door slammed shut. The engine roared. There was a hiss from the brakes, then the huge monster eased forward. It slowly built up speed as it nosed into the desert, and a few minutes later Grant was alone in a landscape so bleak he wondered why anybody wanted to build a town there in the first place.

He took his orange windcheater off, slung it over one shoulder, and walked to the ticket office. The boards creaked underfoot. He felt like he should be wearing spurs. Dust puffed up around his feet. The office was just that, a small, square garden shed in the middle of nowhere. There was no waiting room or restroom or any other kind of room apart from enough space for one man to sit inside selling tickets. Back when anyone caught the train from here. Grant guessed that was a long time ago.

He glanced over his shoulder toward the town.

Absolution was just a row of uneven rooftops breaking the smooth lines of the horizon. Not as far away as they seemed. Not close enough to pick out any detail. Just flat, featureless buildings among the scrub and rock. He squinted against the blazing sunlight. Even the blue sky looked bleached and unfriendly. When he looked closer, Grant could see there were more buildings than he first thought. Smaller and lower than what passed for the main street. A couple of water towers in the distance. A few weather vanes beyond them.

Nothing moved. There was no sound apart from the wind coming in off the flatlands. Then Grant heard pounding footsteps from the other side of the ticket office. He stepped to one side so he could see. A cloud of dust broke the stillness. A man was running toward him. He didn't look happy.

"WHAT YOU THINK YOU'RE doin' here, fella?"

The man was out of breath. His words came out in a rasping voice that sounded like a smoker's but was probably just desert dry from a hard life. He carried a key to the ticket office but didn't offer to open it. Grant was visiting, not leaving. He didn't need a ticket. He held the leather holdall in one hand and nodded his head toward the departing train. Explaining the obvious seemed the way to go.

"Just got off the train."

"I can see that. How come?"

Grant could see this was going to be hard.

"Well, it just kinda stopped. Then I got off."

"No need to be flippant, young man."

The man spat on the boards to prove he could spit.

"This ain't no place for getting shirty."

The parchment face looked like it was shaped from stripped hide. It was lined and cracked and as dry as the voice. There was no twinkle in the eye to soften the harshness. It was impossible to guess his age but Grant figured somewhere between old and ancient. Running from town hadn't helped. When he got his breath back, his voice leveled out.

"Sunset Limited hasn't stopped here in years."

Grant tried a smile to lighten the atmosphere.

"That's a step up from never."

The man looked puzzled.

"What?"

"Conductor said it never stopped here."

"Weren't far short. Seems like never."

Grant let out a sigh. This conversation was going nowhere. He glanced along the rails at the disappearing train. The long silver streak was banking to the right as it took the long, slow bend around the distant foothills. He turned back to the man with the ticket office key.

"Looks like never was wrong and the years have rolled by, 'cause it sure as shit stopped today. And here I am."

The eyes turned to flint in the parchment face.

"Yes, you are. And that begs the question, don't it?"

Grant waited for the question it begged, but it didn't come. This fella was as inscrutable as Charlie Chan but not as friendly. The black trousers, white shirt, and faded waistcoat suggested an official position, but if his job was to sell tickets he must have been on short time. He was no great shakes as a meeter and greeter either.

"You're not much of a welcoming committee."

The parched skin tightened.

"Who said you're welcome?"

Grant nodded.

"Nobody, I guess."

The town was only a short walk from the station but it felt like miles away. The buildings were gray and dull, without any hint of life or color. No smoke from the chimneys. No glints of sunlight from moving vehicles. Place was as barren as a long-shit turd. Dried up and dead and full of crap. The station attendant pressed home his point.

"Nobody asked you to come here."

Grant kept calm but couldn't leave that one unanswered.

"How do you know?"

Then he set off walking toward town.

THE MAIN STREET WAS a long stretch of nothing much. A dozen buildings at most on one side of the road, a couple more across the street. Grant stopped on the dirt track from the station before stepping onto the wider dirt track that was First Street. Swirls of sand blew across the road and he realized it was tarmacked, but the two-lane blacktop was so faded it looked like cracked earth. The center line was unbroken yellow stained brown with the passage of time. A smell of mint drifted on the wind, and Grant noticed the first piece of greenery since getting off the train. A straggly plant behind a low picket fence surrounding a low-slung bungalow. Like a gatekeeper's house guarding the track to the station.

Grant stepped onto the sidewalk. Nobody was out walking. A handful of people were dotted about across the street. Some sitting on chairs outside the only two-story building, leaning the chairs back on two legs against the wall. Couple more standing in shop doorways farther along the street. Two or three staring out through plate-glass windows coated in dust. Nobody moved. Nobody raised a hand in greeting.

The building he wanted was obvious. He ticked off the others anyway. Standard practice when entering hostile territory. There was a pharmacy, a grocery store, the ever-present hardware store, and some kind of eatery. The Famous Burro. Grant wondered if that should have been burrito, then remembered a burro was a donkey. He didn't fancy eating donkey. A bit farther down the street there was a US Post Office and a clean-looking shop marked Front Street Books. There wasn't anything that looked like a bank. He turned the other way. More of the same, not amounting to much. The town petered out. A few dried-up houses, a gas station, and a railroad car diner beyond them.

He turned back to the two-story building. The Gage Hotel. The place with the two fellas leaning back in their chairs. Cowboy boots and faded blue jeans. One had a cowboy hat pulled low to shade his eyes. The only thing missing was a piece of straw hanging out the corner of his mouth. Or maybe chewing a matchstick. Neither man spoke. They just stared.

First order of business was accommodation. Looked like the Gage Hotel had the monopoly. Grant left the smell of mint behind and crossed the street. Time to see if the booking clerk was any friendlier than the ticket seller.

THE HOTEL LOBBY SMELLED of cracked leather and coffee. It was dark and dingy and should have been filled with smoke. The overall impression was of a gentlemen's club. Half a dozen leather chairs were grouped in pairs on either side of three glass-topped coffee tables. Two leather sofas against the wall complemented the chairs next to a cigarette machine at the bottom of a carved wooden staircase. The stairs started beside a reception counter that had a heavy-bound ledger and a manual bell that you pressed for attention. The kind that dinged once when the internal hammer struck.

Reception was unmanned.

A smoke-stained wooden fan spun slowly from the ceiling. The gentle *thwup, thwup, thwup* of the blades reminded Grant of something bigger, but he pushed the thought aside and focused on the reception counter. Patchwork shelving divided into pigeonholes covered the sidewall against the staircase. Each pigeonhole had a hook out front, and each hook held a key. Room numbers went from 1 to 25. None of the keys were missing. All the rooms were vacant.

Grant crossed the lobby and dropped the holdall on the floor. He spun the register on its rotating stand and looked for a pen. The squiggly writing looked faded and old. Proper fountain pen ink, not Biro. He tried to make out the date of the last guest, but it was smudged and indistinct. Didn't look like yesterday though. An old-fashioned quill pen jutted from an inkwell on the counter. He picked it up and studied the ink-crusted nib.

"You is about to deface a historical document there, son."

The voice came from the office door behind the counter. The face that went with the voice was drier and more parchmentlike than the ticket seller at the station. The desk clerk limped into the room and spun the register back around. He indicated a desktop computer that Grant hadn't seen below the level of the counter.

"We've gone all newfangled for checkin' in."

The desk clerk scrutinized Grant's face.

"You must be the fella got off the Sunset."

"That obvious, is it?"

"Sure is. First time the Sunset's stopped here in over a year. First new face in town for almost the same."

"I guess I've got a choice of rooms, then."

"Ain't got no rooms."

Grant let that sink in. This fella was no more welcoming than the welcoming committee at the station. Only difference was, where the ticket seller had nobody to sell tickets to, the desk clerk had a customer right in front of him but wasn't about to rent him a room. Grant figured that made him even less of a welcoming committee. The elephant in the room was the keys hanging from each pigeon-hole. Grant nodded at them.

"Got a lot of keys though."

"That I do. But each one's taken."

Grant felt like he should fold one arm up his sleeve. This was playing like an homage to Spencer Tracy in *Bad Day at Black Rock*. He wondered briefly if the clerk was having him on—a little gentle humor—then he dismissed the thought. The lines etched into the clerk's face were more from grimaces and frowns than smiles and laughter. His voice was gravel dry.

"Block bookings."

Grant smiled just to show the clerk how to do it.

"Let me guess. Cattlemen from the local ranch. For when they come in town after driving the herd."

"Ain't no cattle ranches in Absolution."

"Oil men then. For a break from the rigs."

"No oil neither."

Grant kept his voice conversational.

"Place hasn't got a lot going for it, then, has it?"

"It's got enough. We like it the way it is. Don't need strangers comin' in and tellin' us our business."

Grant leaned forward and rested his elbows on the counter.

"And what business is that?"

"None of yours. That's what."

"Tourism maybe? You've got Big Bend National Park just south of you."

The man tensed. Grant had touched a nerve. Maybe the lack of tourists was part of the reason the town looked so dry and lifeless. The clerk didn't expand on the theory.

"We get by."

Grant shifted his weight to one elbow and reached over the counter with the other hand. He slipped the nearest key from its hook and tossed it in his palm.

"Well, you just got by with one extra guest. I'll take this one."

The clerk looked indignant.

"That room's taken."

"I know. By me. If the fella who's block booked it drifts into town, I'll change rooms. Name's Grant. Jim Grant."

Grant picked the holdall up, grabbed a town map from the display stand on the counter, and turned for the stairs. The fan continued to *thwup, thwup, thwup*. Grant continued to ignore the memory. There was a thump outside as one of the chair-leaners on the porch stood up. Grant was on the second step before the front door opened, but he didn't look back. He already knew who it was. The one in the boots and cowboy hat. The clerk finally found his voice.

"I need more than that. For the register."

Grant leaned over the banister rail.

"Thought you'd gone all newfangled."

"Same applies. Name won't do. Where you from?"

Grant set off up the stairs again and spoke over his shoulder.

"Out of town."

The stairs creaked all the way up.

CHECKING THE MAP IN his room explained why tourists didn't stop here on their way to Big Bend. The founding fathers had pinned their hopes on the Southern Pacific and built the town on either side of the railroad tracks. Road traffic used the 90 just north. The 385 ran north to south all the way down into Big Bend National Park. The crossing of those two roads was at Marathon, west of Absolution. The road through Absolution went nowhere.

Grant picked all that up from the inset map of the area in the corner. A small square indicated the desert town's position, and the rest of the page was taken up by the Absolution street plan. It didn't really need a full page, but there were more streets than Grant had first noticed. Traditional US grid pattern. Streets running east to west and avenues north to south. The main road was First Street with North Second to North Eighth spreading one way and South Second to South Fifth the other. The main crossroad was Avenue D, the rest being Avenues A to K. If there were any more shops, they'd be on Avenue D.

The Trans Pecos Bank was on Avenue D.

Grant left the map on the bed and unpacked his bag. The hold-all had traveled the world with him, and he knew how to fold his clothes to best effect. Partly military training and partly the boarding school his father had dumped him at as soon as he was old enough. The British Army and Moor Grange School for Boys had a lot to answer for. He hung the orange windcheater on the back of the door and put the T-shirts and jeans in the drawers. He slid the long velvet box from the bag between the T-shirts. His fingers played gently over the scarred fabric, then it was gone. Living in the present was Grant's preferred modus operandi, but sometimes the past wouldn't stay buried. An ironic thought, considering why he was here.

With his normal preparations complete, if not necessarily in the usual order, it was time for a shower. First thing was always to get a map. Second was scout the location. Third was check for enemy personnel. That was from his army days. As a cop, the third option was more wide reaching. As a tourist, all but number one were moot points. He just couldn't turn them off. Getting laid wasn't an option this time. Not in his current mindset.

The en-suite shower was hot and roomy. He could stand tall and not bump into the showerhead. That was pretty tall. His shoulders didn't bang the sides. As hotel showers went, this was built for size. He guessed what he'd heard about Texas was right. It was big country for big men. He toweled dry and walked, naked, back into his room.

He stopped in the doorway. The muscles of his thighs turned to knotted ropes and his shoulders tensed. He wasn't alone. The man in the cowboy hat was sitting in the bedside chair, leaning it back on two legs against the wall.